Janet MacLeod Trotter was born in Newcastle and grew up in Durham. She at one time edited the Clan MacLeod magazine and has also had a number of short stories published in women's magazines. Her first saga, *The Hungry Hills*, gained her a place on the shortlist of The *Sunday Times* Young Writers' Award. Janet MacLeod Trotter lives in Morpeth, Northumberland with her husband and their two children. She is currently a TV reviewer for the *Newcastle Journal* and has an author website on the internet. Find out more about Janet and her other popular novels on:
www.the-trotters.demon.co.uk

Praise for Janet MacLeod Trotter's previous novels:

'Well-researched, highly readable . . . compelling and utterly convincing' *Northern Review*

'Brings a time and a place vividly to life and makes compulsive reading' *Northern Echo*

'Not only a good read but a vivid picture of the coal-field . . . You'll believe you're there' Denise Robertson

For Love and Glory

Janet MacLeod Trotter

headline

First published in 1999
by HEADLINE BOOK PUBLISHING

First published in paperback in 2000
by HEADLINE BOOK PUBLISHING

4

ISBN 0 7472 6003 6

Typeset by Avon Dataset Ltd, Bidford-on-Avon, Warks

Printed and bound in Great Britain by
Mackays of Chatham plc, Chatham, Kent

HEADLINE BOOK PUBLISHING
A division of the Hodder Headline Group
338 Euston Road
London NW1 3BH

www.headline.co.uk
www.hodderheadline.com

To Heather, Jill and Graeme, who grew up in Wallsend
– with lots of love

Chapter One

1966

Jo ran out of the school gates, dragging her friend Marilyn with her.

'Race you to Dodds'!' Jo grinned, giving herself a head start.

'I've got no money,' Marilyn complained, her attempts at sprinting hampered by her new slip-on plastic shoes.

'I'll treat you,' Jo called over her shoulder, kicking up neat piles of orange leaves that the road sweeper had collected. 'Dad gave me a tanner.'

Marilyn panted behind. 'Wait, man, I've got a stone in me shoe.'

Jo turned, hands on hips, her unruly red hair glinting like burnished copper in the October afternoon sun. 'You were daft to buy them,' she pronounced, watching her friend hopping along the pavement, one shoe in hand, fair ponytail bouncing. It was the one thing they differed over – clothes, Jo thought. She was content to run around in wellies and her brother Colin's old gabardine. Shorts in summer, dungarees in winter were the only choices worth bothering about. Every Sunday her father tried to coax her into a dress for Sunday

1

School at the Methodist Hall, and every Sunday she refused. Jo would deign to put on a tartan skirt whenever her Auntie Pearl returned from sea, but they were rare and special occasions. She would do anything for her beloved aunt – except wear a frock, of course. Whereas Marilyn showed a baffling amount of interest in the latest craze for miniskirts and plastic clothing. But then her mother, Mrs Leishman, was a seamstress at the co-op and was doing a nice side-line at home, taking up the hems of fashion-conscious neighbours.

Jo linked her arm through her friend's and pulled her into Dodds' corner shop where they spent her sixpence on sherbet fountains and a piece of bubblegum each. Thanking the cheerful Mrs Craney, they sauntered out into the late sunshine, blowing large bubbles that popped in the sharp air.

'Let's gan to the park,' Jo suggested, passing the end of Jericho Street where they lived.

'Mam'll be expecting us,' Marilyn replied, unsure.

'We'll not stay long,' Jo assured, steering her forward, 'just pick up a few bits for the bonfire.' She was reluctant to return too early, for Mrs Leishman would keep them in the house and fuss if they made a mess or knocked into her nest of tables and china ornaments. In her own house, she and Colin could leave things lying about or make crumbs on the bed without anyone telling them off. Her father did not seem to notice and she did not have a mother. Jo thought she was lucky that her mother had died so long ago she could not remember her, so it did not hurt. In fact she gloried in having one tragic parent, who had died 'of a weak heart', as her father put it, while her friends had mothers who nagged at them to brush their hair and tidy the house.

Besides, she had Auntie Pearl, who, when she wasn't

sailing the world on a merchant ship, breezed in with exotic presents of painted camels and gaudy dolls and took them out to Carrick's for tea. And there was Ivy Duggan, Mark's grandmother, who lived in Nile Street down by the docks and opened her door and biscuit tin to all her grandson's friends.

Thinking about Mark Duggan seemed to conjure him up, for as they took a short cut across the Green, they found him playing football with Colin and Skippy. All summer, the streets of Wallsend had resounded to the thud of ball on brick as boys re-enacted England's four–two win over Germany in the World Cup. Jo ran forward and whacked the loose ball so hard her wellie flew off and hit Skippy Jackson.

'Nick off!' Skippy yelled and hurled the boot back at her. 'Girls can't play footie!'

'Well I can,' she replied, pulling a face at him. He had never been as friendly towards her since his year away in Australia. His parents had gone out on a £10 ticket, but grown homesick so quickly they were back in thirteen months. Mark had nicknamed him Skippy after the TV kangaroo and now no one ever called him Billy. He took a swipe at Jo.

'Leave her alone, Skippy man,' Colin intercepted at once, but gave his sister a warning look. 'Shouldn't you be round at the Leishmans'?'

Jo gave him an evasive shrug. 'We're looking for firewood, want to come?'

Just then, the window of the house opposite flew open and old Ma West bawled out, 'I've warned you lot about playing on there! Be off with you!' Mark spun round, flicking the ball in the air, and headed it pro-vocatively towards the angry woman. 'Clear off, you little beggars or I'll call the police!' she yelled.

Colin, sensing their time had run out, picked up the ball. 'Haway, we'll go and look for firewood down the Burn.' As they drifted off, chucking the ball between them, Mark turned, determined to have the last word.

'There's only one thing worse than you, missus,' he shouted over, 'and that's *two* of you!'

Jo sniggered and caught Mark's look. He grinned back and threw the ball at her. She caught it and ran ahead. 'Race you to the park!' she cried, giving herself a head start and hurling the ball back at her brother's friend.

Mark took up the challenge, knowing that Jo always won the sprinting races in the Jericho Street games. She was fast, but her wellies slowed her down and they reached the park gates in a dead heat. They raced each other through the park and on down the dene, heading for their favourite tree. Hauling each other up into the branches of a horse chestnut, they prepared to shower the others with conkers when they caught up.

Of all her brother's friends, Jo got on best with the restless, quick-talking Mark. He had always treated her like one of the lads, which was what she wanted, preferring to hang around with them than play 'houses' or skipping games with the girls in Jericho Street. Mark was cheeky and funny, his dark eyes full of mischief under a fringe of coarse black hair.

And she sensed that they shared something else, that the world saw them both as being slightly different. She was a girl without a mother, a tomboy set apart from the other girls. Marilyn was her friend because she lived next door and was easy to lead, but apart from her, all Jo's friends were boys. As for Mark, he looked different from the rest of his family, leaner and darker-skinned. She had once heard Mrs Leishman say to Auntie Pearl,

'That one's touched with the tar brush,' and had wondered what she meant. It sounded unpleasant and her neighbour had said it with that disapproving downturn of her mouth that Jo knew so well. But Mark was a Duggan, a fighter like his bad-tempered father and handsome older brother Gordon. He had a wild streak in him, as if a slow fire burned away under his laughing exterior and occasionally burst into flames – like the time he had bloodied Kevin McManners's nose for suggesting Mark had been left on his parents' doorstep by the gypsies.

'I heard you got sent to Toddy's room today,' Jo said, swinging her legs to keep warm. Mark grunted and cracked open a horse chestnut. 'What for?' Jo persisted, interested to know what had annoyed the headmaster this time.

'Set off a banger behind the girls' toilets,' Mark sniffed.

Jo looked at him admiringly. 'Have you got any left?'

'Aye, but I'm saving them to use on me dad,' Mark said with a bitter little smile.

Jo felt a twist of unease in her stomach. She knew that big Matty Duggan, who worked off and on at the yards, had a ferocious temper and a large leather belt that he used on both his sons. Gordon, at fourteen, was growing tall and brawny, his hair touching his collar. He was at the grammar school and beginning to stand up for himself. But lately, Jo had noticed that the red weals on Mark's upper legs were appearing more frequently and she felt he should be keeping out of his father's way.

'Why your dad?' Jo asked

'To stop him hitting me mam,' Mark said in a low voice that Jo could hardly catch.

Jo felt queasy. The last time she had called at Nana

5

Ivy's, Norma Duggan had been there, sitting smoking by the open fire with dark glasses on. Jo had wanted to laugh, thinking Mark's mother was trying to be trendy. Her hair was always blonder and more lacquered than anyone else's, her skirts shorter, her nails brighter. Jo had assumed the sunglasses with the sparkling winged frames were just the latest fashion. Only when Jo was leaving, munching one of Ivy's rock buns, had she glanced back and seen Norma take off her glasses. One eye had looked closed and ringed with colour like Chi-Chi the panda at London Zoo.

'Eeh, Mrs Duggan!' Jo had gasped. Norma had quickly slipped the glasses back on and reached for another cigarette.

'It's nothing. I banged into the doorframe,' she said quickly.

'Looks sore,' Jo had continued, glancing at Ivy to see what she made of it.

'It's not,' Mark's mother had snapped. 'And it's none of your business.'

Jo had felt rebuked and rather baffled that Ivy had remained silent. Mark's grandmother usually had an opinion on everything, especially matters which went on in her own kitchen.

Now she scrutinised Mark's brooding expression. 'Did your dad give her that black eye?' she asked. Mark nodded. 'Why?' Jo questioned.

He looked at her, his dark eyes angry and defiant. ' 'Cos of me.'

'What did you do?' Jo asked, puzzled.

'Nowt,' Mark hissed. 'Just for being the way I am.'

Jo didn't understand. 'That's not fair on your mam – or you!' she declared.

'He's not fair,' Mark replied with a harsh laugh. 'He's

6

a big bastard who's going to get a banger up his backside if he carries on hurting me mam.'

Jo started to giggle at the mental image. 'Send him into orbit!' she laughed.

Mark glanced at her, then laughed too. 'Aye, first man on the moon!' he cried.

Jo, relieved that Mark's dark mood was broken, fished out her sherbet fountain, bit off the liquorice top and offered him first suck of the tart, powdery sherbet. 'Anyways, I think you're canny, whatever your dad says,' she said, with a bashful sidelong glance. She didn't want him to think her soppy.

He gave her a strange, intense look, then took the yellow package. 'Ta,' was all he said, as he sucked sherbet up the liquorice straw. When he handed it back, they sat in companionable silence, each thinking their own thoughts. Jo put the straw to her mouth and felt it sticky and warm where his mouth had been. She let the sherbet tingle her tongue and froth in her mouth. Why had Norma Duggan pretended she had walked into a door when her husband had hit her? Jo puzzled. She should have told Ivy, for she was Matty Duggan's mother and Jo was sure she would have given him a telling-off. Instead, Ivy had been drinking tea and smoking cigarettes, thinking her daughter-in-law had merely walked into a door. Either way, Jo decided, they should have taken it more seriously – called out the doctor or gone to that clinic in the newly opened Forum. Wearing sunglasses wasn't going to make it better, Jo was fairly sure.

Still trying to fathom the behaviour of grown-ups, she felt a nudge from Mark, who whispered. 'Here they come! Get ready. Fire!' Mark threw the ball on top of Colin and the two of them began to shake the branches of the tree frantically, loosening a shower of conkers and leaves on their friends below. In retaliation, Colin and Skippy hurled sticks at their hideout and Marilyn screamed with excitement as she chucked conkers back at them. Skippy attempted to reach them by swinging on a lower branch, which snapped under his weight, landing him in a puddle of mud.

'You can tell he's Australian,' Mark teased. 'Can't stay the right way up, can you, Skippy man?'

After that, as dusk fell, they shinned down the tree and hunted around for firewood and conkers, filling their pockets with the smooth gleaming nuts. Between them, Colin and Mark carried Skippy's long branch, while Skippy used a piece of old fence as a bat, throwing up conker husks and hitting them into the twilight. As they entered Jericho Street, they could see Mrs Leishman standing in her slippers in a pool of electric light at her door, looking anxiously up the street.

'Eeh, we're for it now.' Marilyn grimaced and started to quicken her step, her new white shoes scuffed and mud-splattered. The boys swiftly melted into the gloom with their firewood, heading down the back lane to where the bonfire was being built.

'Cowards!' Jo called after them, refusing to hurry.

'Is that you, Marilyn? Joanne?' Mary Leishman barked. 'What time do you call this? You've had me worried sick. Where the devil have you been?' There was a screech as they passed under the street lamp. 'Look at the state of you! You'll take those off your feet, Joanne Elliot, before you come in here. I'll not have you trailing mud through my house. Marilyn! You've *ruined* those shoes . . . !' She administered a sharp slap on her daughter's bottom and pushed her through the door.

'It was Jo's idea to go down the Burn,' Marilyn

8

wailed as her mother continued to scold.

'You could've been got by some bad man – like that Ian Brady they've just put away for murder,' she berated.

'I'll be off home then, Mrs Leishman,' Jo called after them, recognising it was time to retreat. 'Dad'll be home shortly.' She dived past the neatly scrubbed doorstep and the illuminated net curtains in the front window and rushed for the safety of her own front door.

'Don't think I won't have words with your dad, mind!' Mary shouted. 'You'll not go leading my Marilyn astray again, do you hear?'

'No, Mrs Leishman, sorry we were late. Ta-ra.' Jo waved and darted indoors. She slammed the door behind her and fumbled for the brown electric switch, kicking off her wellies at the same time. The hall light flickered and came on, sending a dull yellow glow from under the dusty fringed lampshade. Throwing her coat over the brown banisters, she padded along to the kitchen. She was met by the warm glow of the banked-up fire and the comforting smell of cinders and ham soup, old toast and vinegar. Her father had a passion for polishing their ancient table and cumbersome sideboard with vinegar, saying that was how Jo's mother had always treated them. Jo thought it would be quicker to use the new spray polishes that Mrs Leishman was forever brandishing, yet she preferred the smell of vinegar on mellow wood.

Jo busied herself setting the table for tea, stirring the large pan of soup that had been simmering all day on the old range and filling up the kettle. They were the only household she knew of who still used a black range; everyone else had gas cookers.

'Don't trust gas,' her father would say, 'it's unstable,' as if it were a person to be wary of and not let inside the house. 'That range has done us proud – I remember me granny cooking broth on a stove like that.'

Colin would mutter to Jo, 'Aye, and I think we're still eating it.'

Jo laughed now as she stirred the pan again, feeling a thick sludge of lentils and barley sticking to the bottom. It was true the soup pan rarely got a clean-out; her father just seemed to add a bit of what he fancied to it each day. His other specialities were lamb hotpot and rabbit stew, but these too often metamorphosed in time into 'Granny's broth'. What Jo loved best were his scrambled eggs and rice pudding, both of which he had learnt from an Indian cook when he'd been in the Merchant Navy. They were spiced with nutmeg and cinnamon and were the most exotic variety served in Jericho Street.

While the tea brewed, Jo dashed out into the dark backyard, letting the kitchen light spill out and illuminate her way to the outside toilet. Hurrying as quickly as she could, she peed, flushed and hopped back in holey socks across the cold, slippery concrete. The yard door banged behind her and Colin appeared.

'Did the Alsatian get you?' he grinned, clomping into the kitchen with shoes caked in mud. 'The Alsatian' was his nickname for Mary Leishman.

Jo shook her head and laughed. 'I came straight home. Not that you were much help, mind,' she added, giving him a shove.

He unlaced his shoes and washed his hands in the scullery. 'Have you got the tea ready?'

'Aye, and I've even cut the bread,' Jo said proudly, pointing at the uneven hunks on the breadboard.

Colin emerged. 'You know Dad doesn't like you using the carving knife – it's too sharp.'

'I've still got all me fingers, look.' Jo held up her

hands with the thumbs hidden. 'Just a couple of thumbs missing!'

'Ha, ha,' Colin said with a roll of his eyes. They both dived for some bread, too hungry to wait any longer. Jo went over to the old radiogram, wedge of bread in her mouth, and put on a Beatles single. Last year, Pearl had given her the money to buy her first record and she still recalled the thrill of going into the shop clutching the ten-shilling note. She had carried the single home like a piece of china, thrilling at the feel of the crisp green sleeve and the hiss of the needle as it made contact with the shiny black disc.

As the opening beats of 'Help!' boomed across the cosy room, Colin stoked the fire into flame and used the poker handle as a microphone. Jo seized the hearth shovel and, holding it like a guitar, jumped on to the battered green settee and started to sing. They were yelling out the chorus when their father trudged in the back door. Jack Elliot was greeted by the sight of his two children leaping around the furniture, shaking their heads wildly and screaming Beatles lyrics. Things are normal, Jack thought, pulling off his cap and throwing it at them.

'Thank you, thank you,' Colin said, clutching the poker, 'the audience is going wild!'

'And now for our second song.' Jo grinned at her father, jumping down and rushing over to change the record.

Colin shouted, 'put on "Day Tripper".'

'Aye,' Jo agreed, and soon they were belting out the lyrics, which they knew off by heart. As they came to a screaming crescendo, their father covered his ears.

'That's enough!' he ordered. 'By heck, you'll both be growing your hair next and wearing pink trousers.'

'Hipsters, Dad,' Jo corrected and went to give him a

kiss. 'You're filthy, where've you been today?'

'Knocking down half the West End – least it feels like it,' Jack said, achingly tired. Demolition work was a come-down from his time at sea, but these days there was plenty of it. Newcastle was turning into one large building site, he thought. He couldn't fathom the attraction of these new buildings of concrete and glass, or the need for a motorway cutting right through the city, but a job was a job. So every day he laboured on the planners' vision, dismantling overhead trolley cables, digging up cobbles, shovelling away bricks from demolished terraces and watching the people move out. The thought made him suddenly depressed.

'You smell of beer too,' Jo commented.

Jack sighed. 'You're as bad as your Auntie Pearl. A man's allowed a pint at the end of a working day.' He looked at his daughter's impish face and remembered he was supposed to be cross with her. 'And you, young madam, have some explaining to do,' he said severely. 'Why didn't you go straight to Marilyn's after school? Mrs Leishman's in a right state. You know I don't like you wandering around on your own.'

'I wasn't on me own,' Jo insisted, 'I was with Marilyn.'

'Don't be cheeky, you know what I mean.' Jack glowered. 'I like to know where you are, know that you're safe, 'specially now it's getting dark early.'

Colin piped up. 'She was all right, Dad. She was with me and the lads. It was us made her late – we wanted a bit help collecting firewood for the bonfire.'

Jo threw her brother a grateful look. Jack grunted. He was not sure if Colin was telling the whole truth, but he knew his son would always look out for his sister. He was not yet eleven, less than two years older than Joanne, but the boy was sensible beyond his age, Jack thought gratefully. He eased off his jacket and lowered his braces, preparing to strip-wash in the sink. As he did so, a postcard fell to the floor from his inner pocket. Jo pounced on it like a jackdaw, seeing the exotic picture of some gold-roofed palace. She turned the thin cardboard in anticipation.

'It's from Auntie Pearl!' she cried. 'Is she coming home soon? You never said she'd written.' Jo flung an accusing look at her father.

'I forgot,' Jack answered, flushing.

'Forgot!' Jo exclaimed.

'It came this morning . . . we were all in a hurry . . . you were late for school,' he blustered, but his daughter's look told him his excuses were lame.

'When's she coming?' Colin asked excitedly, his fair face flushing.

'Should be home in time for Bonfire Night.' Jack smiled to see their enthusiasm.

Jo gave him a funny look. 'You don't sound very pleased. Normally you're happy when a card comes from Auntie Pearl. Aren't you happy, Dad?'

He put an arm around her and kissed the top of her head. 'Of course I'm happy your auntie's coming to stay. It's just something else's been worrying me . . .'

'Oh,' Jo said, giving him a cautious glance. 'It's not about me making Mrs Leishman cross, is it?'

'No,' her father assured her, 'I wish that were all it was.'

'What's wrong, Dad?' Colin asked, looking up anxiously from stirring the soup.

Jack sighed heavily, his boyish face looking drawn. 'I've heard talk among the lads. They're going to start knocking down around here soon. Compulsory purchase.'

13

'What does that mean?' Jo said, her nose wrinkling.

'It means folk've got to clear out whether they want to or not. They say Jericho Street is going to be demolished for a new library,' her father explained.

'But how can we live in a library?' Jo puzzled.

Her father smiled, but Colin thumped her. 'Don't be daft! It means we'll have to move so they can build a library!'

'Aye,' her father confirmed, as he watched his son begin to dole out the soup. 'Street's been standing here for eighty years, but it's no longer good enough, so the council says. People want inside toilets and modern kitchens these days. That's why they haven't done any work on our street for years – just been waiting to knock it down rather than modernise. It's happening all over the city.'

Jo's face fell. Move from Jericho Street? she thought in shock. Impossible! She could not imagine living anywhere else. She loved her home. Her friends lived all around her. She knew every inch of this street, from its uneven pavements chalked with hopscotch to its towering lamp that was 'den' for games of tig. Jo's eyes welled up with tears.

'But I don't want to go anywhere else!' she quavered, realising with horror that she was about to cry. She buried her face in her father's grimy shirt and felt his arms tighten about her in comfort.

'Neither do I, pet, neither do I.' And although she could not bear to look him in the face, Jo could hear deep sadness in his voice too.

'When will it happen, Dad?' Colin asked, taking the news in his stride.

'Might not be for ages – couple of years even,' Jack replied. 'So don't worry yourself, pet.' He kissed

14

Jo's head. 'I shouldn't have said anything.'

'I wonder what Auntie Pearl will have to say about it,' Colin commented, as he plonked bowls of soup on the table.

Jo looked up suddenly and wiped her nose on her jumper. Of course! Auntie Pearl would make things better! She watched her father cross to the scullery and strip off his shirt. His back looked taut and muscular like a wrestler's, milky pale in contrast to his weathered brown neck.

'Auntie Pearl will know what to do, won't she, Dad?' Jo cried. But all she heard in reply were sharp grunts as he doused himself in cold water.

Then he turned, rubbing himself down. His face looked young again, rejuvenated. 'Aye, your Auntie Pearl will have her opinion, that's for sure,' he answered with a wink.

Chapter Two

A week or so before Auntie Pearl was due home, Jo came in from playing to find her father crying in front of the television. She had never seen tears on his face before and it shocked her deeply.

Rushing to his side, she seized his hand. 'What's wrong, Dad?'

He wiped his eyes quickly, embarrassed to be caught weeping. 'Those poor bairns!' he croaked, then cleared his throat and stood up. Just before he switched off the set, Jo saw a glimpse of a collapsed building, people standing around grim-faced.

'What's happened?' she asked.

He looked at her, his green eyes red-rimmed. 'There's been a terrible accident at a pit in Wales. Spoil heap's slid down and covered a school . . .'

Jo gasped. 'Were the children inside?' He nodded. 'Can they not get out?' she persisted. Jack pulled out a large handkerchief and blew into it vigorously. 'Are they dead then?' she demanded. 'How many are dead, Dad? Were those the parents standing about?'

Jack moved quickly towards her and squeezed her tight. 'Give us a hug, pet,' he said in a hoarse voice. She did as he asked, but could not get him to tell her more about the disaster with the children.

That night, lying in bed in the room she shared with

Colin, her brother supplied the details. He had seen it all on television at the Duggans' house: over a hundred children trapped and missing under the pit sludge, along with teachers and some other adults.

'Most of the schoolchildren in Aberfan were caught,' Colin told an appalled Jo. 'Just our age, an' all.'

Jo peered over the covers at the familiar walls, covered in cut-out magazine pictures of the Beatles and the Rolling Stones that she and Colin had collected. Next to the window was a poster of *Mary Poppins* from Pearl, given after Jo had pestered her to take them to see the film three times in one week. Her mind was in turmoil about the suffocating children lying under the slag in a Welsh village instead of tucked up in bed like she was. She wished Mary Poppins could be sent to get them out, do her magic to save them and make the parents happy again. But Mary Poppins was not real, whereas Aberfan was, and Jo lay awake a long time, imagining the empty bedrooms and the crying grown-ups in Wales.

The next day, running to school with Colin, she kept peering into the distance to see if the pit heap beyond Wallsend was on the move. But it was far away and they did not live on a mountainside, so Jo tried to stop worrying. That afternoon her father was standing at the school gates waiting for them. Colin slunk off with his friends, embarrassed to be met, but Jo took his hand, surprised and pleased that he had finished work early.

'Can we go to the baths?' she asked eagerly.

'If that's what you want,' Jack agreed, gripping her hand tightly. She persuaded him to take Marilyn too, and Colin and Mark.

All that week, her father turned up to see her out of school. She sensed it was something to do with the children in Wales, although she did not understand why this should make her father worry about her so much. Still, Jo soon realised she could ask for any treat and it was granted. They went ice skating and bowling; they went on the bus into Newcastle and even had tea at Fenwick's. Then, to cap it all, they were to go on the early train into town one Saturday morning to meet Pearl at Central Station.

Jo lay awake half the night, but this time it was excitement at seeing her aunt that made her sleepless, not the spectre of Aberfan. They had tidied and vacuumed her father's bedroom, changed the sheets and taken blankets downstairs to where Jack would sleep on the settee. She and Colin had put a collection of their best conkers into a bowl and placed these on the dressing table, beside a home-made card saying, 'Welcome Home, Auntie Pearl!'

Jo put on her tartan skirt without any fuss. 'It's a mini on you now,' her father exclaimed. 'Shows how long it's been since you last wore it. Maybes we'll have time to go and buy a new one before the train gets in . . .'

'It's fine, Dad!' Jo answered impatiently, yanking her skirt down. 'We don't want to be late.' She felt he was taking far too long shaving and ironing a clean shirt and slapping on Brylcreem in front of the mirror while he sang songs from *South Pacific*. Mark turned up on the doorstep just as they were leaving and was swept into going to meet Pearl too. They ran up and down the carriage in excitement, until Jack ordered them to sit still, and by the time they reached the huge echoing station in Newcastle, Jo was almost sick with anticipation.

Finally the London train pulled in and they rushed around behind the barrier, craning for a view of their aunt. 'Is that her?' Colin queried, pointing at a distant figure dressed in yellow and black, piling luggage on to a porter's trolley.

'That's her!' Jo cried.

'Looks like a bumble-bee,' laughed Mark, starting to make a buzzing noise.

Jo gave him a shove. 'Auntie Pearl!' she shouted, gesticulating madly. 'Over here!'

The figure in the brightly striped outfit waved back and hurried towards them, the porter trailing behind. She came through the barrier fumbling for her ticket, spilling half the contents from her PVC handbag, laughing and apologising breathlessly to the ticket collector. Jo rushed forward and flung her arms up around her neck. Pearl spun her round.

'Look at the size of you! You've legs like Twiggy's!' She showered her with kisses.

'You smell like a flower shop,' giggled Jo, 'and I love your cap. Can I try it on?'

Pearl pulled off the large black and yellow peaked hat and plonked it on Jo's head. 'Course you can. Well, let's have a kiss from me favourite lad, then!' she ordered Colin, and smothered him in a perfumed hug before he could resist. He flushed with embarrassed pleasure, a red beacon from his neck to his ginger hair.

Pearl ruffled Mark's black hair and kissed him too. 'By, you're turning into a handsome young man. I bet you'll kiss the girls and make them cry!'

Mark snorted, half amused, half disgusted. 'You'll not catch me kissing lasses,' he protested as Jo and Colin hooted with laughter.

Pearl patted her own stiff brown hair that was flicked up in glamorous waves. 'Jack,' she smiled at her brother-in-law. Smiling back, he nodded at her, reminding Jo of one of Colin's nervous zebra finches he kept in the backyard.

'You're looking grand,' he said. 'Let me take some of this luggage. Full of contraband, is it?'

'Did a bit of shopping in London. Got you some clobber from Carnaby Street,' Pearl said, winking at the children.

'I draw the line at hipsters,' Jack replied, looking merry.

'Ooh, I'm impressed,' Pearl teased. 'We'll make a trendy man out of you yet, Jack Elliot.'

They chattered non-stop all the way back to Wallsend, hearing about Pearl's voyage to East Africa and the Indian Ocean as a stewardess, and telling her their news from the past months.

'We had a street party after England won the World Cup,' Colin told her.

'Fancy having a party without me!' Pearl exclaimed.

'Don't worry, Auntie Pearl,' Jo assured her, 'you're home in time for Bonfire Night.'

'Aye,' Mark enthused, keen to please her too. 'Mam and Dad are having a party for grown-ups if you'd like to come to that.'

'That sounds grand,' Pearl smiled, swinging an arm round him. 'How is your mam?'

She felt his sinewy body tense under her hold, and his large dark eyes looked away from hers to Jo's. 'All right,' he mumbled.

'Well, tell her I'll be round to see her,' Pearl said lightly, and changed the subject.

Soon they were back in Wallsend, walking up to the high street and past the shops. Jo was proud of her popular aunt, who stopped every two minutes to talk to someone she knew.

'Look, the Forum's open,' Pearl commented on the new shopping centre as they passed. 'You'll have to take me in there soon.'

'It's just shops,' Jo said with impatience, eager to have her home. 'Will you take us swimming this afternoon? Or to the matinée? *My Fair Lady*'s on again.'

'Ugh, soppy!' cried Colin and Mark together.

'Listen to the pair of you! Well, we like a good musical, don't we, Jo?' Pearl defended her niece. 'Us girls will go to the flicks together.'

Jo felt special at being chosen and pulled a triumphant face at the boys.

'I think we should let Pearl get home and settled first before you bully her into anything,' Jack decreed. But it took them twenty minutes to get up Jericho Street and into number eleven, for all the neighbours were out to welcome Pearl Rimmer. Mrs Leishman spent ages admiring her outfit and quizzing her about the clothes being worn in London, until Jo wanted to scream with impatience. Finally they got her inside and had her opening up her bags to see what treasures she had brought. There was a pair of curved brass daggers for Colin, which he and Mark dashed away with. 'I'll be Bond,' Colin cried, 'and you be the villain.'

'This is for you,' Pearl said, handing a package to Jo. 'From Carnaby Street.'

Jo opened it suspiciously, fearing it was a dress. She did not want to hurt her aunt's feelings, but she would have loved a pair of daggers like Colin's. Unwrapping it, however, she found a small waistcoat made out of dark leather. It smelled like new boots and was just the sort of thing Mick Jagger might wear.

'It's fab!' Jo cried, and flung her arms round her aunt. 'I love it!' She put it on over her old jumper, ignoring

22

the fact that it was too big for her skinny frame. Jack and Pearl laughed indulgently. 'I'm off to show Marilyn.'

By the time she had shown off to her friend and cycled up and down the street so that everyone could see her new waistcoat, Jack had returned with fish and chips for them all. Later Jo went with her father and aunt to see *My Fair Lady*, while Colin went with Mark to watch Mark's older brother, Gordon, play football for Wallsend Boys' Club. Jo felt a momentary pang that she was missing out on something, for she secretly liked to watch the strong, long-haired Gordon play. She was rather in awe of Mark's big brother, who completely ignored her presence, but she admired him for being a good footballer and for playing the electric guitar like Paul McCartney.

But having Pearl and her father's undivided attention was even better and she revelled in an afternoon in front of the big colour screen, eating sweets and losing herself in the story and songs. The heroine, Eliza was like her, a poor girl without a mother who was good at singing. She rose from the backstreets to be a celebrity, invited out to parties. Maybe one day, Jo herself would be a famous singer, a pop star, she fantasised in the cosy dark of the auditorium.

Sitting between her father and Pearl, feeling happy and safe, she wondered if this was what it felt like to have two parents. Was Pearl anything like her real mother? she mused. After all, they had been sisters. It comforted her to think her mother might have been as nice as Pearl, but then she didn't really know. Her father rarely talked about her dead mother, and neither did her aunt. Apart from the photograph of her on the sideboard and a wedding picture of her parents on the mantelpiece in the front room, she had no idea what her mother was

23

like. All they revealed was an impression of fair wavy hair and a dreamy smile, a remote fairy-tale figure in a flowing white dress. She imagined her mother as soft and gentle, like the mother in the washing-up-liquid advert on TV, who never got cross or laughed too loud. Not very like Pearl at all really, Jo thought.

If only Pearl didn't have to go sailing round the world, she sighed as the film ended, they could be like this always. For the first time it crossed Jo's mind that there was nothing to stop Pearl marrying her father. But then Pearl would become her stepmother, and Jo's mind filled with all the fairy tales where stepmothers were cruel and wicked to children. She would hate Pearl to change into one of those creatures, so perhaps it was best if she stayed as an auntie, Jo decided.

On the way home they bought chestnuts from the fruit shop and roasted them in the fire at teatime. Colin came back with Mark and Skippy and they all stayed for sausages and beans and spicy rice pudding, washed down with a special bottle of dandelion and burdock. They played Pearl all their Beatles singles and Mark dashed home and returned with his brother's new Rolling Stones LP, *Aftermath*. Pearl clapped and laughed at their impersonations of the bands, then insisted on hunting out and playing her collection of Cliff Richard and Tom Jones records that they kept in the sideboard. Mark screwed up his face and mimicked Tom Jones, until Pearl swiped him with a cushion.

'Isn't it time you lads were off home?' Jack finally said. Skippy said his goodbyes and disappeared, but Mark seemed reluctant to go. Jo knew he was wanting to stop the night, but her father seemed keen to get them all to bed.

'Can't he stay?' Jo asked her father.

'Another night when we're not so full,' Jack promised.

Colin said casually, 'If we get to move house, can I have a room of me own where Mark can come and stay?'

Pearl looked at Jack in surprise. 'You're moving? When?'

Jack flushed. 'Never, if I can help it,' he blustered. 'It's just rumours at the moment.'

'What rumours?' Pearl asked. 'Come on, Mr Secretive. I need to know if I'm on the move.'

'They're going to knock down Jericho Street,' Colin said.

'But you needn't worry, it won't happen for ages,' Jack insisted. 'Your home is still here.'

Jo saw Mark's troubled look. She knew he did not want to move away from his friends either. He had told her that his parents had rowed all week over where they might go. Matty wanted to stay near the docks for work, while Norma yearned for a large semi with a garden on one of the green-belt estates beyond the coast road.

'You won't let it happen, will you?' Jo asked anxiously. 'Dad says they can't force us to go if we really don't want to. You don't want to, do you, Auntie Pearl?'

Pearl did not answer her, but looked challengingly at Jack. 'Where are they talking of rehousing you?'

Jack's flushed face looked wary as he replied. 'Could be a block of flats – or a new estate up by the coast road. Away from the heart of things either way.'

Pearl gave an exasperated laugh. 'Well, what are all the long faces for?' she cried. 'I think knocking down Jericho Street's the best idea I've heard in ages. It's a slum! We could have a house with a garden, a proper bathroom! Or a nice clean flat with an electric cooker.'

Jo gawped in shock; this was not what she had

expected. Her aunt was attacking their beloved home – *Pearl*'s own home, for she had no other family but them. Fancy calling it a slum!

Jack was offended. 'We don't need anything fancy,' he scowled. 'This place has done us proud since—' He checked himself. 'Since Jo was a baby,' he said carefully. 'Why should we want to move?'

Pearl was suddenly cross. 'Because everything's out of the ark! That kitchen range should be in a museum – and that filthy fire. Having to wash in the sink and trek out in the rain to go to the toilet. Think of the kids, Jack. You could give them a grand home somewhere else – a new start.'

'They've got a good home here,' he snapped. 'I do the best I can for them. They like it here, damn it! Don't you go interfering!'

Pearl gave him a furious look and jumped to her feet. 'Oh, I don't believe I'm hearing this! Come on, Mark, I'll walk you home.'

'I can manage on me own,' Mark said, awkward at the sudden argument. But Pearl was not going to be diverted.

'I want to say hello to your mam – and I need a breath of air,' she said pointedly to Jack.

'Too warm and cosy for you with a real fire, is it?' Jack needled.

'Yes, too stifling by half!' Pearl retorted, glaring at him. She bundled Mark out ahead of her and slammed the door. There was shocked silence in the room for a moment, and then Jack told them gruffly to get to bed.

'I thought Auntie Pearl liked it here with us?' Jo said, quite bewildered.

'That's enough,' Jack said curtly. 'I don't want to hear any more about moving or what your aunt's opinion is. She lets her mouth go too much.'

They scrambled upstairs and quickly got ready for bed in the icy bedroom. Jo lay shivering under the covers, wondering how such a happy day had ended so badly. She waited for her father to come and kiss her goodnight, but eventually heard the back door close and his footsteps clomp off down the street.

'He's gone and left us!' she hissed to Colin.

Her brother grunted sleepily. 'He'll be looking for Auntie Pearl.'

'What if a burglar comes in while he's out?' Jo imagined.

'Not in this street,' Colin yawned. 'Nowt worth nicking.'

'What if the house burns down?' Jo persisted.

'Then we'll *have* to move,' Colin said in a muffled voice from under his covers. 'Now shut your gob and go to sleep.'

After a pause, Jo whispered, 'I've never heard Dad and Auntie Pearl shout at each other like that before. Do you think she'll come back?'

'She'll have to – her things are here,' Colin reasoned. 'Now will you shurrup!'

By the time Jo heard her father return, Colin was asleep, but she still wanted a proper goodnight. When he did not come up, she decided she needed a trip to the outside toilet and climbed out of bed anyway. As she tiptoed across the cold linoleum, she heard the tap of thin heels across the yard and the back door latch lift again.

Crouching in the dark on the stairs, she heard Pearl's voice. Jo edged down the banisters, wondering if she should make a dash through the kitchen or hang on until Pearl came upstairs. But her aunt did not come. As she crept closer, she could hear their voices, soft and apologetic, and realised with relief that they were making up. She heard the rattle of the poker in the fire and someone pouring tea. Then the murmur of voices changed. There was a comment from Pearl, then an abrupt answer from Jack, and their voices grew louder. Now Jo could not help listening.

'Why don't you just go and look at some of the new houses?' Pearl asked. 'It wouldn't do any harm. Take the bairns, see what they think.'

'Leave the bairns out of this,' Jack replied. 'They're too young to know what they want.'

'Joanne's nine now – and Colin's nearly eleven,' Pearl cried, 'and they both know their minds! They're growing up, Jack. They're not babies any longer. They should be having their own rooms soon.'

Her father's voice sounded agitated. 'We're happy here, we don't want change. Don't you go filling their heads with ideas of grand houses we can't afford.'

'You know I could help pay for a new place,' Pearl offered. 'It could be a fresh start for all of us, Jack.' Her voice was pleading.

'I don't want your money,' Jack said, offended.

Jo heard Pearl make an impatient noise. 'And I'm sick of living off your charity!' There was a pause and then she went on quickly, 'I'm sorry, Jack, I don't mean to sound ungrateful, but I've always lived in someone else's home – first Aunt Julia's, and then it became yours and Gloria's. I don't remember what me parents' home was like, it was that long ago they died. But I'm thirty-two now, Jack. I'm not Gloria's little sister any more. I'm a grown woman and I want what grown women want! Has it never occurred to you how I might feel about all this?'

Jo was hopping around by this time, desperate for the

toilet. But if she emerged now they would know she had been eavesdropping on their conversation.

'I've always tried to make you feel welcome here,' Jack said defensively. 'What more do you want of me?'

'Oh! Nothing, Jack,' Pearl said angrily. 'You'll still be here when they're knocking this place down around your ears, I can see that! And I know why. You're still torturing yourself over my sister. You see this place as some sort of sanctuary where you don't have to remember what happened. But Jericho Street's never been the escape you thought it would be. Gloria's been dead over eight years, yet you still let her rule your life, don't you? You tiptoe around her photograph like she's some sort of saint. Saint bloody Gloria!'

'No!' Jack cried. 'How dare you talk about your sister like that!'

'Well, it's true. Sometimes I really hate her,' Pearl said heatedly, 'for the way she wrecked all our lives! When I think of those lovely bairns, Colin and Jo . . . !'

'Shut up!' Jack shouted. 'How dare you blame her!'

'You can stew in the past,' Pearl continued, unabashed, 'but I'll not be made to feel guilty any more. The future's all that matters. You've got to live for tomorrow. And I'm going to buy myself a flat if you won't budge from here!'

Jo could hang on no longer. She burst into the kitchen. 'I need a wee! I wasn't listening,' she gasped as she dived across the room and out of the back door. They gawped at her in astonishment. Jo skidded over the freezing yard and plonked herself on the icy seat. She was shaking hard, partly from the cold and partly from overhearing the terrible row in the kitchen. She did not understand it all, but she knew that the argument had not just been about moving. It had been about her mother, Gloria, the fairy-tale princess. Auntie Pearl had spoken about hating her, Jo thought with shock. It made her feel sick inside. Perhaps her aunt was just like a wicked stepmother after all, having bad thoughts about people. How could she hate her mother, Jo wondered, when Dad had always said she was so good and with the angels?

When Jo darted back into the house, both adults were looking warily at her. Pearl held out her arms. 'Come here, pet.' But Jo side-stepped and bolted for the door into the passage. She could not look at either of them. She felt strange inside, as if she had eaten something she should not have.

A few minutes later, she heard someone come up the stairs after her. She buried herself under the covers and pretended to be asleep. When her father bent over and kissed the top of her head, she held her breath. She wished more than anything that she had never heard the argument downstairs or the frightening words, but she had. Jo was aware that there were secrets she knew nothing about that her father kept from her – something to do with this house and the memory of her young mother. Auntie Pearl had talked about her mother as if she still lived with them and would not let them move.

Maybe her aunt was just jealous because her mother had been pretty and had worn a long white dress like a princess, all around Wallsend. Jo was hurt by Pearl's words about hating her mother, and for making her father so angry that he had come too late to kiss her goodnight. But worst of all, the disdain her aunt had shown for their home in Jericho Street had tarnished Jo's unquestioning love for the house. She stared through the dark at the damp walls where her pictures of the Beatles were crinkling and lifting, and was filled with a strange hankering after something better.

Chapter Three

Jo was glad to get back to school on Monday, for a bad atmosphere choked the house like smoke from a blocked chimney. After school, she tried to talk to Colin about it, but he brushed off her questions and went to band practice at the Boys' Brigade. She found Mark kicking a football around in the back lane.

'Things still bad?' Mark asked, seeing Jo's glum expression. She nodded. 'I've never heard your dad raise his voice like that before,' he added. 'It was a bit of a shock, but.'

'I know,' Jo agreed, and found herself confiding in him about the row she had overheard later the same night. 'I don't think it's just the house Auntie Pearl doesn't like,' she puzzled. 'She was saying things about me mam – nasty things – really making me dad upset.' Jo remembered how wretched it had made her feel inside. 'Now she's trying to be all nice to me, but I don't want to speak to her. Auntie Pearl shouldn't have said those things, should she?'

Mark shook his head. 'It's not like her to be nasty about anyone. Mind, I've heard a lot worse at my house. Me dad never has a good word to say about anybody – except maybes Gordon. But then our Gordon's good at everything and I'm not.'

'Yes you are!' Jo defended him. 'You're dead good at

footie – and conker fights, and climbing trees.'

Mark gave her a sheepish grin and laughed. 'That'll really get me into the grammar school!'

It suddenly dawned on Jo that next summer Mark and her brother and Skippy would be leaving her primary school and moving on to big school. She could not imagine them not being around in the playground. Her father was hopeful that Colin would pass the eleven-plus and go to the grammar, but she had often heard Matty Duggan tell Mark that he was 'thick as a plank' and bound to fail. It already seemed taken for granted by his parents and headmaster that Mark would be going to the secondary modern.

They squatted by the wall in the fading light, sharing Jo's cinder toffee, both reluctant to go home. Mark suddenly asked, 'Do you want to come down to me Nana's the night? She said I could dunk some apples for Hallowe'en.'

'Fab!' cried Jo, remembering how Ivy liked to celebrate Hallowe'en. She had been married to a Scotsman, who had kept up the tradition where everyone else made a big thing of Guy Fawkes Night instead. But Ivy hated fireworks.

'Fab? You sound just like Pearl,' Mark teased.

Jo pulled a face. She knew she was going to need her aunt's cooperation in making a turnip lantern and persuading Jack that she could stay out late on a school night. 'Haway! Let's ask Auntie Pearl if she'll cut out a turnip for us.'

Pearl seemed delighted to help. As she gouged out the turnip and cut holes for the eyes she told them about the flat she'd been to see. 'It's on the ninth floor and you can see right up the river in both directions – Tynemouth and the sea in one, and the Tyne Bridge in the other. It's fab!' Mark and Jo caught each other's look and smirked as Pearl chattered on. 'I'll take you to see it if you like and you can come and stay when I'm back on leave.'

Jo felt a flicker of excitement. It would be like going on holiday to stay in a new flat halfway to the sky, with a view like a bird over Wallsend and far beyond. But she was still cross with Pearl and was not going to show her enthusiasm.

'So you're really going to move then?' Mark asked.

'Yes,' said Pearl firmly. 'It's time I got somewhere of my own. I've been like a cuckoo living in someone else's nest all my life.'

Jo didn't really know what she meant, but she could not help her reproachful question. 'Won't you miss being here with us, then?'

Pearl swung an arm around her at once. 'I'll not have to miss you if you come and stay with me when I'm home, will I?'

Jo wriggled out of her hold. 'Depends what me dad says,' she answered, feeling torn.

Pearl continued digging out the turnip. 'They'll have to remove your dad with a bulldozer. But I'm not stopping in this place any longer. You've got to look ahead, not live in the past like your dad. Besides,' she grinned, 'I need somewhere where I can cover the walls with all my souvenirs that your dad hates!'

Jack returned weary from labouring and allowed Jo to go to Ivy's as long as Pearl went too. 'I'll stop in and wait for Colin – don't you be too late, mind.' Pearl walked them down to Nile Street, carrying the lantern. She seemed just as keen to get out as Jack was to stay in, Jo noticed.

Jo breathed in the smell of burnt turnip in the dank

air and skipped ahead excitedly. There were other lanterns glowing in front windows and occasionally they would hear the bang and fizz of early fireworks going off in the distance. Crossing the high street aglow with shop lights, they descended the bank towards the docks. In the dark, the huge hulk of a half-built tanker loomed over the end of the street, like a ghostly monster. Ivy's door was open and a gaggle of children were gathered outside waving sparklers. There were two lanterns balanced on the windowsill and two more sitting on the hearth either side of a roaring fire. On the table was spread an array of treats: home-made fairy cakes, gingerbread men and toffee apples.

'Haway in, hinnies!' Ivy welcomed with a cheery smile. 'Eeh, it's grand to see you back, Pearl. Sit yourself down. I told the bairns we couldn't start without you, bonny lad,' she told Mark, hugging him to her faded apron. Mark grinned and rushed to turn out the electric light so that the room suddenly leapt with shadows and their faces were bathed in soft firelight. The neighbours' children squeezed in and began to help themselves to the food in the dark.

'Will you tell us one of your scary stories, Nana Ivy?' Jo asked through a mouthful of cake.

Ivy obliged as they munched their way through toffee apples, the thick gooey toffee sticking to their teeth. It was all about a shipwreck and a ghostly crew, and Ivy claimed it was a true story passed on by her seafaring father from South Shields. Mark's eyes widened into huge dark pools as he hung on every word.

'. . . And no one ever saw the captain again!' Ivy concluded. 'Aye, your great-grandfather Matthias was a great one for a tale.'

Afterwards they dunked for apples in Ivy's zinc bath

that usually hung on a nail in her backyard. Mark and Jo gave up trying to drop forks from their teeth into the bobbing apples and instead plunged their faces into the chilly water, soaking their hair and clothes. By the finish, Ivy's floor was awash with water and the apples ended up being thrown around the street outside. But no one told them off and Ivy seemed content to share a bottle of barley wine with Pearl beside the fire while the children rampaged outside. When Jo rushed in for a drink of Ivy's home-made lemonade, she heard Pearl telling Ivy about the new flats.

'Well, it sounds canny for you young'uns,' Ivy wheezed, her stout body filling the chair by the fire, 'but you'll not catch me living that far above the ground. Where do you hang your washing? And how does the milkman deliver your pint if you don't have a doorstep?' She shook her head in bafflement. 'No, I like a front door on to the street where you can have a bit crack with your neighbours and the tradesmen. You know where you are with a front doorstep.'

Pearl rolled her eyes. 'Ivy, you sound just like Jack. I like everything that's new. I need a bit of change in my life now and then – but not him.'

Ivy gave a sympathetic nod. 'Aye, it's a shame you two . . .' Then she saw Jo in the gloom and stopped. 'All right, hinny?'

'Aye,' Jo said, gulping down her drink and dashing for the door again.

But Pearl decided it was time to go and soon they were off up the street with their lantern burnt out and clutching small parcels of food for Colin and Jack. Jo went to bed with her mind still vivid with Ivy's stories of ghostly ships and missing captains, but she did not end up creeping into Pearl's bed for comfort, as she often did when her aunt was home. Somehow she felt it would be disloyal to her father or her dead mother, she was not sure which. For despite Pearl's attempts to win her round, she knew something had changed between them.

The week did not pass quickly enough for Jo, as excitement grew for Bonfire Night. Their street bonfire was the biggest she could remember, with bits of stolen garden fence supplementing the large branches and debris from the Burn. To their satisfaction it was bigger than the one built by Kevin McManners's gang two streets away. It was to be lit at six thirty when everyone was back from work, and then the grown-ups were invited to a party at the Duggans', after the fireworks had been let off.

At last Saturday came, and all day they roamed the park and the Burn collecting final barrowloads of firewood. Mrs Leishman had helped make a guy by providing material to stuff into an old pair of Colin's trousers and a jumper of Skippy's. She sewed them together and they added a head made out of newspaper stuffed into a brown paper bag. Mark drew on the face, with a black moustache and a big nose.

'Looks like me dad, doesn't it?' he said with satisfaction.

Gordon, overhearing, gave his brother a cuff, but climbed on to the Duggans' back wall to put it on top of the bonfire for them. Jo felt her insides twisting at the sight of Gordon in his denim jacket and flared jeans. His shaggy hair fell into his eyes and she loved the way he looked at her with sultry disdain. He was the nearest thing to a Rolling Stone she had ever met.

Jo had refused to go shopping with Pearl that after-noon, even though her aunt had promised her a treat from Woolworth's. Jo had felt bad at the look of disappointment on Pearl's face, but she could not rid herself of the memory of her poisonous words against her mother.

When Jo and Colin clattered in for tea, Pearl had fried egg and chips waiting for them, and a bag each by their place on the table. Jack came in from feeding Colin's finches, looking more cheerful than he had done all week. Pearl had put her name down for one of the high-rise flats and there had been no more talk about the rest of them moving. They appeared to have come to a wary truce on the matter.

'See your aunt's been spoiling you again,' Jack smiled.

Jo tore into the paper bag on her side plate. She got a whiff of plastic and gasped in delight. 'It's a Beatles wig!' she cried, pulling the black plastic dome over her auburn hair. Leaping on to an armchair, she craned to view herself in the mirror over the mantelpiece. The plastic sideburns dug painfully into her high cheekbones, but she loved what she saw.

'I look like Paul McCartney, don't I?' she demanded.

'More like Ringo,' Colin teased, for they both thought Ringo Starr the ugly one.

Pearl had bought Colin one too, which he put on self-consciously. It was too small for his square head and perched like a hat on his thick red hair. Jo burst out laughing.

'Well, you can't talk!' she exclaimed.

As Colin whipped it off, Pearl said hastily, 'I'll take it back and change it.'

'No,' Colin assured her, not wanting to sound un-grateful. 'I'll take it to school and swap it. It's great.'

They bolted their tea, anxious to be outside again. Jack made them wrap up in scarves and balaclavas and gloves, as well as their gabardines. But once they escaped into the lane, Jo whipped off her hat and stuffed it in a pocket so she could show off her plastic wig. She was delighted when Mrs Leishman failed to recognise her.

Soon the bonfire was lit and their faces glowed hot in the heat from the blaze, while their toes went numb with cold. Jo did not care, for she was brimming over with excitement as the sky lit up with multicoloured fireworks and Catherine wheels spun crazily on yard posts. She ran around with the others, brandishing sparklers like swords, ignoring her father's warnings to be careful. Matty Duggan came into the street waving a bottle of beer in either hand and called the men in for a drink. Pearl persuaded Jack to go in for one. 'Colin will keep an eye on our Jo for a few minutes while we go into the Duggans', won't you?' she asked the boy. 'I want a chat with Norma.'

When the fireworks ran out, they drifted into the surrounding lanes to criticise other bonfires and set off bangers outside the big houses near the Green. Mark shinned up one high garden wall at the back of a large villa belonging to a bank manager called Bewick. 'Dare you to follow!' he hissed and dropped out of sight. It was a long garden with an orchard from which Mark and Colin often stole apples. Grumpy Bewick, as they called him, had threatened them with the police if he ever caught them.

Colin turned to Jo, saying, 'Wait here and don't wander off.' He swung himself up on the overhanging tree.

'But I want to come!' Jo protested, as he disappeared over the high brick wall. She could hear them rustling about in the undergrowth on the other side, laughing under their breath. Her heart began to hammer at the risk they were taking. Jo got a toe-hold in the wall and began to heave herself up.

She had just pulled herself into the tree when she heard noisy footsteps echoing down the pavement and a girl's throaty laughter. Jo froze on her perch as a couple stopped under the tree in the dark shadow of the wall. They were talking in whispers, sharing a cigarette. With her ears muffled by her Beatles wig, she could not catch what they were saying, but there was something intimate about the way they laughed together. Jo held her breath, not daring to make a move.

In the dark it was impossible to identify them, then one of them flicked the cigarette into the gutter and the whispering stopped. For a moment, Jo wondered what they were doing, until she heard a sucking noise like someone eating an orange. She peered down and saw the two heads welded together and arms fumbling as if someone had put itching powder down their clothes.

They're snogging! Jo thought in horror. She had seen couples doing it in the park if the keeper wasn't in view, but she had always looked quickly away in distaste. Part of her wished she was safely on the other side of the wall with the lads, but part of her kept watching in fascination. The boy's arm seemed to be stuck inside the girl's jacket. Maybe he's keeping his hand warm, Jo puzzled. They were both making soft sighing noises as if they were slightly out of breath.

Just when she was wondering how long the snogging could go on, there was a cry from Colin on the other side of the wall. 'He's coming out!'

'When I chuck it, run for the tree!' It was Mark's command. A moment later there was an ear-splitting bang and a frantic scrabbling and giggling among the bushes.

The girl snogger cried out, 'What's going on?'

The boy snogger swore and pulled her away from the wall. 'Haway, we'll find somewhere in the park,' he said, his voice deep and slightly breathless.

As they stepped out of the deep shadows, Jo smothered a gasp to see who it was. She recognised Gordon's broad denimed shoulders and his collar-length hair. He had his arms firmly clamped around the full figure of Barbara Thornton, who worked at the laundry and was at least two years older than him. Jo's heart began to hammer even harder at the thought of having witnessed such an intimate moment in Gordon Duggan's life. It made her feel quite peculiar, a touch excited.

Then all hell broke loose behind her as Mark and Colin came crashing through the bushes beyond the wall, pursued by angry shouts down the garden.

'I'll wring your necks, you little buggers!' a man hollered, and a rotten apple flew past Jo's head. A second one caught Colin on the shoulder as he flung himself at the wall.

Jo tumbled out of the tree almost on top of Gordon, skinning her knees. 'What the bloody hell . . . ?' Gordon said, astonished. Jo tried not to cry out with the pain.

'Eeh, that lad's been spying on us!' Barbara cried indignantly.

Gordon pulled Jo roughly to her feet, peering hard. 'It's not a lad – it's Joanne Elliot.' He stared at her. 'What's that plastic thing on your head?'

'It's me new Beatles wig, of course,' Jo answered, going red in the face.

Suddenly Gordon laughed. 'Looks more like a crash helmet than a wig!' And then Barbara was laughing at her too.

Jo felt tears of humiliation sting her eyes, but her

words of protest never came as Colin scrambled out of the tree above. From over the wall they could hear Grumpy bawling that he was going for the police. 'By God, I'll get you this time!' A moment later Mark appeared in the tree above, laughing helplessly.

Gordon cursed him. 'I might've known you'd be behind this.'

Barbara started to pull him away. 'Come on, Gordon, let's gan before there's trouble.' They were already moving off down the street when another apple came whistling over the wall and hit Mark on the cheek. He leapt, slightly off balance, and landed awkwardly on the pavement.

'Agh-ya!' he cried, clutching his ankle.

'Run!' Colin ordered, pushing Jo in front of him.

She resisted. 'Are you all right, Mark?' she demanded.

Mark tried to stand up but his face creased in pain. 'I've twisted me ankle,' he gasped.

Jo rushed to his side as Colin called up the street, 'Gordon, wait on! Mark's hurt himself.'

There was a rattling of bolts on the other side of the garden gate. Grumpy was still in pursuit.

Gordon turned round and shouted, 'Serves the little bugger right!' Then he carried on, disappearing into the dark with Barbara.

'Get up!' Jo cried. 'We'll help you.'

Colin gripped Mark's other arm. 'Hang on to us and start hopping.'

With groans from Mark and encouragement from Colin and Jo, the threesome began to hobble away as quickly as they could. But they had hardly got across the street when the garden door burst open and out pounced Mr Bewick.

'Stop where you are!' he ordered, lunging forward

and seizing Colin and Mark by their coats. 'Now which little beggar threw that firework into my garden?'

'Ah-ya! I did,' Mark admitted at once.

'We both did,' Colin said.

'Your parents are going to hear about this!' Grumpy barked. 'Where do you live?'

Jo began to feel sick. Nobody answered. 'Do you want the police involved?' he threatened.

'Jericho Street,' Colin mumbled.

Grumpy grunted. 'Might've known. Well, you're going to take me there, so start walking!' he ordered.

They trailed ahead, a subdued trio, with Mark limping in pain and their captor prodding them in the back to be quick. As they approached the Duggans' house, Mark began to panic.

'We could come and do jobs for you after school, mister,' he offered. 'Tidy up your garden.'

'Do you think I'd let your sort loose in my garden?' he answered with disdain.

'Wash your car, then?' Mark suggested. 'Only please don't tell me dad!'

Grumpy gave a grim smile of triumph. 'You should have thought about that before. Now tell me where you live.'

His mother came to the door, looking flushed and slightly tipsy. She gawped in surprise at the solemn children and the irate bank manager, who was in full flow at their bad behaviour. As Norma fled to get her husband, Pearl suddenly appeared.

'What are you doing here? Your father's just gone home expecting you to be there,' she exclaimed.

Jo began to gabble. 'It was just for a laugh, but we're really sorry, and Mark's hurt his ankle . . .'

Pearl spoke quickly. 'I'm sure the children really are

sorry for what they've done.' She smiled apologetically at Mr Bewick. 'And I promise you, they'll do nothing like this again.' She gave them a warning look. 'I'll take these two home now to their dad. He'll be wondering where they are.'

The bank manager seemed slightly mollified. 'Very well, as long as this is the last of it . . .' He turned to go.

Just then Matty barged past Pearl, his drunken face puce with anger.

'What's the little runt been up to now?' he bellowed. And before Jo's appalled eyes he seized Mark viciously by the hair. Jo could see the terror in her friend's eyes. 'Trespassing and thieving, were you? Showing me up again!'

'I'm sorry, Dad,' Mark squealed. But Matty slapped the side of his head so hard it sent him staggering.

'You will be by the time I'm finished with you!' And he kicked his son, making him yell with pain.

The bank manager looked startled at the violence. 'I don't think that's necessary—'

'You bugger off!' Matty roared.

Norma stepped forward and quickly ushered Jo and Colin out of the door, along with Mr Bewick. 'Best if you go now,' she said to Pearl. Jo thought she looked frightened too and did not want them to see any more.

'I'll come back, Norma,' Pearl offered in alarm. Matty was swearing at Mark to get upstairs and the boy was hobbling as fast as he could to escape.

'No you won't,' Matty growled, turning his drunken abuse on her. 'You stop interfering and get back to your fancy man – little Jackie Elliot,' he sneered. 'Turned him into a right doormat – can't even drink like a man any more.'

'Don't talk about Jack like that – and in front of his

43

bairns,' Pearl answered indignantly. 'At least he can take his drink!'

'What do you mean by that?' Matty leered at her, threateningly.

Norma tried to calm him. 'She means nothing, Matty.' She gave Pearl a pleading look. 'Please go,' she whispered.

But Matty pushed her aside and swore foully at Pearl. 'Get out of my house! And take Jack's filthy brats with you an' all! I don't want to see any of you round here again, do you hear?'

Pearl put a protective arm around Colin and Jo. 'Don't worry. I wouldn't want them anywhere near a foul-mouthed drunk like you!' She steered them quickly away, just before the door slammed on them.

Jo was shaking. 'But what about Mark . . . ?' she asked in fear. 'He's got a twisted ankle.'

'His mam'll see to him,' Pearl snapped. Then, seeing Jo's anxious face, added, 'I'll check on him tomorrow when things have calmed down.' She sighed. 'If you hadn't been where you shouldn't, none of this would have happened.'

'That's right,' Mr Bewick said from the shadows. Jo had forgotten he was still there. 'I really think you should keep those children of yours away from such people. Like father, like son, they say.'

Pearl bristled. 'Mark's not a bad lad, just high-spirited. But I'm sorry for the trouble that's been caused tonight. Colin and Jo will come round tomorrow and clear up any mess they've made in your garden.'

'Well, that's not necessary . . .' Mr Bewick blustered.

'No, I insist.' Pearl was firm. 'And so will their father, when he hears of this.'

They parted quickly and Pearl marched the children

in silence down the street to number eleven. Jack seemed so relieved to see them home safely that they did not receive the scolding they'd expected, and they hurried up to bed without a word. Lying in the dark, thinking about Mark, Jo heard Colin whisper, 'Are you still awake?'

'Aye,' she whispered back. 'I can't stop thinking about what might be happening to Mark.'

'Me too,' Colin admitted. 'I've seen Matty give him a thumping before. He says terrible things to him an' all.'

'What sort of things?' Jo asked in confusion. 'And why?'

Colin sat up in bed. 'It's to do with his mam. If I tell you, promise you won't tell anybody? Not even Mark that I've told you.'

'Promise,' Jo answered, leaning closer to hear.

Mark lay huddled under his bed, still fully clothed, curled up as small as he could. He had rolled under there to escape the kicking his father was giving him, until Matty had tired of hurling abuse at him and had staggered off to find his mother. His heart still hammered and his body ached all over. He could not stop shivering, yet he dared not come out. His mind was branded with horrible images of what had just happened.

Soon after the row on the doorstep, the last of the neighbours had swiftly departed and he and his mother had been left to bear the brunt of his father's temper. They were both to blame for the party ending too soon. The abuse had started in the usual way, with Mark being called worse than useless and constantly compared with Gordon.

'At least Gordon takes after me,' Matty had boasted. 'He's got my brains and brawn. That lad's going to make something of himself – he'll get a good job at the yards like I did.'

His mother had made the mistake of answering back. 'As long as he stays off the drink, you mean.'

'What did you say, woman?' Matty had shouted.

'Well, when's the last time you put in a full week's work?' she demanded. 'It's a good job I'm working. Cleaning offices might not be much, but we need it.'

Matty lunged at her and struck her across the mouth. 'Don't you speak to me like that!' Mark instinctively shrank back as his mother clasped her mouth in pain and tried to dodge her husband. But Matty pursued her into the bedroom. 'And we all know what you do in those offices after hours, don't we? Screw the bosses, don't you?'

Norma groaned in denial and shook her head. He had her pinned against the bulky wardrobe. 'Slut!' he shouted. 'Just like you've always been.'

'Leave me alone,' she whimpered.

'You like coloured men best, don't you? That's how we've got a little darkie bastard in the family. Whore!' He seized her face in a vice-like grip.

'No, I never!' Norma wailed. 'He's your bairn, no one else's. I've told you that a hundred times.'

But Matty seemed to thrill at the power he now had over his cowering wife. He smacked her again. 'You'd do it anywhere, wouldn't you? On the floor, eh, is that where you do it?'

'No!' she screamed as he began to hit her with both fists, pummelling her to the ground. 'Please, Matty . . . !'

Mark watched in horror as his mother tried to protect herself with her thin arms, her pink crocheted dress riding up over her thighs. Matty tore at her tights. Mark wanted to run from the room like he usually did if there was a fight, hoping that Gordon would intervene. But Gordon was somewhere in the park with Barbara Thornton and he was the only one who could help his mother.

His heart pounding in fear, Mark croaked, 'Leave her alone!'

He leapt at his father and tried to pull him away. But he had none of the strength in his slim shoulders that Matty had, and all he could do was cling on to his father's broad back. Matty appeared not to notice until Mark sank his teeth into his shoulder.

'Agh, you little bastard!' Matty turned in shock and sent Mark flying. But it had the effect of diverting his father's drunken wrath on to him. Matty went after Mark, kicking him where he sprawled on the floor. Mark was too winded to scream, as he tried to roll out of the way. 'You're a disgrace,' his father shouted. 'You've made a laughing stock of me round here! Just look at you – everyone can tell you're no son of mine. You've a whore for a mother!'

Sobbing, Mark managed to scramble out of the room and dive into his own bedroom. Behind him, he could hear his mother weeping and begging Matty to stop. Crawling under the bed he shared with Gordon, Mark knew he was out of range of his father's blows. For a few minutes, Matty bawled at him to come out, but he was too drunk to reach him. Eventually he gave up and staggered out of the room. Mark lay, shaking and crying, listening to his mother's protests. He covered his ears, wanting to block out the sound of her pain and his father's violence.

Finally the noises died down, but still he lay in his dark hiding place, as if paralysed. He thought he heard his mother quietly weeping and then a low rhythmic droning that was his father snoring. Just as he was considering whether it was safe to come out, he heard a banging noise downstairs. Someone was knocking on the back door, just below his window.

With a huge effort, he crawled from under the bed and on to all fours. The knocking came again. He pulled himself up to the window and peered out, just in time to see Pearl retreating across the backyard, believing them to be all peacefully asleep. Mark tapped at the window, wanting to attract her attention but fearful of waking his father. He did not have the strength to run down the stairs and stop her. Then he thought of the brutal scene in his parents' bedroom and the cruel words, and his paralysing fear turned to deep anger. Someone must know what his father had done.

Just as she reached the lane, Pearl glanced back. She did not see him at first as she peered at the house. Then she caught sight of his frantic waving. He mouthed that the door was unlocked and beckoned her in. By the time Pearl had reached the stairs, he had limped on to the landing.

'Are you all right?' she whispered.

'Aye,' Mark answered, his body throbbing with bruises. 'But I'm worried about Mam.' He saw Pearl hesitate. 'Me dad's asleep now,' he assured her. Just as Pearl was about to mount the stairs, the front door opened quietly.

Gordon gasped in shock to find a figure standing in the darkened hallway. 'What the . . . ?'

Pearl put her finger up to her lips to silence him. 'I might need your help, pet,' she whispered as she turned and climbed the stairs. Gordon, catching sight of Mark's tense face above, followed without a word. When she reached the landing, Pearl put her arms

48

protectively around Mark. He winced in pain.

'Has he hurt you bad?' she asked. When Mark did not answer, she shuddered. 'I'm sorry I left you, pet. Jo wanted me to make sure you were all right.'

'Please help Mam,' Mark urged.

The boys followed Pearl into their parents' bedroom. Matty was sprawled across the bed, half undressed, snoring. At first Mark could not see his mother, then a small voice whispered, 'I'm over here.'

They turned to see Norma huddled in a chair beyond the chimney breast. She was wrapped in a pale blue dressing-gown, her legs bare, but Mark could see she still wore her party dress underneath. Pearl went straight to her, putting out a trembling hand to her swollen face.

'My God, what's he done to you this time?' she gasped.

Mark saw his mother crumple into Pearl's arms and start to sob. She could not speak. Her sons stood rooted by the open doorway, feeling a mixture of fear and revulsion. But Pearl acted swiftly.

'Come here, Gordon, and take your mother's arm. Mark, you fill a bag with some clothes for you and your brother. I'll get some for you, Norma. You're all coming to stay with us.' Norma shook her head, looking in panic at her comatose husband, but Pearl was firm. 'You're not stopping with him – not after what he's done to you. And look at Mark, he's covered in bruises too.'

Gordon murmured, 'He'll only come and fetch her back. He does when she goes to Nana Ivy's.'

Pearl was brisk. 'Just let him try. Now come on, lads, and let's get your mam out of here.'

Mark hurried as quickly as he could to grab a few possessions and bundled them into Gordon's haversack. He felt a wave of relief as he led the way downstairs,

Pearl and Gordon following with his mother. He grabbed a pile of coats from the closet under the stairs and hobbled out into the night. He marvelled at Pearl's bravery. She was the only person he knew who seemed willing to stand up to his father, and he felt suddenly close to Jo's spirited aunt. They would be safe and cared for at the Elliots'. Mark longed for that with a deep, hungry need.

Chapter Four

Jo was amazed to find Mark and Gordon downstairs the following morning, camped either side of the kitchen fire. Gordon seemed awkward about being there, but Mark was cheerful. Pearl came down to say that Norma was still sleeping and made them a large breakfast of sausage, eggs and beans. Jo heard her talking in a low, urgent voice with her father, but no one seemed able to answer her own string of questions: 'How long are you going to stay here? Does Mr Duggan not mind? Can we all have Christmas together?'

Jo thought it a dream come true to have their best friend Mark to stay. As for waking up to find the handsome Gordon under the roof, looking all surly with his hair ruffled . . . ! Jo's tummy did a somersault. She must have been staring too hard, for Gordon pulled a face at her and said, 'What you looking at, Beatle wig?'

Jo blushed furiously and he laughed. Vowing she would never wear the hateful plastic wig again, she slunk to the door to the scullery, where Pearl was washing up with Jack.

'It's up to you to go round and have it out with him,' Pearl was insisting.

Her father looked agitated. 'You're in over your head. We can't go interfering in folk's marriages . . .'

Pearl gave him a sharp look. 'Why not? You've seen

the state of her – like a punchbag. I want Norma to go to the police, but she's saying no.'

'There you are,' Jack said. 'She doesn't want us to interfere. There are some things a husband and wife have to sort out for themselves.'

Pearl's look was withering. 'And what about Mark?' she hissed. 'Who's going to protect him?' When Jack gave a helpless shrug, Pearl added, 'Imagine it was your bairn got thumped last night. Now how do you feel about it?'

Jack flinched with shame. 'Aye, you're right. I'm sorry. I'll go and talk to Matty if you think it'll do any good.'

Pearl put out a hand and touched his slim face affectionately. 'Talk some sense into him – he might take it from another man. He certainly won't from me.'

Jo felt sure Pearl was about to kiss her father, but he caught sight of her hovering in the doorway and stepped abruptly away. They both gawped at her, wondering how much she had overheard, and then busied themselves quickly.

That day, Mark went with them to Sunday School, though Gordon refused and went out on his own. 'Bet he's gone round to Barbara's,' Mark snorted, hobbling along on his bandaged ankle.

'Aye, for a snog,' Colin laughed.

But Jo did not like to think of it and changed the subject. 'Remember Auntie Pearl says we've to go round to Grumpy Bewick's after church.'

Strangely, the idea seemed more appealing than it had done the night before, for it would get them out of Jericho Street all day. The boys seemed happy too. They went the long way round to the chapel so as to avoid Mark's house, chattering expectantly about what it would be like inside Bewick's place.

By the time they headed home, it was getting dark. Grumpy had put them to work clearing leaves, but they had had a grand bonfire and his wife had treated them to crumpets and lemon sponge cake for tea. They decided Grumpy was not so grumpy after all. They found Norma sitting by the fire smoking with Pearl and Jack.

'You all right, Mam?' Mark went over to her at once.

Norma nodded, her face puffy and bruised like a boxer's.

'We're just telling your mam you can stay as long as you need,' Pearl smiled.

'We're not going back, are we?' Mark asked, his face tense. Norma's face crumpled and she began to cry. Mark patted her awkwardly on the shoulder.

Jack said, 'I went to talk to your father. He doesn't remember much about last night. Says it's all been a mistake. He thinks we're making too much fuss.'

'Too much fuss!' Pearl snorted.

'But he's agreed to let you stay here till you feel like going home,' Jack added quickly. 'He'll not bother you here.'

'Mam,' Mark said, his look urgent, 'I don't want to go back.'

She gazed at him bleakly. 'I'm so a-ashamed,' she whispered through her tears.

Pearl said at once, 'You've nothing to be ashamed of! You've had to put up with that man for too long. He's a drunkard and a bully—'

'Pearl!' Jack warned.

'Well, she can't possibly go back to him,' Pearl exclaimed. She touched Mark on the arm. 'I've told your mam you're welcome to live in the flat I'm renting. It'll be ready in a fortnight and I'll be back to sea at the end of the month, so it'll be nice for me to have someone keeping an eye on the place.'

Mark smiled in relief. 'That's great, isn't it, Mam?' Norma tried to smile, but it hurt her face too much. 'Can me and Gordon go up and see it after school tomorrow?'

Jo noticed a look pass between the adults. Jack answered, 'Your brother's gone back home. He was there when I went round. Says he's stopping with your father.'

Mark's face fell. He put his hand on his mother's shoulder again. 'Mam? That doesn't mean we have to, does it?'

Jo was puzzled by the look Mark's mother gave him. It was almost resentful. She pulled away from him and with a querulous 'No!' started to cry again.

For a week, Norma did not venture outside, though all the neighbours knew where she was. At first Matty kept away, but by Friday he was drunk and ranting outside the house.

'You get yourself back home, woman! You'll not make a fool of me. Come out, do you hear?' He cursed foully then shouted for Jack. 'Show your face, you coward! You've no right to keep me wife in there.'

Pearl stuck her head out of the upstairs window and threatened to call the police. Matty released a string of invective and she banged the window shut so the children could not hear. Eventually, after the Leishmans complained about the noise, Gordon appeared and helped his father home.

That weekend, Ivy came to visit, but she grew so distressed at the situation that Pearl could see she was just upsetting her daughter-in-law the more. Pearl coaxed Norma upstairs to lie down.

'Can't you have words with your Matty?' she demanded when she returned to the kitchen. 'He's been round here calling us all worse than muck.'

But Ivy grew defensive. 'It's not all his fault. I know he's got a bad temper, but Norma's not always been the perfect wife to him either, by any means. She's had affairs, you know.'

'No, I don't know. Anyway, that's no excuse to raise his fists to her!' Pearl retorted. 'And he shouldn't take it out on Mark either.'

Ivy flushed. 'Oh, the poor lad!' But then she went on the attack, blaming Pearl for making the situation worse. 'I don't think they should be going to live in one of them flats – it's too far away from family.'

'Exactly,' Pearl replied. 'Where they'll be safe.'

'No.' Ivy shook her head. 'We should be trying to get them back together as a family.' Pearl gave a cry of exasperation. By the time Jack came back with the children from the fish and chip shop, Ivy had gone and Pearl was in an angry mood. She announced she would take them ten-pin bowling that afternoon to cheer them all up.

'Smashin'!' cried Jo, leaping around the cramped kitchen with the boys. Norma refused to be coaxed out in broad daylight and Jack went off to put a bet on the dogs and have a quiet drink with Mr Leishman. Jo noticed her father was unusually impatient with them and kept muttering that the house was 'too crowded by half'.

'Don't fuss,' Pearl answered. 'We'll all be out from under your feet by next week, when the flat's ready.'

After Jo's pleadings, they went round to look at the flat on the way to the bowling alley. They rode up and down in the lift three times, before Pearl called a halt to the game. There were workmen in the flat putting up kitchen cupboards, and the rooms smelt of drying paint. Jo gasped at the view. 'It makes me dizzy!'

'Isn't it grand?' Pearl grinned. 'And look at the bathroom – all the mod cons! No more heating up water in a copper boiler for Auntie Pearl.' She took Mark by the hand. 'You can have this little room,' she told him. 'Your mam can share with me until I go back to sea.'

'What about when *we* stay?' Jo queried.

'I'll get two settees,' Pearl promised, 'one for each of you to sleep on.'

They spent the rest of the afternoon on a high of excitement, planning future stays at the flat together. After bowling, Pearl treated them to pie and peas for their tea, so it was late by the time they got home. Strangely the house was in darkness, and they found Jack sitting in the firelight, listening to the wireless.

Pearl flicked on the electric light, making Jack squint and cover his eyes.

She laughed. 'Getting a bit of shut-eye while we were out?'

Jo looked at her father's groggy face and thought he looked much older than when they had left him.

'Where's Mam?' Mark asked quickly. 'Is she asleep?'

Jack got to his feet and looked at the boy pityingly. 'Your dad came round while you were out,' he said gently.

'What?' Pearl cried.

'He didn't hurt her, did he?' Mark demanded.

Jack held up his hand to Pearl, who looked about to burst with questions. 'No, lad, he didn't hurt your mam. He came round to say sorry – brought her a bunch of chrysanthemums.'

'So where is she?' Pearl asked impatiently.

Jack continued to address Mark. 'He's fetched her home.'

Pearl exploded. 'You let her go . . . ?'

Jack turned on her. 'I couldn't stop her,' he replied crossly. 'When she saw how sorry he was, she wanted to go back. He was being nice as ninepence. I could hardly tie her up and keep her here against her will, could I?' They glared at each other.

Jo looked at Mark and saw his confusion.

'What am I to do?' he asked. 'Is Mam coming back for me?'

Jack struggled to compose his face. 'She asked if I would keep you here a bit longer – until they sorted things out at home.'

'How long?' Mark persisted.

Jack tried to reassure him. 'You can stay here as long as needs be. Your mam thinks you'll be better off here until she sees how things go with your dad.'

But Mark was ashen. 'I can't believe she's gone without waiting for me,' he said.

Jo piped up. 'Well, I think it's great, you staying on here. Isn't it, Dad?'

'It won't be forever,' Jack warned, wanting to curb Jo's expectations.

Mark tensed and his voice hardened. 'They don't want me living with them, do they?'

'Of course they do,' Pearl said quickly. 'Your mam's just a bit confused at the moment – she's had a real shock. She's doing what she thinks is best for you.'

'No she isn't!' Mark cried. 'Neither of them want me. I'm the reason they fight. It's *me* that me dad can't stand. Now Mam doesn't want me either!'

Jo reached over to touch him. 'We want you.'

'That's right,' Pearl agreed.

But he shook Jo off, glaring at them all. 'Why should you when me own family can't stand me? I can't stay here for ever, there's no room for me!'

'We'll make room.' Jack tried to calm him. 'Listen, I'll do us all some hot milk and we can talk about it tomorrow. I'll have another word with your father.'

'No!' Mark cried angrily. 'What's the use? You didn't manage to stop me mam going, did you?' Abruptly, he turned and fled out of the kitchen and down the passageway.

Pearl moved to follow him, but Jack stopped her. 'Leave the lad be. He wants to be on his own.' They heard him running upstairs. Jo looked at her brother in desperation. If anyone could comfort him, it was Colin.

He nodded. 'I'll go up and see he's all right.'

By the next day, Mark was calmer, and after Sunday School they went off to see the Bewicks again. But the following week he was in trouble at school, and Jack found him increasingly difficult to handle at home. The boy seemed intent on disruption, enticing the others to roam the Burn instead of coming home, and challenging them to dares. Soon, Colin and Jo were answering back like he did, challenging Jack's orders and trying his patience. Even Pearl was finding it difficult to keep her temper, and she spent her time out of the house, buying furniture and crockery for her new flat. Neither Matty nor Norma came near them, and on the Saturday, Gordon was sent round with another bag of Mark's clothes.

'Thought he might want these,' Gordon said awkwardly, thrusting the parcel at Jack. 'There's a pair of me old football boots he can have. Will you tell him I'm playing this afternoon? On second thoughts, he better not turn up in case me dad's there.'

Jack was appalled. 'How's your mother?' he asked.

Gordon gave him a cautious look. 'Canny.'

'Have things calmed down with your dad?' When the boy nodded, Jack continued, 'Mark's missing his mam. If things are better now, he should be with his own family. When's she going to fetch him?'

But Gordon merely shrugged. 'Better be off.' He glanced over his shoulder as if he was being watched.

'Stay and wait for Mark,' Jack urged. 'He'll be back from the baths any minute. Pearl's taken them.'

'Sorry,' Gordon answered, with a toss of his shaggy fringe, 'I can't stop.'

Jack stared after him, worried by the boy's words. For the first time it seemed possible that the Duggans might never reclaim their youngest son. He determined to have words with Matty before any more damage was done.

That afternoon, Colin had his first real fight with Mark. Jo was sure it had something to do with the bag of clothes that Gordon had brought round, for they had both been in high spirits at the baths. So much so that the attendants had threatened to ban them from the pool for dive-bombing each other, before Pearl had intervened. But after Mark had discovered the bag of crumpled jumpers and his brother's old boots, he had gone into a mood and started baiting Colin. Finally, he got hold of Colin's bugle and began to play it, though Jo knew her brother hated anyone else to touch it. When Colin told him to stop, Mark blew it harder and then ran out of the house, taking the instrument with him.

Colin chased him, shouting furiously, 'That belongs to the Brigade! Bring it back, man!'

But Mark was faster than his friend and soon disappeared into the park. Jo had followed. 'I think I know where he'll be. Do you want me to go after him?'

Colin looked at her, his square face puce with anger and running. 'He better bring it back or I'll kill him!'

'I'll make sure he does,' Jo promised. She ran on down the bank and found Mark where she expected, in their favourite tree. It was easy to spot him now that the leaves had almost fallen. He was swinging his legs disconsolately, the bugle hanging round his neck.

As Jo began to scale the tree, he shouted down, 'Colin sent his little sister after me, has he? Crying like a baby, I bet!'

Jo stopped and squinted up into the low wintry sun. 'Give it back, Mark man. You know what he's like about the bugle.'

'Come and get it then,' Mark grinned.

Jo continued to scramble up, but he edged along the branch and dangled the bugle out of her reach. 'Don't be daft!' she called. She knew she could not climb out after him, so she tried to divert him. 'Eeh, look at that spaceship landing over there!'

Mark did not even look round. 'Not fooled,' he laughed.

Jo regretted her next words almost before they were spoken. 'Hey, there's your mam, behind you!'

Mark craned round at once and Jo lunged for the bugle. Realising he had been tricked, Mark gave her a shove. 'You little cow!' he yelled, and hurled the bugle out of the tree in fury. Jo screamed, losing her footing in the fork of the tree, and slithered down the trunk, skinning her knees and chin on the way. She landed with a thud on her back, quite winded. For a moment she could not breathe, and gasped like a fish for air.

'Jo! Are you all right?' Mark shouted down, scrabbling out of the tree and dropping to the ground. Just as he did, Colin reached her, having witnessed her fall and his

60

bugle hurtling into the undergrowth.

Colin hurled himself at Mark. 'You scabby bastard! I hate you!' he yelled. At once the two of them were on the ground, rolling around, trying to punch each other. They tore at the other's hair and kicked with their feet. Jo, regaining her breath, screamed at them to stop. But within minutes a small crowd of children had gathered to watch, and word was going round: 'There's a scrap down the Burn!'

Jo watched in distress as her brother and her best friend gouged and bruised each other as if they were sworn enemies. How could this have got out of hand so quickly? she wondered in fright. To her relief the fight was stopped by the appearance of her father, who had come out looking for them. Both boys were caked in mud and nearly sobbing with the pain they had inflicted on one another.

Jack marched them all back home, grim-faced, and ordered the boys into the scullery to wash off the dirt and blood. Jo was hugging her ribs, which were still sore, but no one seemed bothered when she tried to describe her dramatic fall from the tree.

'I'm off to see Matty,' Jack told Pearl as she dabbed iodine on their cuts.

They sat subdued around the fire, Colin fretting that his bugle might be lost for ever. 'We'll search for it in the light,' Pearl promised him, throwing Mark a disappointed look.

When Jack came back, it was with a harrowed face. He shook his head at them. 'Your dad won't have you back just yet,' he said, keeping to himself the filthy words that Matty had spoken about his son. Jack found it hard to imagine the man could harbour so much hate against a child, even if, as local gossip would have it, he was

61

another man's son. Mark hung his head, but this time the news was greeted with silence. Even Jo felt too weary to give him comforting words, though she was still feeling guilty about the way she had provoked him in the tree by pretending to have seen his mother. Everyone else was still too cross with him about the bugle and the fight.

That night, Jo stirred sleepily, thinking she heard something in the yard below. But the sound was so soft, she thought it must be next door's cat and drifted off to sleep again.

Mark stole out of the back door without disturbing Jack, who slept upright in the fireside chair. He wore three jumpers and carried Gordon's boots around his neck. Luckily there was a bright frosty moon shining over the dene as he shivered through the dark. Still, it took him over an hour to find the bugle, lodged in a thorn bush, glinting in the moonlight. The thorns pricked and tore his hands as he delved among them to pull it out, cursing his own impetuousness.

Mark gazed up at his chestnut tree and tried to fathom what had got into him. He had been filled with a destructive rage when he had heard about Gordon's visit and the meagre bag of clothes dumped on the doorstep. Was that what he amounted to? he thought miserably. A pile of old jumpers and a pair of cast-off boots? But that was what he was, a cast-off. No one wanted him, least of all his own family. Or were they his family at all? he wondered. His father did not think so. So where did he come from? Where *did* he belong?

Now his best friend hated him and even Jo was tired of speaking up for him. How could he have pushed her out of the tree like that? Mark felt shame engulf him. Wretchedly, he trudged back to Jericho Street and, in the dead hours of the night, laid Colin's bugle on the back doorstep. Glancing up one last time at Colin and Jo's bedroom, his eyes blurred with tears. Then he was gone into the night.

Just before dawn, Ivy heard the creak of her front door. She was a light sleeper and was about to rise and make herself a pot of tea. 'Is that you, Poppins?' she called out to her cat, as she entered the kitchen.

'It's me, Nana,' Mark answered quietly. Ivy gasped to hear another voice and peered short-sightedly through the dark. She saw the huddled shape of her grandson in the chair by the fire.

'Hinny, is that you?' she said in surprise, fumbling for the electric switch. Mark squinted at her in the light, his face forlorn.

'Neebody wants me, Nana,' he said in a dull voice.

Ivy's heart squeezed at the sound of his pain. She bustled over to him in her billowing nightgown and thrust her arms around him, feeling a sob catch in her throat.

'I want you, hinny,' she told him, hugging him fiercely, 'don't you ever forget that.' Mark buried his weary head in her large comforting bosom and let himself cry. Ivy felt her own tears brimming over as she vowed, 'Let others think what they want, but I'll never turn you away, bonny lad, not ever!'

Chapter Five

1968

A year after Mark went to live with Ivy Duggan, they began to pull down the end of Jericho Street. Jack remained adamant he would not move until forced, and the demolition went on around them, the street cut in half like a loaf, the upper end a scavenger's paradise of planks and bricks and discarded trinkets. Jo and Marilyn laid claim to an old sofa wedged in the rubble below an end wall that still wore shreds of flowery wallpaper. The whole summer of 1968, they had it as their den, dressing up as flower people in Mrs Leishman's curtains and Auntie Pearl's chain belts. They rang bicycle bells and pretended they were meditating with the Maharishi like the Beatles.

Jo had created this new world of make-believe in retaliation for the boys shunning her company. Once Colin and Skippy had gone to the grammar school they no longer wanted her hanging around them. 'Nick off, Wig!' Skippy had said, using the derogatory nickname that had stuck ever since Gordon had coined it. He had chased her away from their football game, and this time Colin had not defended her. By then, there had been no

Mark to stick up for her either. Once he was living down in Nile Street, he was never around to play football in their back lane.

Although Colin and he had made up after their quarrel, Mark avoided Jericho Street and they began to see less of him. Norma would call to see him at Ivy's and take him shopping for new clothes, but the day of his return home was always put off until the next week or the next month, until finally no one mentioned it any more. The Duggans were the first to move out of the street, taking a semi in Walkerville as a compromise between the docks and a new estate. Matty could still get easily to work and Norma had a patch of garden where she could sunbathe. Jo never saw Mark's mother with a black eye again, but then she hardly ever saw her out at all. Norma never came back to visit any of the neighbours and never answered the door when Pearl tried to call.

Pearl blamed Matty for the rift. He would cross the high street rather than talk to any of them. 'He's got Norma terrified of speaking to us,' Jo's aunt declared in disgust.

'He's never forgiven us for taking her and Mark in after that fight,' Jack commented. 'Shamed him in front of the neighbours. That's why he avoids us like the plague.'

Pearl snorted. 'Matty wouldn't know what shame felt like if it jumped up and bit him!'

Once Mark had started at the secondary modern, the drift away from his old friends increased further. Jo began to see him hanging around with his old enemy, Kevin McManners, and an older group of boys. He was friendly enough when she went to visit Ivy's and teased her about the scarves she had begun to wear around her

66

neck. But both of them had stopped climbing trees, and when Jo went to the park now it was to try out the new tennis racquet that her father had bought her for her eleventh birthday.

That September of '68, Pearl was on leave for Jo's birthday. At Jo's request the girls stayed over at her aunt's flat and Pearl took them out to a new Chinese restaurant, where they sat under coloured lanterns eating chow mein and feeling grown-up. Pearl wore a purple silk dress she had had made in the Far East and Jo had on her first miniskirt, made of green suede, which buttoned down the middle.

'You suit your hair longer,' Pearl told her in approval, as she picked up food deftly with her chopsticks. The girls were allowed to use forks.

'I'm growing out me fringe too,' Jo said. 'I can't stand it getting in me eyes any longer.' They talked about the rumour that Paul McCartney had an American girl-friend, and discussed the new musical, *Hair*, that Pearl had seen in London.

'Is it true they take off *all* their clothes?' Marilyn whispered, not wanting the waiter to hear. Pearl nodded and the girls smirked.

'But they do it behind this netting stuff,' she explained.

'Fancy being naked in front of all those people,' Jo puzzled. 'What they want to do that for?'

Pearl laughed. 'Well, I promised your dad there would be nothing like that tonight.' It had been her aunt's idea to take them to a play at a local hall after the meal, instead of to the pictures. Jo had been dubious, not having been to the theatre before, but she was infected by her aunt's enthusiasm. Pearl went to musicals in London and took Jack to watch seaside players at Whitley

Bay in the summer. This was just a local amateur group performing *Time and the Conways*, but Pearl promised they would enjoy it. 'Not Burton and Taylor, but you've got to start somewhere.'

They bought a box of chocolates and settled into their seats. 'It's a play by J.B. Priestley,' Pearl explained. 'He was fascinated by time.'

Jo thought this sounded particularly boring, but once the lights dimmed and the curtains were pulled back, she was transfixed by the lavish costumes and scenery. Before her mesmerised eyes unfolded a tale of family strife, a privileged olden-day world. It was like eaves-dropping on a family's intimate secrets, except she felt no guilt, for these people were revelling in the telling. Jo agonised for them, sharing their joys and tragedies, wanting to turn back the clocks for them so they could avoid the sad future that lay in store. Imagine if the real world was like that! thought Jo. She could go back to a time when her mother was alive, or before Jericho Street was knocked down, or when Mark was Colin's closest friend . . .

At the end she stayed in her seat, overwhelmed by the experience.

'Never seen you so stuck for words,' Marilyn teased.

'Did you not enjoy it then?' Pearl frowned.

Jo dragged her gaze away from the stage and looked at her aunt. Her eyes shone with emotion. 'It was fantastic!' she gasped. 'So real. I felt I was right there in the room with them. Not like at the flicks where you know it's just made up.'

Pearl was delighted. 'Do you want to go round the back and meet some of the actors coming out? You could get their autographs on your programme.'

'Magic! Yes, please!' both girls chorused.

They waited by the back entrance to the hall, feeling bashful, but Pearl pushed them forward when two of the actors appeared.

'You've won two new fans tonight,' she told them.

'Would you sign me programme?' Jo asked, thrusting it in front of the woman who had played the mother. The actress seemed taken aback by the request but was quick to oblige, signing 'Martha Jones' in huge capitals.

'If you're interested you should come along on Wednesday evenings when we have readings or rehearsals.'

'Oh, I'd be no good at that.' Jo blushed.

'Yes you would,' Pearl encouraged. 'She's got a voice as loud as a hooter when she wants.'

'We can always do with helping hands behind the scenes if you don't want to act,' Martha smiled. 'You're very welcome.'

'Ta,' Jo grinned.

'I might come along myself,' Pearl said, giving Jo an affectionate hug. 'I used to tap-dance at your age, you know.'

That night, at Pearl's flat, they chatted late into the night about the performance. Jo found it almost impossible to sleep. She wanted to go back and see the play again, and she imagined herself on the brilliantly lit stage, acting in front of a packed hall and signing programmes for eager fans. This was even better than playing at being the Beatles, she thought drowsily, as sleep finally claimed her.

Throughout the winter, she dragged Marilyn along to the Wednesday-night meetings of the Dees Players, and at Christmas they had a walk-on part in the pantomime as the cow in *Jack and the Beanstalk*. The girls argued over who should be the front end, until

Martha decreed that they should take it in turns. To Jo's disappointment, Pearl was away, but she thrilled at the thought of her father and Colin in the audience while she sweated inside the cow's head.

Jack came every night, and on the final one, Mark and Ivy turned up too. Jo was embarrassed that she was playing the back of the cow that evening.

Mark teased her afterwards. 'It doesn't say anything in the programme about you being the cow's arse!'

Jo gave him a shove. 'I've been the front end an' all!'

Mark whistled. 'You'll be in next year's Royal Variety Performance at this rate.'

Jack treated them all to fish and chips back at number eleven. Jo glanced at Mark as they walked past the space where his home had once been, wondering what he was thinking. But his face was impassive.

'Do you ever go over to your mam's place?' she asked him quietly, as they lagged behind the adults.

'I've been a couple of times – when I've known *he's* been at work,' Mark answered stiffly. 'It's a lot smarter than Jericho Street. Mam says Matty's bringing in better wages these days.'

Jo noticed how he referred to his father by his first name and no longer as Dad. 'Do you see much of Gordon?' she asked.

Mark pulled a face. 'Na, he doesn't bother with me or Nana. I asked him to teach me the guitar, but he's too scared of *him* coming back and finding me there. So I have a play on his guitar when neither of them are around – teaching myself.'

'Good for you,' Jo encouraged 'So might Gordon let you be in his band?'

'Not a chance,' Mark snorted. 'Not that I'd want to be – not after the way he's sided with Matty.' His face looked bitter for a moment and then he smiled at her. 'Anyways, I've only learnt three chords so far – not exactly Jimi Hendrix yet.'

'Might get on the Royal Variety next year then,' Jo teased back and was glad when he laughed. 'I sometimes see Gordon in the distance at school. It's good he's staying on to do A levels.' Then she blushed to think of how Marilyn teased her when she craned for a view of Mark's brother walking past the classroom windows, his hair defiantly long and his tie triple-knotted. But it was the wrong thing to say, for mention of his brother exasperated Mark.

'I couldn't care less what he does. I'll not be stopping on to do more exams – waste of time,' he said dismissively. 'Three more years and I'll be out in the world.'

'What do you want to do?' Jo asked, as they neared home. 'Get an apprenticeship at the yards?'

'Na! I'm not stopping round here. I'll go to sea like me great-grandfather – or to London,' he answered, his dark eyes fierce. 'As far away as possible.'

Jo felt heavy inside at his words, and a little hurt that he should want to reject them all. She could understand him wanting to get away from his father, but he seemed to be dismissing his friends and their shared past too. She could not imagine leaving Wallsend and all the familiar places. Jo loved it all, even the half-torn-down Jericho Street. She glanced away from his burning look, not sure what she was supposed to say, and led the way into the house.

The following summer, Jo was in the chorus of *Hello Dolly*. She spent much of the holidays riding her bike down to the coast with Marilyn and swimming at Whitley Bay. Pearl was home briefly and they went together to watch a touring show do an Agatha Christie thriller in Newcastle. Coming home late on the bus, they gazed up at the moon, full of wonder that Neil Armstrong had walked on it, which sparked Pearl into singing 'Paper Moon' along the high street.

That August, there was much debate about where they should move to, for the rest of Jericho Street was about to be knocked down. Jo was secretly relieved that they would not have to suffer another winter of half-dug-up road and traipsing through a sea of liquid mud to get into the house. It also worried her that her father had been plagued by a bout of arthritis in his hands during the cold weather, and she knew he found labouring increasingly tiring. More of the burden of running the house was falling on her shoulders, and she decided to add her voice to Pearl's campaign to get them to move to the flats. Time spent doing housework or cooking was wasted time in Jo's view.

Pearl came round one evening full of excitement. 'I've just heard on the grapevine that the caretaker's flat is going to be vacant soon. Old Nelson's moving to be near his daughter. It's ground floor, two bedrooms, Jack. You won't even feel like you're in a flat!'

'Caretaking job would be good, Dad,' Colin encouraged. 'Regular, and less grafting.'

'And you'd always be home when we come in from school,' Jo enthused.

Jack looked at them all suspiciously, then burst out laughing. 'Seems like you've made up your minds on this one. Maybes I'll take a look at the caretaker's flat.'

'Good,' Pearl beamed, ' 'cos I've made an appointment for you to go round on Friday and talk about the job.'

Jo asked Pearl if she would come round and help

72

clear out the yard shed and sort out the cupboards, as Jack could not bring himself to throw anything out. Colin dragged out the mouldering contents of the old wash-house: a rusting trunk, a battered pram, some worn clippy mats and a clothes horse. Everything was caked in coal dust and cobwebs, making them cough and splutter.

'Better look through your dad's old trunk before we hoy this lot out,' Pearl said, sneezing loudly. 'He must have had this at sea.'

Colin helped her haul it inside then disappeared to play football. Prising it open, they found its contents covered over with Jack's old seaman's duffel coat. But underneath were piles of women's clothes: utility dresses, a stiff net petticoat, a mauve twin set and tweed skirts. Jo saw Pearl go pale as she covered her mouth with her hand.

'These are Gloria's,' she whispered, drawing back. 'I should have guessed.'

'Me mam's?' Jo questioned. Pearl nodded, overcome. Jo put out a tentative hand and touched the soft cardigan. It smelt of mothballs. She thought how old-fashioned the clothes seemed, compared to Pearl's jazzy outfits. These staid jumpers and skirts were so dull, the sort of thing Ivy would stop and admire in old ladies' clothes shops on the high street. Jo felt a stab of disappointment. She could not relate their ordinariness to the wedding-dress princess who lived in her head.

'Why has he kept them?' she asked, thinking it rather macabre to store her dead mother's clothes all this time.

Pearl's voice trembled. 'He couldn't bear to throw them out, I suppose. It's all that's left of your mother. He loved her that much, you see . . .' She looked away and fumbled for a handkerchief. Jo was shocked to see

73

her crying. She wanted to look further into the trunk, but did not want to upset her aunt any further.

'Don't be sad, Auntie Pearl,' she tried to comfort, putting her arm around her shoulder. 'It doesn't make me upset.' Pearl blew her nose and made an effort not to cry. 'I thought you didn't care much for me mother?' Jo said, with a quizzical look.

Pearl sniffed. 'Oh, that silly argument with your dad . . . ! I never meant it.' She looked at Jo with her bright blue eyes. 'I thought the world of your mother when we were growing up,' she confided. 'Gloria mothered me after our parents died. Aunt Julia wasn't very maternal, but Gloria made up for it. She always had me turned out nice, hair brushed, hands clean. When I had nightmares, she'd sing me to sleep again, and she used to tell me stories – wonderful stories that she made up in her own head. You must get your imagination from your mam,' Pearl smiled wistfully, 'though you're head-strong like your dad, as well!'

Jo held her breath. She had never heard anyone say so much about her dead parent before. 'Tell me more,' she urged, stroking the woollen clothes. 'How did she meet me dad?'

Pearl gave an embarrassed laugh. 'Through me, really. I'd sneaked out to a dance during Race Week and Jack walked me home. I was much too young for him, of course, but he got introduced to Gloria and kept calling round when he was back on leave. She loved all those stories of your dad's about life on the ocean waves! Head over heels, they were.' Her look was faraway. 'They didn't take long to marry. When Aunt Julia died, Gloria took me under her wing again. They moved back into Aunt Julia's flat because it was bigger than the place they were in. That's where you were born.'

Jo looked at her in astonishment. 'I always thought I was born here, in Jericho Street!'

Pearl shook her head. 'No, your dad chose to come here after your mam died. Staying in the old place – well, it was a bit upsetting. And he wanted somewhere for you and Colin to play outside with other bairns. I'd decided by then to go off to sea, so I was just as happy to sell Aunt Julia's flat.' She glanced around. 'This place became my home too. It was always nice coming back to a bit of family life after months at sea – seeing you bairns.'

Pearl gently pulled down the lid of the trunk. 'Jack worked so hard at making it a happy home . . .' She gave Jo a painful little smile and touched her long coppery hair. 'We'll let your dad decide what to do with these, eh?'

Jo nodded. As she got to her feet, her mind bursting with all this new information about her mother, she noticed something bundled in a pillowcase that Colin had leant against the wall. 'What's this?' she asked, already unwrapping it. It was a heavy mahogany picture frame, with a photograph inside the filthy glass. Jo sneezed. 'Looks a bit like you, Auntie Pearl.'

Pearl leaned over and wiped the glass. 'Eeh, it is! I remember that dress – it was pink and white candy stripes with a silver belt—' Then she caught her breath.

'Who's the little lass?' Jo asked. A young Pearl with permed hair and a sticky-out dress was holding the hand of a round-faced infant with pale hair in a spotted dress and ankle socks. The small child was squinting at the camera, a quizzical smile on her lips.

Pearl said softly, 'That was my goddaughter.' She clutched the frame.

'What's she called?' Jo asked, curious.

Pearl stared hard. After a pause she said, 'Joy.'

'You've never mentioned her before. Where's she now?' Jo persisted.

For a long moment her aunt said nothing. Then, in a hushed voice, 'Oh, I don't see her now.' Pearl put the photo down. When she saw Jo's puzzled face, she tried to explain it away. 'I was good friends with Joy's father – a navy friend. We lost touch. Best not to mention it to your dad.' She wrapped the picture up again quickly.

'Why not?' Jo was surprised.

'Well, he didn't approve – not of my friend. He'd be upset. It was all a long time ago,' Pearl said, quite flustered.

'What's it doing in our wash-house, then?' Jo asked, none of it making much sense to her.

Pearl hesitated a fraction, then shrugged. 'I must have put it there years ago with some of my stuff – to be out of the way. I'll take it round to my flat now.'

Nothing more was said about the photograph, and when her father came home there was a heated dispute about what to do with the trunk.

'Wouldn't you like to keep your mam's clothes?' he asked Jo. 'They might come in use . . .'

'Dad!' Jo protested. 'I wouldn't be seen dead—' Then she clapped a hand over her mouth, realising what she had said. She saw the pain in his eyes. 'Sorry,' she said quickly, 'I didn't mean that.'

But Jack shook his head. 'No, you're right,' he answered in a heavy voice. 'We'll give them to a jumble.'

'They're better than jumble,' Jo insisted. 'I've an idea. Would you let me give them to the Players? They're always on the lookout for costumes. Then they'd still be sort of in the family.'

Jack agreed, and so Gloria's dated clothing was given

to the wardrobe mistress at the dowdy Dees Theatre, which the Players shared with a local scout group and a spiritualist church.

In the last week of the summer holidays, the Elliots moved to the caretaker's flat and Jack settled into his new job. The following week, Jo and Marilyn moved up to the grammar school. A month later, Jo went with Colin to watch the final part of Jericho Street being knocked down. Sitting on a wall beyond the cordoned-off street, Jo watched in awe the relentless pounding of the giant weight against the old brick walls and the speed at which her old home collapsed in a cloud of dust and was gone. She felt strange inside, as if she had just witnessed the end of her childhood as well as her home.

'I'll treat you to a bag of sweets from Dodds',' Colin offered, as if he knew how empty she was feeling. Jo just nodded and they made their way silently to their favourite corner shop.

After that, her father would detour around the area rather than walk past where they had once lived, but Jo soon got used to passing by the waste ground that had once been Jericho Street and its surrounding lanes. Before long, a modern airy library of concrete and glass had grown up in its place, and by the following year, Jo often stopped to do her homework there after school. The flat was cosy but cramped, and she always seemed to be in Colin's way. They argued over trivial things, accusing each other of using or losing the other's pen. Besides, it was more fun going with Marilyn and the other girls to the library, and joining in their whispered comments about the boys who strutted past the large windows swinging their haversacks full of school books.

'Look, there's Gordon Duggan,' Marilyn would laugh, and nudge Jo.

'So!' Jo replied, pretending not to care, but colouring all the same.

'Looks a bit like Paul McCartney with those big eyes, if you ask me,' said Brenda, a new friend from the flats. She wore a long maroon maxi-coat and midi–skirts and was generally listened to when it came to opinions on fashion or lads.

'He doesn't look anything like Paul McCartney. Anyway, I've gone off Paul,' Jo declared, pushing her lengthening red hair behind her ears, 'ever since he married that Linda. And now the Beatles have split up . . .'

That spring, they had talked about the break-up at length, and Jo had felt that yet another strand of her childhood had finally snapped. Now they were supposed to be writing arguments for a school debate on the coming General Election. To her father's annoyance, Jo had been chosen to represent the Tories. 'They'll not get back in,' Jack muttered, 'you haven't a chance.' He was half right. In June of 1970, Jo was roundly defeated in the class elections, but Ted Heath led the Conservatives to a surprise victory. Undaunted by her failure, Jo got involved in school productions as well as plays at the Dees Theatre, and another year sped by.

The Christmas of '71, Pearl was home and took Jo on a shopping spree, buying her a long sheepskin waistcoat which she wore with her wide jeans, while her aunt chose for herself a garish long poncho with slits for the arms which clashed with her orange crimplene trousers. Pearl persuaded Jo to go to Trotter's hairdresser's on Station Road and have her hair trimmed for the first time in two years, but Jo resisted the perm to which Pearl treated herself.

On New Year's Eve, Pearl galvanised them all into going 'first-footing'. It annoyed Jo that Colin was allowed to go where he pleased now that he was nearly sixteen, but her father was still so protective of her. Her brother was getting ready to go and hear Gordon's rock band play, but Jack would not allow Jo to go too. So Pearl had intervened before another argument sparked between them all.

'I shouldn't really leave the building.' Jack was hesitant.

'For one night in the year you can,' Pearl insisted, worried that he was becoming too reclusive. He had taken to the caretaking job far better than anyone had imagined, but seemed reluctant to venture out of his self-contained domain. 'We'll call round to a few of the old neighbours.'

'As long as it's not the Duggans,' Jack had decreed. Her father had not spoken to Matty since the terrible rift over his treatment of Norma and Mark. Too many cruel things had been said for either of them to patch up their quarrel.

They started with the Leishmans, who lived now in one of the low blocks of flats behind the Forum. The girls soon got bored drinking sherry and advocaat with Marilyn's parents, and Marilyn was disappointed that Colin had not come, so when the adults were all merry, Jo suggested they went on ahead to Ivy's. Pearl allayed Jack's fears. 'They're teenagers now, and it's only five minutes' walk. Let them go, Jack. We'll follow on in a bit.'

'As long as you go straight there,' Mary Leishman said, with a warning wag of her finger.

They escaped before anyone changed their mind, clattering out into the frosty night. Jo had not been to see Ivy since the autumn half-term, for her time had been taken up with school and the Christmas pantomime, *Cinderella*. At fourteen she was tall, with gangly legs and hair that drooped in her eyes, and she had been given the part of the Prince's equerry, who went around flourishing the slipper on a cushion. Mark had not come to see her perform this year and she was secretly hoping he might be at Ivy's, although she thought it unlikely. He was bound to be out with Kevin McManners's skinhead gang. The last time Jo had seen Ivy, she had been struck by how old and fretful Mark's grandmother had become. She worried about the new decimal currency that she could not fathom even when Jo tried to teach her. But most of all she worried over Mark, who was increasingly beyond her control.

'It's the bad company he keeps,' she had clucked in disapproval. 'Is it any wonder that he's always getting into trouble? I've had the police knocking on me door all summer, and the truancy officer – the school was that glad to see the back of him when he left. I don't know what he's going to do, mind. All he thinks about is drinking and fighting and playing loud music. He's getting too much for me to manage . . .' Ivy had fought back tears and Jo had tried to comfort her.

'It'll be a phase, Nana Ivy,' she had said, making her a soothing cup of tea.

'I wish you were right,' Ivy sniffed in distress. 'I love that lad.' Then she lost the struggle not to weep. 'Oh, it's all my fault . . . !'

'Don't be daft.' Jo had hugged her in concern. 'You're the only one of his family that's tret him right. Don't you go blaming yourself.'

Emerging from the Leishmans', Jo wished she had found time to visit Mark's grandmother more often, but somehow the weeks had sped by. It had begun to snow while they were indoors, and Jo whooped in excitement, scraping the wet layer of snow off a stationary car and hurling it at Marilyn. She screamed and threw snow back, skidding down the lane towards the high street. Crossing it, they heard the thud of bass music coming from a pub. They stopped and listened.

Marilyn giggled. 'Sounds like Gordon's band.'

Jo was seized by an impulse. 'Should we gan in? Just for a minute. I bet Colin's in there.'

Marilyn was shocked. 'They'd never let us in! Even dressed like this we don't look anything like eighteen. Mam would go light! And your dad . . .'

'All right, yella-belly,' Jo teased. 'I was just joking.'

'I wouldn't put it past you,' Marilyn replied, with a suspicious look. 'What you doing now?'

Jo was fumbling in her long sheepskin waistcoat. 'I've pinched a couple of Pearl's fags. Thought we could smoke them on the way to Ivy's,' she grinned.

'I hate them,' Marilyn said quickly.

'Bet you've never tried one, Miss Goody-Goody,' Jo mocked as she lit up. 'Here, you have this one.' She lit the second from the first and passed it to her friend.

Marilyn took it gingerly. 'Let's get off the main street in case anyone sees us,' she hissed. They dived down a back lane, puffing and coughing and shrieking with laughter. Behind them, Jo was vaguely aware of the back door of the pub banging open and raised voices spilling into the dark.

Then suddenly the girls stopped as the sound of arguing grew more strident. There was cursing and shouting and threats of retaliation. Marilyn gripped Jo's arm in fear. 'Sounds like a fight,' she whispered. 'Let's get going.'

Jo was about to turn and escape when she heard her brother's voice being called. Someone was taunting him about the school he went to. She recognised Kevin McManners's menacing voice, and peering up the lane she saw a ring of skinheads milling around the back steps of the pub. Her heart began to hammer at the shadowed figures with their shaven heads. It was a new sight around the town – lads of Colin's age strutting in heavy lace-up boots, braces and baggy trousers, their once shaggy hair now shorn down to the scalp. In a group, Jo found them frightening and could not understand why Mark should want to hang around with the likes of Kevin, who had tattoos across his knuckles.

Jo edged nearer and glimpsed her brother being pushed around on the steps. Skippy was with him, mouthing off at McManners. Colin was trying to calm him and pull him back into the pub, but someone was blocking his way. As Jo crept to the end of the lane, her pulse pounding, she saw that it was Mark, and her heart thumped in shock. Her mouth went dry with fear as the gang jostled around their victims, egging them on to fight. She knew it would be no equal contest, for her brother and Skippy were well outnumbered. Kevin jabbed out with a steel-capped boot and caught Colin on the shin. Her brother shoved back, but someone else hit him from the side.

Jo saw Colin lose his footing and stumble. Skippy began to lash out aimlessly in fear. The gang crowded around, all except Mark, who hung back indecisively in the shadow of the doorway. Then the kicking started, heavy boots flying as if passing a ball between them. Behind her Jo could hear Marilyn begging her to run for help, but instinct told her it would be too late. Colin had disappeared from view.

Feeling sick with terror, she ran out from the dark lane, screaming her head off for them to stop. 'Leave them alone! Stop! Stop, you bastards! You're just a bunch of cowards – bullies! Someone help!' She ranted on hysterically, the noise echoing around the snow-lined street.

Kevin and a couple of the others looked round in surprise. They looked amused and then irritated when the din did not stop.

'Look who's come to the rescue – little Wiggy Elliot!' Kevin cried in scorn. Jo felt her legs lose all their strength at the sight of his aggressive, contorted face. 'Do you think this lass can save you, eh, Elliot? You're just a tart anyway, with your little Boys' Brigade trumpet!'

Jo was almost hoarse with her screeching, but they had stopped the attack momentarily. She was shaking from head to foot as Kevin turned his attention on her.

'What's a bairn like you doing out at this time of night? Hanging round pubs an' all,' he leered.

'I'm not a bairn,' Jo rasped. He stepped towards her, laughing harshly.

'No, you're not, are you?' he jeered. 'What are you looking for then?' He lunged out and grabbed her arm. Jo froze, looking round wildly for help. Marilyn was nowhere to be seen. Suddenly she fixed on Mark, who had stepped forward. He looked so different with his dark hair gone, his scalp gleaming in the street light. His cheekbones were accentuated and his dark eyes looked huge in his stark face. There was a raw handsomeness about his brutal looks, but he seemed a stranger. How could he allow an attack on his old friends? Somewhere in all her fear she managed to feel angry, and gave him a furious look. As Kevin's grip dug into her arm and he began to make lewd suggestions about what he might do to her, she saw Mark move.

In one swift movement he was over to them. 'Leave her alone,' he ordered. 'She's still a kid.' Kevin just laughed; he was having fun. 'Haway, man!' Mark said angrily. When Kevin still did not leave go, he pulled him off roughly. 'I said leave off!'

It had all happened in seconds, but it was long enough to allow Colin and Skippy to scramble to their feet, their faces bloodied. Kevin turned on Mark, thumping him instead. 'Don't tell me what to do, darkie bastard!'

Jo saw Mark react with fury, and he was on Kevin in a flash. They punched and rolled on the ground, cursing each other with venom. The others circled, not knowing quite what to do. A moment later, there was noise from behind as revellers from a nearby house responded to Marilyn's frantic knocking for help. At the same time, the landlord appeared on the steps of the pub, bawling at them to clear off, and then there was the sound of a police siren wailing down the street.

The gang scattered into the back lanes, shouting at Kevin to follow. Levering himself up quickly, he gave Mark one last kick in the head and ran off. Jo, watching in horror, went to help her old friend, who was writhing on the ground, clutching his head and groaning.

'Mark! Are you all right?' she asked in agitation. Then there were people swarming around them, hands reaching to steer her away. Everywhere was commotion. Pulling Mark roughly up by his jacket, a policeman called out, 'There's one still here!'

'Careful!' Jo cried. 'Can't you see he's hurt?'

But in the confusion she was ignored. The neighbours who had responded to Marilyn's cries insisted Jo come with them. She tried to resist but everything was happening too quickly. Mark was hauled to his feet and pushed towards a police car. Another constable was questioning Colin and Skippy.

In desperation, she tried to shout, 'He saved me!' But her voice was cracked and hoarse from so much screaming, and she dissolved into uncontrollable tears. Mark glanced towards her as he was bundled into the car. She met his look for a snatched moment and thought she saw the trace of a smile, an attempt at reassurance. Then he was gone and she let herself be led into the warmth by her rescuers, numb with shock.

Chapter Six

1972

They never got to Ivy's that terrible night. Someone went for Jack and the Leishmans and there were emotional tears and furious arguments over Pearl's idea of letting the girls walk through Wallsend alone.

'I'm not letting you out of me sight again!' Jack declared, hugging Jo to him. When he heard Mark had been mixed up in the attack on Colin, he forbade either of them to see him. 'He's not right in the head!' he raged. 'He's nothing but trouble these days – even Ivy's at her wits' end with the lad.'

'It wasn't him that gave me a kicking.' Colin tried to defend his old friend, as Pearl cleaned up his face and bandaged his hand, which had been raked by a boot.

'And he stopped Kevin from . . .' Jo tried to tell her father, but found herself in tears again.

'Hush! I don't want to think what might have happened!' Jack fussed. 'Mark was one of that gang and as long as he's mixed up with them skinheads you'll steer clear of him.' He cradled Jo in his arms like a child. 'To think of all the kindness this family has shown him over the years – we've been more family to him than his own!

And he betrays us like this – turning on his own childhood friends.' Jo was too shaken to protest further, and only Pearl was brave enough to show her concern.

'Well, I'm going down the police station tomorrow to explain he wasn't the one that started it,' she insisted.

'You're wasting your time.' Jack was dismissive. 'Leave it to the coppers to deal with him. A night in the cells'll give him the fright he needs.'

Over the following days, news filtered through that Mark was being charged with affray and breach of the peace. By then, Kevin McManners had been brought in and charged with assault. Jo and Colin went back to school, but Jo could tell her brother was edgy about giving evidence against Kevin. He was tetchy at home and the niggling arguments between brother and sister escalated once Pearl was back at sea, until Jack despaired of them.

'Can't you agree on anything?' he pleaded. 'You used to be that close . . .'

'She won't leave me alone,' Colin grumbled, 'always poking her nose in me business.'

'No I don't!' Jo protested. 'I just wanted to know if you're going to speak up for Mark. Tell the whole story about what happened inside the pub – before the fight. Mark was being picked on by some drunks, Dad, but no one stood up for him. Did they, Colin? That's why they all got chucked out.'

'I couldn't have done anything,' Colin said, stung by her accusation. 'Anyway, he had his skinhead mates to protect him.'

'Oh aye? And look how they turned on him and called him worse than muck!' Jo replied. 'Skippy said they were spoiling for a fight. They just picked on you as the first ones to come out. Mark had nothing to do with it.'

'Don't waste your pity on that lad,' Jack said firmly. 'I used to feel sorry for him, but it seems he's turning out just like his father – only interested in drinking and fighting. He's a bad influence and beyond our help.'

Jo silently wished that Pearl was still at home so that she could confide in her. She knew her aunt had been to see Mark and had tried to comfort Ivy, but she did not know what had been said. Finally the boys were dealt with by the juvenile court. To everyone's surprise, Mark was saved by the intervention of Mr Bewick, who attested to his good character and said he employed him as a part-time gardener. Mark was put on six months' probation, while Kevin was sent to a young offenders' institution for nine months.

'I didn't know he still went to Grumpy's house,' Jo said in amazement.

Colin shook his head. 'Me neither.' He was relieved that Kevin would be off the scene for a while, but Jo could tell he was anxious about what might happen come the end of summer.

'Are you going to go round and see Mark?' Jo questioned.

'Why should I?' Colin answered defensively. 'He was part of Kevin's gang, wasn't he? And he's never bothered to see me since New Year's Eve.'

Jo let the matter drop, but she agonised over whether to go and see Mark herself. Her father would be angry if she did, for he still blamed Mark for being part of the trouble. But she wanted to thank him for saving her from Kevin. She talked it over with Marilyn, but her friend was cautious.

'He's still a skinhead,' she reminded Jo. 'He's not the same lad we grew up with. How can he be if he hangs around with that lot? My mam says I'm not even to visit

Ivy's any more in case he's there. Just forget about him.'

But Jo could not. She put off making contact until Easter, when it occurred to her that she could go round to Ivy's and invite her to the play in which she would be performing over the holidays. Jo was getting good parts now at the Dees Theatre. She had stuck at the acting, whereas Marilyn had grown bored with the time taken up with rehearsing. Her friend preferred sport and, increasingly, hanging around the Forum or the park with Brenda and chatting to boys.

To Jo's disappointment, Mark was not at Ivy's when she called.

'He's hardly ever here,' Ivy confided, 'he's that restless. But he's keeping out of trouble as far as I know,' she said, as if trying to convince herself. 'I've told him he'll shame me into an early grave if he gets into any more bother with the police.'

But Jo's visit cheered the old woman and she broke into a packet of caramel wafers in celebration. 'By, you're looking bonny these days with your wavy hair. I can't believe how quickly you're growing. When I think of how you bairns used to be always round here . . .' Her hazel eyes shone behind her pink-framed National Health spectacles. 'I miss all that,' she sighed. Jo, feeling guilty at staying away, promised to call more often.

As she was going, Jo paused. 'Tell Mark I was asking for him,' she said with a bashful look.

Ivy nodded. 'He'll come in telling me he's spent the day working for Mr Bewick, but I think he's found another interest.' She tapped the side of her nose conspiratorially.

'What's that?' Jo asked, intrigued.

'I think he's courtin',' Ivy answered with a wink.

Jo's jaw dropped. 'Courting? Who with?'

'I'll be the last to be told!' Ivy chuckled. 'But I think it's a lass from Joan Street – Christine they call her. Anyways, that's who he's been seen with.'

Jo left, feeling a tightness in her stomach. She could not think why the news was such a shock; Mark was sixteen after all, and not bad-looking. Maybe it was because he had always been like an older brother to her and she felt piqued that she knew so little of what he did any more.

Ivy came to see her in the play, but there was no sign of Mark or the mystery girlfriend. Jo determined she had done all she could to try and make amends and would waste no more energy fretting over her wayward former friend. Her life was taken up with school and acting and going up to Brenda's on the fourth floor and listening to 'Maggie May' on her record player. She and Brenda loved Rod Stewart, whereas Marilyn's choice of music – the Osmonds and David Cassidy – was to be avoided at all costs. They would sprawl on Brenda's bed and floor reading copies of the new *Cosmopolitan*, a magazine that Jo would not have dared bring home, going into fits of embarrassed laughter over the articles on sex and men.

'Me dad left Auntie Pearl to tell me the facts of life,' Jo confided. 'She explained about periods, but when it came to sex she said, "If you don't want babies, go to bed with both legs stuck down one leg of your tights!" '

The girls fell about laughing. Brenda was always keen to discuss how far they would go with a boy, and they would try out magazine questionnaires to gauge their love lives. Brenda was told she was a bad judge of character and would get hurt, Marilyn that she was incurably romantic and Jo that she was too choosy and likely to end up a nun.

'That would probably suit me dad!' Jo said wryly. 'Even if I was interested in a lad, I wouldn't dare bring him home. Dad still thinks of me as six, not nearly fifteen.'

'Well, at least you've got a trendy aunt,' Marilyn consoled her. 'She'll always fight your corner.'

'Aye, you could always keep a lad in Pearl's cosy love nest on the ninth floor!' Brenda fantasised.

To Jo's delight, her aunt came home unexpectedly at the beginning of May, just in time to see the launch of a supertanker at the Wallsend yards. They all went down to gaze at the *World Unicorn*, which towered over Nile Street and the surrounding terraces that dipped steeply down the bank. Thousands of people had turned out to watch, and there were police cordoning off the route for the arrival of Princess Anne. Some of the children, who had been allowed off school for the occasion, had union flags to wave, and a band played jauntily above the din of voices.

In the press of people, Jo and Pearl got separated from Jack and found themselves squashed up against the fence at the bottom of Nile Street, craning for a view of the slipway and the launch platform.

'Can you see anything?' Jo asked, stretching on tiptoe.

'Not really,' Pearl answered. 'I can see the top of the flags . . . Here, you're taller than me.' Pearl squeezed Jo in front of her. She could see the bows of the monster ship, lined with proud workers, and shadowing all around it. There was a lot of activity around the berth, a clanging of chains as the beast-like ship was unshackled. In the distance she could just see tiny figures gathered under the awning of the launch platform, one of which must be the princess.

Suddenly a hush came over the crowd and Jo could

clearly hear the metallic shudder of the ship as it stirred. Slowly at first, like a lumbering whale, it slid backwards down the slipway, sighing and groaning with the effort. The awestruck crowd seemed to echo its groans, as if no one could quite believe that a ship of this size could possibly stay afloat. But as it moved and dipped its huge flanks into the murky river with a triumphant splash, a deafening spontaneous cheer went round. Jo felt her heart hammering with pride at the sight of what Wallsend had produced. She waved and shouted at the top of her voice and noticed that people on the far bank of the river were waving in admiration too.

They waited around for a while, enjoying the sound of a brass band and chatting to the people beside them. Then Pearl suggested they call in at Ivy's. 'It'll be useless trying to find Jack in the crowd now, he's probably headed home already.'

Turning, Jo suddenly caught sight of Mark. Her stomach lurched to see his arm around a fair-haired girl in a yellow minidress. Pearl saw him at the same time and beckoned him over. Mark hesitated, then pushed his way towards them, holding on to the girl's hand. His hair was growing out again and he was dressed simply, in jeans and T-shirt. The boots and braces were gone. He looked broad-shouldered and fit from hours of strenuous outdoor work. For months Jo had imagined what she would say on meeting him, but for the first time in her life, she was tongue-tied before him. So she let her hair fall in front of her eyes and left Pearl to do the talking.

'You're looking well, pet,' she enthused. 'Isn't this a fab day? And who's your friend?'

Mark grinned sheepishly. 'This is Christine.'

'Please to meet you, pet,' Pearl smiled. 'Mark's an old

friend of our family. Isn't that right, Joanne?'

Jo squirmed at the formal use of her name, but nodded. She saw the other girl give her a suspicious look, but as Mark ignored her, Christine seemed to relax. Both girls looked uninterested while Pearl chatted on to Mark. She was encouraging him to join the Merchant Navy.

'You'd love it,' she assured him, 'a fit lad like you. And you'd see so much of the world. It's a wonderful life.' She put a hand on Mark's arm. 'You haven't been given much of a start, but I know you've got it in you.' She smiled at him. 'Give yourself a second chance, eh? You deserve it, pet.'

Jo was embarrassed by her aunt's forthright words and thought they were not being well received by Christine, judging by the downturn of her lipsticked mouth. But Mark was staring back at Pearl, as if struggling to answer. Eventually, he simply muttered, 'Ta. I'll think about it.' Then Christine was dragging him off and they were soon part of the crowd again, disappearing from view.

When Pearl and Jo reached Ivy's, they found Jack there, fretting.

'Where've you been? I thought you'd've come here when we got separated.'

'Hello, Ivy,' Pearl beamed, ignoring Jack's fussing. 'It's lighter in here already with the Unicorn away!'

'You know what I think of crowds?' Jack carried on.

'Stop going on,' Pearl said, losing patience. 'Jo was with me all the time. She's not a bairn any more and the sooner you realise that, the more peace we'll get!'

'Well, it's canny to see you all,' Ivy interrupted, 'I never see enough of you now you live up at the flats.'

She calmed everyone down with some warm beer for the adults and a Pepsi for Jo, but the arguing started again on the way home when Jack heard they had been speaking to Mark.

'I thought I told you—' he began, but Pearl cut him off.

'Don't be so daft! She can't go avoiding the lad for ever. Colin and Jo are old enough now to know their own minds and choose their own friends without us interfering. Besides, Mark seems to be calming down – got a girlfriend – he's not going to lead our two astray any more. There's no harm in being civil to the poor lad if we see him.'

Jack finally admitted he might have overreacted, and the subject was dropped. Jo wished Pearl was always around to defuse the squabbles at home, especially between her father and Colin. Her brother was about to sit his O levels and was constantly being badgered to decide what he was going to do afterwards. Jack wanted him to get an apprenticeship in the shipyards, while Pearl thought he was bright enough to stay on and do A levels. Colin refused to be drawn on either option, and it led to constant battles.

That evening, Pearl took her nephew and niece for a walk along the river. Jo had the feeling she was trying to tell them something but didn't know how.

'I know sometimes he's a right nuisance, but don't be resentful towards your dad,' she said, linking arms with the two of them like friends. 'He's only this protective because . . . well, with losing your mam so young. It's sometimes been hard for him bringing you up and knowing what's best. If you've lost someone that close – you're always more anxious about the others you love. Can you understand that?'

Colin grunted. 'Aye, but why does he have to make every decision for me?'

'He doesn't,' Pearl admitted. 'Only you can do that. Just let him know what you're thinking.'

They walked along in silence, until Colin stopped and said, 'I want to join the army, Auntie Pearl.'

'The army?' she said, amazed.

'Aye, I want to play in an army band – see a bit of the world like me dad did when he was young,' Colin enthused.

Pearl was doubtful. 'I can't see him being keen on that – you going away. And with all the troubles going on in Northern Ireland just now. It's not just about playing the trumpet.'

Colin protested, 'Auntie Pearl, you sound just like Dad!'

Pearl flushed. 'I'm sorry, pet. I didn't mean to put you off, it's just . . .'

'You were telling Mark he should get away from here and see a bit of life,' Jo pointed out, 'so why shouldn't Colin?'

Pearl laughed. 'You're right, I was.'

'So you'll stand up for me when Dad says no?' Colin persisted.

Pearl looked at him fondly. 'If that's what you really want – of course I will.'

'Champion!' Colin cried. 'You're the only one he'll listen to.'

Jo kept out of the way that summer while the battle over Colin's career raged. 'What's wrong with stopping at home and getting a steady job?' Jack demanded. But eventually, with Pearl's help and Colin's dogged persistence, they wore down his opposition. He was helped by the news from Ivy that Mark, his probation over, had taken Pearl's advice and joined a ship. 'If he can do it, then so can I,' Colin insisted. So, having passed his exams, he went off to a training camp in Yorkshire in the autumn, writing home enthusiastic letters that eased his father's worries.

Jo said to her friends, 'If Dad's like that with Colin, imagine what he'd say if I decided to leave home!' But unlike her aunt and brother, Jo was content where she was. Although she missed Colin, things at home were calmer once her brother was gone, and there seemed more space in the small flat. She and her father settled into a comfortable routine, enjoying each other's company more than they had in recent months.

That autumn Jo got her biggest part yet at the theatre, playing St Joan in the Bernard Shaw play. She worked hard at her studies and decided to stay on and do English at A level with Marilyn. At sixteen they both decided to become teachers, with Jo harbouring dreams of making it on the stage as well. 'Teaching will be my fallback,' she announced grandly.

As they grew older, Jo looked forward to when Colin was home on leave, for the flat would grow lively with visitors and Jack would allow them out together. A group of them would go bowling or to the pictures, or the lads would sneak them into the pub for an illegal drink, as Jo and her friends had not yet turned eighteen. Sometimes they would go to hear Gordon Duggan play bass guitar for a rock band, and dance at the front of the smoke-filled room. Their ears rang with the music all the way home and Jo was left with an excited yearning for something more.

On one occasion, Colin came home at the same time as Mark, and they found themselves playing on the same side in a football tournament. To Jo's amazement and their relief, it was as if the rift between them had never been. Their time away had helped the bad memories fade and made their differences seem trivial. They quickly discovered that their friendship was as strong as ever, brought back to the fore by playing football together as they had done so often in the past. By the end of their leave they were firm friends again and it gladdened Jo to see them reconciled. Both lads were far happier than they had been before leaving home, full of a new confidence and enthusiasm for life that was infectious.

Over the summer of '75 they had trips to the coast, playing the amusement arcades, pub-crawling and swimming in the icy sea with their clothes on. Mark risked arrest by streaking up the beach clad only in Marilyn's Bay City Roller tartan bonnet. Luckily it was pouring with rain and the promenade was almost deserted.

That summer, Brenda went out with Mark and Jo paired off briefly with Skippy. She thought it was probably more out of convenience than for love, but he was passably good-looking, with shaggy fair hair and the beginnings of a moustache, and was out to have fun. He was an apprentice joiner at the yards, mad about Genesis and Ten Years After and devoted to Newcastle United. They had a few passionate, experimental clinches in bus shelters and the back rooms of pubs that summer.

Skippy would take her back to his parents' for Sunday tea, and Mrs Jackson would fill her with watercress sandwiches and cake. Jo liked his quiet, kind parents, but wondered from where Skippy's boisterous nature had sprung. She would have been content to carry on going out together, but when the football season started again, Skippy's interest reverted to Saturday afternoons at St James's Park and Jo went back to her acting with her feelings momentarily bruised.

'You two always used to fall out over football,' Marilyn reminded her, when the girls got together to discuss their love lives. 'Remember how you used to annoy him and Colin by supporting Sunderland?'

'Aye, I did,' Jo laughed ruefully. 'Suppose it's amazing he went out with me as long as he did.'

'Well, I'm in love,' Brenda declared, and the others groaned, 'Not again!' Brenda's infatuations waxed and waned as regularly as the moon.

'This time I really am,' she insisted with a laugh. 'Mark's a fantastic – well, you know!'

'Spare us the details,' Jo said quickly, feeling uncomfortable with the conversation.

'No, I like details,' said Marilyn dreamily. 'It's so romantic.'

'So when are you and my brother going to get romantic?' Jo teased her oldest friend.

'He's not interested.' Marilyn flushed puce.

'Course he is!' Brenda cried. 'He's daft about you. Isn't he, Jo?'

'First thing he asks about when he gets home – "Is Marilyn seeing anyone?" ' Jo grinned.

'Liars!' Marilyn pouted, clutching her hands to her burning cheeks.

'Well, maybe not in so many words,' Jo admitted, 'but I think he's keen. You've just got to show him you're interested.'

'Who says I am?' Marilyn protested.

Brenda threw a pillow at her. 'We do!'

But to Jo's disappointment, Colin and Marilyn never quite seemed to find the right moment, and the following summer, as they were hard at work revising for their A levels, it was Brenda that her brother started courting. Brenda worked as a clerk at the town hall and had lost interest in Mark when she discovered he would be away at sea for six months. She had briefly shown an interest in a mechanic at the Fina garage, but a fit-looking Colin arriving home in uniform with plenty of money was far more interesting. Jo could tell that her shy brother was bowled over by the attention of her extrovert friend, and she had to console Marilyn.

'Just think of all the choice of lads there'll be at college in September!' She enthused. 'We'll have our pick.'

'Who cares about lads?' Marilyn said dismissively. 'I'll be concentrating on my studies like Mam says I should.'

Neither of them had wavered from their desire to train as teachers of English and drama, and now they had the rest of the summer to earn some money for college and wait to hear if they had got the right grades. Jo was looking forward to a break from studying and a summer of being able to help out more at the theatre. On the afternoon of their final exam, the girls left the school euphoric, bought a bottle of cider and went down the Burn to drink it under Jo's favourite tree, chatting excitedly about the future. Brenda found them there after work.

'You'll come and visit for the weekend as soon as we're settled in college, won't you?' Jo encouraged.

'Try and stop me!' Brenda laughed.

They had grown giggly, then maudlin, at this sudden ending to their old life. For no matter how much they insisted on staying in touch, Jo knew that once they, as well as Colin and Mark, were away, the easy intimacy of their circle of friends would never be quite the same again. Feeling tipsy, they wandered into Wallsend along the hot, dusty high street and into the Coach and Eight, where they had done much of their under-age drinking a year or two before.

'I'm not serving you in uniform, lasses,' Ted the landlord growled at them.

Jo pulled off her tie. 'Haway, Ted, we've been eighteen for nearly a year.'

'What you celebrating?' he grunted.

'No more school,' Marilyn smiled, and then crumpled into tears. Ted let them stay.

'If you're kicking your heels over the summer,' he told them, 'I could do with a hand behind the bar – specially at weekends when the bands are in.'

Jo and Marilyn agreed at once. Jo knew her father would object, but she needed a job and it would be more fun than the laundry. That evening she changed into jeans and a lacy Indian top, put on some make-up and went straight back to start work before the euphoria wore off, promising her father she would take a taxi home. To her amusement, Jack came in for a pint to make sure she was all right and to instruct Ted that she was to get home safely.

It was crowded and people spilled on to the street with their drinks in the stuffy, still night air. Jo found herself enjoying pulling pints and snatching conversations with people she knew.

'I'm having a night out and getting paid for it,' she grinned at Nancy, the chief barmaid, who was showing her what to do. Nancy, with her greying beehive, was a friend of Pearl's and had been a fixture behind the bar as long as Jo and her friends had been sneaking in.

'Not too much chatting with the customers,' Nancy warned her, 'or it'll get back to your aunt.'

'Well, that's you told,' said a familiar voice above the

noise. Jo looked up from concentrating on the pump handle she was pulling. There, in front of her, was Gordon Duggan looking like Rod Stewart. Her heart thumped at she took in his wolfish face regarding her with interest under his mane of tawny hair. He was slightly unshaven, his knowing brown eyes taking in her slim flushed face as she pushed back her waves of long hair. In her platform shoes she was as tall as him, and from behind the protection of the bar she felt bold. She smiled at him broadly, pushing her hair behind her ears, aware that he was looking at her in a way he never had done before. 'Are you allowed to serve an old friend?' he asked.

Jo's green eyes widened in surprise. Gordon had hardly spoken to her before and now he was claiming her as a friend! 'As long as you don't distract me from me work,' she grinned, trying to smother her nervousness.

He gave her a flash of a smile, reminding her momentarily of Mark. 'I can't promise you that,' he answered.

'Well, just don't call me Wig,' she replied with a challenging look.

He shot her a look of surprise. 'Why would I call you that?' he asked.

'Don't you remember?' Jo asked in amazement. 'Me up a tree with a plastic Beatles wig on? When you were with Barbara Thornton . . . ?' She could feel herself burning with embarrassment, wishing she hadn't started. She could recall it all like yesterday, yet he was looking bemused. To think of the agony she had suffered because of the nickname, and he didn't even realise he had coined it!

'What a memory you've got,' he laughed. 'You certainly don't need to hide under a plastic wig now,' he grinned.

She poured him the pint of lager he asked for, and a rum and Coke which he was fetching for someone else. She wondered who he was with. He seemed in no hurry to move from the bar, taking his time finding the right money.

'Are you playing tonight?' Jo found herself asking, wishing she could empty her head of the thought of him and Barbara Thornton.

'No, but we are tomorrow. Will you be working here then?'

Jo felt her mouth going dry at the direct look he was giving her, as if it was more than just a casual question. 'Aye, I expect so.'

'She won't be if she doesn't hurry up and serve someone else,' Nancy butted in.

Jo rolled her eyes and Gordon nodded. 'I'll see you then,' he said, picking up the drinks.

Jo smiled and nodded, then hurried to serve someone else. She felt ridiculously light-headed at the short exchange with Gordon and she craned to see where he went. Over in the corner she saw him sit down next to Christine, the blonde from Joan Street that Mark used to see. She was looking tanned and glamorous, and Jo's heart sank a bit.

'Don't even think about it,' Nancy warned her.

'About what?' Jo coloured again.

'You know,' she said, jangling a bangled hand at her in warning. 'Keep your eyes off that one. He's in here with a different girl each week. Like a praying mantis!'

Jo laughed. 'He's not the least bit interested anyway,' she protested. 'It's just I used to be friendly with his brother.'

Nancy gave her one of her 'I'm not fooled' looks. 'Well, don't say I didn't warn you.'

Jo was too busy to do much more than glance in their direction, and after half an hour, Gordon and Christine were gone. She felt a stab of disappointment that he hadn't come back to the bar, but reminded herself that she would see him tomorrow night. The thought was intoxicating, and Jo felt with a thrill that this summer of transition between school and college was going to be more exciting than she had hoped.

Chapter Seven

The following evening saw the pub packed with weekend revellers and supporters of Gordon's band, Red Serpent, who were playing upstairs. Jo and Marilyn were rushed off their feet, with Nancy giving out orders while Ted chatted to his regulars. They could hear the pounding of the bass guitars overhead, and Jo wished she were able to watch. She tried to notice who had gone upstairs, but had not spotted Christine among them. Perhaps, she dared to hope, she was not going out with Gordon after all. Then she told herself not to be so ridiculous. Even if Gordon was unattached, he would hardly be looking in her direction – his younger brother's tomboy friend. He was twenty-four and worldly and could have his pick of older girls as far as she could see.

But it did not stop her heart thudding when the band came downstairs for a drink just before closing and she caught sight of Gordon in leather jacket and cowboy boots. Marilyn nudged her playfully. 'Looks like he's on his own,' she whispered.

Jo blushed with pleasure when he came straight over and asked her for his drink. She had put on her favourite cheesecloth shirt and taken extra care applying some eye make-up and lipstick to make herself look older. Her hair, which gleamed like burnished copper in the electric light, was tied back with an Indian silk scarf to reveal long silver and jade earrings. For once, the shape of her high cheekbones and slim chin were not shrouded in hair and Gordon gave her an appreciative look. Jo felt the same quickening of excitement she had experienced the night before.

He seemed to want to chat to her, but the press at the bar for last orders was too great and he disappeared to join his friends. After that, he must have gone back upstairs to pack up because Jo lost sight of him and, to her disappointment, he did not reappear.

'Do you want me to order you a taxi, lasses?' Ted asked.

Jo shook her head. 'We'll walk up the road together,' she assured him, wanting to save her wages.

They picked up their jackets and left, welcoming the cool air after the fug of inside. Walking through the town, they saw groups of people sitting on walls eating takeaways, and calling to each other as they caught the last bus home.

'Me feet are killing me,' groaned Marilyn. 'Let's catch the bus.' Jo hesitated, preferring to walk. She had taken off her platforms and was enjoying the cold pavement on her feet.

'Fresh air'll do you good,' she answered, pulling on her friend's arm. They dithered too long, and the bus pulled away from the stop with a group bellowing the words to 'Bohemian Rhapsody' on board. Marilyn took off her chunky shoes and walked barefoot like Jo.

'Hippie!' she grumbled, tagging along. But they had just drawn level with the library where their old homes used to be when a car hooted at them. It stopped a little way up the road, waiting.

'I'm sure that's Gordon's Mazda,' Marilyn gasped, peering at the dark-blue car in the dim street light. It looked sleek though slightly battered. 'He hasn't stopped for us, has he?'

Jo looked around for someone else but saw no one. 'Looks like it,' she laughed. 'Come on then,' she said impulsively. 'You wanted a lift home.'

'And you wanted to walk,' Marilyn reminded, her look cautious. But Jo was already padding up the pavement towards the waiting car. She leaned in at the open passenger window and saw Gordon eyeing her.

'Having a trip down memory lane?' he asked, nodding at the open space behind, where Jericho Street used to be.

'No, just thinking it would be handier if we still lived here,' Jo said wryly.

'But then I wouldn't have the excuse to give you a lift home,' Gordon said with a flicker of a smile. 'Haway and get in.'

Jo glanced in the back, where half the seat was taken up with a large guitar case. She pulled open the front passenger door and slipped into the seat beside him. Marilyn arrived hobbling and climbed into the back. Radio Luxembourg was playing 'Sailing' by Rod Stewart, and it struck Jo suddenly that Gordon was looking more like her favourite singer than ever. She sank back into the deep seat, letting the music calm her racing pulse. He chatted about the gig and asked them about their exams and the college they would be going to in the autumn. Jo had never heard him say as much before, or certainly not to her. As Marilyn seemed to have been struck dumb in the back, Jo found herself gabbling about everything from Pearl's latest trip to the Far East to drinking cider down the Burn in celebration at the end of school.

'Three whole months of summer to have some fun,'

she said. 'I'm not going to open another book until the end of September. Are you, Marilyn?'

Her friend gave a squeak in reply that could have been either yes or no, and then said hastily, 'This is my street – just drop me at the end.' She was opening the door as the car came to a halt. 'Ta very much.' Then she was out and slamming it shut.

'I'll give you a ring,' Jo called, and waved at her retreating friend. 'She'll be worried her mam spots the car and jumps to the wrong conclusions,' Jo tried to explain, not wanting Gordon to think her rude. 'Mrs Leishman's as bad as my dad. Colin used to call her the Alsatian.'

Gordon did not seem concerned. He gave her a bold look. 'And will your dad be hanging out the window waiting for his little lass to come home?' he mocked.

Jo flushed. 'No, he'll be watching the football highlights.' To her relief, Gordon chuckled softly. He briefly rested a hand on her knee.

'Time for a spin then,' he said. It wasn't a question, more a statement of fact, and Jo's pulse quickened in alarm.

'I can't be too late home,' she said half-heartedly, as he swung the car round. She sat tensely as they turned on to the coast road, wondering where on earth he was taking her. But the niggle of doubt was smothered by her excitement at being alone with the lad she had had such a crush on for as long as she could remember. The radio crackled and hissed and he retuned it as they sped towards the coast. To break the silence that had settled between them, she asked him about his mother. 'I never see her,' she commented. 'Is she still cleaning at Procter and Gamble?'

Gordon flicked her a look. 'No, me dad doesn't like

her going out to work. She's just a housewife these days,' he answered. Jo thought his tone dismissive.

'Do you still live at home then?' she asked.

'Aye, it's handy enough for work – but I stay out as much as possible. Let them get on with their arguing,' he grunted.

'Do they still not get on?' Jo asked in concern, wondering why Norma still put up with it. In the past, she had heard Pearl and Jack discussing her several times. Pearl had given up suggesting to Norma that she get divorced now that the new law had come in and made it easier. 'Easier for him to leave me with nothing,' had been her friend's jaded reply, according to Pearl.

'What married couple does get on?' Gordon said with derision. 'Rowing's just part and parcel of getting wed, as far as I can see.'

'I wouldn't know,' Jo mused. 'I don't remember me mam, so I don't remember any arguments even if there were any.'

'Lucky for you,' Gordon replied. 'Make love not war, that's my motto.'

His tone was casual, but Jo's heart jolted just the same. They said no more as he drove through the deserted streets of Tynemouth and parked looking on to the river mouth and the pier. The water glinted molten under a bright moon and the smell of the sea infiltrated the car. Gordon turned up the radio and lit them both cigarettes.

'I like to come here and unwind after playing,' he told her, leaning back and flicking ash out of the window. 'Just me and the sea.'

Jo doubted he ever came here just on his own, but found herself relaxing in his company. He was quite different from Mark, more detached, more cynical, with an underlying edge of hardness. He oozed self-confidence, as if he expected to get his own way. Yet there was something that reminded her of his brother, flashes of the same wicked smile.

It prompted her to ask, 'Do you see much of Mark when he's home?'

Gordon gave her an appraising look. 'No, why should I?'

Jo felt herself blushing. 'You used to get on, before . . .'

'Before me dad threw the little bugger out?' Gordon finished for her. Jo squirmed at the harsh words, wishing she had never mentioned Mark. But he didn't seem to care. 'We've never been close, not really. Not like you and Colin. Different peas out of different pods, more than likely. Anyway, it was the best thing could have happened to him, going to live with me nana – being out of the firing line. Ivy's always spoilt him rotten. It's me who's had to put up with all the shit at home for years. Not that I've had any thanks out of Mark for it.'

Jo was surprised at his bitterness. She had always thought of him as the favoured one. The thought of Gordon showing a touch of vulnerability under his hard-man image only made him the more desirable. She let him go on without interrupting.

'I was surprised when he took off to sea, mind. Bit envious really. Made me dad sit up an' all. He'd gone on for years about Mark being ripe for a career in the nick and then he was suddenly in the Merchant Navy – something me dad had never done. He didn't know what to say. But he's still too proud to have him round the house like Mam wants. It would kill him to have to admit he was wrong all along about Mark being worse than useless. And it's a way of getting at Mam, refusing to see him. He'll punish her for ever for having it off with someone else. You know he thinks Mark's another man's bastard, don't you?'

Jo nodded uncomfortably. 'What do you think?' she asked quietly.

'Well, you can tell by just looking at him, can't you? Looks like Omar Sharif.' Gordon flicked his cigarette out of the window and shifted closer. 'So, do you see much of the prodigal when he's on leave?'

Jo gulped. 'Well, now and then. When Colin's home mostly. We go out as a group. He and Brenda were courting for a bit.'

'Aye,' Gordon laughed, 'Mark and half of Wallsend.'

'That's not true!' Jo said hotly.

Gordon leaned over and stroked a strand of hair from her burning cheek. It sent a shiver through her. 'That's nice,' he smiled. 'I like to see loyalty.' Pushing her hair behind her ear, he probed. 'But Mark's never been out with you?'

'No,' she whispered, as his fingers trailed down her neck. He reached behind her head and pulled her towards him.

'Never kissed you then?' he murmured in her ear.

'No,' she croaked, feeling her heart pounding as his breath tickled.

'I bet he's wanted to,' Gordon said, and then his mouth was on hers and she closed her eyes. Compared to Skippy and the other boys from school she had kissed half-heartedly in the past, he was an expert. She felt the deftness of his fingers in her hair and the taste of his tongue in her mouth. She wanted it to go on and on, but after a minute he drew away.

He smiled at her, then started up the engine as if nothing had happened. 'Don't want your dad calling out the police, do we?'

She was too shaken to speak, wondering if he could hear her heart thumping. He had stirred something in her and she yearned for him to kiss her again, but already they were cruising out of Tynemouth and heading homewards.

They hardly spoke, but as he drew up outside the flats, she forced herself to ask, 'Are you seeing that Christine? The one Mark used to . . .'

He shot her a look. 'Not especially. Just for the odd drink.' Then he smiled and touched her face. 'Does that bother you?'

'No, why should it?' Jo tried to sound unconcerned and opened the door.

'Good,' he said. 'Are you doing anything tomorrow?' She shook her head, holding her breath. 'I'll pick you up at twelve then. We can go up the coast or something.'

Jo had a sudden panic about what her father would think. 'Great, but I'll meet you on the high street – by the garage. Save a lot of questions from me dad,' she grinned.

He nodded and blew her a kiss. 'Don't be late.'

She watched him drive off, the sound of the car radio fading quickly, and took deep breaths to still her trembling. She let herself in as quietly as possible and was thankful to find her father sound asleep in his chair. Creeping to bed, she lay for a long time, savouring the unexpected end to her evening and wondering impatiently what tomorrow would bring. She had never felt so strongly for a lad before. It was as if her childish infatuation with Gordon had been fanned into a real passion by his sudden attention. He made her feel vital and alive. Just the way he looked at her made her feel desirable, like a fully grown woman. It was a heady, explosive feeling.

The next morning, she told her father she was going to the beach with friends and would be out all day.

'You got in late last night,' he commented.

'Aye, there was a band on, so we were late clearing up,' Jo said, as she forced down some toast. She could hardly eat for anticipation at seeing Gordon again. 'I didn't like to wake you when I came in.' She packed a towel in a patchwork shoulder bag, put on denim shorts and jacket over her bikini and tied her hair in a bright scarf, peasant-style.

'You'll take a picnic?' fussed her father. Jo seized some fruit from the basket on the sideboard and a chocolate biscuit to keep him happy.

'Not working today then?' he persisted.

'No, Sunday's going to be me day off,' Jo assured him. 'I'll be in tomorrow though.'

'Maybe we can go out together next Sunday,' Jack suggested, 'have our dinner at Shields or some'at?'

'Yes, Dad,' Jo agreed distractedly, squirting on some more perfume. She ignored the odd look he gave her and kissed his cheek quickly. 'I'll get me tea at Marilyn's or someone's, so don't keep anything for me. Ta-ra, Dad. See you later.'

Then she was out of the door before he asked any more searching questions about who she was going with or how she was getting there. Jo wished that Pearl was around this summer to take his mind off fretting over her. But then again, her aunt was just as likely to ask awkward questions, and her opinion of Gordon was little higher than Jack's. 'Treats his mother like a skivvy just as much as Matty does,' Pearl had said. 'He's a Duggan through and through, that one.' But Jo dismissed her aunt's unkind words. Pearl was just prejudiced against him because of Matty; she didn't know Gordon at all. If it was Gordon's way of surviving in that warring, unhappy household, who could blame him?

The streets were baking in unaccustomed heat by midday, and Jo sat on the wall by the Fina garage wishing she had put on a long skirt to stop her legs burning. Gordon drove up twenty minutes late.

'Sorry, slept in,' he smiled beneath dark glasses as she got in. He leaned over to brush her hot cheek with a kiss and glanced at her long pale legs. 'You've kept them well hidden.'

Jo grimaced. 'I don't have any false tan either.'

'You don't need to cover them up,' he said, touching them lightly, 'they're beautiful.' Jo felt a flush of heat that had nothing to do with the temperature outside.

She laughed bashfully. 'I'm not used to compliments – especially from you!'

He laughed as he accelerated out of town. 'I'll have to change that, won't I?'

They headed up the coast, northwards into Northumberland, the radio blasting out of the open windows. Stopping in the market town of Alnwick, they had a couple of drinks at the White Swan and then headed for the beach. Gordon knew of a quiet cove with a small caravan park on the cliffs above. He took her hand and they scrambled down the dunes on to the beach, picking a spot near some rocks away from the holidaying families. Jo felt quite tipsy from the lunchtime drink.

'Let's go in the sea!' she cried, stripping off down to her bikini. Gordon laughed, shedding his clothes on the warm sand and pulling on a pair of cut-off shorts. He raced her down to the sea and they splashed each other and gasped at the cold. They swam about for several minutes, then he said he'd had enough and hauled her out of the water.

'Let's get warmed up,' he grinned, putting his arm around her dripping waist and giving it a squeeze. Back at the rocks they rubbed themselves down and then lay on their towels, listening to Gordon's portable cassette player. He had brought a tape of Red Serpent that they had recorded in Jerry the drummer's attic, and they lay close together listening to its heavy beat.

'I think it's fantastic,' Jo murmured, resting her head on his arm, enjoying the feel of the warm hairs on her cheek. 'Why don't you try to go professional?'

He smiled with pleasure. 'It's not that easy. You need someone behind you with money. It's just something the lads like to do for kicks at the weekend. I'm better off having a regular job at the yards. I'm doing all right. Got enough to get me own place when I want to – when I find the right lass.' She could not read his expression behind his sunglasses, but she knew he was looking at her intently.

'What sort of lass would that be?' she asked.

'Someone who likes my music,' he smirked, tracing a rough finger across the dip of her waist and over her thigh.

'Not Christine then?' Jo said with a quizzical smile. 'She's not one of your groupies, is she?'

'No, she has no taste in music,' Gordon grinned. He shuffled closer. 'Anyway, I haven't brought you all the way here to talk about her.' He kissed her drying shoulder, then her arm. 'You taste of the sea,' he murmured, running his tongue along the rim of her bikini top. Jo could feel her heart jumping under his touch and knew that he must feel it too. Then he was over her, his mouth firmly on her own, devouring her with kisses. She responded enthusiastically, running her hands over his back, revelling at the feel of his skin.

They lay embracing and touching each other for what seemed like an age, Jo hardly aware of the call of children further down the beach. Eventually, they lay entwined and fell asleep, Gordon's arm resting heavily across her thigh. When she woke, she felt shivery, their spot now lying in shadow. The beach was emptying. Gordon pulled her up and threw his leather jacket around her shoulders.

'Haway, we need to warm up,' he ordered. Gathering up their clothes, Jo followed him back up the rocky path to the dunes above, wondering vaguely why he was not heading back to the car. He led her through a small gate and into a field of caravans. In the far corner was a small green caravan that looked as if it had taken root there many years ago. Grass grew up around its steps, and when Gordon tried the handle it was unlocked. Inside, the flowery curtains were drawn and it was dim and cool.

'Whose is it?' Jo whispered nervously.

'Jerry in the band – it belongs to his family, but they hardly ever come here,' Gordon replied. Jo stood at the door, not moving. 'Haway,' he smiled, 'no one'll disturb us here.' He reached out and took her hand, guiding her over to the bench seat and plonking her down on a damp cushion. He rummaged in the cupboard next to it. 'He sometimes leaves a few cans . . . Here we are.' Pulling out a couple of cans of Tennant's lager, Gordon handed her one and opened the other, taking a long swig.

Jo did the same, shivering inside his jacket. He reached towards her and she flinched, but he fished in his jacket pocket and brought out his battered cigarettes, offering her one with a grin 'Relax,' he said gently, taking off his sunglasses, 'I'm not going to pounce.'

Jo laughed nervously and took another swig from the

can. They looked at each other for a long moment and she knew she wanted him. It was like a deep, gnawing hunger that would not go away. She had tasted his kisses and felt the strength in his arms and shoulders, and she wanted more. Jo wanted all of him with a sweet, aching longing. Before her courage failed her, she put down her can and said, 'I want you to pounce.' She was shaking with nerves and cold, wondering what he would say.

Gordon laughed softly and put down his drink. 'I hoped you would. Come here, then.' He held out his arms to her and she squeezed round the Formica table.

'I've never done it before,' she whispered.

He looked surprised. 'Well, aren't I the lucky one?' he smiled, and pulled her to him. 'The lads of Wallsend must be blind.'

They began kissing at once, urgently, as he guided them to the back of the caravan behind a thin curtain where a mattress lay on the floor. There was a pile of grey blankets to the side and everything smelled musty, but neither of them cared. Gordon's jacket fell off her shoulders as they went down. Jo gasped as he touched her, aroused her. They made love in the muted light. He was practised and vigorous and she marvelled that Gordon Duggan should be the one to make her a woman.

Later, they lay wrapped in the blankets, listening to fractious parents shouting at their children to come in for tea to the surrounding caravans. 'We should go soon,' Gordon said, sharing a cigarette. But a few minutes later they were making love again and Jo thought she never wanted to go home. She was drunk with desire for him.

When he finally made a move to get dressed, she asked, 'When can we do this again?'

He smiled. 'We'll find a time. Haway, it's getting late.'

117

As they made their way to the car, Jo said, 'Are we going out now – you and me?'

Gordon did not answer directly. 'Best if we keep it quiet, don't you think? The last thing I need is your father giving me a hard time. He doesn't care for us Duggans, and my dad feels the same about you lot. He'd make me life hell.'

'I don't want that,' Jo said quickly, 'not because of me.'

He kissed her in satisfaction. 'It's our secret, then? We'll keep prying noses like Nancy out as well, eh? Stop word getting back to your dad.' He must have seen her disappointment, for he added, 'Just for a bit – till we see how things work out.'

Jo swallowed hard. 'Okay.' She wanted everyone to know she was going out with Gordon and didn't care what they thought. But if that was what he wanted, she would have to be content with keeping it secret. It would certainly make it easier with her father. And with no Colin or Pearl around this summer, he was even less likely to find out. Speeding home, listening to the Top Twenty on the radio, she consoled herself with the astonishing thought that, secret or not, Gordon was her man.

Chapter Eight

Jo spent the next month in a lovesick daze. Every minute she was not with Gordon felt wasted. She ached with longing for him, day-dreamed about him and woke up at night in a sweat thinking of him. She loved her job at the pub, for there was always a chance that he would walk in and order a drink with that knowing look and secretive smile that set her heart pounding. Band nights were the best, for under the noise of the crowd they exchanged words and planned where to meet. To her satisfaction she never saw him in the Coach and Eight with Christine.

'Why would I want to see her when I've got my Jo-Jo?' he teased.

He would pick her up in his car and take her to quiet places after she finished work for snatched lovemaking. Occasionally, when she had an evening off, they would drive into Newcastle to hear a band or go to a nightclub, and she would give her father the impression that she was out with a group of friends. Marilyn was the only person she confided in, for she had guessed quickly that there was something going on. Marilyn knew that Gordon picked her up at nights and she allowed Jack to think that Jo stayed late at her house.

'Why can't you tell anyone?' Marilyn puzzled.

'We don't want any strife from our fathers,' Jo

explained, hiding her own dissatisfaction at the situation. 'It's just easier this way.'

They agreed not to tell Brenda. 'Might as well put it in the paper as tell Brenda a secret,' Marilyn joked. Jo knew she could rely on her best friend to be discreet, for they were going to share their future together at college and told each other everything.

'I can't believe I'm going out with him,' Jo would sigh. 'All those years when he never gave me the time of day – thought me a right nuisance. And now . . .' She hugged herself in delight.

Marilyn would roll her eyes. 'I hope you're not going to be this bad once we're at teacher training. I've never known you like this over a lad!'

'Oh, don't talk about the end of the summer.' Jo shivered. 'I don't want to think about that.'

Gordon took complete possession of her mind. She hardly even thought about Colin, who was now in Northern Ireland. While her father fretted over news of an ambush in County Down and a bomb blast on the Shankill Road, Jo found herself detached from the outside world. A letter came from Pearl, but Jo hardly took in any of the news. Normally she would rush to the atlas and track where her aunt had been, but this time the letter lay around half read.

On Sundays Jo was in heaven. Gordon would pick her up away from the flat and they would leave town for the day and drive up the Tyne into the countryside or up the coast to the caravan. They would lie together for hours, making love to tapes of Red Serpent, smoking and drinking. On the way home they would stop for fish and chips or a bar meal and Jo would eat ravenously after their afternoons of passion.

Then, during the last few minutes of the ride, as the

cranes of Wallsend poked into view, she would feel desolate and go quiet. Before she got out of the car, her craving to see him again would already have started. It amazed her that he could kiss her calmly and wave her away with a smile and a promise to come into the bar during the week. She did not like to think that he did not love her with the same intensity. Jo knew that he wanted her and enjoyed their trips, but did he *need* her in the same way that she needed him?

He would whisper his desire for her as they made love, and give her compliments, but he never spoke of love. When she asked him about it, he would laugh it off.

'Love is for school bairns, Jo-Jo,' he scoffed. 'What we've got is pure lust.'

She did not like it when he said that, though she had to admit she felt it too. But she was sure it was more than just physical attraction. She loved him more than anyone else in the world and now could not bear to think of a life without him. She began to worry about what he did on the nights she did not see him, when she was tied up working in the pub. She became obsessed with wanting to know his every move, to be reassured he was seeing no one else. But her questions led to small rankling arguments, so she tried to curb her curiosity, knowing it only annoyed him.

'We're free spirits, you and me,' Gordon told her with a warning glance. 'That's what I like about you. You get on with everyone – you're out to enjoy yourself and so am I. Let's just leave it at that.'

But Jo couldn't. It was early August, and as they lay on the riverbank outside Hexham, Jo was thinking of her nineteenth birthday the following month. 'Why don't we have a big party at the pub for it?' she suggested. 'Then we can tell everyone about us. I'm getting tired of sneaking around as if we've got something to hide. Sod what our dads think!' She gave him a challenging look.

'It's just a birthday. You make it sound like an engagement party or some'at.' Gordon grunted and sat up. 'I don't think it's a good idea.'

'Why not?' Jo demanded.

He gave her a sidelong look. 'It's over a month away. You might be sick of me by then,' he joked.

'I'll never be sick of you,' Jo insisted. 'I love you!'

'Haway,' he said impatiently, 'don't say that. Anyways, you've got college in October – you'll be living hundreds of miles away.'

'Just Yorkshire,' Jo said, dismayed at his reluctance.

'Well, it'll still not be the same once you've gone,' Gordon pointed out. 'You can't expect me to hang around for months waiting for you to come back.'

Jo's stomach felt leaden at his words. 'I won't go then,' she said in panic.

'Don't be daft,' he said sharply, 'of course you must go. You're going to be a teacher. It's important you make something of your life – something to make your family proud of you. I might be a selfish bastard, but at least I can see what's best for you and I'll not be the one to spoil it.'

Jo felt wretched. She grabbed his arm. 'We can still go on seeing each other after the summer. You can come and stay at weekends.'

The look he gave her was cool. 'I thought you understood me better than that. I don't go chasing lasses around the country. What we've got is a summer affair, Joanne, let's just enjoy it while it lasts. You're too young to go getting serious about me.'

She felt winded. 'I'm not too young!' she croaked, tears springing to her eyes.

'You'll probably meet someone else your first week at college. I've heard what students are like,' he teased.

Tears welled up and trickled down her cheeks. 'Don't say that,' she cried. 'It's you I want, just you!'

'Hey, Jo-Jo,' he said, suddenly softening and reaching over to wipe away her tears with a rough hand. 'I've never seen you cry before!' He gave her a cuddle. 'You're in too deep. I didn't mean for you to get this bothered about me.'

'What did you mean then?' Jo accused.

Gordon shrugged. 'I don't know. I just go after lasses I fancy. And you were so sexy in your little lacy top standing behind the bar. I couldn't resist you.' He was grinning at her. Then he added, 'And I must admit, I got a kick out of scoring with Mark's childhood sweetheart an' all.'

Jo gaped at him, the words wounding her more deeply than his trivialising of their relationship. Was this whole affair just a petty game to get back at his brother? she thought, quite stunned. Was she really nothing more than a casual victim of Gordon's jealousy of Mark? Did their rivalry go that deep? Jo was appalled. She would not believe he could be so callous.

'I was never his sweetheart,' she whispered hoarsely. 'Please tell me I mean more to you than that.' Her green eyes were pleading.

Gordon gave her a hard look as he drew away. 'You're bonny and I like having sex with you,' he answered brutally, 'but that's all. I don't love you, Joanne.'

Jo forced herself not to cry as they drove home in a tense silence, digging her nails into the palms of her hands. She had ruined everything with her childish idea of wanting a big birthday party. If she had only kept quiet, they would still be enjoying each other's company in Hexham, but she had opened her big mouth once too often. She should have given him more time to do it his way, for she was sure he would have come to feel just as strongly about her, given time. Instead, as they cut short their day out, he had suggested they cool it off for a bit, see other people. See other people! Jo agonised. She could not bear the thought of letting someone else touch her, let alone not being with Gordon again. And the thought of him going with other girls made her mad with jealousy.

But bursting into tears on their arrival back to Wallsend just seemed to annoy him more. 'You see what I mean? I don't want you seeing me if it's going to upset you all the time. We'll give it a break for a couple of weeks and see how we both feel, eh?'

By his look she knew that he thought her immature and not old enough to be taken seriously. She was devastated by the sudden reality. She had been his summer fling, nothing more; a little act of spite against his brother. She stumbled out of the car, blind with tears, and watched him drive away up the road with an impatient acceleration. She hardly remembered the walk home, where she locked herself in the bathroom and wept for hours until exhausted, cauterising the pain of his rejection.

When her father came in from having tea with Ivy, she had already put herself to bed, mumbling at him in the darkened room that she had a splitting headache. She slept for hours, waking with the dawn and the rattle of a milk float outside her window. And then the pain came, relentless and all-consuming. Gordon had finished with her and she did not know how she would ever get over it.

Chapter Nine

For several days Jo felt completely numb. Somehow she managed to drag herself to work and force a happy appearance for a few hours. But it was a façade, for underneath she felt as fragile as a china doll. Marilyn guessed before she was told and tried to shield her from Nancy's inquisitive questioning. 'Why's she looking so peaky all of a sudden? Not getting to bed early enough? Boy trouble?'

'She's worrying about her brother in Northern Ireland,' Marilyn replied, and, 'It's that time of the month,' in a low voice so Ted didn't hear.

'How can I face him again after the things he said?' Jo confided weepily round at Marilyn's house. 'He's just used me. I never meant anything more to him than a roll in the sack.' She hung her head. 'I feel so ashamed.'

'You've got nothing to be ashamed about,' her friend insisted, passing her another wodge of tissues.

Jo tried to smile. 'Ta. I wish I had shares in Kleenex.'

'You just ignore him when he comes in the bar – I'll serve him. You deserve better than his type. The way he made you keep it all hush-hush, it wasn't right. I bet he's been seeing someone else all the time.'

Jo shuddered. 'Oh, don't say that! I still love him.'

'Jo!' Marilyn protested.

'I'm sorry, but I can't help it. I wish I could just

forget him, but I'm aching all the time.'

'I'm taking you out this weekend,' her friend declared. 'I'll get some of the gang together. You're going to stop making yourself ill over that Duggan lad.'

It was the last thing Jo felt like doing, but she allowed Marilyn to bully her into it. They negotiated Saturday night off, thankful that they would miss Gordon's band, and went into Newcastle. Jo got very drunk and collapsed on the disco floor of the Mayfair, and they all taxied home. She stayed at Marilyn's and in the morning found Skippy on the settee downstairs.

'I didn't say anything daft last night, did I?' Jo winced at the pain in her head.

'Nothing in English,' Skippy joked. 'A lot in Gibberish.'

They all went for a walk along the Burn. 'You did burst into tears when I told you Mark was coming home next week,' Skippy told her. 'That'll be a canny welcome for him.'

Jo exchanged glances with Marilyn. 'I don't remember you saying that.' Jo was not sure she could bear to see Mark so soon. He would be a painful reminder of her failure with Gordon. She had made such a fool of herself over him! she agonised.

But there was no escaping either Duggan for long. Gordon seemed to be avoiding the Coach and Eight, but one afternoon she saw his car on the high street and her stomach lurched to see a woman in the passenger seat. As he sped past, Gordon waved to her. Jo was left with her heart thumping painfully, wondering who the woman was. It did not look like Christine.

When she mentioned it to Marilyn, her friend was cagey. 'Who do you think it was?' Jo fretted.

'Does it matter?' Marilyn replied.

126

'You know, don't you?' Jo accused.

Marilyn shrugged. 'It's just something Mam said . . . She said Mrs Thornton was in the store on Saturday.'

'Mrs Thornton?' Jo was baffled

'You know. Barbara's mam.'

'Barbara who used to work at the laundry?'

'Yes,' Marilyn said, 'but she hasn't worked there for years. She's been down London, nannying or something.' She gave Jo a pitying look. 'But now she's back.'

Jo felt her stomach twist. 'And she's seeing Gordon.'

Marilyn nodded. 'That's what her mam told mine.' Something about her awkwardness made Jo persist.

'What else did she say? There's something else, isn't there? You've got to tell me!'

Marilyn said in a quiet voice, 'Mrs Thornton says Barbara's been courting Gordon for six months – every time she comes home she sees him.'

Jo was stunned. 'Six months! It's not possible . . .' She felt seized with a sudden rage. 'All the time he was having his way with me!' She clasped her head and started to howl.

'Stop it, man!' Marilyn said in alarm, glancing around them in the park where they had gone for a smoke. People were staring.

But Jo took the can of Coke she was drinking and crushed it under her foot. 'I hate him! The bastard!' she yelled, stamping on the can until its contents spewed and frothed all over the ground. 'The lying, cheating . . . !' Then she burst into tears.

Marilyn looked on in dismay, not knowing what to say to this new, emotional Jo whom she did not recognise. She produced tissues and waited for her friend to calm down.

'Well, it just proves he wasn't worth bothering about,'

Marilyn concluded. 'You should get yourself out with other lads and show him you don't give a toss.'

Jo nodded, her eyes sore and swollen from too much crying. 'Aye, you're right. I'll show him.'

That evening, Jo went round to the theatre for the first time in a month. She had neglected her friends there and refused a part in the summer musical so as to be around for Gordon. Now she worked behind the scenes and helped people learn their lines, filling every waking hour with activity so that she did not dwell on her foolish affair. When she wasn't working or helping at the theatre, she would go out partying with her friends, stifling any craving she felt for Gordon. On band night, she steeled herself to act coolly towards him, as if their brief passion had never been. She was polite but aloof, so that no one should guess they had ever been more than on nodding terms. Jo even managed to be civil to Barbara when she came in to listen to Red Serpent, noticing with a pang how mature and sophisticated she was in her linen trouser suit and with her shoulder-length permed hair.

The night Mark came home, he came into the bar with Skippy and Brenda and Jo's spirits lifted to see his grinning face and hear his cheerful banter. He was full of his time away and the trips ashore in American ports.

'Makes a change to see you lasses on that side of the bar,' he teased. 'Not drinking all Ted's profits, are you?'

'Not if you offer to buy us drinks,' Jo quipped back.

'You're looking well on it, anyways,' Mark smiled, and Jo's insides twisted at the fleeting likeness to Gordon.

'I am,' she lied, thankful at what a bit of make-up could hide.

'We thought we'd head down to the coast tomorrow,'

Brenda shouted over Mark's shoulder in the jostle. 'Want to come?'

Last Sunday Jo had spent moping at home, thinking back to the week before and the terrible trip to Hexham. Looking at her friends' enthusiasm, she determined she was never going to waste her day off like that again. 'Count me in,' she smiled.

'And me,' Marilyn nodded.

'Champion!' Mark replied. 'We'll all go in Skippy's car. Come round to Nana's for breakfast – she's complaining she never sees you.'

'Aye, I'd like that,' Jo agreed, feeling guilty that Ivy was yet another old friend she had neglected over the past month.

She was up early the next day, packing for the beach and pulling on her denims as it was blustery and threatening rain. Jack seemed pleased that she was going to Ivy's. He had begun to go down to Nile Street regularly at weekends since Pearl had been away such a long stretch. He said it reminded him of Jericho Street, and he and Ivy liked to chat about the old days without the young complaining. Jo wondered if they ever discussed Gordon or his parents. She knew Ivy tried to keep in touch with Matty, but there had been a stand-off since Mark had gone to live with her and she was largely snubbed by her son and his wife. To Ivy's distress, Gordon made no effort to see her either. Jo knew this was because of his jealousy over Mark and the way he saw his grandmother favouring the younger grandson, but Ivy would not understand that.

'She's always asking after you,' Jack said pointedly.

'I know,' Jo said, giving him a quick kiss. 'I'm going to make up for it now,' she promised. Meeting Marilyn on the way, they hurried to Ivy's, Jo feeling more like her old self for the first time in two weeks. Ivy had bacon and eggs, toast and tea ready for them and sent them off in Skippy's car with a picnic of ham sandwiches and crisps, ordering them to return for their tea if it poured with rain.

'I like nothing better than having you bairns around again,' she beamed from behind her steamed-up glasses.

'You'll be calling us bairns when we're turning grey,' Mark teased his grandmother, and gave her a smacking kiss.

With David Bowie blaring out of Skippy's battered Vauxhall Viva, the five friends rattled off towards Whitley Bay. They walked along the prom to St Mary's lighthouse and clambered around the rocks. Almost missing the tide, they waded back across the causeway, soaking their shoes and jeans, and headed back to the funfair at Spanish City. They went to a pub for lunchtime last orders and then took their sandwiches to the beach, where they buried Skippy in the sand when he dozed off. Later, it began to rain, so they sheltered in a café eating chips and playing noughts and crosses on the steamed-up window.

Jo realised she had not been so relaxed or enjoyed a day out as much all summer. It was just like past summers when they had hung around together; only Colin was missing from the group. She could tell how the others missed his company by their constant reference to past things he had done or said, and she felt suddenly ashamed that she had thought so little about her brother these past weeks. When Mark asked her for news, she tried to remember what her father had told her. There was Colin facing danger every day in Northern Ireland, while she had been too consumed with her own selfish passion for Gordon to care.

By the end of the day, when they had returned to Ivy's for tea and then gone for a drink on the high street, Jo began to wonder what madness had gripped her these past few weeks. It was as if she was waking from a trance, a spell that Gordon had put on her. Now she could see how blinkered she had been about him, too eager to overlook his faults and ignore the casual way he treated her and others. Looking at Mark, with his unfashionably short hair and the lively warmth of his eyes, she saw how different the brothers were. She had always thought of Mark as the wild, dangerous one, but she was wrong. Despite all the bad treatment he had received in the past, he was not bitter like Gordon. He was kind and funny and good to be with, just like he had always been when they were children.

Mark caught her staring at him and gave her a quizzical look. Jo blushed and glanced away, but he put out a friendly hand.

'Haven't grown another head while I've been at sea, have I?' he joked.

Jo laughed. 'No, it's just good to see you again, that's all,' she answered, wondering why she felt so bashful.

He gave her knee a quick squeeze. 'You too,' he smiled, and Jo felt a warmth creep through her like the comforting glow from a fire. Not the passion she had felt for Gordon, but a deep feeling of well-being that came from years of friendship.

All that following week, towards the end of August, Mark called into the Coach and Eight for a drink and a game of pool with Skippy during his friend's lunch hour. Jo found herself looking forward to their appearance, watching out for them coming through the door with their constant joking chat. She wished that Colin was there too to share in the fun, but his tour of Northern

Ireland would not be over until just before Christmas, which seemed an age away.

One afternoon, when she was walking home after three o'clock closing, she found Mark waiting for her on the road up to the flats. He was dressed in jeans and a white T-shirt that accentuated his muscled arms and the darkness of his skin. Jo's heart skipped a beat.

'Fancy a walk down the Burn?' he asked, and she thought he seemed nervous. She hesitated a moment, looking around for a sign of the others, but Mark was alone.

'Aye, why not?' she agreed, sensing there was something different happening between them. He grinned with relief and fell into step with her. Descending into the dene, they began to reminisce about their escapades there as children.

'Reckon you can still climb that tree?' Mark challenged, nodding towards the vast horse chestnut.

'Why-aye!' Jo replied at once, thankful that she had put on dungarees that morning. She reached for the old familiar branches and hauled herself up, scrabbling against the trunk with her chunky sandals and finding it much harder than she had remembered. Mark laughed and gave her a shove from below.

'You're not as fit as you used to be,' he commented, 'but you're a cannier shape!'

Jo blushed and took a swipe at him. 'Just 'cos you've got muscles like Popeye!'

'Glad you've noticed,' Mark grinned, swinging himself up easily beside her.

They sat astride the thick branch, half hidden by rustling leaves, listening to the sound of an ice-cream van jingling in the distance.

'This takes me back,' Jo mused, swinging her legs.

'Aye,' Mark said softly, 'some of me happiest times were up here.' He looked at her with his large dark eyes and Jo was suddenly aware of how close they were sitting, knees touching, hands clasping the same stretch of branch. 'With you, I mean,' he added. The smile he gave her was so warm and tender that Jo felt tears prick her eyes.

'Me too,' she whispered. Then it happened. Mark leaned across and kissed her gently, tentatively on the lips. In all the years they had been friends, he had never done that before. Deep inside, she felt something hard and bitter melt at his touch, as if the disappointment and shame with which Gordon had filled her was dispelled, and she bent her head and began to cry.

Mark stared in alarm. 'I'm sorry, Jo . . .' he said, bewildered, drawing back. Jo could not speak, but shook her head and stretched out a hand to him, grasping his firm shoulder. He put an arm around her and stroked the hair from her face. 'Hey, I didn't mean to spoil things between us.'

'You haven't,' Jo rasped. 'It's me – I'm sorry.'

Mark shushed her and held on as she wept against his shoulder. At last he lifted her chin gently. 'I think we should get down before we fall out of this tree,' he said. He swung down from the branch first and then helped Jo down. She found herself standing under the tree, clinging on to him. Mark steered her round the trunk and sat her down in its shade, away from the path.

'I don't know why I did that,' he said bashfully. 'Trying to kiss you. It just seemed right . . .'

Jo put out a hand and touched his face. 'I felt it too,' she said quietly.

'But you don't want it to go any further?' Mark asked.

'I don't know,' Jo said, confused. 'I've never thought of you like that until now.'

Mark gave a rueful smile. 'I shouldn't have listened to Marilyn. She thought I might stand a chance with you.'

'Marilyn's been talking about me to you?' Jo said, aghast. 'What did she say?'

'Said you'd been hurt by someone recently. That it would do you good to go out with someone who cared for you.' He gave her one of his penetrating looks. 'And I do care for you, Jo. I have for a long time. But I don't think you feel the same. Have I ruined me chances up that tree?' he asked, with a smile of regret.

Jo was overwhelmed by his words. She took his handsome face between her hands and kissed him back gratefully. 'You're so canny,' she said, smiling at him tearfully. 'I do care for you, Mark.'

She felt his arms go round her in a tight hug and then they kissed again, a longer, more confident kiss. It filled Jo with tenderness and surprise that their friendship had come to this moment. It was nothing like the intensity she had felt for Gordon, but it soothed her like a balm and she clung on to him afterwards, happy in their new intimacy.

They went for a long walk and then back to the flat, where Jack was making tea. Jo dreaded some tactless comment from her father, knowing he was still wary of Mark since his skinhead days. But after an awkward few minutes, Mark put Jack at his ease, asking after Colin and talking about past voyages. Mark stayed for tea, and by the time Jo had to return to the pub, she was finding it difficult to stop them talking about life at sea.

At the end of the evening, Mark was waiting to walk her home with a bunch of flowers he had picked from Bewick's garden. They kissed under the stars by the park railings and Jo was amazed to find him so romantic.

'How many other lasses have had this treatment in other ports?' she teased.

'None,' he declared, then added mischievously, 'as bonny as you!'

'I could get used to this,' she smiled as they walked up the road, arm in arm.

'Did this other lad not treat you right?' Mark asked.

Jo tensed. 'I made a big mistake with him,' she confessed. 'I thought I was really in love. But whatever it was, it wasn't that. I found out afterwards he had another lass all the time he was seeing me. You've got more kindness and understanding in your little finger than he'll ever have.'

'Who was he?' Mark asked.

Jo could not look at him as she agonised over whether she should tell him. But she was still too hurt by the affair, and her courage failed her. 'I don't want to talk about him any more,' she gulped.

She felt him squeeze her tight. 'Well, whoever he was, he must have been daft to throw you over. But his loss is my gain.'

Jo had a sudden image of Gordon's mocking smile and wondered uncomfortably what he would think when he heard she was seeing Mark. She imagined he would take a perverse pleasure in knowing he had gone out with her first, and she felt a niggling dread at Mark finding out. She told herself it didn't matter; Gordon couldn't hurt either of them with his petty point-scoring, it wouldn't change the way Mark felt about her. But all the way home she had the uncomfortable feeling that she had missed the right moment to tell him.

She lay awake that night, wondering if she was right to encourage Mark so readily. Was she doing it because she really loved him, or was there an element of wanting to get back at Gordon? she asked herself brutally. Her uncertainty at her motives made her cautious in their courtship, and for a couple of weeks she kept Mark's ardour in check. She knew he wanted to take their relationship further, and part of her longed for that intimacy too. But she was scared of getting hurt again and guilty that she might in turn hurt Mark if her feelings were not as strong as his. What if her new-found love should fade once he was back at sea, as it had done for Brenda? Was she guilty of using him for a summer fling in the same way as Gordon had used her? she agonised.

Then, one night, Mark took her out for an Indian meal, for he liked exotic food since his travels. They got dressed up and Jo felt there was an edge to their chat, a charged atmosphere that she could not ignore. He walked her back to the flat, but at the doorway she said impulsively, 'Let's go for a walk down the Burn.'

They both knew then that it was going to happen, and they hurried, nervousness and excitement gripping them, each unusually silent. It was a windy night and the trees were swaying and moaning in the stiff breeze. Mark laid out his jacket on the damp grass under their chestnut tree, which was already tinged with the yellow of the end of summer. They lay down and embraced, fumbling at each other's clothes and laughing with embarrassment at their attempts to undress each other. But Mark covered her in kisses and took his time. He was such a tender lover that Jo wanted to weep at the contrast with his brother, then chided herself that she still compared them. She wondered bleakly if she would ever rid herself of thoughts of Gordon, or would he always have a malign hold over her?

Jo clung to Mark, hoping desperately that his caring,

loving nature would protect them both from his brother.

'I love you!' Mark whispered as he made love to her in the dark.

Jo let the tears flow down her face, thankful for his love. She wanted to say it back, but instead found herself saying, 'You make me so happy!'

She was filled with relief that this was the moment she could put the affair with Gordon behind her. Mark's new-found love would make everything right, she determined. She was crying because she was happy, she assured herself. Yet inside, a small, poisonous voice struck at her peace of mind.

'You're just fooling yourself,' it said, 'and sooner or later you'll regret this night.'

Chapter Ten

That September was the happiest Jo could remember. She was enjoying her job and helping at the theatre, and looking forward in anticipation to starting college with Marilyn. And to cap it all, she was 'courting', as Ivy and her father kept saying. But this time there was no sneaking behind people's backs like with Gordon. Mark made a fuss of her wherever they went, as if he enjoyed showing her off, and their other friends seemed happy for them too. He made her feel loved and wanted and restored her self-esteem after the trauma of being dumped by Gordon. In return, she wanted to make his leave happy too, and they went everywhere together.

They had days at the coast, borrowing Skippy's car to visit places, and went to the football together. Unlike her solitary expeditions with Gordon, they often went in a group with their friends, for Mark was sociable and out to have as much fun as they could cram into the final days of his leave.

He was due to join a cargo ship at the end of September, when Jo and Marilyn would be heading for college. They talked of what they would do when they met up at Christmas time, when Colin would be back too. Jo revelled in thoughts of the future and no longer dwelled on the mistakes and heartache of the summer. The nearer October drew, the more impatient she became about becoming a student. She was keen to start her course and go back to her books again, and talked excitedly about the drama she would be doing. Although the thought of leaving Wallsend made her nervous, she felt she was ready to see more of the world.

Mark seemed happy for her and encouraged her desire to become a teacher. 'I might have paid more attention in class if I'd had a teacher like you,' he joked.

So she was not prepared for what he had to say on one of their walks along the promenade one chilly late-September day.

'Will you miss me as much as I'll miss you?' he asked, hugging her tight.

'Of course I will,' Jo replied.

'How will I know?' he pressed.

'I'll write to you,' she smiled, 'in between all the essays.' But she could see by his expression that something was worrying him. 'What's wrong?'

Mark flushed. 'It's just . . . all those other students – the male ones.'

Jo touched his face affectionately. 'If I promise not to speak to any other lads, will you be happy?' she teased.

'I'd be happier if you agreed to get engaged before you went,' he blurted out.

Jo stared at him. 'Engaged?' she repeated. 'But we've only being going out a month.' The idea made her flustered.

'But we've known each other since we were bairns, Jo,' Mark reminded her. 'I know what *I* want.'

Jo floundered. 'But now . . . ? I'm at the start of a three-year course – I'm going to be away a lot, and so are you. I don't think we should be tying ourselves down just yet.'

He looked hurt. 'I don't see it as being tied down,' he

protested. 'I'm sorry you see it that way. I just thought it would show we belonged together.'

He began to walk off. Jo took his arm. 'We do belong together. But I don't see that we need to make it so official. I'm going to be nineteen in two days' time. I don't want to think about getting wed yet. I want to prove I can make something of myself first – get qualified.' He looked at her silently. 'You chose to go away and do something you enjoy, Mark. Why can't I?'

For a moment his face looked stormy, a deep frown carved between his lively eyes. Then he gave a regretful shrug. 'Aye, you're right. I was just being selfish. Course you must gan to college – I never meant to stand in your way.'

It was the nearest they had come to an argument, and Jo put her arms around him, thankful that the subject was dropped and a row averted. Still she was left with an uncomfortable thought: why had she been so panicked by his idea? An engagement would have been a bit sudden, but no one would have been that surprised, since they had been friends for such a long time. She told herself she was just being cautious after the hurt over Gordon, and buried the disloyal thought that she might still feel something for Mark's older brother.

She agreed to meet Mark the following afternoon, but that night she began to feel unwell and in the early hours of the morning was sick. She struggled to get up for work, but was instantly sick again. Her father, worried at her pasty look and her vomiting, forbade her to get out of bed.

'It's a bug,' Jo groaned, curling up in bed to stem the dizziness and nausea. 'I'll be all right by tomorrow.' She hated the thought of being unwell for her birthday, for Mark had arranged a disco in the room above the pub and invited their friends.

He came round full of concern and wanted to call the doctor, but Jo told them both to stop fussing and leave her alone. Her birthday came and Jo got up, feeling much better, but after half an hour on her feet behind the bar she began to feel strange again. The smoke and the smell of the hot pies on the counter made her want to retch, and she kept having to dive outside for fresh air. Nancy was giving her funny looks, and eventually Ted told Marilyn to take her home.

'I'm sorry,' Jo apologised weakly, 'it must be something I've eaten.'

'Go and have a lie-down before your party,' said the easy-going landlord as Nancy sniffed her disapproval at being left to serve on her own. Marilyn stayed a while to keep her company, sitting on the end of her bed flicking through a magazine Brenda had left the day before.

'Do you want me to cancel the party? You're not going to enjoy it in this condition,' her friend commented. Jo groaned in disappointment; everything had been going so well up until now, and the party was her big chance to see all her friends before starting college. 'Mark's right, you should let the doctor take a look at you.' Marilyn gave her a sideways glance.

'What is it?' Jo asked weakly, knowing by that look that her friend had something to say. Marilyn kept flicking the pages of the magazine nervously. 'Spit it out,' Jo said, her green eyes looking like dark pools in her pale face.

'It was just . . . well, I was wondering . . .' She tossed the magazine down. 'Oh, nothing. Just make sure you go to the doctor's. I'm worried about you, that's all.'

Jo closed her eyes, baffled by her friend's reticence. 'Aye, maybes I will.'

The party was cancelled, and after another day of not feeling well, Jo went down to the clinic at the Forum. Dr Samson checked her over, but could find nothing wrong.

'You may be a touch anaemic,' he suggested, and took a couple of samples.

The following day, Jo went back to work, finding that she could keep the nausea at bay by eating small amounts regularly. The day after, feeling much better, she went into Newcastle with Marilyn to buy some clothes for college and a new set of mugs and a teapot for her room. 'We'll all go for a final night out next week – make up for not having the party,' she suggested brightly. On her return, Jack told her that someone from the clinic had been on and wanted her to ring back. He was preoccupied with the thought of Pearl returning in a couple of weeks' time and was constantly checking her flat and doing small jobs around it, as if being there would make her come back all the quicker.

Jo rang the clinic. 'Just a minute, Doctor wants a word with you,' she was told. She hung on, beginning to feel nervous. Eventually Dr Samson answered.

'You are slightly anaemic,' he told her, 'so I'm going to give you iron tablets.' Jo felt instant relief. Then he added, 'But the urine test has shown up positive – that's why you've been feeling sick.'

'What do you mean, positive?' Jo asked.

He cleared his throat. 'It means you're pregnant, Joanne,' he explained. She gaped at the receiver.

'*Pregnant?*' She began to shake. 'Are you sure?' It simply had not occurred to her that she might be. Mark had been so careful.

'Quite sure,' he confirmed. 'It's showing up strongly,

so you must be a good couple of months into the pregnancy. When was your last period?'

Jo struggled to think. She was never regular and could go for weeks without having one. Come to think of it, she had not had one since early in the summer holidays – when she started going out with Gordon. Her heart began to hammer in fright. She and Gordon had not always been so careful. A good couple of months meant that the baby could not be Mark's. She began to tremble at the implications.

Dr Samson cleared his throat again. 'Do you have a boyfriend?'

Jo flushed puce. 'Yes,' she gulped, deeply embarrassed to be discussing this with the family doctor who had dealt with all her childhood ailments.

'Good. Have you discussed with him the possibility of you being pregnant?' he asked matter-of-factly.

'No,' Jo said faintly.

'Well, I think you should,' the doctor said briskly. 'Contact me if there's anything more you'd like to ask. Otherwise we must make plans for your antenatal care. Come in and see me next week.'

'Yes,' Jo said meekly and put down the telephone. Her head was spinning from the news. Next week! She should be packing for college and saying goodbye to her friends. Next week was the start of a new, exciting future . . . Jo felt a wave of nausea flood through her and rushed for the bathroom, retching into the rose-pink toilet bowl. This could not be happening to her! she thought in distress. A pregnancy was the last thing she needed: it would ruin everything. But the thought of whose baby she was carrying made her feel even worse. It must be Gordon's. She had thought she was rid of him, but now this had happened to spite her again. How could she possibly tell Mark?

Jo slumped to the floor, burying her face in her hands, and sobbed uncontrollably. Try as she might, she could not stop crying. When she heard her father coming back in ten minutes later, she made a huge effort to pull herself together, dousing her swollen face in cold water and wiping at her smudged mascara. She knew she must get out of the flat and go to Marilyn's, for she was sure her friend suspected and had been trying to talk to her about it a few days before. But her father took one look at her and stopped her.

'What in the world's the matter?' he asked anxiously. Jo's attempt at a smile disintegrated. 'Was it something you heard from the doctor's?' He was gripping her by the arm and steering her into a chair before she could protest. 'Tell me, Joanne. Are you ill? They wouldn't tell me. What did he say?'

'No, Dad, I'm not ill,' Jo reassured him, alarmed by his reaction.

'What then?' he demanded.

Jo hung her head, feeling tears of shame and anger at her situation welling up again. 'I can't tell you,' she whispered.

Suddenly he was putting his arms about her shaking shoulders and hugging her to him, stroking her hair like he used to do if she'd skinned her knees or had a nightmare as a child. 'Don't be daft, you can tell me,' he encouraged gently. 'Whatever it is, we'll face it together, like we always have.'

'Not this,' Jo wept into his shoulder. 'You'll hate me for this.'

'Never,' Jack insisted. 'No matter how bad it is, I'd never turn me back on you, pet.'

She looked at him, still fearing his reaction. 'I've

ruined me life,' she said unhappily. 'I'm pregnant.'

He looked at her blankly for a moment and then she saw his jaw tighten. 'Oh, lass!' he cried.

'I'm sorry, Dad,' she said, feeling the burden of having let him down.

'Does Mark know?' he asked in a strained voice. Jo shook her head. 'Well, he sharp will!' Jack declared. 'He'll face up to his responsibilities.'

Jo felt panic flood her. 'It's not his fault,' she blurted out. Her father gave her a sharp look. 'I mean, it was an accident,' she stammered. 'Don't be hard on him.'

Jack sighed. 'Well, don't think you're the first. There're plenty of marriages have begun by jumping the starting gun.'

Jo looked at him. 'Marriage?' she echoed uncomfortably. 'Dad, I'm not sure about that. It's all a bit of a shock. I don't know what I'm going to do yet. Dr Samson said to go and see him next week to discuss it.'

'Discuss what?' Jack said sharply. 'It seems perfectly straightforward from where I'm standing! You're not thinking of getting rid . . . ?' His look was appalled. He stood up, agitated, and ran a hand through his thinning hair. 'Listen to me,' he ordered. 'You've decided you're grown-up enough to go having a relationship with that lad, and this is the result. Maybe it's unplanned, but that's the risk you both took. I can't pretend I'm happy about it, but it's happened. You can't just think about your own future now – there's someone else involved: your future bairn, my grandbairn! By heck! You'll give it the best start in life you can.' He glared at her. 'And in my eyes that means marrying that Duggan lad sharpish!'

Jo flinched, an image of Gordon floating like a spectre before her eyes. But of course her father meant Mark. Poor Mark! she thought guiltily. The trouble was being heaped at his feet when none of it was his doing. Whatever her father said, she would not allow him to be bullied into marriage because of her mistake. She would have to find the courage to tell him the truth. For a fleeting moment she felt a malicious stab of revenge. What if she should force Gordon to marry her because of the baby? But as soon as she thought it, she discounted such an outcome. No doubt Gordon would deny all responsibility. Then, to her surprise, Jo realised for the first time that she did not want to be tied to Mark's older brother. It would be a disastrous, loveless marriage. She could imagine him turning out as callous as Matty, treating her with the contempt Norma received. Jo shuddered at such a vision.

'I'll talk to Mark about it,' she promised. 'Just let me do it in me own way, Dad.'

For twenty-four hours she avoided Mark, as she struggled with her own feelings. Marilyn was the only friend she confided in about her guilty secret, but even there Jo did not find the help she sought. To her dismay her old friend seemed to be annoyed that she was spoiling their start at college together.

'I'd guessed as much,' Marilyn told her. 'Honestly, Jo! I was really looking forward to us going away together, but now . . . !' Jo gave her a desperate look. 'Oh, I'm sorry, but it's so disappointing. I always told you that Gordon Duggan was trouble.'

'Don't mention him!' Jo winced. 'Please don't tell – you're the only one who knows about him.'

Marilyn gave her a wary look. 'Are you going to tell Mark?'

Jo felt sick with dread. 'Aye, I'll have to – it's only fair. I can't let him think the bairn's his.'

'Why not?' said Marilyn. 'It might be kinder. You know

how much bad feeling there is between him and his brother.'

'I know,' Jo said unhappily, wondering what on earth she should do.

Unable to stand her father's badgering to 'have it out with the lad', she went in search of Mark. She found him down at Ivy's, filling her coal hod from the bunker in the yard. The look of relief on his face at seeing her made her heart ache. She refused Ivy's offer of a cup of tea and asked Mark to walk with her. They made their way along the rough track beside the railway line and Jo broke the news of her pregnancy.

At first Mark just gawped at her in disbelief. He seemed stunned, and Jo waited for his astonishment to turn to suspicion. She felt leaden inside. But instead of questions or recriminations, he hugged her excitedly. 'By, that's a bit quick,' he laughed. 'But it changes things, doesn't it? Don't look so worried, Jo. I'll marry you, of course. You know I will. A bairn, eh!'

Jo paled. 'Mark, stop . . .'

'What's wrong? Is it the thought of not going to college?' he asked in concern. 'I know how much it meant to you, but maybes you could still do the course somewhere local. Once the baby comes Ivy would help you out – and your dad, and Pearl. Or maybe I could find a job back on land—'

'Stop it!' Jo cried. 'Listen to me!' She was shaking with distress. 'There's something I've got to tell you and I don't know how.' She looked at him helplessly.

He watched her warily now. 'Go on,' he said, stepping back.

Jo took a deep breath, knowing how much it was going to hurt him. 'Dr Samson says I'm at least two months pregnant.' She looked at him while the news sank in. Mark struggled to compose his features and she saw a flicker of anger in his dark eyes.

'So the bairn's not mine,' he said quietly. Jo felt her chin tremble and shook her head, unable to speak. His shoulders sagged as if weighted down with disappointment. 'That lad you went out with before me, then?' he asked. 'It's his?' Jo nodded. 'Does he know?' Mark frowned.

'No,' Jo rasped. 'And I'll not tell him. That's all over. He wouldn't want me or the baby. And I don't want him.'

'What *do* you want, Jo?' Mark demanded, his eyes blazing with some emotion she could not fathom.

'I don't know,' she whispered, her thoughts in turmoil. 'I need time to get used to what's happened.' She saw his bleak look and stretched out her hand to touch him. 'The last thing I want is to hurt you,' she said, 'but I know I've already done that.'

She saw the brightness in his eyes as he denied the pain she'd inflicted on him. 'I'll not be the one to judge you for making a mistake you regret — I've made enough in me time.' He gave her a rueful look. 'But do you want to keep the baby?'

Jo gulped. Like him she was already thinking of it as a baby and not just a pregnancy. In the short time she had known about its existence, its potential for life, she had already projected ahead, visualising a child in her arms. The idea scared her, and yet deep inside she experienced a small thrill. She would be someone's mother, able to lavish on them the love that she had been cheated of by her mother's premature death. Mark's direct question made her see that quite clearly.

'Aye, I do,' she admitted.

Mark's eyes shone as he forced himself to say, 'Maybes

I care for you more than you do for me, Jo. But if you want me, I'd still marry you. My feelings for you aren't changed just because the bairn isn't mine – though I wish it was,' he said fervently. 'I'd treat it like me own – care for you both, if you'd let me.'

Jo was overwhelmed by his compassion and forgiveness. What was the point in hurting him further by telling him who the real father was? she thought with relief. He had shown that her past was not important and had never pressed her to know the identity of her former lover. If she accepted Mark's offer to stand by her, no one else apart from Marilyn need ever know that he was not the father, she assured herself. Her mistake with Gordon could be turned into something positive. She would probably have married Mark in time anyway, she reasoned, and her career in teaching would just be delayed, not abandoned for ever.

She reached out quickly to embrace him, a sob catching in her throat. 'You're so good to me, Mark!' she cried gratefully. 'I don't deserve you.' Tears began to stream down her face. She felt his comforting arms go around her, holding her tight in his strong embrace.

'You'll marry me then?' he insisted.

'Aye, let's get wed,' she said impulsively, and was gladdened by his broad smile of pleasure. She lifted her lips to his and he kissed her hard and long, until her tears stopped and she felt filled with courage to face what lay ahead.

Chapter Eleven

It was hard waving Marilyn off at Central Station in Newcastle. Jo felt her emotions see-sawing all day between regret at not going with her friend and sudden excitement at the thought of why she was not going. There was life growing within her and she and Mark were planning their future together. Hasty decisions had been made all week. Jo had pulled out of her course and Mark had decided not to go back to sea. He had already applied for a job with a local removal firm and was having an interview at that very moment. Arrangements for a December wedding were underway, when Colin would be home, and Marilyn and Brenda had agreed to be bridesmaids.

'Have a good time for me too,' Jo said, hugging her friend and trying not to cry.

'I will,' Marilyn said, in tears at the thought of starting out alone.

'And you'll come back for the fitting next month?' Jo urged.

'Only if your studies allow,' interrupted Mary Leishman.

'I'll try,' Marilyn assured her friend. 'You take care of yourself.' Jo nodded; neither of them could speak any more. Marilyn climbed hastily on board the train where her father had stowed her cases and kissed him goodbye.

Her mother burst into tears as they waved at the departing train. Jo felt suddenly bereft.

'You should've been on there with our Marilyn,' Mary said reproachfully, mopping her face with a scented handkerchief. 'It'll be hard for her not knowing anyone.'

'I know.' Jo flushed. 'And it's hard for me not going.'

Mary humphed. 'Pity you didn't think about that before you went getting into trouble with that Duggan boy. I thought you would've had more sense – a lass with your brains.'

Jo felt angry and humiliated that Marilyn's mother was still telling her off at the age of nineteen. She was thankful Mark was not there to hear her unkind words.

'I'm not in trouble!' Jo protested. 'I'm happy to be having this baby, not ashamed. And Mark's happy too. It's what we want.'

'That's right,' Mr Leishman said, patting them both on the back. 'Our Marilyn will be fine. Now we've got shopping to do.' He smiled awkwardly at Jo and quickly steered his wife under the vast archway into the bustling city.

Jo wished their other friends had not been at work, for now she felt totally alone. She should have let the Leishmans see Marilyn off by themselves. It was obvious they resented her presence, but her friend had asked her to go. Jo wandered out into the blustery streets and walked aimlessly along to the high-level bridge. She looked out over the murky River Tyne and the snaking railway line heading south, then to the distant cranes of Wallsend, and was overwhelmed with doubt. What had she done? she panicked. Mary Leishman was right: she had thrown her future away and that was why she had reacted so angrily to the woman's slights. She put her head down on her arms and tried to stem the panic that rose within. This feeling would pass, she told herself firmly. There was no point regretting the past; she must fix her mind on the future and being a mother.

Mark must have guessed how she would be feeling, for he came round to the pub at afternoon closing time and took her out for tea. He was full of excitement at having got the job. 'I start Monday and I'm going to take me PSV so I can drive the vans an' all.' Jo was heartened by his enthusiasm, though the money would not be enough to buy them a house of their own. She would carry on at the pub as long as possible and save to buy things for the baby. 'We can rent a Tyneside flat to begin with,' Mark suggested, squeezing her hand. 'Being together is what matters.'

After that day, Jo's optimism returned, and gradually her sickness lessened. Her spirits rose further when Pearl came home. She had longed to see her aunt again and yet had feared her disapproval of the mess she had created. But Pearl was quick to reassure her.

'Doesn't matter what others say, as long as you and Mark are happy,' she said stoutly.

'I thought Dad would've been really mad at me for ruining me chance of going to college,' Jo confided. 'But it was the opposite. He wouldn't hear of me giving up the baby – said he'd disown me if I did. I've never seen him so upset.'

Pearl looked thoughtful. 'Well, it was probably just the shock . . .'

'Do you think I'm doing the right thing?' Jo asked quietly.

Pearl put her arm around her niece. 'Mark's a good lad – he's right for you. It's always struck me how close you were as bairns. It might not be the start you were looking for, but I know you'll both make the best of it.

You're young, but you'll make canny parents, I'm sure of that.'

Jo felt a wave of gratitude towards her aunt. 'Thanks for saying that,' she smiled.

Pearl kissed her head. 'But promise me one thing.'

'What?' Jo asked.

'Don't give up the idea of becoming a teacher for ever,' she answered. 'Lasses of your generation should expect more from life than just a home and family. Besides, I might be around more to help out when the baby comes.'

'Really?' Jo looked at her in surprise.

'Yes,' Pearl smiled. 'I'm thinking of retiring from stewarding. It's a young person's job, all the travelling. I've seen all the places I want to see, now I fancy a bit more time at home. Especially now you're going to make me a great-aunt – that makes me feel old!'

'Never!' Jo cried. 'You'll always be young in my eyes, Auntie Pearl. But I'd love you to come home for good. Does Dad know?'

'Not yet,' she admitted.

'Oh, he'll be dead pleased,' Jo assured her. 'He's been checking on your flat daily – like a pining dog.'

'That surprises me,' Pearl laughed. 'But then that's his job – he is the caretaker!'

'You know it's more than that,' Jo replied. She gave her aunt a searching look. 'Is there any chance of you two . . . ?' She saw Pearl colour. 'How about a double wedding?' she teased.

Pearl seemed quite flustered by the idea. 'Not with your dad! It's never been like that between us two,' she insisted. 'Jack doesn't feel about me in that way. No, we're just good friends for each other, that's all.'

Jo thought she detected regret in her aunt's voice.

'Pity,' she said. 'It would get him out of my hair.' Pearl laughed and swiftly changed the subject.

The next few weeks were spent viewing flats and making arrangements for the winter wedding. Jo was thankful to have Pearl at home, for they went together on shopping trips and Jo sought her advice on where to live. Mark's enthusiasm about the baby was infectious and she enjoyed his protective concern for her health. It was as if he had forgotten his disappointment that the baby was not his. A month after Marilyn had gone away, Jo had overcome her envy at her friend's new life and was enjoying the anticipation of a first baby on the way.

Then one day in early November, Pearl sprang a surprise on her. 'I went round to see Norma the other day,' she said. 'I really think it's time some bridges were mended before the wedding. You're going to be the Duggans' daughter-in-law whether they like it or not, and Norma's quite keen on the thought of her first grandchild.'

Jo felt a sinking feeling. She had been thankful when Mark had declared he did not want his family at the wedding, except for Ivy. 'They've disowned me up till now,' he had said bitterly, 'so why should we put ourselves out for them? Ivy says Matty wouldn't come even if he were asked – just because I'm marrying an Elliot. You don't want them there, do you?' Jo had hastily said no. 'Not after the way they've treated you,' she had insisted.

'What have you been up to?' Jo asked Pearl.

'Don't go all defensive,' Pearl warned. 'Norma's an old friend of mine and I just thought you two should get together – make the peace. She seemed keen on the idea – she's inviting us round one morning if you want.'

'Why should I?' Jo said indignantly. 'She turned her

back on Mark years ago – what sort of mother would do that to her own son?'

'A frightened one,' Pearl answered. 'I know what she did was wrong, but she really believed Mark would be safer with Ivy than with her. It broke her heart to do it.'

'I don't believe that!' Jo cried. 'She rejected him just like Mark's dad and brother have done. She didn't have to stay with that bully.'

Pearl gave her a pleading look. 'I know it looks that way, and I don't understand myself why Norma hangs on with Matty. Goodness knows, I've tried to make her see sense. But he has a hold over her – emotional and financial. I think the thought of leaving him frightens her more than staying. But that doesn't mean she should be denied the chance to see Mark wed and to be a grandmother to your baby, does it?'

Jo felt suddenly churlish to deny her aunt's request. Norma was to be pitied, living on in that loveless house with men who despised her. She was weak rather than malicious for not standing up for her younger son.

'What about Mark's dad?' she countered. 'He won't approve.'

'No, he doesn't,' Pearl admitted. 'But this would be for Norma. She's sticking her neck out for Mark for once. Please, Joanne!'

'Only if Mark agrees. I won't do anything to hurt him,' Jo insisted. 'If he doesn't want me to see his mam, then I won't.'

But to her surprise, Mark did not dismiss the idea. 'Maybe Pearl has a point. Nana's always trying to get me to make it up with Mam. But I've never seen why I should make the effort when she doesn't,' he defended himself.

Jo was quick to support him. 'I don't blame you in

the least. I'll not go if you think it's a bad idea.' But as she searched his troubled face, she felt instinctively that he wanted to find some way back to the mother who had abandoned him.

'Well, going round for a cup of coffee isn't doing any harm, I suppose,' he said tentatively.

Jo was filled with dread at the thought of going to the Duggans', but this was something she could do for Mark and she buried her own reluctance.

She chose a time to go with Pearl when she knew Matty and Gordon would be out at work, for she had no intention of seeing them. Making amends with Norma was one thing; forgiving Matty for his abuse of Mark or Gordon for his treatment of her was quite another. The house was a neat semi in a long row of similar houses with small front gardens and lots of lacy net curtains to screen the interiors from prying eyes.

Norma welcomed them in with a nervous smile and apologies about the weather, as if the rain were her fault. Jo let the older women chatter on while she sipped at a weak tea, nauseous at the smell of coffee in the spotless sitting room. She gazed around at the plush velvet suite, the reproduction furniture and the myriad ornaments and wondered if Norma thought it had all been worth it – this ordered, comfortable house, instead of poverty and precarious living with her youngest son.

'Joanne?' Pearl was demanding her attention. 'Norma was asking after Mark.'

Jo saw Mark's mother shredding a paper serviette in her lap as she waited.

'He's well.' Jo forced herself to smile. 'Loving his new job. He's down to Durham today with a house move. And he's really pleased about the baby coming.'

Norma gave a trembling smile and to Jo's alarm

looked on the verge of tears. 'So am I,' she confessed. 'I hope you'll let me help out when the time comes – in any way. I'd like to make up for . . .' She faltered.

A moment later she was in floods of tears. Pearl went to her and put a comforting arm about her shoulders. 'I'm sorry, Joanne,' Norma sobbed. 'I know I've been a t-terrible mam. P-please let me try and be a good grandma.'

Pearl looked across appealingly. Jo put down her cup and reached over to touch Norma's arm. 'It's not me you should be saying this to,' she told her gently, 'it's Mark.'

'I know,' she wept, clutching at Jo's hand. 'I want to . . .'

Just then there was the sound of a key in the lock and the front door opened and banged shut. They all jumped. Jo looked at the door in horror as it swung open bringing a blast of cold air. Gordon stood staring at them, nonplussed.

'Oh, it's only you.' Norma breathed a sigh of relief. But Jo's heart was hammering painfully. She felt her throat drying in fear. His long hair was tousled in the wind, his face as leanly handsome as ever. His brown eyes narrowed in suspicion, then a small smile lifted his sensual lips as he recognised her. She sensed the danger in that smile and her heart turned cold.

'I didn't expect you back for your dinner,' Norma said, trying to compose herself.

'Obviously,' Gordon commented. 'I forgot me bait.'

'You remember Pearl and Joanne, don't you?' his mother said, fidgeting nervously.

'Oh, aye,' he smiled, 'I remember.' He gave Jo a mocking look and she glanced away, her cheeks burning. 'I hear you're to be congratulated,' he persisted. Jo nodded, forcing a smile. 'Childhood sweethearts, eh? And a baby on the way, Mam says.'

'Gordon!' Norma protested weakly.

'Sorry, am I not supposed to know?' he asked.

Pearl was looking between them, rather puzzled. 'Half of Wallsend seems to,' her aunt intercepted. 'But Jo and Mark are very happy about it – we all are, now we've had time to get used to the idea. So you'll be Uncle Gordon, how does that suit you?'

Gordon shrugged. 'I can't see me having much to do with Mark's bairn,' he answered. Then he gave Jo one of his appraising looks. 'So when's it due?'

She felt faint and her pulse raced uncomfortably as she forced herself to answer as casually as possible. 'In the spring,' she said, deliberately vague.

'Early May, isn't it, pet?' Pearl queried. Jo nodded, knowing it for a lie.

Gordon gave her a sardonic smile before heading for the kitchen. 'Good luck,' he called over his shoulder, in a tone that said he couldn't care less. Shortly afterwards he banged out of the door again and was gone, leaving Jo shaking from the encounter.

Pearl noticed. 'You don't look well, pet.'

'I'm still not over the queasy bit.' Jo pulled a face. 'I'll have a lie-down before going into work.'

Pearl and Norma fussed over her and Jo was thankful to leave the Duggans' house and the atmosphere of tense claustrophobia that she sensed. 'I don't know how she stands it there,' she said afterwards to Pearl, gulping in the cold autumnal air.

'No, I could see you were upset,' Pearl said with a scrutinising look. 'Is there anything you want to talk about?' Jo shook her head. 'Maybe I shouldn't have taken you,' Pearl worried.

'No,' Jo assured her, 'it's not your fault. It's just the pregnancy making me feel funny, that's all.'

She was glad her aunt did not question her further, but she could not throw off her feeling of disquiet about Gordon. She felt odd for the rest of the day and rang in sick to work. Mark came rushing round to see her, but she could not begin to tell him what preyed on her mind. She slept badly, images of Gordon's threatening smile haunting her in the dark hours. In the morning things seemed better and her fears receded. Why should Gordon want to cause trouble between her and Mark? she reasoned. If he boasted of their affair, he would be wrecking his relationship with Barbara too. Besides, he did not know the baby was his and not Mark's, and from his attitude she knew he would not care.

Still, at times anxiety would seize her and spoil her anticipation of the future. It would leave her feeling sick and wretched, making her distant and preoccupied.

Mark was baffled by her moods, but put it down to being pregnant. He seemed as relieved as she was when Marilyn returned from college one weekend in November to go for the dress fitting. She, Jo and Brenda had a happy day out in Newcastle, trying on the dresses, going for lunch and looking round the shops. The wedding was only a month away and Jo's excitement grew daily. She and Mark had taken a six-month lease on a flat on Hedley Street, just off the high street. They had already started to collect pieces of equipment for the baby: a pram that had been advertised in the corner shop and a high chair from a second-hand baby shop. Jo had decided all the clothes must be new and she could not resist dragging her friends into Mothercare to browse. But Marilyn was bubbling over with her experiences at college and Jo felt a stab of envy at the freedom and challenges she was describing.

'Never mind the course and the communal kitchens,' Brenda said, tiring of the monologue. 'What about the lads?'

'Canny,' Marilyn smirked. 'I've been out with three already.'

'Three? Eeh, I bet you haven't told that to your mam!' Brenda exclaimed.

'No, and neither will you,' Marilyn laughed.

Eventually they headed home, Jo feeling exhausted but glad of the day out.

At the pub that evening, Marilyn was given a royal welcome by Ted and there was a party atmosphere, until Gordon walked in. Jo got a shock, because his band were not booked to play and she knew he usually kept away from the Coach and Eight when Mark was back on leave. But now, of course, Mark was never away, so they were bound to bump into each other sometime. Jo wished anxiously that it had not been in front of her.

'Look what the cat dragged in,' Mark muttered. The two brothers scowled at each other with hardly a word exchanged.

'Haven't seen you in here for weeks, Gordon lad,' Ted grunted at him. 'Pint, is it?'

'Aye,' Gordon nodded, ignoring the others.

Ted served Gordon quickly, but he hung around at the bar, making Jo feel increasingly nervous. She realised after several minutes that he was quite drunk.

As no one else was speaking to him, Ted said, 'So where's the beautiful Barbara tonight?'

Gordon grunted. 'Not with me.' He took a long gulp of his pint. 'Finished with her. Wanted to get married, silly tart,' he slurred. Jo's heart thumped in dread, suddenly realising the danger of the situation. She tried to move off to the other end of the bar, but Gordon called her back.

'So when am I getting my invite to the wedding of the year?' he sneered.

'You're not,' Mark said shortly and turned his back. This inflamed his brother, who pulled at Mark's shoulder.

'Don't turn your back on me, you toe-rag! Mam thinks she's going,' he slurred. 'Ever since little copperhead here went tappy-lappying round to see her. Cosy little scene I interrupted. Can't wait to be a grandma. Isn't that right, Jo-Jo?'

Jo's heart was pounding; she felt hot and cold at the same time.

'Don't speak to her like that!' Mark rounded on him.

'Mark, it doesn't matter . . .' Jo began. She exchanged a look of alarm with Marilyn, but her friend could only watch helplessly as the argument escalated in seconds.

'Like what?' Gordon said, thrusting his face at Mark's. Mark pushed him away, but Gordon persisted, eager to rile him. 'Like I know her too well?' He turned and focused drunken eyes on Jo, reminding her of Matty. 'But I do, don't I? We're old friends, aren't we, Jo-Jo?'

Mark looked furious. 'Stay away from her,' he threatened, grabbing Gordon by his leather jacket.

'Steady, lads,' Ted tried to calm them.

But Gordon laughed savagely. 'Stay away?' he derided. 'I couldn't keep her off me half the summer!'

Jo felt her head reel. Sickness and faintness gripped her. 'Leave us alone!' she gasped.

'Right little raver, weren't you, Jo-Jo?' he taunted. Mark's face changed from anger to horror as Gordon's words sank in. He looked at Jo in disbelief. Everyone around had fallen silent. 'All summer,' Gordon repeated, sloshing his drink at them, 'couldn't get enough of me . . .'

'Tell me it isn't true?' Mark rasped. 'Jo! Say it wasn't *him*!'

She would have given anything to be able to reassure him, to stop him looking at her with that angry hurt in his eyes. But all she could do was stare back in total humiliation as Gordon shouted. 'Aye, it was me! I had her first. She's probably carrying my bastard, not yours!'

A howl tore out of Mark, and in an instant he had head-butted his brother. Gordon crashed to the floor. Skippy intervened to pull Mark away as people backed off in panic, but Mark shrugged him off and turned to glare accusingly at Jo. 'Why didn't you tell me it was him?' he demanded furiously. 'You should've told me it was him!'

'Get him out,' Ted ordered, grim-faced. 'I'll deal with Gordon.' As the landlord went round to haul Gordon to his feet, Skippy pushed Mark to the door. Jo gripped the counter to stop herself collapsing to her knees.

Everyone was staring at her as if it was all her doing. Marilyn came to her rescue.

'Jo?' she said in concern. 'Are you all right?' Jo shook her head. 'I'll get you out of here. Brenda, you take over until I come back.' Marilyn rushed round to support her friend and steered her into a back room. Jo crumpled on to an upturned crate and began to shake violently.

'I hate him!' she said, grinding her teeth. 'He's ruined everything. I should have told Mark the whole story . . . !' She looked agonised. 'Why didn't I have the courage to tell him?' she wailed.

'Gordon was drunk. Mark might just think he was winding him up,' Marilyn said, but neither girl believed it. Grabbing Jo's knitted jacket, she chivvied her along. 'Come on, I'll get you home.'

They went for a bus, but none came, so they just kept walking until they arrived exhausted at the block of flats.

'I can't face me dad,' Jo pleaded, her face swollen from crying.

'Pearl's then,' Marilyn said, and bundled Jo into the lift. To their relief, Pearl was in on her own, watching TV, and saw at once her niece's distress. Jo was almost hysterical as she tried to explain, but Pearl hushed and calmed her. She put her to bed in the tiny second bedroom, the one that, years ago, she had promised to Mark had he come to live there with his mother. Jo lay on the bed, unable to undress, feeling drained and ill. Pearl covered her with an eiderdown, and she was aware of Marilyn telling Pearl what had happened, then she must have fallen asleep. When she woke, disorientated in the dark, there was no sound of voices beyond the open door.

Jo turned over and gasped in pain. She felt as if her insides were gripped by a vice. She wanted to scream, but no sound came. Crawling out from under the cover, she fumbled towards the door. The door to the sitting room was ajar and she glimpsed Pearl curled up asleep on the sofa. She staggered into the bathroom and switched on the light. Her image in the mirror was ghostly, gaunt and pale, her eyes ringed like a panda's from mascara and tears.

Images of the terrible scene in the pub rose up and tortured her: Mark's aghast, accusing face, Gordon's leering one. Jo covered her face in fear as pain stabbed like needles between her legs again. She crouched down on the floor, doubled up in agony. Pearl must have removed her skirt, because she saw at once what was happening. Her pants were soaked in blood.

For a long moment, Jo stared in confusion. Then terror filled her very being.

'Please God, no!' she cried out. 'Please don't let me lose the baby!' Then she started to scream like a wild animal. 'Pearl! Oh, no, please . . . Auntie Pearl, *help me*!'

Chapter Twelve

By the time the ambulance came to fetch her, Jo knew the worst was happening. Pearl had tried to calm her and make her lie still on the bed, but blood was seeping everywhere. The more her stomach cramps eased, the more her womb seemed to spill out its contents on to Pearl's pink nylon sheets. Jo squeezed her eyes tight shut and willed it all to stop, terrified of moving or looking at the mess.

Of all the worries that had plagued her since discovering herself pregnant, losing the baby had never entered her head. Now fear gripped her at the thought. She realised just how much she wanted it – wanted it with a passion even if it was Gordon's baby. She had day-dreamed of pushing a pram round the park – the pram she had already bought – and of being a mother. How she yearned to be a mother! she realised. Her life had been turned upside down: she had given up college and a teaching career for the baby, while Mark had given up his life at sea . . . Oh, Mark! Jo thought in an agony of guilt, remembering the furious hurt on his face that evening. What would become of them now?

Hot tears squeezed from beneath her clenched eyelids as she thought of her fiancé. She wished that he was with her now, holding her in his comforting arms. But after the scene in the pub, he might never want to hold her again.

She could hear Pearl speaking in a low, urgent voice to the ambulancemen. 'She's miscarrying. Do what you can for her, please.'

Within minutes they had bundled her in blankets and lifted her from the bed on to a collapsible metal chair. Jo was too embarrassed to look them in the face as they wheeled her to the lift. She looked pleadingly at Pearl, frightened of going alone.

'Please come with me,' she whispered.

'Of course. But what about your father?' Pearl asked, hesitating.

Jo shook her head in panic. 'I can't face him yet.' Pearl nodded and took Jo's hand.

But Jack had been roused by the noise of lifts and seen the ambulance waiting outside the flats. When the grim party emerged from the opening doors, he went pale with shock. 'What the—Joanne!' he cried. She burst into tears and Pearl quickly explained, while Jo was manoeuvred into the ambulance.

Pulling on his overcoat over his pyjamas, Jack jumped into the back with her. She braced herself for fretful questions, but his look was full of compassion. He sat stroking his daughter's hair and repeating. 'Don't worry, your dad's here,' and Jo clung to him, grateful for his presence, yet full of dread at him finding out her guilty secret.

'Mark,' she tried to explain, 'we had a row . . .' She convulsed in tears again.

'Hush!' he soothed. 'You don't have to tell me now.'

At the casualty department, Jo was wheeled into a side room and helped on to a bed. A nurse came and changed her into a hospital gown and a doctor checked her over. She wanted to ask what was happening to her, but did not dare, for fear of what they might say. She lay alone, comforted only by the thought that her father and Pearl were sitting somewhere nearby, waiting. She was given something to ease her cramps and it made her drowsy, for she dozed off to sleep.

She woke to a strange sensation and cried out for the nurse.

'That's it,' the woman said, removing the mess from between her legs and depositing it into a metal bowl. 'Sorry, pet, but it's over now.'

Jo lay shaking uncontrollably, too stunned to cry. Shortly afterwards she was taken on to a ward full of women eating breakfast. The smell made her want to vomit. The doctor was explaining something about having to go into theatre to clear out her womb. She felt numb and bewildered and wondered where her father was. Maybe Pearl had told him about the fight at the pub and the baby being Gordon's and he was too disgusted with her to stay and wait around the hospital. Then, just before she was taken to theatre, Jack and Pearl appeared.

'I'm sorry, pet,' he said, stretching out his arms to her. She hugged him tight as she had not done for an age, unable to speak for the tears flooding her throat. All that mattered at that moment was her father's arms around her and his kind, sympathetic face.

Pearl kissed her cheek. 'We'll be here when you wake up after the op,' she promised.

Jo remembered being taken into the theatre and a friendly anaesthetist asking her to count to ten. The next thing she knew, she was back on the ward, staring at a sunbeam on the ceiling and feeling strangely detached and content. She watched herself smiling at her father and heard her own slow voice telling him that she felt fine. She vaguely recalled chatting about what was on the menu for tea, and then Jack and Pearl were gone.

Sleep claimed her and she woke to find it dark and the lights out. Someone was moaning in the corner. Jo dozed off again. Later she was disturbed by someone being moved hurriedly in the ghostly light of the ward, and she could not get back to sleep. By then the numbing anaesthetic had worn off and the full brunt of the miscarriage hit her.

Her dreams of married life with Mark and their first baby lay in shreds. In a few painful hours, their future had been torn from them. What use now was the flat they had chosen, with its second bedroom for the baby? Even if the nightmare of losing it had not happened, Mark might have washed his hands of them anyway. He had been prepared to raise another man's child as his own for her sake, but not his hated older brother's child.

Gordon had humiliated Mark in front of all their friends. He could have borne it from another man, Jo thought, but not Gordon. He was the brother who had rejected Mark when he most needed him, the betrayer who had sided with his father in turfing him out of the family home. The resentment was long-running and deep. In Mark's eyes, Gordon had had everything in life that he ever wanted, especially the attention of his parents. Useless to tell him now that Gordon had felt the same envy at his brother's closeness to Ivy, or that Gordon believed he and not Mark had been the main victim of his parents' warring.

And now, Jo winced, Mark knew that Gordon had slept with her and fathered her baby. Gordon had snatched his future dreams too. Jo wept into her pillow, in the full rawness of her loss, knowing that Mark would blame her for not telling him herself. She was a worse betrayer than Gordon, she accused herself brutally.

So it came as a shock when Mark appeared at her bedside at visiting time that evening, with a small bunch of flowers. They stared at each other, not knowing what to say, too aware of the other people around them. Others on the ward had looked at her askance for being unmarried, and she had overheard one of them muttering that losing such a baby was for the best. Jo was painfully aware that they were glancing with hostility at Mark, believing him to be the cause of her shame. It left her unable to say what she really felt, that she had missed him and wanted him so badly through the terrible ordeal.

Instead she joked lamely, 'Did these come from Bewick's garden?'

'Nowt grows there in November,' Mark answe wryly. 'I had to pay for these.'

She took them. 'Ta.'

'How you feeling?' he asked.

Jo felt like saying 'Awful,' but wanted to spare him her private torture. 'All right,' she managed.

He began to gnaw on a finger and Jo knew he was trying to bring himself to say something. 'Look,' he began.

'No, I know what you're thinking,' Jo broke in. 'It must be difficult for you to come here.' She dropped her voice. 'I'm sorry I never told you about . . . you know. I should have done. But it doesn't really matter any more, does it?'

He gave her a long, questioning look. Jo was aware of the people at the next bed falling quiet, listening. She should have said she had not wanted to hurt him with

171

the truth, that she had really wanted to marry him anyhow. But the words would not come and she felt inhibited in this large ward with its eavesdropping patients.

Mark seemed about to say something when Jo noticed Pearl and her father crossing the room towards them. 'Here's me dad,' she gulped. Mark stood up, looking awkward. They exchanged embarrassed greetings, the men not knowing what to say to each other. Pearl gave Mark a kiss. 'Sorry for you, pet, an' all.'

Jo watched them helplessly, consumed with guilt that she was putting them all through this purgatory. She could see Mark glancing to the door, desperate to escape.

'You don't have to stay,' she told him quietly.

He shot her a bitter little look and nodded. 'Aye, well, I'll call round when you're home – if you want.' Jo nodded back, aware that she had handled their meeting ~dly. Miserably, she watched him go.

Mark hurried from the ward, making aimlessly for the stairs. He felt wretched at leaving Jo. She had looked so pale and withdrawn, as if she were already putting the past behind her, cutting him out. He had been so angry with her after Gordon's taunts. She had strung him along and made a fool of him. Why had she not told him it was Gordon's baby? he had railed.

But as he had calmed down later that night, he began to question what he would have done if he had known. Would he have offered to marry her at all? He doubted it. He would probably have left her to fend for herself. He had lain all night plagued with thoughts of how Jo had been his brother's lover. He knew from Marilyn that Jo had been in love with this other man and hurt by his rejection, and it was agony to discover it had been Gordon. He had merely been second best. Was that always to be his lot in life, to be runner-up to his older brother? Mark had raged.

Then news had come about Jo's miscarriage and he had been shocked to the core. Pearl had come round to see him, but he had been out all day, wandering around a cold and windswept Whitley Bay. By the time Ivy had given him the news, it had been too late to go to hospital to see Jo. Part of him had wanted to rush straight to her, to comfort her in her loss – in *their* loss.

Yet a small, mean thought niggled deep inside. It was not his loss, it was Gordon's baby. If it would have caused his brother any pain, he would almost have derived a vindictive pleasure from the miscarriage. Jo too was being punished for hiding the truth from him and for using him. Then Mark had been overwhelmed with remorse at such thoughts. He began to wonder if his own violent reaction to Gordon's revelation had brought about the miscarriage. He hardly slept all night, torturing himself that he was somehow responsible for Jo losing the baby.

Now, as he clattered down the hospital stairs, unaware of those around him, he thought about Jo's reaction to his visit. He had come to say to her that he would still marry her if that was what she wanted. He had wanted to say sorry if the upset had caused her to miscarry, but she had not let him say it. She had kept him at arm's length, almost eager to see him gone as soon as her family arrived. And she had talked as if it was already over between them.

He saw now that it probably was. Jo had only ever agreed to marry him for the baby's sake and because Jack had been adamant that she should. When he had mentioned getting engaged before, had she not put him off? he questioned. She did not seem as distressed at losing the baby as he had feared either. Maybe for her it was a relief, a way out of a reluctant marriage. Gordon had been the one she had really wanted, not him, he told himself harshly. Now she could get on with the life she had planned without him – her college course and a teaching career.

He went out into the twilight, gulping down treacherous tears in his throat. Why did he feel so wretched about the loss of someone else's bairn? he thought in bewilderment. And why did his heart ache so much for the woman upstairs who had hurt him so badly two nights ago that he had sworn to himself never to see her again?

'Mark!' A voice called to him out of the dark and Brenda almost bumped into him. 'I thought you hadn't seen me.' She was clutching a box of chocolates.

'Been in to see . . . ?' she began, then laughed at herself. 'Well, of course you have – stupid question!' She put out a hand and touched his arm. 'Is she all right?'

Mark shrugged. 'Seems canny. Jack and Pearl are in.'

They exchanged awkward smiles and he suddenly felt his exclusion. Nobody knew what to say to him any more, and he wondered if Brenda had known about Jo's affair with Gordon all along. Maybe he was the only one to have been kept in the dark about it, while half of Wallsend chewed over the gossip. He felt a surge of renewed anger towards Jo for the humiliation and misery that he felt. Even old friends did not seem comfortable with him any more. She had robbed him of that too.

Turning from Brenda with a grunt for a goodbye, Mark pulled up his jacket collar and marched into the dark. He walked into the first pub he came across and drank himself into a numbing stupor.

★ ★ ★

It was nearly two weeks before Jo saw Mark again. When she came out of hospital, she went to recuperate at Pearl's flat, where she could gaze out of the ninth-floor windows over the grey docklands and the bare trees of the park. She found her father's fussing attention touching but wearing. Worst of all, he would not stop fretting about the wedding arrangements.

'Where is that lad?' he demanded. 'Is he going to wed you or not?'

'I can't blame him if he doesn't, can I?' Jo had cried in distraction.

Her father had blustered: 'From what Ivy says, he's spending his whole time drinking. He'll lose his job if he's not careful. I've sometimes wondered if he's up to the responsibility of marriage. Always had a bit of a screw loose, if you ask me. Like all those Duggans.'

So Jo had taken refuge at Pearl's, where her aunt had protected her from Jack's questions. 'He doesn't always think before he speaks,' Pearl defended her brother-in-law. 'But he's hurting too over you losing the bairn. He wants the best for you – to protect you. He hates to see you so unhappy.'

In the peace of Pearl's bright flat, Jo came to a decision. While her aunt was out at the supermarket, she went looking for Mark. Wrapped against the biting cold of an east wind that funnelled up the river, she made her way down Nile Street and knocked on Ivy's door. It was the first time she had seen Mark's grandmother since the miscarriage, and the plump old woman hesitated a moment before giving her a warm hug and pulling her inside. Ivy's kindness made Jo feel renewed guilt at the pain she had caused everyone.

'I'm not stopping,' Jo said, keeping on her purple coat and crocheted hat. 'I just wondered if Mark . . .'

'He's down to Hartlepool today, not back till teatime,' Ivy explained. 'Just stop for a cuppa.'

Jo plonked herself down by the cheery fire and found herself telling Ivy everything. 'In a way it's a relief that the truth came out,' she admitted sadly when she'd finished. 'I don't think I could have gone through with the marriage keeping the secret that the bairn was Gordon's. It would have destroyed me, bottling up a secret like that for years, don't you think?' Ivy was pensive and did not reply. Jo went on, 'And there would always have been the chance of Gordon wrecking things much later, when it was all too late. He would have always had a hold over me. At least now he can't do that.'

Ivy seemed upset by her words, so Jo stopped. The older woman went to stoke the fire, then asked, 'You've made up your mind to call the wedding off, haven't you?'

Jo answered quietly, 'Aye, I have. I've spoilt things between us. At least I can release Mark from having to marry me now there's no point. He can go back to sea, do something that makes him happy.'

'And you, hinny?' Ivy asked with eyes glinting with emotion.

Jo shook her head. 'I don't know yet. I find it hard enough deciding what to wear in the morning, let alone thinking of the future.'

Ivy trembled. 'Eeh, it breaks me heart, hinny!'

Jo left before either of them broke down crying. Since coming home, she found tears came all too easily. She hurried through the town, wishing to avoid seeing anyone she knew. Ted had been understanding about giving her time off, but she had written a letter telling him she would not be coming back to the pub. Like the winter drawing in around her, she wanted to hibernate and hide herself away from the world.

Mark came that evening to Pearl's flat, and her aunt left them alone and went down to Jack's. He looked haggard, his eyes dark-ringed and haunted.

'Nana's already told me you're calling off the wedding,' he said in a stony voice.

'Aye,' she gabbled. 'I meant to tell you first, but Ivy got me chatting. I'm sure Ted'll give us back the deposit on the room. And I'll pay for anything owing on the flat – Pearl said she'd lend me—'

'To hell with the bloody deposits!' Mark exploded. 'I don't give a toss about the money!'

Jo stared at him in alarm. 'I'm sorry. I know how you must feel.'

He glared at her. 'No you don't! You haven't a bloody clue how I feel.'

She grew agitated. 'Well, it hasn't been easy for me either! I'm the one who lost the baby, not you—' She broke off, covering her face in distress. She yearned for him to make a move towards her, some sign that he understood what she had been through. There wasn't an hour when she didn't think about the baby, wonder if it was a boy or a girl she had lost. At times she drove herself mad with thinking what should have been. But he did not go to her. Looking up, she saw the empty expression in his eyes.

'I thought you'd be glad to be let off the wedding,' Jo said in a brittle voice. 'I was the one caused this whole mess, so I'm trying to clear it up. At least this way you can go back to sea – start again.'

'You mean you can go back to college like you always wanted,' he said harshly.

'Maybe I will,' Jo replied shortly.

He paced to the door, throwing her a stormy look. 'Well, there's no point me stopping any longer if you've made your mind up.'

Jo sprang up, angry that he should make her feel guilty at her decision. She thought he would have been relieved, yet he seemed more angry with her than ever. 'Tell me this before you go, Mark,' she demanded. 'If I'd told you about me and Gordon at the beginning, would you still have wanted to marry me and take care of his bairn?'

He was stung by her question for it was the one that had plagued his fitful sleep for the past fortnight. He could not answer her.

She gave him a bitter look. 'No, I didn't think you would have.' Her eyes shone with angry tears. 'Maybe it was for the best then, as Brenda keeps saying. Better to find out now than after we were wed.'

'Maybes,' Mark echoed, his face stormy. 'At least now I know what you really feel about me. Gordon was the one you wanted, wasn't he? But good old Mark, he'd have done as second best – a consolation prize. Except now you don't need me any more.'

'That's not true!' Jo cried.

'Isn't it?'

Jo sobbed, 'I wanted that baby . . . !'

Mark stared at her in misery, unable to offer the comforting words he knew he should. He had wanted the baby too. But all he could think of was that he was being rejected again, only this time by the one person he had loved and trusted all his life. He could not stem the desire to hurt her back, hating himself even as he did so.

'Aye, but you didn't want me, did you, Joanne?' he said coldly. 'You're not the lass I thought you were – so I don't want you any longer either.'

His look was full of contempt as he turned and slammed the door behind him. Jo gave a gasp of pain and crumpled on to a chair, letting out a howl of distress. What had she expected? she asked herself harshly. She was the one who had called it off, hurting him again instead of making things better. She had vaguely imagined that he would be grateful to her for breaking off the engagement, that now he would have the freedom to go where he wished and not resent her for tying him down. Deep down she had hoped that time would heal the hurt between them and that they might be able to make a fresh start, without the pressure of a rushed wedding and a new baby.

How stupid she had been! Jo thought in misery. The seeds of destruction of their love had been sown even before they had started courting – Gordon had unwittingly seen to that.

When Pearl came back, she found Jo sitting staring out of the window at the lights along the river. One of the cranes had a line of coloured Christmas lights strung along it. Her aunt took one look at her face and said, 'Bad, is it?'

'Aye,' Jo said bleakly. 'We've split up.'

Pearl came over and gave her a hug. 'I'm sorry, pet. I wish things could have worked out differently. But at least this way you're both free to do what you want.'

Jo was numb, amazed at her own calmness after so many bitter tears. 'Well, I'm sure of one thing,' she said. 'I was right to call it off. He doesn't love me any more, you see. In fact I think he hates me for what's happened.'

'No!' Pearl protested.

'It's true. But one day he'll thank me for it,' Jo whispered, and went back to gazing out of the window.

* * *

The following week, Jo's spirits rose at the thought of Colin returning from Northern Ireland and of Marilyn coming home from college. It was an emotional reunion with both of them, but her joy at seeing Colin was marred by his criticism of her. He blamed her for the state that he found his old friend in. Mark had lost his job and was spending his time on drinking binges around the town.

'I was looking forward to the weddin',' Colin accused her. 'Why did you call it off after the way he stuck by you? And you and Gordon . . . ! I can't believe the carry-on!'

'Leave her alone,' Jack ordered. 'She's been through enough.'

'Aye, well so's Mark from what I can see.' Colin was indignant. 'You've really screwed the lad up, Joanne.'

When he had gone, Jack tried to excuse his rudeness. 'Pearl says Brenda's finished with him since he got back. He's just a bit sensitive at the moment.'

'Oh no,' Jo said sadly, 'he never said. No one told me . . .' She realised how isolated she had become.

Jo found herself excluded from the nights out with her old friends, who were rallying round Mark. Not that she had any appetite for going out. She tried to talk it over with Marilyn, who came round frequently to see Colin. Although Marilyn was more sympathetic, Jo felt there was a distance between them that she could not bridge. Her friend was so full of her time at college, so obviously happy, that Jo did not like to spoil her holiday. As Christmas neared, she noticed how inseparable Colin and Marilyn had become, while Jo herself withdrew more and more into a twilight world of silent mourning.

The date of the wedding came and went, with no one mentioning it. Pearl took Jo shopping into Newcastle, but the packed, brightly lit shops only served to heighten the forlorn emptiness she felt inside. She just wanted to get the festive season over with as quickly and quietly as possible. Then, one afternoon, Martha from the theatre group called round to see her in a hurry.

'We need someone to stand in for the prompter,' she told her. 'Dan's gone down with flu. Will you do it?'

'Course she will,' Pearl replied before Jo could turn down the request. Jo had lost the confidence to go anywhere on her own, but her aunt chivvied her along. 'I'll take over if you get tired,' Pearl bargained, going with her.

Later, after the performance, when Jo had managed to prompt without ending in a gibbering heap in the wings, she wondered if Pearl and Martha had plotted the whole thing. She relaxed in their company in the makeshift bar, realising just how much she had missed the theatre these past months since the upheaval of the summer.

For the rest of the holiday period, Jo came to the theatre and helped out behind the scenes, working long hours to take her mind off grieving for her baby. She found it hard that no one spoke of it, as if she had never had a life growing within her. It was the loneliest feeling in the world and at times she felt as if her depression would overwhelm her while all those about her seemed to be enjoying themselves.

But it helped to be at the theatre with friends who knew little about the trauma with Mark, save that her engagement had been called off. Losing herself in the make-believe of drama was the best therapy she could find for her wounded heart. At times she found herself dwelling on Mark and wondering how he was coping. She wished she had the courage to go round and see him, try to make up for the harsh words they had thrown at each other. She hated to think that he should be left believing she had not really cared for him. There were moments when she yearned to see him again, and wished herself back to the time when they had been together. Perhaps after Christmas she would go round and see him, put the record straight.

Jo made an effort on Christmas Day, doing the major share of the cooking and trying to get close to Colin. But she sensed his disapproval and knew that he felt let down by her too. On Boxing Day, he disappeared round to Marilyn's house without her. Jack and Pearl went to Ivy's while Jo escaped to the theatre to help with the matinée.

When she got home that evening, Colin was spread out on the settee with Marilyn snuggled under his arm. They were watching TV with a nearly empty bottle of wine at their feet.

'Do you want a drink?' Marilyn asked, moving over to make room for her.

'Ta, I will,' Jo said, flopping down on the floor, as Colin did not move his feet.

'Has Pearl told you?' Colin asked, his face flushed with alcohol.

'I haven't seen her all day,' Jo answered. 'Told me what?'

' 'Bout Mark,' Colin said.

'No,' Jo said, her heart twisting at the mention of his name.

'I must have told him too many stories about the forces,' he grunted.

'Why? What's he done?' Jo asked.

'He and Skippy marched into a recruiting office on Christmas Eve,' Colin laughed. 'Drunk as skunks, no doubt.'

Jo looked at them in astonishment. Marilyn explained. 'They've signed up for the Navy.'

'They're having a leaving drink on Friday night at the Coach and Eight,' Colin told her.

Jo gave him a questioning look. 'Am I . . . ? Could I . . . ?'

Her brother's look silenced her. 'You're kiddin'!'

Marilyn gave her a pitying look. 'Thing is, Jo – he's been seeing Brenda again since you two split and it might be awkward if you came along – for you as well.'

'Oh, I see,' Jo gulped, her heart freezing over. She got up quickly. 'Think I'll spend the night at Pearl's,' she said hoarsely and escaped from their cosy togetherness. Standing on the open walkway of the ninth floor a few minutes later, Jo took deep breaths to calm herself as she stared out over a frozen Wallsend.

Well, at least that was the end of it, she thought numbly. Mark was leaving, just like she had encouraged him to do. Now that it was happening, she felt engulfed with sadness at the thought. Yet a small part of her cried out with relief. This awful limbo might come to an end and they could move on and get over it, she thought. While they both remained in Wallsend, likely to bump into each other, it was impossible, and Jo knew she was still too fragile to be the one who made the break.

But Mark had taken the decision for them both. With that small glimmer of hope in her heart that she would one day get over all this, Jo blew a trembling kiss into the dark – a kiss for Mark, wherever he was, and the baby who was never to be. Then she bent her head on the frozen parapet and wept.

Chapter Thirteen

New Year's Eve, 1981

It was the first time Jo had been out in Wallsend celebrating New Year in three years. Usually she was touring with her community drama group in draughty village halls, performing pantomimes, or stuck in a strange town unable to get a bus home in time. She had not gone to college, but had found escape in drama and among her acting friends. Two years ago, she had found herself stranded with company director, Alan Wilson, in a Yorkshire mill town. Alan had suggested a curry and later they had gatecrashed a party of some Trotskyite mime artists and stayed for three days.

She found Alan attractive, though he was nearly forty and his beard was turning grizzled. But he was charming and articulate, knowledgeable about his art and passionate about politics. He had lived in Paris and been on the barricades in 1968 before becoming a pacifist. He was well travelled, drank too much red wine and swore in six languages. For a year Jo had resisted his persistent attempts to get her into bed, for she had shunned any involvement since the traumatic break-up with Mark over five years ago. Two things changed that.

In November 1980, almost four years to the day after Jo miscarried, Brenda and Mark got married. According to Marilyn, their relationship had been more off than on, but Brenda was tiring of the single life and rushed Mark to the registry office one leave. Marilyn and Skippy had been witnesses and Colin had been furious to miss both the stag night and the wedding celebration. Jo was more upset by the news than she cared to admit.

Then John Lennon had been assassinated, and Jo felt as if one of the family had died. She would have rung Colin, because they had always shared their Beatles passion, but he was in Belize. She struggled through a tiring day of performing in school to five-year-olds, then Alan came round with two bottles of claret and insisted on comforting her.

Now they were lovers and Alan had settled in Newcastle, where he worked at one of the big theatres. He had a bohemian flat in Sandyford, full of Marxist paperbacks and windowsills covered in expensive wine bottles holding dripping candles. Jo continued with her drama-in-education group, which struggled to survive with ever-decreasing funds. To eke out a living, she had gone back this past year to work in Ted's pub.

'It would be cheaper to move in with me,' Alan kept tempting her. 'I wouldn't charge for the use of my bed,' he teased, 'and I'd promise to cook you curry at least once a week.'

But so far, Jo had refused. She suspected Alan had had many such arrangements in chaotic flats from Newcastle to Paris, and was not convinced of his ability to stick with her. Besides, she enjoyed being courted by this sophisticated, sensual older man who was so different from Mark or Gordon. Alan gently ridiculed her for still living with her father in his 'petit bourgeois' flat with the china poodles on either side of the electric fire.

'You're about as liberated as a battery hen,' he laughed.

He did not begin to understand that for a long time after the miscarriage she had needed to stay close to both Jack and Pearl. They were the only ones who accepted her without criticism for what she had done, who gave her comfort when black bouts of grieving took hold of her many months after losing the baby. Pearl had retired from sea and often Jo would spend as much time in her flat as Jack's. While her old friends and Colin had distanced themselves for a while and sided with Mark, her father and aunt had told her to hold her head high and not be afraid to face the world.

'You've done nothing wrong,' Pearl would insist, when Jo was plagued with guilty feelings.

'You're the one who's been wronged,' Jack would defend her. 'And you've lost your bairn – nobody deserves that.' Jo was taken aback at how emotional her father was on the subject, and was deeply touched by his concern. She grew closer than ever to both Jack and Pearl, wondering what she would have done without them.

As Jo emerged from her depression, grateful for their support, she began to wish that her father and Pearl would finally marry. She knew each cared deeply for the other, and yet there was always a reserve to their relationship, a holding-back. They went ballroom-dancing together and enjoyed the occasional outing to the dog track. Pearl even dragged Jack along to the theatre now and again. But they maintained their separate lives and flats. Pearl helped out at the Seamen's Mission and went to keep-fit classes, while Jack did his caretaking and kept around the home. He always had a bed made up for Colin's return and he seemed reluctant to let Jo go.

'I'm twenty-four now, Dad,' Jo had joked recently. 'Most fathers would be glad to see the back of a pest like me.'

'There's no point moving out for the sake of it,' he declared. 'You're happy here, aren't you? I thought we got along canny.'

Jo kissed his gaunt cheek. 'Course we do. I just thought – well, maybe, you might want a bit more room.'

'What for?' Jack asked.

Jo gave a conspiratorial smile. 'Isn't it about time you and Pearl . . . ?'

Jack had flushed. 'There's nowt like that between your aunt and me. No, this is your home, Joanne, and I want you and Colin to always see it that way. Unless either of you get wed, of course. I don't know why he hasn't done anything about Marilyn,' he blustered on. 'She's a grand lass – smart too, teaching those strapping eighteen-year-olds. She'll not hang on for ever.'

'Knowing Marilyn, she probably will,' Jo smiled wryly. 'She's been sweet on our Colin since primary school.' Jo thought she would be as happy as her father if her brother and old friend did marry, for Marilyn had helped Jo's reconciliation with Colin after she qualified as a teacher and returned to live in the area. As long as they didn't talk about the Duggans, she and Colin did not argue about much. Jo realised it was the best she could hope for with her stubborn older brother. But Colin appeared married to the army and loved his itinerant life and the camaraderie. He had been all over the world.

'And are you sweet on this lad of yours – the actor?' her father asked anxiously. Jo laughed to think of Alan

188

being called a lad. He was as near her father's age as hers.

'He's a director, Dad,' Jo smiled. 'And yes, I'm in love with him.'

'Is he going to marry you?' Jack asked bluntly.

Jo shrugged. 'I doubt it. He's been married before. Doesn't believe in it any more. Thinks it's "bourgeois and repressive"!' she parodied.

Jack snorted. 'What does the bugger mean by that?'

'It means he likes to keep his options open, I suppose,' Jo said drily.

Her father gave her a direct look. 'Well, I hope you've got a healthier view on marriage.'

Jo laughed shortly. 'I think marriage is grand – for people your age, or Pearl's,' she teased.

Jack turned from her with a grunt of impatience. 'I just don't want to see you getting hurt again, that's all.'

But this New Year's Eve, Jo was more optimistic than she had been for a long time. She had worked the previous night at the pub and now she was having a night off with Alan, wanting to show him the sights of Wallsend. He seldom ventured this far out of the city, despite his rhetoric about the rights of shipyard workers and the 'diabolical' Mrs Thatcher, who was busy making anyone who moved unemployed. Tonight Jo was going to enjoy having him hugging her possessively in the crush of revellers in the pubs along the high street.

Since coming back to work at the Coach and Eight, Jo felt she had been accepted again by her old friends. This past year she had even felt comfortable with Brenda when she came in the pub. Brenda had refused to stay on the naval base while Mark was away at sea and continued to live with her mother, who had moved into a newer flat across the coast road. Now Brenda would include Jo in the gossip like old times with no awkwardness between them. Jo had even found it possible to chat normally to Mark and Skippy when they had returned on leave that summer. Now that Mark was married and she was in a relationship with someone else, both of them seemed to have regained confidence and an echo of their old, teasing friendship had returned.

Jo took Alan into the Coach and Eight and he was soon propped up at the bar discussing football and politics with Ted. She marvelled at the easy way Alan had with people, always finding something in common. He would draw them out like flowers in sunshine, making them feel special. He knew that Ted liked a good argument and he was doing his best to stir him up about Newcastle United.

'Don't listen to him, Ted,' Jo laughed. 'He doesn't even watch footie. He's a rugby supporter.'

'Ah, now there's a game that isn't ruled by money,' Alan declared.

'Hello, Jo-Jo.' A familiar voice made Jo's smile freeze on her lips.

She turned to see Gordon in the throng behind her. She had not set eyes on him for over two years, for he had moved down to the coast to work at the Tyne Dock and seldom came home. Ivy had told her that he had fallen out with his father for taking a management course and becoming a foreman instead of remaining a docker like Matty. But Ivy had been pleased. 'Well, he's got a wife and a bairn to look after now, hasn't he?'

Jo's stomach twisted to remember how quickly Gordon had married after his damaging revelations about their affair. He had made it up with Barbara and married her in the summer of '77. One year later, they'd had a dark-eyed girl named Michelle. Jo had told herself she didn't care, but she felt pangs of envy to see Barbara pushing the baby around the town and down to Ivy's. She could not help wondering whether her baby might have looked a bit like Michelle, and so had been thankful when they had moved away. Jo was sure it was Barbara who had chivvied Gordon into getting qualifications and leaving Wallsend and his father's malign influence. 'Doesn't get on with Norma,' Brenda had said, 'or Matty – but then who does? Me and Mark don't bother with his parents either.'

Now Jo turned and faced Gordon. His hair, cut shorter, was receding slightly at the temples, and he had grown a moustache, which suited him. He gave her that familiar appraising look that used to make her stomach somersault. Instinctively, she leaned towards Alan.

'Hello, Gordon,' she said coolly. 'Where's Barbara?'

'Not feeling well – and she doesn't like drinking round here anyway,' he answered. 'How about you? You're looking canny.'

'Fine. This is Alan, by the way,' she said hastily, slipping her arm through his. The men exchanged looks, then Alan put out a friendly hand. She knew that he had guessed who this was, for he knew all about her bitter affair and traumatic miscarriage.

Gordon shook hands warily. 'You two work together?' he asked.

Alan gave a sardonic smile. 'Yes, we work together very well.' To Jo's dismay he added, 'Can I buy you a drink?' Gordon accepted and soon Alan was chatting to him about the state of the yards.

'Everything's changing on the river,' Gordon told him. 'Cargoes coming in on the big roll-on-roll-offs – can't get up the Tyne to the old docks any more. That's why Newcastle's got to close. But try telling that to me dad.

191

The dock labour scheme will have to go – along with stubborn buggers like me dad who think everyone owes them a living.'

'And why shouldn't he?' Alan demanded. 'Don't the dockers deserve a bit of security after decades of casualisation? Would you have them go back to jostling like cattle at the gates for work twice a day, at the mercy of the bosses?'

Gordon gave him a disparaging look. 'And what would you know about the life of a docker?'

'I did a documentary on the Clydebank Work-in of '71,' Alan said proudly. 'I wasn't born yesterday.'

Gordon grunted. 'Aye, I can see that.'

Jo was annoyed at his look of derision. 'Come on, Alan, it's time to move on. Gordon wouldn't understand about empathy for those in a worse situation than himself.' She gave him a hostile look, but Gordon just laughed and Alan seemed intent on escalating the discussion.

'We'll not go until I've educated this fool in some of his own class struggle!' he insisted. They ordered another round, argued some more and then Alan wended his way to the toilet.

'Not used to drinking pints, is he?' Gordon mocked. He saw Jo's furious look and put out a hand. 'Sorry, I'm just jealous,' he grinned.

'You've got a cheek,' Jo hissed. 'After what you did . . . !'

'I've often felt bad about the way it all came out,' Gordon said, his expression contrite. 'I'd been going through a bad patch with Barbara – story of me life! And I suppose I was annoyed you'd never told me we had a bairn together.'

'We didn't,' Jo said angrily. 'You'd already dumped me by the time I found out.'

'Aye, but I've often thought that was my big mistake.' He covered her hand again. 'By heck, we were good together, weren't we? Don't you remember?'

She pulled away quickly. 'Get lost.'

He laughed. 'I've missed you, Jo-Jo. What you doing with an old man like him?'

'He's not old,' Jo said hotly, 'and he's—'

'Yeah, yeah! He's worth ten of me, I know,' Gordon interrupted. 'Well, I think he's a patronising bastard with a bladder problem. Why stick with him when you could have me?' he added softly.

'You're married, remember,' Jo said sharply.

'As good as separated,' Gordon countered. His flippant look vanished. 'Things are bad at home – me job's uncertain and we're always rowing these days. It was never like that with us, was it, Jo-Jo? I wish I could start again with you.'

Jo's pulse was thudding. How dare he make such an outrageous suggestion? This was the man who had ruined her life, and now he was propositioning her as if none of it had ever been. But worst of all was the treacherous quickening of her heart at the idea. She could still recall what a hold he had once had over her.

'You've got a daughter,' Jo said pointedly, feeling a surge of envy at the reminder. 'It would be impossible to start again.'

Thankfully Alan returned to put an end to the dangerous conversation. They left quickly, but the evening had been marred by the encounter. Alan, who was not usually bothered by criticism other than for his drama, seemed put out, and sulked as she dragged him around Wallsend. It suddenly struck her that he was jealous. He didn't like being confronted by another man from her past.

'Gordon means nothing to me,' Jo insisted as they munched a Chinese takeaway on the way back to the flats.

'Well, the feeling's obviously not mutual – he couldn't keep his eyes off you,' Alan complained.

'Oh, rubbish!' Jo protested, uncomfortable with the thought. But Alan went on.

'And you were the same with the other one in the summer – making jokes about things that happened years ago that I couldn't feel part of. Have you any idea how maddening that is for me?'

'Mark?' Jo looked at him in astonishment. She'd had no idea he had felt excluded. 'But you have loads of friends from your past. I've never once complained at having to socialise with them. In fact I enjoy meeting them – it helps me know you better.'

He gave her a satisfied look. 'That's the difference, Jo. I don't think your old friends are particularly interesting. You rise head and shoulders above them. I can see how drama has helped you blossom, while your so-called friends have remained ordinary. I mean, that Marilyn – as goody-goody as Mary Poppins. And Brenda's like a Venus flytrap when it comes to men!'

'Stop it!' Jo said, hurt. 'You hardly know them.'

'I've seen as much as I want to. Like many of the proletariat, their souls are corrupted by petit bourgeois ambitions and desires,' Alan said. Jo wondered if he was drunker than she'd imagined. She would excuse him because of that; he was normally so charming to her friends.

'You sometimes talk a load of crap, Alan,' she answered, tossing her carton into a bin and walking up the path.

'Well, prove that you feel nothing for either of those

Duggan boys,' he shouted after her. She turned round to shush him. 'I won't be silenced!' he cried, dropping to his knees dramatically. 'Declare yourself, or I'll fall on my sword this instant!'

Jo started to giggle. 'Get up and come here. Melodrama doesn't suit you.'

But Alan rolled around in the frost, groaning and gasping, until Jo went back to haul him up. He seized her hand and pulled her down on to the frozen concrete, kissing her urgently. 'Prove it,' he challenged. 'Move in with me. We're meant for each other. I could do so much to help you in your acting career.'

Jo smiled, flattered by his persistence. Maybe it was time she made more of a commitment. Gordon's predatory face came to mind. She did not like to think of him hanging around the pub, tempting her with another affair, bringing the past alive to haunt her again. And she resented his insinuations that Alan was too old for her. Moving in with Alan would be a clear signal to Gordon that she was not interested, that she was over him forever. Suddenly it seemed the best way to put the past firmly behind her. She and Alan had much in common and she could learn so much more from him. It excited her to think that with Alan's help and contacts she could go far in the theatre.

'Okay.' She kissed him. 'I will.'

'Wonderful!' he cried in triumph. 'Let's go and break the news to your doting father.'

Chapter Fourteen

1982

That spring, Jo found contentment. Dismissing her father's concerns at her drifting into a live-in relationship with Alan, she was enjoying being at the Sandyford flat, where people were always dropping in for a late drink after performances or for cups of Alan's thick black espresso coffee. They would discuss politics and art late into the night and often she would get up in the morning to find friends sleeping on the sofas or floor. Things were never as tidy or as ordered as at her father's, but the homely chaos reminded her vaguely of Jericho Street.

Most exciting of all, Alan had secured her a part as a First World War nurse in a new play to be premiered in Newcastle, based on the life and writings of the poet Siegfried Sassoon. 'In *Counter-Attack*, I become a peace campaigner after nursing Sassoon and other war veterans,' she told Pearl. 'It has a very strong pacifist message – highlighting the futility of war. Alan helped work on the script. He's very excited about it too.'

Pearl sounded less enthusiastic on the telephone than Jo thought she should. 'It's lucky for you pacifists that there are those willing to fight to protect you,' she said drily.

'But if everyone took on the pacifist message, we wouldn't need people to kill each other – or spend the ridiculous amounts of money we do on arms,' Jo pointed out impatiently. 'That's why I joined CND – to fight for nuclear disarmament. We're in the middle of the world's worst arms race – a nuclear one that's going to blow us all off the planet if we don't stand up and say enough is enough.' Jo thought proudly of the rally they had been to in Hyde Park to listen to Michael Foot, where she had taken courage from the thousands of ordinary people like her who wanted to stop the madness.

Pearl, however, refused to argue with her further and Jo was frustrated by her aunt's apparent lack of interest. Her aunt ended with a wistful, 'Well, it would be grand to see you when you get a spare minute. Take care, pet.'

The early spring was taken up with rehearsals, and Jo thrilled at this chance to be noticed more widely. It was intoxicating to be living with a man who had so much experience in the theatre and to be the centre of attention wherever they socialised.

At Alan's suggestion, Jo gave up her job at the pub to concentrate on her real work, so her visits to Wallsend became infrequent. When she did go back to her father's flat, there was an awkwardness between them that had never existed before. Jo saw that he did not share her new interests in art and politics and felt herself growing away from him. Perhaps, she consoled herself, it was merely a period of adjustment they were going through, but it made her less enthusiastic about visiting and she tended to ring him up instead.

'I'm rehearsing all weekend,' she would say,

making excuses not to come down, knowing that Alan would find a reason not to go with her.

'Pearl's missing you,' Jack would say reproachfully. 'A visit from you would cheer her up.'

'Why does she need cheering up?' Jo asked, masking her impatience. 'I speak to her every week, she sounds fine.'

'She's been a bit off colour lately – you'd be just the tonic,' her father persisted.

'Pearl always hates the cold winters,' Jo said. 'But it's nearly spring, and you can both come and see the play when it opens – I've got tickets. Tell Pearl I'll give her a ring soon.'

To her relief, Pearl sounded her old self the next time they spoke, and Jo concluded it was just her father fussing as usual.

'Don't listen to Jack,' her aunt said breezily. 'There's nothing wrong with me. I know how busy you are. You just come when you can – and we'll see you at the play anyway. Got a bit of a surprise for you!'

Pearl would not tell her what it was, but Jo was reassured that all was well and dismissed her guilt at not seeing them more often. When the end of March came, bringing with it the opening week of the play, Jo was at fever pitch. There were favourable press reviews of the opening night, but what really mattered to her was what her father and aunt thought of her performance. Friday night came, and she knew they were sitting out in the audience. It gave that extra edge to her performance, and instinctively she felt she had done her best. Alan had arranged that they would meet in the bar afterwards, but when Jo emerged, her stage paint hurriedly removed, she gasped in shock.

'Colin!' she cried in delight. 'I didn't think you'd be

back in time!' She rushed to her brother and gave him a hug.

'Hello, bonny lass. Wouldn't have missed this for anything,' he grinned. 'You're quite good, aren't you?'

'She was fantastic,' Marilyn corrected, patting her friend on the back.

Jo beamed and turned to kiss her father and Pearl. It was then that she realised there were other familiar faces in the throng around the bar. Brenda's flushed face beamed at her. And there stood Mark and Skippy. Jo was overwhelmed by the support.

'You were great,' Brenda said, shoving a half-pint of lager into her hand. 'I didn't think I'd enjoy it – all about war and that – but I did.'

Alan said indulgently, 'Actually, it's not about war at all. It's anti-war. The battle sequences are just to highlight war's brutality – how ordinary people are exploited by greedy tyrants and benign rulers alike.'

Brenda gave him a dismissive look. 'Well, there were plenty of soldiers in uniform, as far as I could see.' Jo laughed with her.

Mark put a hand on his wife's shoulder and smiled shyly at Jo. 'Anyway, you were grand.'

'Aye,' Skippy agreed, leaning over and kissing her cheek, 'we all enjoyed it.'

'Thanks.' Jo smiled gratefully, basking in their approval. A couple of drinks later, she suggested impulsively, 'Why don't you all come back to the flat for a last drink? Cup of coffee?'

She saw from Alan's look that he was not enthusiastic, but he quickly smiled. 'Of course you must.' When her father seemed reluctant, Alan insisted. 'Come on, Jack, it's time you saw where I've locked up your daughter.' Pearl needed no persuasion, and the others seemed happy to extend the evening. Jo slipped her arm happily through Colin's and they hurried out into the dank night, hailing taxis to take them to Sandyford.

Back at the flat they lit the fire, put jazz on the record player and a pot of coffee on to boil. Jo got a thrill to see her family and friends settling into Alan's comfortable worn sofas, while he handed round tumblers of wine or whisky. She saw Colin and Mark exchange amused looks, but they took what they were offered. She did not like to admit how glad she was to see Mark again, to have him here in her new home, squatting near the fire with her brother. It reminded her of old times, long before fate had driven them apart. Noticing that Brenda was in loud conversation with Skippy and Marilyn on the couch, she plonked herself down by Colin on the floor.

'I didn't think you'd be home,' she said, smiling tentatively at Mark.

'Skippy and me are joining a new ship in April – HMS *Gateshead*. We're heading for the Med,' he said, his eyes lighting up as he spoke.

'That was built at Wallsend, wasn't it?' Jo asked.

'Aye.' Mark nodded. 'Launched at Wallsend, then fitted out at the Walker yard.'

'How long will you be away?' Jo asked, wondering what Brenda thought of the move.

'Till the summer probably,' Mark said. 'So I'll be back in time to see your summer performance, whatever it is.' He winked.

Jo's insides twisted at his warm look and felt a disloyal pang of longing. 'I'm glad you came to the play,' she said quietly and got up quickly to pour out the coffee.

Later, after they had all gone, Alan flopped on the sofa. 'Stop tidying up, for God's sake, and come and sit down.'

Jo joined him, overwhelmed by exhaustion. 'Thanks for having them all back,' she smiled, settling under his arm.

Alan snorted. 'You don't need my permission, girl. This is your home too, remember?'

'Of course,' Jo said hastily. 'I know that.'

'Don't see that you have anything in common with that brother of yours,' Alan mused. 'He's such an old reactionary.'

'We are quite different now, I suppose,' Jo said, thinking privately that they had never regained their old closeness since the fall-out over Mark. 'But he's still me brother and I like to see him when he's home.'

Jo did not see much of her family the following week because of the play, but arranged that they would go out for a meal together once it was finished. She was just getting ready to go to the theatre for Friday night's performance when she caught the end of a news bulletin on the radio. Alan preferred radio to the TV and Jo had got used to listening to Radio Four. She was still rubbing her hair dry when they announced that Argentina had invaded the Falkland Islands and that Parliament was to sit in emergency session on Saturday to consider a response.

'Emergency session?' Jo repeated in astonishment. 'Why should they do that?'

'Because the Falklands are a British territory, I suppose,' Alan answered distractedly. 'Come on, it's time we went.'

'Where *are* the Falkland Islands?' Jo said, puzzled.

'Somewhere near Argentina, presumably. Hurry up, girl,' Alan urged, grabbing his cigarettes and jacket and heading out of the flat. Jo followed him, feeling uneasy but not quite knowing why. Soon she was immersed in the performance and thought no more of it, but once home she flicked on the television for the late news. Scant details were given, except that a company of British Royal Marines had surrendered to an Argentine force that was now in control of the Falklands capital, Port Stanley.

'I'm glad Colin's not in the Marines,' Jo said, feeling strangely depressed.

'Come to bed,' Alan advised. 'You seemed tired in your performance tonight. Let's give it your best for the last night, eh?' He seemed so unconcerned about the news of invasion that Jo thought she must be over-reacting. She knew her nerves were stretched by the past two weeks of adrenalin and late nights and the best thing would be sleep. Curling up next to Alan's warm body was comforting, and she was soon in an exhausted sleep.

Jo slept right through to lunchtime and was only woken by the telephone. She heard Alan have a short conversation and then put the receiver back.

'Who was it?' Jo yawned.

'Jack,' he said shortly. 'I said you'd ring him tonight after the play.'

'What did he want?' Jo asked.

Alan shrugged and poured her coffee. 'Just getting a bit het up about this Falklands lark. Thinks it'll mean Colin's leave might be cancelled.'

'Has Colin heard anything?' Jo asked, suddenly anxious, going for the telephone.

'No,' Alan assured her, 'and I can't imagine he will. Even macho Thatcher won't think of going to war over a few rocks in the South Atlantic. Don't worry yourself.'

But Jo rang anyway. She felt reassured to hear Pearl's sunny voice. 'Alan's right to say not to worry. But we thought it might be nice to all meet up after your play and go out, just in case Colin's recalled.'

Jo agreed immediately, but Alan was cross when she told him. 'For goodness' sake, we've got the party afterwards – it's a big thank-you to everyone.'

'Big booze-up, you mean,' Jo answered shortly. 'I'm not stopping you going, but I want to see Colin tonight. Pearl's arranged to meet at the Rawalpindi because she knows you love curry.'

Alan went out in a huff to put a bet on the Grand National, but by the time he came home the news was growing more serious. It was being announced that a Task Force was being assembled to send to the South Atlantic. The aircraft carriers *Hermes* and *Invincible* were already being prepared. Diplomatic relations had been broken off and the UN Security Council had called for the Argentinians to withdraw.

That evening Jo could not concentrate and missed out a whole speech that ruined one of the scenes. 'Damn Thatcher and her Task Force,' Alan said afterwards, putting a consoling arm around her shoulders. 'Let's get this meal over with and then we can meet up with the others at the party and let our hair down a bit.'

When they reached the restaurant, Colin was at the head of a table of family and friends which took Jo by surprise. Mark and Brenda were celebrating having backed Grittar, the Grand National winner, and Jo could tell that they had all been drinking for a good while. There was almost a desperation in Skippy and Mark's determination to have a good time, but Colin's mood was quieter as he observed them all, Marilyn sitting close beside him. 'I'm glad you could come, I'm returning to the regiment tomorrow,' he told Jo. She gave him a quick kiss, not wanting to show her anxiety for him.

'It's bound to be settled soon,' she said with an encouraging smile. Jo and Alan sat down next to Pearl and Jack, opposite Mark and Brenda. The talk quickly turned to the invasion.

Alan started holding forth. 'It's old-fashioned gunboat diplomacy – the Tories are living out a fantasy of giving Johnny Foreigner a bloody nose. But it won't come to anything. They must reach a diplomatic solution, it's the only civilised way.'

'I hope you're right,' Mark said, 'but we're prepared to go and do our bit whatever.'

'God, you sound like a tabloid headline,' Alan mocked.

Brenda said in annoyance, 'It's all right for you to scoff, sitting there swigging your red wine while others do the dirty work. But Mark and Skippy have to join their ship next week and I don't know when I'll see me husband again!'

Jo felt her insides twist as she looked at Mark. 'What have you heard?'

'Ship's been diverted from duties in the Med,' Mark told her.

Skippy broke in excitedly, 'We're joining her at Plymouth as part of the Task Force.' She could see his eyes alight with the possibility of adventure, and it made her scared.

'What a waste of bloody money,' Alan continued. 'I bet they'll be working overtime in the yards to kit out Thatcher's merry escapade – when she couldn't lay them off quick enough before.'

'Well, you should be glad of that at least,' Mark answered, giving him a hostile look, 'seeing how you care about the working man so much.'

'War is always the capitalists' answer to economic depression,' Alan said, leaning aggressively across the table. 'But it's a criminal waste of resources – material and human. Thatcher's as bad as Galtieri – she's using this to gain popularity and deflect criticism away from making a mess of the economy.'

'Alan has a point there,' Jo intercepted. 'It all seems far too hasty sending off ships and jump jets and things before any sort of diplomacy. I mean, what are the Foreign Office lot paid for?'

'Well, it's nice to know whose side you're on,' Brenda said, offended. 'Once upon a time you would've stuck up for your mates.'

'I resent that,' Jo said in annoyance. 'I'm on the side of a peaceful settlement, that's all.'

'And what if the Argies won't budge?' Colin joined in.

'It's still not worth going to war over a handful of sheep farmers,' Alan insisted, 'and I bet they'd be just as happy resettled somewhere like the Highlands.'

'But they're Brits,' Colin argued, 'and the Argies don't have the right to tell them that they can't be British.'

'Stop calling them Argies,' Jo said irritably, hurt by the way they were rounding on her and Alan.

'Well, let's call them fascists then,' Mark said, giving her a hard look. 'That's a word you and Alan like to use. I can't believe you're defending a military Junta against your own people. Galtieri's a thug – people disappear in Argentina. That's what we'd be fighting against – dictatorship.'

'No you wouldn't!' Alan protested. 'You'd be fighting against young conscripts who are just as much pawns in the game as you are.'

Mark was furious. 'I'm no pawn in anyone's game!' he cried. 'I joined the Navy willingly and I'm not afraid to fight for me country. I know where me loyalties lie.'

'Well, I'm more concerned with promoting world peace,' Alan said angrily. 'Nationalism is an ugly, out-dated emotion that brings more harm than good – whether it's British or Argentine.'

Mark's eyes narrowed at them both. 'And you, Joanne? Do you believe that crap?'

She was stung by his attack, deeply angry that it should come from him. 'It's not crap!' she said hotly. 'I stand with Alan on this. Neither of us believe the Falklands are worth risking hundreds of lives over. I don't believe the islanders would want that either. I don't want Colin to go and fight for some disputed islands eight thousand miles away. The whole idea's crazy! They're just a leftover from our imperial past. For all I know, Argentina might have more claim to them than we do.'

Everyone had gone quiet before her last remark, but now the table erupted in argument. Even Jack and Pearl were remonstrating with her for saying such things. Alan was the only one coming out with rational arguments, as her family and friends threw angry accusations of disloyalty.

'I never thought you would be so unpatriotic!' her father complained.

'You just think you're better than us, now you're living with Mr High-and-Mighty!' Brenda declared.

Colin gave her a filthy look. 'Ta for spoiling me last night,' he said, pushing his plate away and calling for the bill. Jo forced back tears of anger.

'And thanks for spoiling me last performance! I forgot half the words for worrying over you and the thought of you going away!' she accused.

'Well, don't bother,' he said, standing up. 'I can look after myself.'

'That's what countless Argentine boys will be saying to their families tonight as well,' Alan said. 'Doesn't that make you realise how futile the whole thing is?'

'And what about the Falklanders?' Mark demanded. 'What will they be saying to each other tonight? I'm glad they can't hear you two going on about how they don't count for anything.'

'That's not what we're saying!' Jo replied, trembling with indignation. At that moment she hated him. She was glad she hadn't married him; their marriage would have been a disaster! Alan and she never rowed like this.

'What are you saying then, Joanne?' he glared. 'All I can hear is you being snide about us lads for being proud of our country – and proud of being Geordie.'

She glared back. 'And why are you so patriotic, Mark?' she goaded. 'Is it because really you're insecure about who you are and where you come from?' She saw him flinch away from her and regretted the words instantly.

'Jo!' Pearl gasped in shock.

Mark pushed back his chair. 'Maybe it is,' he said, his eyes blazing. 'Maybe I don't know who me real father is. But I know now who me real friends are. And I don't have to sit here and be insulted by the likes of you and that patronising bastard!'

'Oh, don't be so melodramatic,' Alan laughed impatiently. 'Sit down and we'll order another round of drinks.'

But everyone else was getting up and leaving, throwing money into a pile on the table. Jo felt terrible, but she was equally incensed at the way she had been attacked for her opinions. They were treating her worse than a stranger.

'I'm ashamed of you,' Colin told her stonily. 'My own sister saying such things! Don't bother coming to see me off.' He turned from her and marched to the door without looking back.

Brenda scowled at her as she took Mark's arm. 'How could you say that to him? You of all people!' Mark did not even look at her as they left, Skippy tagging along awkwardly behind, wondering how the celebrations had collapsed so quickly. He at least gave Jo a shrug and a mumbled goodbye.

Her father's sad, reproachful look was the worst of all. 'Best to let tempers cool a bit, eh?' he said uncomfortably.

Marilyn and Pearl were the only ones who said a proper goodnight. 'I'm sorry. . .' Jo said helplessly. She felt miserable, yet still angry.

Pearl just gave her a regretful look. 'So am I,' she said quietly, and Jo was left acutely aware that she had hurt and disappointed them all.

But Alan comforted her. 'Don't go feeling guilty for sticking to your beliefs,' he told her. 'I was proud of the way you stood up for yourself. It's always hardest trying to convince your own family – sometimes it just isn't worth the pain. A prophet reviled in his own country and all that.' He gave her an encouraging hug. 'Come on. What we need is to get roaring drunk at the end-of-play party and say to hell with them all!'

Chapter Fifteen

Jo remembered little of Sunday, except that she nursed a hangover and a feeling of anti-climax after the end of the play. At least that was what she put her depression down to. She was vaguely aware of the news seeping into her consciousness that Argentina had overcome the last British military unit on the Falklands and had taken another island called South Georgia. But Alan switched off the radio and dragged her out for a walk through Jesmond Dene and a 'hair of the dog' at the Millstone pub.

She tried to recall what exactly she had said to Mark and the others that had caused so much anger, but Alan would not help her and did not want to talk about it. 'Put it behind you, girl,' he encouraged. 'They had no right to attack your pacifist beliefs like they did. This is supposed to be a democracy. If they can't enjoy a healthy debate then that's their problem, not ours.'

But the week stretched ahead aimlessly. Jo had no more work lined up for a fortnight, when she would be going into schools again with a May Day project. While Alan was out at the theatre on Monday, she found herself turning on the television and watching the emotional scenes of the Navy Task Force setting sail from Portsmouth Harbour. Marines and paratroopers were boarding, and the huge hangar of the flagship HMS

Hermes was crammed with Harrier jets and helicopters.

Jo watched in awe the vast decks of the aircraft carriers *Hermes* and *Invincible* lined by sailors. The harbour was full of ships and the dockside a mass of people waving hands and union flags. Military bands were playing. The commentator was saying something about this being the greatest display of naval strength since Suez, and that more ships would link up from Gibraltar.

The captain of HMS *Invincible* was being interviewed. 'Nobody wants to get involved in military action, but we are training to do so if the nation requires it,' he said.

Jo was struck by how familiar those words sounded, and then she had a flash of memory. It was virtually what Mark had been trying to say. At the time, Jo had thought he was revelling in the anticipation of conflict and dismissed his opinions just as Alan had. But now she wondered if she had been right. Had Mark not agreed with Alan that a diplomatic solution would be best, but that he was prepared to go into battle if called on to do so? Was there not a world of difference in the two stances? Jo challenged herself.

She turned up the volume and began to scan the screen for signs of Mark. What had he said about joining his ship? Was it here, or had Skippy mentioned something about Plymouth? she tried to remember. The camera focused in on the face of a young woman looking wistfully up at the stick-like figures on board, trying to pick out her loved one. Husband? Brother? Lover? Jo wondered. The woman's eyes were bright with tears, yet her face was stoical, her expression full of love and anxiety and acceptance.

Jo found her own eyes pricking at the thought of what the woman was feeling at that moment, and the thousands of other family and friends gathered around on the quayside. Up until then, it was as if she had been watching some historical pageant, a drama that did not touch her. But now she felt a leaden weight in her stomach as she realised these ships really could be off to war.

She was seized by a sudden panic. Why had she argued with Mark so bitterly when he and Skippy were on the verge of leaving home for unknown dangers? And how could she have spoilt Colin's party so badly? she fretted. She and Alan had treated it like any other night out, willing to argue and philosophise as they normally did with his friends. But for Mark and Colin and Skippy it had been no idle debate; for them the prospect of war was a real one.

Jo was about to reach for the telephone when Alan came back in and saw the television pictures.

'For God's sake, Joanne!' he cried, crossing the room. 'Look at all that flag-waving jingoism! It makes me sick.' He turned the television off and looked at her, seeing the emotion on her face. 'Hey, don't upset yourself, girl,' he said, swiftly moving to hug her.

'It's all happening so quickly,' Jo whispered in fright. 'I bet it'll be Colin going off next. I don't want to think about what might . . .'

'Then don't think about it,' Alan urged. 'It won't come to war. This is just the sabre-rattling I talked about. It'll take them weeks to get down there, and by that time it'll all have been resolved.'

'I need to speak to Colin,' Jo said stubbornly.

Alan's look turned stern. 'You're not going to go grovelling for Saturday night, are you? Because he's the one who should be apologising if anyone does. He's the one who said he didn't want to see you, remember?'

Jo's courage failed her. She had no desire to get into

another slanging match with her brother. 'He's probably already gone,' she said lamely.

'Yes, he said he was going back to barracks yesterday, didn't he?' Alan agreed. 'Leave it a couple of days and let things cool off, then ring Marilyn. She seems like a sensible type.' Jo nodded, beginning to think she had overreacted because of the stirring pictures on television. She was working herself up over nothing. Alan brightened. 'Listen, I'm going to take you away for a couple of days' holiday.'

'Holiday?' Jo puzzled.

'Yes, you deserve it after all your hard work. I'm so proud of the way your acting is maturing, Jo.' He kissed her forehead. 'We'll head for the Highlands or somewhere romantic. Lots of fresh air and big meals. What do you say?'

Jo smiled at him, relieved at the thought of getting away and having a breathing space. Alan always seemed to know what she needed most. What would she do without his guidance and care? she wondered gratefully. 'Sounds perfect,' she answered, and kissed his warm lips.

They had four wonderful days at a country hotel that Alan knew of, that served gargantuan breakfasts and evening dinners, with the host piping them into the baronial dining room each night. Afterwards they would sink into vast chairs by a roaring wood fire, drinking whisky and yawning contentedly after their day's exploring around the lochside. Alan was not as fit as he liked to make out, and their walks were meandering rather than arduous, but they stayed out long enough to justify the large amounts of food and good wine that they consumed.

The only other fellow guests were a Dutch ornithologist and a touring American couple, who only wanted to talk history, so they were quite cocooned from what was happening in the world. But on the way home they caught a news bulletin on the car radio saying that the American Secretary of State, Alexander Haig, was mediating in the Falklands crisis and that the EEC was approving a ban on Argentinian imports in support of Britain.

'See,' said Alan in satisfaction, 'things are going to be settled amicably. Sanctions and diplomacy – that's the only real option.'

Jo felt optimistic at his words and refreshed by their time away. She rang her father that night, for the first time since the family row. To her relief, he sounded pleased to hear from her.

'I've been away – recovering from the play,' she told him.

'With Alan?' he asked.

'Of course,' Jo answered. When he said nothing, she asked, 'Any news from Colin?'

'Aye, he's been attached to Field Ambulance,' Jack said. 'They're away training somewhere in Wales.'

Jo's heart sank at his words. 'He's going to be sent out then?'

'Sounds like it,' he replied quietly.

'When?' Jo gulped.

'We don't know yet,' Jack sighed.

'You'll let me know when you hear something, won't you?' Jo asked, and Jack agreed. There was a silence between them and then she forced herself to ask, 'Did Mark and Skippy get away all right?'

'Aye, they went off on the train the day after . . .' His voice trailed off.

'Did Brenda go too?' Jo asked, feeling wretched at the memory of their last night out.

'No, Mark wouldn't let her. Said he hated goodbyes and there was no point going all the way to Plymouth just to turn right back again,' Jack explained. 'Course, I never understood why she wouldn't live on the naval base in the first place. At least she'd have had the comfort of the other wives around her now to keep her chirpy.'

'She's always been a home bird,' Jo mused. 'She and her mam are like best friends really.'.

'You could go and see her,' Jack suggested. 'Make up, eh?'

Jo felt a flood of remorse. 'Aye, maybe I will.' She felt her voice trembling. 'Dad, I'm sorry for falling out with you all over this stupid Falklands thing. I didn't mean to hurt Colin's feelings – or Mark's . . .'

'I didn't think you did,' Jack answered. 'It's not like you. Maybe you could write to the lads and tell them yourself?'

'Aye, maybe,' Jo mumbled, and rang off, thinking how annoyed Alan would be if he caught her writing grovelling letters to her brother and friend – especially Mark. It reminded her of how jealous Alan had appeared of her continuing friendship with Mark. It probably suited him that she had ended up rowing with Mark and insulting him, so that their friendship would wither, Jo thought. Maybe he had deliberately provoked the argument? Then she chided herself for such disloyal thoughts. Alan had merely been expressing his own strong moral opinions, and he had deserved her support.

Before the end of the week she went to see Brenda, but received a frosty reception from her friend's mother, who told her that Brenda was out but would not want to see her anyway. Discouraged by this, she called on Pearl, to find her aunt in bed.

'Oh, it's just a silly cold,' Pearl said. 'I can't seem to shake it off. Probably just the worry over Colin and the other lads.'

'But it won't come to anything,' Jo tried to reassure her. 'Alan thinks . . .'

'Alan!' Pearl snorted. 'Since when has he been an expert on military tactics?'

'He's very knowledgeable about international affairs and the situation in South America,' Jo bristled.

'Well, he ought to be more worried then,' Pearl retorted, then started to cough. Jo rushed to get her a glass of water. When the coughing had stopped, Pearl went on: 'Did you not see the pictures of all those celebrating crowds in Buenos Aires, cheering Galtieri? They've gone Falklands daft – or Las Malvinas, as they call them. I've been to Argentina. Even in the sixties they used to go on about those islands being theirs. The Junta may have organised the invasion to save their own skins, but that makes it the more dangerous. If they back down now, they know they'll be kicked out at home.'

Jo looked at her, feeling anxiety rise at the words. 'But the Americans won't let it continue,' she suggested. 'Mediation must work.'

Pearl gave her a direct look. 'Like Mark said, we're dealing with a dictatorship. They're used to getting their own way. We came back here after that terrible meal out and watched those Argentinian crowds on the telly. Mark said, "Look at that. It's like they've already won a war. They'll not give up those islands without a fight." That's what he said, and I think he's right.'

Jo felt sick. 'Did he say anything else? About the evening . . . ?' she asked with difficulty.

'Not a lot,' Pearl answered. 'He was that quiet after the restaurant. Brenda was calling you all the names under the sun, but that just seemed to annoy him more. He told her to lay off and then they argued. It was a bad evening all round. I think he was almost glad to get away, poor lad. Poor Brenda too!'

Jo felt a wave of remorse engulf her at the memory of her harsh words to Mark. How was it that she kept hurting him, when he was one of the people she cared for most deeply? She realised that now. She was not sure she had ever been truly in love with him, but she cared what happened to him. And it grieved her to think he had left with her callous words ringing in his ears. She knew how sensitive he was about his parentage under his I-don't-care attitude. How could she have been so cruel as to taunt him about it in front of the others? Jo promised herself that when Mark returned, she would apologise and make it up to him.

That night she wrote a brief note to Brenda saying sorry, and posted it the next day. When she heard nothing back, she fretted over the incident all the more. She rang Marilyn at her flat to ask to meet up, but her friend was working late each evening on a school play. 'It helps to keep busy, I find,' said Marilyn rather brusquely.

'Let me know when you're free,' Jo said, but doubting that she would get in touch. For the first time she felt really cut off from her old world. A few months ago it had been her choice to see less of them all, but only now did she see how far she had drifted. She did not like her exclusion.

Jo was thankful that she was going back to work on the following Monday, for it stopped her moping around the flat getting on Alan's nerves, or finding herself glued to the news bulletins when he was out. And the news was not optimistic. The Government had rejected Haig's peace deal and plans were going ahead to send further troops down to the South Atlantic. Jo threw herself into her work, banishing thoughts of conflict and hoping that good news would soon come. But that Saturday a British casualty was reported: a Sea King helicopter had crashed, killing one of those on board. The next day, Jack rang.

'Colin's heard – he'll be going out with 5th Infantry Brigade on the *QE2*. Says he's always wanted to go on a cruise!' he joked. But Jo's heart felt heavy.

'When, Dad?' she asked.

'As soon as they've got the ship ready, I imagine. Pearl and I said we'd keep Marilyn company and go down to see her sail,' he told her.

Jo felt again that stab of being left out, and her pulse hammered. 'Do you think Colin would want me to come too?' she asked, holding her breath.

'Maybe not.' Jack was frank. 'But he can't stop you if that's what you want to do. And if you-know-who will let you.'

Jo flushed. 'If you mean Alan, he doesn't stop me from doing what I want.'

'I'm glad to hear it,' Jack grunted.

'Honestly! I don't know why you're so against him. He's a very caring man,' Jo defended her lover. 'And he likes you and Pearl.'

Jo was glad when May Day came and she was involved all day with drama in school, the children showing off their maypole dance and marching with May Day banners. That night there were reports of the RAF bombing the airport at Port Stanley, and then next day came the shock news that the large Argentinian cruiser, the *Belgrano*, had been sunk outside the British-imposed exclusion zone. Hundreds of lives had been lost.

Jo and Alan watched in stunned disbelief. 'What the hell are they playing at?' Alan fumed. 'That can't be justified. Now we're the aggressor. It's as if we're asking for war!'

'All those lives . . . !' Jo gasped. 'Their poor families.' All she could think of was that it could have been Colin on a troop ship – or Mark and Skippy blown out of the water. She did not know where HMS *Gateshead* was, but she must have reached the South Atlantic by now.

'It's started now,' Alan said grimly. 'There'll be retaliation for this. God, the senseless waste of it all!'

Jo could tell by the anguish on his face that he sensed the helplessness that she did, the feeling that events were spiralling out of control. It did not matter what they thought, or how much they argued the morals and politics of it all. The conflict had started.

Jo went about with a feeling of dread in her stomach for the next two days. That evening, as she watched the news, a Ministry of Defence spokesman came on and announced in a grave voice that HMS *Sheffield* had been hit by an Exocet missile. Jo had no idea what kind of weapon that was, but lives had been lost. She was filled with a very real fear.

'What did I tell you?' Alan said.

'They won't say how many have been killed,' Jo said anxiously.

'It won't be as many as were slaughtered on the *Belgrano*,' Alan replied. 'Have you seen how the tabloids are revelling in it? Well, this is what their jingoism brings – more young men killed.'

Jo buried her face in her hands in horror. 'I know!' She was seized with anxiety about her brother. 'I want to see Colin before he goes,' she whispered. 'I can't bear the thought of him leaving without being able to say a proper goodbye.'

Alan gave her a worried look. 'I don't want you upsetting yourself over all this.'

Jo shook her head. 'I can't let him leave with bad feeling between us.' Not like she had done with Mark, she thought but did not dare say.

The next day Jo wrote to Colin and asked if she could travel to see him embark at Southampton. A week later she had a scrawled note from him. '*It would be canny to see you one more time. Just don't bring that tosser you live with, okay? Fancy me getting to sail on the* QE2 – *lots of good food and sunbathing on deck, I bet!*'

She hid the note from Alan, embarrassed by her brother's name-calling, but determined she would go down with the others to say her goodbyes. She needed to make up for their last acrimonious parting, for although she did not approve of the warmongering of the Government, she could no longer turn her back on what was happening. She was emotionally involved.

Hasty word came through from Colin late on 11 May. The requisitioned luxury liner would be sailing the next day. There would be no time for a last day of leave or a meal out together before sailing, as originally planned. Jack told her, 'Marilyn's prepared to drive through the night so we can at least wave him off.'

'I'll help with the driving,' Jo offered at once, and rang off to get ready.

'I think I should come with you,' Alan fretted. 'All that driving and you in a state about Colin.'

'No,' Jo replied quickly, 'I'll be fine. There wouldn't be room in the car anyway,' she added, seeing the hurt look on his face. 'But thanks for offering.' He dropped her off at the Tyne Bridge, under the arc of lights, where Jack had said they would pick her up. She kissed him goodbye hurriedly and jumped into the car. At first there was an awkwardness between her and Marilyn, but after an hour of chatting about school work, the coolness thawed and Jo felt at ease. Jo was cheered to see Pearl looking much better, and her aunt helped ease the tension with anecdotes about the Seamen's Mission. The younger women took it in turns to drive or doze in the passenger seat.

While Jack and Pearl fell asleep in the back, Marilyn said in a low voice, 'Well, one good thing's come out of all this.' She smiled ruefully. 'Colin's asked me to marry him at last!'

Jo was overjoyed. 'That's fantastic!' she exclaimed, squeezing her friend's shoulder. 'And about time too!'

'No one else knows yet,' Marilyn continued in a hushed voice. 'We were going to announce it on his next leave. But with him having to go straight to the ship . . .'

'Oh, Marilyn!' Jo felt for her. 'We'll have a celebration anyway – on the dockside if necessary! I'm really pleased for you. I can't think of anyone I'd rather have as a sister-in-law.'

Marilyn looked touched. 'Thanks, Jo, that means a lot.'

After that there was no reserve between them and the journey sped by. They arrived in Southampton in the early morning, shrouded in a drizzly dawn fog. Grabbing a cup of tea and an egg bun in a café on the outskirts, they made their way towards the docks, abandoning the car. The quayside was already teeming with activity. Soldiers were streaming out of a hangar, lugging equipment up the gangplanks, while other cargo was being lifted into the hold. They waited around all morning among the hundreds of other nervous people, jostling for a better view of those embarking. Some had made banners with their loved one's name on; others were shouting as they spotted someone they knew.

The fog began to lift and the sky to clear.

'Can you see him?' Marilyn asked anxiously, squinting short-sightedly at the ship.

'Put your glasses on!' Jo ordered. 'He'll still love you in specs.'

There were journalists pressing around the gangplank, eager for last-minute interviews.

'I can't see him!' Marilyn began to panic as the embarkation came to an end. Jo scanned the decks for any sign of her brother, but there were so many packed by the railings that she thought it impossible. A band was now playing and the gangplanks were being lifted. The noise on the dockside rose in a crescendo of shouts of good luck and unhappy sobbing. All were waving frantically.

Then Jo caught a glimpse of a familiar red head, peering for a view of the ground far below. 'There he is!' she cried. 'Look, up there!' She pointed. 'I'm sure it's Colin.'

'Where?' Marilyn wailed, fumbling with her glasses.

'Aye, you're right,' Jack agreed. He cupped his hands around his mouth and bellowed, 'Colin, down here, lad!'

'He hasn't seen us,' Pearl said, worried. 'Colin!'

They all began to scream his name and wave, but he continued to search the crowd with an anxious frown. Jo's heart squeezed at the familiar expression. So many times in their childhood, when her big brother was trying to look after her, she had seen that protective look, that worried concentration.

'Haway, Dad,' Jo said hastily, 'we'll give Marilyn a leg

up.' Without hesitation the two of them seized her friend and hauled her up between their shoulders.

'Help!' Marilyn said, half laughing, half crying.

'Hang on tight,' Jack ordered.

'Auntie Pearl, give her your shocking-pink scarf to wave,' Jo said. 'He's bound to see that.'

Pearl quickly untied the scarf from her head and Marilyn waved it high in the air, yelling with all the breath in her body. As the ropes began to slip and the huge liner edged away from the dock, the band struck up 'Auld Lang Syne'. At that very moment, Colin spotted them. His serious face broke into an astonished gasp and then a broad smile of delight.

'He's seen us!' Jo croaked, her eyes suddenly flooding with tears at the sight of her brother waving joyously at them. He was trying to shout something, but in the din all around them they could not make out a word. 'Hey, I want to be bridesmaid!' she called out.

'Bridesmaid?' Jack queried.

'Tell them, Marilyn,' Jo urged.

'We're going to get married when he comes back,' she sobbed happily.

Pearl screeched with delight and jumped up and down. 'Better late than never, bonny lad!' she cried.

Jack's eyes glistened. 'By, that's grand!' They cheered and waved all the more desperately.

'I love you, Colin!' Marilyn screamed at him, tears streaming down her cheeks and blurring her glasses.

'Come back safely!' yelled Pearl.

But Jo and Jack were too overcome to speak and could only wave until their arms ached. Colin was grinning and waving hard too. Jo blew him a kiss and hoped she was forgiven. The stately ship bowed out of the harbour, attended by a flotilla of small boats, blaring their horns. When the band began to play Rod Stewart's 'Sailing' and people began to sing along, Jo broke down in floods of tears.

'Put me down, you're soaking me skirt!' Marilyn sobbed and laughed at the same time. They lowered her to the ground, Jo's shoulders burning with the effort of holding her up.

'You should be grateful for a seat in the circle,' Jo teased her. Marilyn passed her a tissue, and Jo smiled tearfully. 'You always did have these at the right moment,' she joked, blowing her nose.

They hugged each other as the ship gradually receded until they could no longer make out the figures on deck. Still they stood and watched, linking arms in comfort.

'I'm glad you came,' Marilyn whispered.

'So am I,' Jo sniffed.

'It'll have pleased Colin so much,' her friend smiled.

'Do you think so?' Jo trembled.

Marilyn nodded. 'It'll help make up for the things that were said.'

'I hurt him badly, didn't I?' Jo whispered sadly. Marilyn nodded. Jo said with remorse, 'I'm sorry – I never meant to.'

'You can tell him that yourself – when he comes home,' Marilyn smiled in encouragement.

Jo felt the heaviness in her heart ease a fraction. 'Yes,' she nodded, 'I will.'

Chapter Sixteen

When Jo got back to Tyneside, she stayed the night at her father's. She rang Alan, but could not begin to express the emotion of the dockside parting, sensing that he would not have approved. 'I think I'll stop here for a couple of days – keep Dad company,' she told him.

'Do you have to?' Alan asked. 'I'm missing you, girl.'

'Me too,' Jo said, 'but I'll be back at the weekend.'

She slept late the next day, back in her old bedroom where the walls were still plastered with her faded Athena posters and tickets from productions at the Dees Theatre. Jack brought her a cup of tea in bed just before noon, the way he used to when she had worked late at the Coach and Eight. He sat on the end of the bed and they talked about Colin, imagining what he was doing on board ship.

'Fitness training up and down all those stairs, I bet,' Jack mused, 'and training some of the squaddies in first aid, maybes.'

They both fell silent. Jo drank her tea thoughtfully.

'Dad—' She hesitated, not knowing how to bring up the subject. He studied her.

'Go on,' he encouraged.

'I feel that bad about the things I said to Mark that night,' she admitted in a small voice, glancing away. 'I don't know what got into me. I suppose I was trying to

227

protect Alan . . . And I do believe that going to war over this whole matter is wrong,' she added more defiantly. He said nothing. 'But I shouldn't have taken it out on Mark like that. I've tried to explain to Brenda but she doesn't want to know.'

'Maybe she's a little jealous of you,' Jack said quietly.

'What on earth for?' Jo asked, surprised. Jack shrugged and would not explain. Jo flushed and said, 'She shouldn't see me as a threat, if that's what you mean. I got over Mark ages ago – and he certainly doesn't think of me that way! Alan's the only man I love now.'

'So why are you so upset?' her father asked gently.

Jo looked at him perplexed. 'I don't know . . . It's just seeing Colin leaving with that fantastic send-off – knowing that his fiancée and family were there to wish him well. I keep thinking of Mark setting sail without anyone to wave or shout for him. All his life he's had to fight his own battles. And there I was ridiculing him about not knowing who he really was. What sort of friend is that?' she agonised. 'I've let him down badly in the past and now I've failed him again as a friend, haven't I?'

Jack considered her. 'Did you write to him like I suggested?'

Jo shook her head. 'It didn't seem right, not when Brenda wasn't speaking to me. I thought if I cleared the air with her first . . . I bottled it, Dad.'

He stretched across the bed and took her hand. 'I know someone you could chat to. Someone who's missing the lad more than most.' She gave him a questioning look. 'Ivy,' Jack smiled.

Jo instantly perked up at the thought of talking to Mark's grandmother. Then her face fell. 'But does she know about the things I said to Mark?' she frowned.

'No doubt Brenda will have told her,' Jack grimaced. 'But you might feel better if you spoke to Ivy about it anyway. Think how anxious she must be feeling. It might comfort her to know you're thinking of him too. You go and pay her a visit.'

Jo leaned over and gave him a kiss. 'You're a wise old man sometimes, aren't you?' she grinned.

'Hey, less of the old!' he smiled back.

Walking down Nile Street listening to the hammering and bustle of the yards, Jo felt transported back fifteen years or more, to when she would run down to Ivy's for jam stotties and glasses of pop after school. The May afternoon was mellow; there was a warmth in the sun that lit the dirty bricks with a promise of summer. In the next street the jingle of an ice-cream van made her smile nostalgically. But when she reached the house near the bottom of the street, she found the door closed and no one answering to her knocking.

On the point of giving up in frustration, a neighbour popped her head out. 'Ivy'll still be at the bingo,' she said. 'She spends a lot of time there these days. It's Joanne Elliot, isn't it?'

'Yes,' Jo smiled. 'I didn't know Ivy was a secret gambler.'

The woman clucked. 'Aye, well, it helps fill in the time and stops her fretting about her grandson.'

Jo nodded. 'I know the feeling – my brother Colin's just gone off on the *QE2*.'

'Aye, I'd heard. Worrying times,' the neighbour sighed. 'Why don't you go on in and wait for her?' she suggested. 'The door's not locked. Pity for her to miss you.'

Jo let herself in. She gazed around the familiar kitchen, with its old-fashioned range and the collection of thimbles on the rack above the dresser that Mark had bought her. The dresser and windowsills were covered in ornaments that her grandson had also brought back from his voyages, and on the mantelpiece there was a large photograph of Mark in uniform. She picked up a smaller one of him as a schoolboy, his impish face grinning and showing two gaps in his teeth. How long ago that seemed now, Jo thought.

Then she noticed a postcard propped against an ebony statue, and turning it over, she saw that it was from Mark. *'Dear Nana, We've reached Ascension Island already. Weather's sweltering. We do a lot of running on deck for exercise – in shorts! Skippy and me play cards at night – it's costing me a fortune! The lads are a grand bunch and we're all in good spirits. Take care, love Mark.'*

'You always did read me postcards,' Ivy said, startling her from behind. She closed the door behind her.

'Sorry, Ivy,' Jo said in a fluster, quickly returning the card to the mantelpiece. But the old woman chuckled, 'Divvn't worry, hinny.' She dumped down her shopping bag and took off her hat and coat. 'I wasn't sure I'd ever see you round here again – now you're so grand!' she teased. 'Read about your play in the papers. I hear you're living with a fancy man in Newcastle an' all.'

Jo laughed in embarrassment. 'He's not a fancy man, Ivy! He's a well-respected actor and director.'

'If you say so,' Ivy snorted. 'I've given up trying to fathom the ways of you youngsters. In my day we had rules and everyone knew where they stood.' She bustled over to the range and reached for the kettle. 'You'll stop for a cuppa, won't you?'

'Love to,' Jo smiled. She watched Ivy's ritual of warming the teapot and reaching for the Coronation tea caddy on the mantelpiece, spooning out three heaps and pouring on boiling water from the simmering kettle. They exchanged pleasantries and Jo wondered if she would ever summon the courage to talk about what troubled her.

But Ivy sensed her unease and turned the conversation to Mark. 'I didn't hear it from him,' Ivy said, 'but I was told about the argument on his last night.'

Jo nodded in distress and unburdened herself to Mark's grandmother. She told her all that she could remember of that night, not glossing over the insults and accusations. She found herself speaking more frankly to Ivy than she had to anyone about it all.

'Perhaps I meant to hurt him,' she whispered. 'Maybe deep down I'm still angry with him for the miscarriage and for hating me because of my mistake with Gordon. I don't know! Am I very terrible?'

She looked across at Ivy in her worn armchair with the crocheted antimacassars and saw the old woman struggling with her emotions. Her face was very flushed and her eyes glistened behind her spectacles. Her fingers were digging into the chair arms as if she were kneading bread. 'He's never hated you, hinny,' she croaked.

'But I knew what would hurt him most, didn't I?' Jo went on, turning back to finger the childhood photograph. 'I knew that any talk about him not knowing who he was – who his dad was – would be a kick in the teeth. He used to go mad at Kevin McManners for teasing him about being a gypsy when we were bairns. All he's ever wanted is just to belong – to be accepted as a Geordie like everyone else round here. It's not much to ask, is it?' Jo's voice quavered. 'Yet I was no better than those skinhead thugs he tried to get in with who called him racist names, am I? I'm sorry, Ivy, and I wish I could have said so to Mark! I'll never forgive myself if he doesn't come back . . . !'

She heard a sob behind her and swinging round was shocked to see Ivy's face streaming with tears. Ivy took off her glasses and mopped her eyes with a handkerchief, letting out a cry as if she had been winded. Jo leapt over and put out her arms in comfort.

'Ivy, I'm sorry, that was a stupid thing to say,' she gasped. 'I didn't mean to upset you too.'

But Ivy clung on to her and shook her head, trying to speak. 'N-no – not your fault.' She was overcome again and sobbed into Jo's shoulder. 'Oh, hinny,' she said in distress, 'it's me. A-all this is m-my doing!'

'Ivy, don't be so daft!' Jo remonstrated, rocking her like a baby in her arms, baffled by her words.

Ivy pulled away and Jo saw the utter desolation in her face. 'It's true,' she whispered. 'I love that lad more than anyone in this whole world,' she gulped. 'But I'm the one who's hurt him most, not you!'

'What do you mean?' Jo asked, holding on to Ivy's thick, veined hands.

'Oh, Joanne, hinny,' she said, with a beseeching look. 'Can I tell you something? I *have* to tell someone. I can't keep it to meself any longer!'

Mark looked out over the deep, dark water rippling and lapping below. In the distance could be seen the blue-white tip of an iceberg drifting by, echoing the colour of the pale sky. It was bitterly cold, the air pinching his face in seconds. He had taken up smoking again and liked to do so on deck. His favourite time out here was when it grew dark and the sea calm. Then he would lean on the railings and gaze at the glittering Southern Cross and marvel at a shooting star among the brilliance of other stars. At home there was always such a glow of artificial light that the night sky was never this clear, yet now he would stare at the vast heavens and feel connected to those back home.

There wasn't an hour when his thoughts didn't drift homewards, however briefly. He saw Ivy making stottie cake, wheezing in her apron. He imagined Brenda dressing for work. He had regretted not letting her come to see him off from Plymouth. He treasured a good-luck card she had sent that had been waiting at Ascension Island, with a photograph that he had stuck on his locker.

Mark wondered where Colin was and whether he was on his way out to join them. Which made him think of Jo. But that made him angry. At times he thought he really hated her. How was she able to aggravate him so easily? And he could not bear that overweight, condescending, sneering Alan she seemed so besotted with. Well, she was welcome to him, Mark decided. She had done him a favour breaking off their engagement when they were younger and more foolish. Just because they had been childhood friends did not mean they would have been happily married. They had nothing in common now and it would have been a disaster. Mark determined to stop dwelling on Jo once and for all.

Today the air was still, and so clear that he could see every fold in the gently rolling hills of East Falkland. Even the whitewashed cottages that huddled on the shore, with their neat red roofs, were visible like pieces of Lego. He could see other frigates dotting the becalmed ocean like watchful beasts. They would be glad of the respite from the stormy seas that could so easily whip up around them, like a crazy rollercoaster. Winter was coming to this side of the world and the weather would worsen sooner or later.

Mark extinguished his cigarette between his fingers and tossed it over the side. There would be action soon, he knew. No one wanted a long winter campaign. He sensed they were building up to something. He looked anxiously into the pearly sky for signs of aircraft. The drawback to clear days was the ease with which enemy planes could pick them out. Mark thought of the luckless *Sheffield* and the loss of twenty-one crew. He shivered and hurried below.

Chapter Seventeen

1919

Ivy remembered the end of the Great War because her father came home from sea. She was eight years old and she had only a vague memory of a very tall man with prickling whiskers and long sideburns who would pick her up and throw her in the air.

'How's my little dumpling?' he bellowed, for as a gunner he was partially deaf. Ivy screamed in alarm as he tossed her at the ceiling, which only made him laugh louder, like the horns that boomed through the fog off South Shields where they lived.

'Put her down!' her mother fretted. 'The neighbours will think you're doing away with her,' and Sarah twitched the blind for a quick anxious look.

'Damn the landlubbers!' Mathias Black boomed. 'I'll play with me pretty plump daughter if I want to, eh, Ivy?' He chuckled and hugged her to his tobacco-smelling cheeks. 'And take down those blackout blinds. The war's over and this old tar is home from the high seas!'

Ivy soon grew used to his boisterous ways and delighted in sitting on his knee and hearing about his days at sea. Her father had started on whaling ships and then been away for years on long voyages to places with exotic names like Sumatra and Penang. Her mother, tired of waiting, had threatened to marry another, but eventually, mature in life, they had been 'spliced', as Mathias put it in his seaman's idiom.

Ivy, living in a day-dream of romantic tales, did not notice the hardship that crept up on them after the war. She was only aware that her father never returned to sea and that they moved away from their neat little cottage near the park that overlooked the golden sands on which she delighted in walking with her father, imagining they were on a tropical island. They moved nearer the teeming docks, where her mother ran a small boarding house as strictly as any sea captain his ship.

'Best do as the captain says,' her father would wink when Sarah shouted at Ivy to help around the house. 'Else we'll be swinging from the yardarm!'

Most of the lodgers were merchantmen off the ships, a transient group who brought the smell of the sea with them and left having shared a bowl of tobacco and a few yarns with Mathias. Ivy remembered clearly the day she answered the door to Hassan Mohammed. She gawped at this lean-faced man with dark oval eyes and skin the colour of toffee, who nodded politely and swung his duffel bag to the ground.

He spoke in a sing-song eccentric English, a mixture of seadog idioms and formal literary expressions. She was captivated. He must have been conjured out of one of Mathias's tropical tales. She ran to fetch her father and tell him the exciting news. By the time Sarah had returned from the market, Hassan's kitbag was installed in one of the rooms and he was conversing with Mathias over a cup of strong sweet tea.

236

Sarah's mouth set in that grim, thin line that Ivy knew meant they had committed some sin, but her mother was far too sensitive to proper decorum to make a scene in front of any of the lodgers. Ivy heard the row later, lying in the boxroom, her ear pressed to the wall of her parents' bedroom.

'. . . But the lad's served this country in the war – just like me,' said Mathias. 'He was a stoker. A lot of his type lost their lives fighting against the Hun. People have short memories round here.'

'Aye, well round here is where we live,' Sarah hissed, 'and coloured men are nowt but trouble! The *Shields Gazette* was full of that Arab riot at Mill Dam – they had to bring in the bluejackets to sort them out. They carry knives like savages! And you've let one of them stay here. What about our Ivy? We're not safe in our beds!'

'Be quiet!' Mathias grew angry. 'Ivy thinks he's a prince from the Orient, she's not the least bit scared of him and neither am I. He's a lad of twenty, a long way from home, and he needs a hammock till he joins another ship.'

'Why can't he live with his own kind?' Sarah protested. 'Them coloureds have got their own boarding houses down Holborn. Let him go there.'

'He says they're all full,' Mathias answered.

She snorted. 'Shows there are too many of them! They're taking over the town – and taking the jobs from our seamen. It's because of them that times are so hard. Why can't they all gan back where they came from?'

'It was our government and shipowners who encouraged them to come in the first place,' he pointed out. 'We lost that many shipmates and vessels, we'd've lost the war at sea if it hadn't been for the likes of them Yemenis stoking our ships. They're good sailors – decent, hard-grafting lads when they're left alone to get on with it.'

'That's not what I've heard,' Sarah said scornfully. 'Thieves and cowards who'll cut your throat in the middle of the night. That's what I've heard!'

Ivy lay fearful and perplexed as the argument raged for an hour or more. At the end of it, she heard her father shout impatiently, 'The lad stays and that's an end to it. If any of your busybody neighbours start their tongues going I'll be the one cutting them out, not that young Mohammedan!'

Ivy had been unable to sleep, lying petrified listening to every creak in the house and turning every shadow into a creeping murderer. She waited for Hassan to come and slit her throat, but he never did. During the following days she kept away from him, watching him cautiously from a distance and wondering where he kept his cutlass. He wore a suit when he went out, just like the other men in the town. Disappointingly, he did not seem to possess a jewelled turban or golden cloak. She would spy on him as he knelt on a small mat and prayed in a strange language, and observed him sitting cross-legged on the floor sharing his Woodbines with her father.

Her mother complained when he did not eat the bacon she served and shouted at him when she found him cooking rice on a small stove in his room. But eventually his quiet politeness and ability to stay out of trouble won her round. The other lodgers tolerated him, calling him Sinbad, and would play cards or back-gammon with him at night. But Hassan never went out drinking with them or getting into brawls. He did not touch alcohol at all.

Then, one day, Ivy found him sitting on the back step

238

in the sun, his head bent in concentration. As she stole up to him, he turned suddenly, his face wary, and she screamed. He was holding a knife! Quickly, before she could run away, Hassan put out a hand to stop her, saying something in Arabic. Ivy felt herself freeze, her eyes wide in terror.

Then he smiled. 'Don't be frightened. I'm not hurting you. Here, see. I fashion this for your papa.' His grip on her arm was warm, his face more handsome than any Eastern prince when he smiled. Ivy looked at the piece of wood in his lap. He was carving a small sailing boat.

'That's clever,' she gasped, and sat down beside him. She watched him whittle away at the wood, creating intricate sails and rigging with his small knife. She marvelled at his supple brown hands and the smoothness of his muscled arms as he worked in his shirt sleeves. He was quiet but strong, dignified and self-contained, yet with flashes of teasing humour. There was a poise about him, a way that he carried himself, a fluency in his movement that Ivy admired and wished that her small, plump body could imitate. It was probably during that quiet moment of companionship, sitting silently in the sun together, that Ivy first fell in love with Hassan.

Throughout the twenties he came and went as their lodger, sometimes being absent for months on end. Ivy would find these times dull and would snap back moodily at her mother, who constantly complained at her lack of interest in housekeeping and her dreamy nature. 'Always got her head in the clouds,' Sarah would grumble to her neighbours, 'or in a book of fairy tales.' Her father would stand as a buffer between his women, defending Ivy's right to take the air with him along the pier or beach.

'We'll up and start a mutiny one of these days,' he would promise her with a wink. They were conspirators against the drudgery of life, ignoring the increasing hardship in the town and the spiteful gossip that they were Arab-lovers.

But Ivy lived for the times when Hassan would reappear smiling at their door, bag slung over his shoulder and a hundred new tales on his sensuous lips. He would bring gifts of oranges, nuts and ribbon to try and please her mother. Ivy would sit close by, demanding to be told of his adventures, listening entranced to his words. Once they had been exhausted, she would entreat him to tell the ancient tales of the Arabian Nights and stories passed on by word of mouth that had never been written in her fairy-tale books.

Her mother would berate her for being so familiar with him, but Mathias was indulgent. 'There's no harm in their friendship,' he said, 'and it helps the lad practise his English.'

'He's not a lad any more,' Sarah replied tartly. 'And it's time she was courting a local boy. Can't you introduce her to some captain's son, or a lad with a trade?'

'Ivy's not interested in courting!' Mathias blustered.

'You mean no lad's interested in her while she goes about with a coloured man,' Sarah railed. 'It makes me ashamed to go out some days, the way the neighbours whisper at their gates.'

'Damn the landlubbers!' Mathias cried, and dismissed the subject.

Then, one cold December day in 1929, while Hassan was away at sea, Mathias dropped down dead from a heart attack. Ivy had been watching him returning from his morning walk and saw him pitch sideways like a listing ship and fall to the cobbles. She dashed out to help him, but in the short time it took to reach him, her

240

father was dead, his cobalt-blue eyes gazing up at the sky.

She wept for weeks and her mother went into mourning, wearing black and drawing down the blinds, shrouding the house in a sepia light. When Hassan next returned, Sarah took satisfaction in telling him he was no longer welcome. Ivy's heart broke at the harsh words and the shouts of approval from the neighbours when her beloved Hassan had to retreat past their doors.

For days afterwards she searched the town in vain for a sight of him, returning to the house that now felt like a prison. She would stroke the delicate carving that the Yemeni had made for her father, remembering the strong, supple hands working on the wood. Then, one day, in the market, she was startled by a fight breaking out by a fruit stall. A group of men who had been idling at a pub door had gravitated over to the stall. They were surrounding two Arab seamen attempting to buy fruit, pushing them and shouting abuse.

Ivy was about to hurry away when she caught a glimpse of Hassan's handsome face trapped in the middle. He looked angry but resolute. It all happened so quickly. One moment there was shouting and jostling; the next the stall was overturned and men were being pummelled to the ground.

Ivy dropped her shopping and screamed, 'Stop! Please stop it!'

Someone tried to steer her away, but she stood transfixed with horror, watching the men's boots swinging against their victims with muffled thuds. Suddenly there was the blast of a policeman's whistle and the attackers scattered into the crowd. Ivy crept towards the groaning men sprawled on the cobbles. Hassan was almost unrecognisable, his face cut and bloodied, his jacket torn. She reached down to touch him and saw the anger in his dark eyes.

'Careful, lass,' the policeman said. 'Stand away from him.' Ivy watched him roughly drag Hassan and his friend to their feet. 'Did anyone see what happened?' he asked, as if the men did not exist. But people just glanced away and got on with their business. 'Right then, you two can simmer down in the cells,' the constable said gruffly.

Ivy stepped forward, finding her voice at last. 'I saw what happened,' she gulped. 'They weren't fighting each other, they were attacked. They weren't doing any harm – just buying fruit. Some men came over and started hitting them for no reason.'

'What men?' the policeman demanded. 'I don't see anyone else.'

Ivy pointed towards the pub. 'They were hanging around over there – the landlord might know them. Scarpered when they heard your whistle. You must've noticed them running off!'

He gave her a sullen look. 'Don't tell me what I saw or didn't see,' he scowled. Then he looked at Hassan. 'Is she telling the truth?' he shouted, as if the Yemeni were deaf or stupid.

'Yeth,' he lisped through swollen lips.

'Well, I'll not catch them now,' grunted the constable. 'Be off with you and don't let me catch you around here again making trouble. Do you hear?' He strolled off, and Ivy and Hassan stood a moment looking at each other awkwardly. Then she stepped towards him.

'You should see to those cuts,' she said. 'Come back to the house and I'll wash them. Your friend too.'

'Your mother?' Hassan was hesitant.

'She's gone to the fish quay,' Ivy replied. 'She needn't find out.'

They both knew that that was unlikely, for the neighbours would notice, but Ivy did not care. She took Hassan and his friend, Abdullah, home and sat them in the kitchen, pulling back their shirts and bathing their wounds. Her heart beat faster to touch Hassan's skin and rub salve on his cuts. Afterwards she made them tea and fetched clean shirts that had belonged to her father which her mother intended to sell. She stitched up the torn seams of Hassan's jacket.

'Where are you living now?' she asked. 'I've not seen you anywhere.'

'You've looked?' Hassan asked in surprise.

Ivy nodded and blushed. 'Everywhere.' she whispered.

He took her hand and pressed it to his lips. 'Marry me, Ivy,' he said, trying to smile.

Ivy gasped in astonishment, glancing at Abdullah to see if he was as taken aback as she was. But he was grinning too. She did not stop to question why or when or how.

'Aye, I will!' she cried in delight.

She knew that she had to leave with him there and then, before her mother returned and forbade her to see him again. She hurried to pack a small bag of clothes and wrapped up the precious carving of the sailing ship and a photograph of her father, then she marched out of the gloomy house, linking her arm in Hassan's possessively, not caring who saw her.

Hassan found her a room in Holborn, and two months later they were married in a Moslem ceremony. Sarah was furious at the elopement. When Ivy went back to see her she would not let her over the doorstep. 'You're not of age! You need my permission to marry and I'll never give it for that heathen! You're not married in the eyes of God or the law of the land, you shameless lass!'

'Well, I'm married in my eyes,' Ivy defended herself, 'and Allah's. I'm Mrs Mohammed now, whether you like it or not!'

'You're a disgrace! Don't ever come here again!' Sarah was vitriolic. 'I wash me hands of you, do you hear?'

Ivy hurried away, humiliated by her mother's scorn and the hostile abuse from the watching neighbours. After that she kept to the Arab district and did not venture into the town unless she had to. Theirs was a precarious livelihood, sharing with other foreign seamen a house owned by a Yemeni, for no one would rent them a flat of their own. Often the landlord would give his lodgers credit to tide them over until they got work. But at night, lying beside Hassan, listening to the plaintive singing of a homesick sailor, Ivy would dream of better times to come, while Hassan would whisper stories of foreign lands of sun-soaked villages and warm, star-filled nights. 'You can pick your own oranges from the trees and eat as many cakes as you want,' he would laugh, knowing her fondness for sweet foods.

'Will you take me there one day?' Ivy pleaded, thinking how romantic it sounded compared to Shields with its raw east winds and rank smells from the river.

'One day, perhaps,' Hassan smiled, and kissed her.

That summer of 1930, Ivy grew to know others of their close community and made friends with Kathy, who had married Abdullah. Occasionally the young couples would escape the dockside and the relentless search for work and borrow bicycles, heading into the countryside or Newcastle. They would go to fairs and ride the carousels, the girls teaching their men to sing traditional songs.

Yet Ivy was aware of a growing tension in the town and an anxiety in Hassan's expression when he came home. 'They try to introduce a rota for coloured seamen,' he told her finally. 'Only few jobs for us.'

'That's not fair!' Ivy cried. 'It doesn't sound legal, saying who can and who can't work.'

'We know what they try and do, Ivy,' he said with an angry look. 'They want to sunder us from the white sailors, use us as – what you say? – scabs.'

'But won't the Seamen's Union stand up for you?' Ivy asked.

Hassan shook his head bitterly. 'They are corrupt. It is the Union who bring in this rota for us. Why do they hate us like this?' he asked perplexed. 'We help make the Empire for them. We die in the Great War – many stokers and firemen. But where are our names on the memorials?'

Ivy could not answer his questions. She did not know where the hatred came from, only that the poverty in the town seemed to feed it. Then he saw her distress and took her hands. 'But we join the Minority Movement. We will have meeting here soon to stop the rota,' he said with a determined look.

'Aren't they the Communists?' Ivy asked anxiously. She did not want her beloved Hassan caught up in revolution.

'Yes, but they are the only friends. They want all seadogs to stand together – black and white,' he insisted. 'Our friend, Ali Said, is a wise man. He is telling us say no to the Union and the rota.'

August came and there was a huge meeting at the Mill Dam to oppose the new scheme. A Communist Party leader called Ferguson spoke to the crowd, and other leaders of the Minority Movement called on white seamen to join the Arab protest. Hassan and his shipmates had refused to sign on.

'Comrades!' they were exhorted. 'Support our coloured brothers. Refuse to sail! You have your own grievances against your corrupt Union. Strike now!'

Ivy watched from a distance, fearing trouble. But the speakers seemed to be swaying the crowds and the ships remained idle at the dock. Hassan came home encouraged. 'They are supporting us,' he said excitedly. 'It is God's will.'

But the next day, blacklegs were brought down to the quay and one called Hamilton goaded the striking Arabs. Insulting them, he strode forward and signed on. There was a scuffle around him and then in an instant the police appeared on all sides and charged with batons. Ivy watched in stunned horror the violent clash between the police and the black sailors. The other strikers stood back, not intervening, while the Minority Movement leaders ran around trying to stem the attacks.

In the confusion, Ivy lost sight of Hassan. The men were driven back into the Holborn area but Ivy could not find her husband. Much later she learned that he had been arrested along with fourteen other Arabs and several of the local Minority Movement leaders. She went along to the police station to try and see him but was refused. There was a menacing crowd outside and Kathy persuaded her to stay away.

In a matter of days they were tried in court and convicted of incitement to riot. Ivy watched numbly from the gallery. Hassan stood in the dock, dignified and impassive, accepting his fate. The constable who had threatened him after the market fight gave testimony against him. 'He's a known troublemaker – and living with a white woman.' Ivy shook with fear and indignation, sensing the antagonism against them.

246

Judge Roche passed sentence. The Arabs would all be deported.

Ivy broke down and wept. The next day she was given a few final minutes with Hassan. She could do little but cry. He was not allowed to comfort her.

'Everything comes from God,' he said quietly. 'We must accept our parting.'

'I don't accept it!' she sobbed. 'What use are you to me halfway across the world?'

His dark eyes looked hurt. 'I will come back for you,' he promised.

But Ivy shook her head. 'They'll never let you! And how will you ever find the money to come back if you cannot work on British ships?' They looked at each other in helpless misery.

At the last moment, they touched hands briefly, and then he was being abruptly led away. She never saw the men being deported and did not know whether they went by ship from Shields or were bundled on a train for the south. Ivy went into a twilight world of grieving as if he had died. For that was how it felt. She had lost him as swiftly and as cruelly as if he had been killed in action or succumbed to a fatal disease. Yet she could not mourn in the usual way, for somewhere, far away out of her reach, Hassan lived.

Kathy noticed it first, Ivy's pallid look and sudden aversion to spicy food. By September, Ivy knew that she was carrying Hassan's child. Her friends had supported her as best they could, but the Yemeni landlord was bankrupt from lending all his money and the unemployed seamen were pawning all they had left. The Public Assistance Committee refused them relief and more men were deported as 'destitute aliens'.

Ivy, fearful for her unborn child, her only precious link with Hassan, knew she would have to beg for the mercy of her estranged mother. Sarah was horrified at her condition.

'We'll send you to Aunt Lydia across the river until it's born,' she said with a look of distaste. 'Then when you're rid of it, you can come back here and start again.'

Ivy was appalled. 'But I want to keep the bairn,' she said in distress. 'I love it already. It's Hassan's child too.'

'That heathen's left you to fend for yourself,' her mother snapped. 'You can't bring up a half-caste bastard child on your own – and certainly not in my house!'

Ivy flinched from her harsh words. 'It's no bastard!' she cried.

'Well, it will be in the eyes of people round here,' her mother warned. 'You'll be an outcast and then how are you going to live? They lock unwed mothers away in the workhouse, you know!'

Ivy was cowed by the spectre of incarceration and of her baby being taken from her. She agreed to go and stay with her father's younger sister in Wallsend, but silently determined that no one was going to take her baby away. Aunt Lydia was brusque in manner, yet kinder than Ivy had expected, given her circumstances. She was a seamstress, and introduced Ivy to one of her customers, Thomas Duggan, a quiet Scots riveter. He was a bachelor and looking for a wife. Ivy suspected that by 'wife', the middle-aged Thomas meant housekeeper, for he had saved enough to buy his own home.

Aunt Lydia saw that he had a liking for Ivy and encouraged his interest.

'The Lord has sent him to you,' Lydia told Ivy, 'to give you another chance.'

'But I'm married to Hassan,' Ivy insisted.

'Not by our laws.' Lydia was blunt.

'But I'm having his baby!' Ivy said.

Lydia said more kindly, 'If you really want to keep the child, getting another man to take you both on is your only hope. Can't you see that? It's no good hoping that foreign sailor's going to appear by magic and save you. Put him from your mind and think of the baby.'

Ivy knew deep down that her aunt's practical words were true. She was never going to see Hassan again and there was nothing he could do to help her even if he knew about her condition. Her days of dreaming and romance were over.

'But what happens if the baby's born the colour of Hassan?' Ivy whispered.

Lydia shrugged. 'You'll be married by then.'

Thomas and Ivy were married swiftly in October, at Lydia's church, and afterwards she laid on a small tea party for them. Sarah was the only guest from South Shields, and she kept quiet about Ivy's pregnant state, only too relieved that her daughter was respectably married and off her hands.

Ivy determined to make the most of her new situation and did her best to turn their terraced house in Nile Street into a welcoming home. To her relief, Thomas did not seem interested in the obligations of the marital bed and they consummated their marriage only twice. After Hassan, she could not bear the thought of being touched by any other man. Luckily for Ivy, her womb did not swell noticeably until late into the pregnancy.

Finally she summoned up the courage to tell her husband that she was expecting. To her surprise, Thomas was delighted.

'I never thought I'd be a father,' he glowed, and made such a fuss of her that Ivy felt ashamed of her deceit. As the time for her confinement drew nearer, her fear mounted at her past being discovered. She had begun to enjoy being accepted as normal by her new neighbours and not the constant source of gossip or abuse she had been in Shields. She had buried her yearning for Hassan and now craved acceptance and an ordinary life. Above all she wanted to love and protect her unborn baby.

When she went into labour, Thomas was taken aback.

'But we've only been man and wife for six months,' he puzzled.

'It's decided to come early,' Ivy told him firmly, and sent him rushing for the local midwife.

At the end of a long night of labour, her son was born at breakfast time. She could have screamed with relief when she saw that his skin was only a shade darker than her own, and his eyes when they opened were blue. He had a mop of dark hair and slim, delicate hands like Hassan's.

'He looks like me, doesn't he?' Thomas crowed, and she did not contradict him.

They called him Thomas Mathias, in memory of her dear father, but he soon became known simply as Matty. As he grew into a healthy, robust infant, her son reminded her more of Sarah in looks, with his dark wavy hair and round blue eyes. Perhaps because they both spoilt him so much and gave him everything he wanted, Ivy had to admit that Matty soon had her mother's stubborn will and short temper if he did not get his way.

There were no further children to compete for attention with young Matty, and Ivy sometimes wondered if Thomas pondered over his son's swift arrival in the world. Even if he had guessed, he never mentioned it or caused her embarrassment. She knew that for a man who did not seek intimacy with a woman, he was pleased to have a son at all. And in the main he was a good husband to her, working hard to provide for them and avoiding the temptation of the pubs after the hooters went at the end of the day.

To the outside world, the Duggans were an ordinary working-class family, and Ivy was a cheerful and helpful neighbour. If she had any vice it was to spend longer chatting at the front door than was necessary, telling yarns.

Her boisterous son was both a deep consolation to her and a terrible disappointment. Matty did not enjoy being taken to pantomimes or the seaside vaudeville that Ivy loved, for he could not sit still long enough. Neither would he snuggle on to her knee to be read fairy tales when she wanted. Sometimes she would look at his round, petulant face and watch his restless rushing about and wonder where he had come from. For, apart from his long, slender fingers, Ivy could see nothing of Hassan in her son at all.

Chapter Eighteen

For a long time after Ivy had confessed her story, Jo sat staring at the photograph of the young Hassan that Ivy had fetched from her bedroom. It was set in a small double frame next to one of the seafaring Mathias. The image had faded with the years and gave only an impression of a slight, handsome man in a suit. But Jo saw instantly the likeness to Mark in the dark eyes and the slim face.

'It was taken at a fair,' Ivy said softly. 'I got rid of ones of us together in case Thomas came across them. That's all I've got to remember him by.'

Jo's throat constricted with tears. 'You've got Mark,' she said hoarsely. 'He looks *so* like his grandfather!'

Ivy put her hands to her mouth and Jo knew she was going to cry again. The old woman had broken down several times in the telling of her story. Jo leaned over and gave her another hug.

'It must've been terrible keeping this secret for so long,' she sympathised. Ivy nodded and wiped her eyes with a sodden handkerchief. 'Did you never feel you could tell Matty about his real father?' Jo asked.

Ivy let out a trembling sigh. 'Not while Thomas was alive. It didn't seem fair. And then Matty was a grown man with a wife of his own. I couldn't tell him then. He has such fixed ideas about coloured people an' all,' Ivy answered sadly. 'I've always been too afraid to tell him. I told myself it was all in the past and he didn't need to know. At times I wondered if I'd dreamt the whole thing – I could hardly remember what Hassan looked like.'

Jo squeezed her hand. 'But you must've known that when Matty had kids there was a chance of them looking like their grandfather?'

Ivy sobbed. 'I know – and it frightened me. But Gordon was just like Norma in colouring, so again I said nothing.'

'But Mark . . . ?' Jo pressed gently.

Ivy nodded and sniffed. 'Matty and Norma were going through a bad patch before he was born. Norma had this affair with a man at work – I know 'cos Matty found out. He was furious – been punishing her ever since.'

Jo said, 'But you knew Mark was Matty's son, yet you let Norma take the blame. You let Matty carry on believing Mark was the result of some affair.'

'Well, she'd been unfaithful to my son!' Ivy said defensively. 'Why shouldn't she take the blame? After all those years of secrecy, the truth would've killed our Matty!'

Jo shook her head. 'But Ivy! Holding back the truth has hurt Mark the most – he's suffered just as much as Norma.'

'I know!' Ivy cried. 'And I love him that much. He's the image of my Hassan. That's why he's always been so special to me . . . !'

'He needs to know that,' Jo encouraged. 'You should tell him, Ivy, the way you've told me.'

'I can't!' Ivy said fearfully. 'I've wanted to many times, but I've never had the courage.'

'You will,' Jo said. 'Keeping secrets is a lot more harmful in the long run – I should know.' She gave a rueful look. 'If my baby had lived, I would have had to tell Mark who the real father was. I know I could never have carried the burden for years like you have. Perhaps Gordon did me a favour telling Mark. At least I found out in time that Mark never really loved me enough.'

Ivy clutched her hand. 'I was heartbroken when you lost the bairn and you two broke up. Mine and Hassan's great-grandbairn . . .'

Jo felt tears sting her eyes and quickly steered the subject away from her lost baby. 'Did you never hear from him again, then?'

Ivy shook her head. 'Not directly. He may have written to our old lodgings, but no one would've known where I'd gone and the people would've changed. Kathy and Abdullah moved to Liverpool when I went home.' Ivy twisted her handkerchief as she struggled to compose herself. 'But when me mother died at the end of the Second World War, I found a letter from Hassan that she'd never passed on – probably kept it to re-use the paper, knowing Mam. But it told me he was on a merchant ship, the *Baltic*, on the convoy runs to Russia. He was hoping to come into the Tyne.' Ivy's look was very far away. 'Maybe he did. But if he turned up at me mother's she would never have told me. Perhaps she took satisfaction in telling him I was married to someone else . . .'

'Might he still be alive?' Jo ventured to ask.

Ivy shook her head. 'I made it me business to discover what I could about the *Baltic* once I found the letter.' She swallowed twice. 'It was sunk in 1944 – no survivors picked up. In them seas they never lasted long.'

Jo's mind sped to Mark in the icy South Atlantic and she found herself shaking. 'I'm so sorry, Ivy,' she said quietly.

Mark's grandmother must have had the same thought, for she said, 'Would you write to Mark for me – tell him what you know?' She looked at Jo in hope.

Jo hesitated. 'I'm not sure it's fair to drop such a bombshell when he's so far from home. It'd be such a shock and no one will be there to talk it through with him. I really think you should be the one to tell him, Ivy,' she insisted, 'when he comes home. I'll be around to help you if you want.'

Ivy sighed. 'Aye, I suppose you're right. Thanks, hinny.'

Jo stayed late with Ivy. 'Will you be all right on your own?' she asked.

'Of course,' Ivy said firmly. 'You get yourself back to your man.'

Jo left Nile Street in the dusk of late evening and went back to her father's. She was too full of what she had learned to think of returning to Alan's. She needed time to come to terms with what she knew, and Alan would not want to hear stories about the Duggans. After Jack had gone to bed, she settled down on the settee watching a late film and began to write a letter to Mark.

Chapter Nineteen

Early June, 1982

The seas had been rough and the weather had worsened over the past two weeks, Mark wrote in a letter to Brenda. Their ship now lay tossing in Falkland Sound, or 'Bomb Alley' as it was grimly nicknamed, rain pounding noisily on deck. But he mentioned nothing of the reality of war, or his private fears. Only to Skippy and his other mates could he talk about such things.

'Our radar system's about as effective as Nelson's telescope,' Skippy joked grimly, 'specially when it's choppy.' Their vulnerability to enemy air attack had been brutally learnt. Time and again they had been exposed to sudden enemy planes swooping so low they went undetected by the ship's radar. The fleet had no airborne early-warning system. Their protection came from the handful of Sea Harriers operating from *Invincible* and *Hermes* and the larger destroyers with their Sea Dart missiles. But even these weapons could not engage targets at low level. On *Gateshead*, they relied mainly on two large guns and a handful of smaller outmoded anti-aircraft cannon.

'I'm sure they had these in that Second World War

film *The Cruel Sea*,' Mark laughed.

Up would go their helicopters, trailing radar decoys, but they had grown used to constant air-raid warnings, the shouts of 'Take cover!' and the scream of Argentinian aircraft whooshing overhead. As one of the Damage Control Party, Mark had lain on a cold steel floor behind watertight doors in flash hood and gloves, ready to deal with fires breaking out should they be hit. It was a time of taut nerves, listening to the din of explosions and the return bang of gunfire from above, helpless to do anything but wait. Skippy always seemed to want a pee at such times and would head for the bucket.

'It's the cold floor,' he complained.

'Haway and get down man!' Mark shouted, knowing his legs could shatter in the aftershock if he was standing up when they were hit.

During those long moments of fear, lying face down with his hands over his ears, Mark's mind often wandered to thoughts of home and those he had left behind. He saw Ivy at her door in the May sunshine, chatting to her neighbours, and Brenda sitting in the park with her workmates eating a lunchtime sandwich. Images of his estranged family came to mind and he thought with a grim satisfaction that he had proved to them that he could make something of himself. If he ever came home safely, he would make them acknowledge what he had done. Like his great-grandfather Mathias, to whom Ivy so fondly referred, he had fought in war and protected others, which was more than his bullying father would ever do, Mark thought fiercely.

At the end of one attack, Skippy nudged him and asked, 'What you covering your ears for?'

'To drown out your terrible singing,' Mark replied with a grin of relief.

His ship had offered valuable protection to the landing of the first British troops to storm San Carlos on East Falkland two weeks ago, he thought with pride. It had been a hellish week of conflict, with the loss of sister ships *Ardent* and *Antelope* and the Type 42 destroyer *Coventry*. Yet it had ended in the decisive retaking of Goose Green by the Paras. That Sunday, a special service had been held on board to remember their dead comrades and it had been a sombre moment, gazing out over the icy swell of Falkland Sound, thinking of those who lay beneath it who would never see home again.

The following day, they had witnessed the arrival of 5th Infantry Brigade on various landing craft being ferried to the beaches in San Carlos Water.

'Colin'll be among them,' Mark had told Skippy excitedly. Their friend had written to Mark from the *QE2*, telling him he was with 16 Field Ambulance. *'Don't know how many miles I've done round this deck in my union jack shorts!'* Colin had joked. *'Grub's good, films are crap. By the way, I've finally popped the question to Marilyn and she's accepted. Or maybe it was the other way round! Anyway, we'll have a bloody big celebration when we all get home!'*

With the replenishing of supplies had come a postcard for each of them from Jo, which had puzzled Mark more than it cheered him. It was a dull picture of Wallsend library and simply said, *'Good luck from Jo.'* Skippy's had a couple of kisses under her name.

'Why the library?' Mark questioned. 'Is it supposed to remind me of that terrible Jericho Street? And just good luck – is she being sarcastic?' Such a short, begrudging message, he thought. Why send one at all?

'You read too much into things, man,' Skippy answered. 'She said the same on mine.'

'So what does it mean?' Mark asked in annoyance.

'It means she still fancies me,' Skippy teased. 'But good luck and good riddance to you!' Mark had dropped the subject and stuffed the postcard in his locker.

Over the next few days, Mark had imagined Colin and the troops of 5th Infantry trekking across the inhospitable barren hills, digging in grimly as the incessant rain filled their trenches. But a few days later, plans appeared to have changed, for the amphibious fleet were preparing to evacuate the troops from San Carlos bay and take them round by sea to Fitzroy. They knew this, for their captain, addressing them in the mess hall, had instructed them that they would be providing cover for the dangerous operation. The land forces had soon become bogged down in the mud in their attempt to march across the island with heavy equipment. All would have to be conveyed by sea. They would be within easy striking range of the airport at Stanley and so the operation would take place overnight.

That night, they sailed with the command ship *Fearless*, which carried the infantry. The chief chef on *Gateshead*, who had been part of the gun crew, had been taken ill with appendicitis and Mark, who had had some gunnery training, was chosen to take his place at an oerlikon gun on the upper deck. In the dead of night, having skirted round the south of the island, they rendezvoused off Fitzroy and waited for landing craft to come out and collect the troops. But as they peered into the darkness through the pitching seas and driving rain, none came.

Eventually, towards dawn, Mark saw two of *Fearless*'s own landing craft set off for the shore, none having appeared from Fitzroy. He could just make out the dark shapes in the water. Then the two ships were turning back for San Carlos, the danger of daylight approaching fast.

'They can't possibly have offloaded all the men,' Mark puzzled to his shipmate on the night watch.

'It's too dangerous to hang around any longer,' the other shrugged. 'They must know what they're doing.'

The next day the tactic seemed to have switched to using Fleet Auxiliary Landing Ships to ferry the men round, but no frigates in the Sound were called on to protect them.

'We're too much of a sitting target,' Skippy said, 'ships of our size.'

'But they will be an' all,' Mark pointed out. Still, they took heart from the lessening of air strikes in the past couple of days, and morale was further raised when the captain ordered that the ship's deep fryers in the galleys be turned on for the day so that they could stoke up with a mountain of chips.

The morning of 8 June dawned bright and still, the pale sun lifting over the stark mountains, dazzling the eyes but giving no heat. It was these mornings of such crystal-clear visibility that they all dreaded. They hugged the coastline of Falkland Sound for shelter, moving slowly in the shallows between the mainland and an island. The waters were so calm and shallow that in the dining hall they could hear the eerie noise of propellers churning up the gravel on the sea bed.

Colin found it strange that they should be gliding into Fitzroy Bay as the sun came up and dropping anchor. Two days before, he had been on a fruitless voyage abroad *Fearless* to the very same inlet but under the cover of darkness. He had drawn courage from thinking of Mark and Skippy aboard HMS *Gateshead* which he

261

had seen escorting them. What tales they would have to tell each other when they got home! he grinned. That night, there had been some confusion over landing craft and he had found himself being ferried back once more to San Carlos and disembarking. Maybe this time they would get ashore, for he could not bear to see San Carlos Water again, he thought impatiently. There had been too many frustrating days and nights dug in around the boggy west of the island, making no progress towards the enemy at Stanley.

At the last minute 16 Field Ambulance had been ordered aboard the *Sir Galahad* to join the Welsh Guards, and it was this which had delayed their departure by several hours. Colin was surprised they had sailed that late, but it was still only seven in the morning, not quite broad daylight, and they would soon be disembarking to the relative safety of land.

He took in the view of low gorse-covered mountains and glassy still water reflecting the early sunlight. Colin wanted to remember it, so that he could tell Marilyn, as she was bound to ask for every detail. He thought with longing of her easy smile and her calm efficiency which would bring the comfort and order to his life that he had always craved. His boyhood had been spent in a chaotic household, where he seemed to be in charge as much as anyone else. But Marilyn was a constant quiet support; someone he could always rely on when his family let him down or got on his nerves. He knew how much she cared for him, just as he had grown to care deeply for her over the years.

Colin was suddenly struck by how Jo would have loved this view. She would have pointed to the highest peak and said, 'Last one up there's a sissy!' and raced him for it. He had received a letter from her three days ago which had greatly cheered him. Now he regretted the way they had argued on their last meeting and how he had made no attempt to patch up their quarrel. He realised he had tried to punish her for going to live with Alan and turning her back on her old friends. Deep down, he was still angry that she had spoilt things with Mark. He would have liked them to have married.

But he saw now that it was impossible to stay angry with Jo for ever; she would not allow it. Other families, like the Duggans, could quarrel and fall out and never speak to each other again, but that would never happen with Jo. He wished now that he had been more sympathetic when she had miscarried, but he had been young and quick to blame. He thought fondly of his infuriating, impulsive, loving sister and how pleased he had been to see her standing waving on the quayside as if there had never been a rift. He vowed he would write to her in his next spare moment. All he wanted now was to get off the landing ship, dig in and get the dressing station established.

'I'll race you to the top, bonny lass,' he whispered, smiling to himself. Whistling cheerfully, Colin looked ashore and waited impatiently to be offloaded from *Sir Galahad*.

Chapter Twenty

'Air-raid warning, green!' came the message over the ship's tannoy in the late morning. Mark and Skippy dropped the dice they had been playing with and scrambled to their action stations.

'Remember you owe me a fiver!' Skippy shouted at him as Mark made for the upper deck.

'I'll win it back.' Mark grinned. 'You just have a nice lie-down while I go and fight the Argies.' Skippy gave him the V-sign and disappeared.

Out on deck in the winter sunshine there was a clear view of an empty sky. After the initial rush of adrenaline, Mark felt the anticlimax of no action. Time crept on and his stomach began to rumble for dinner. He thought of Skippy and the others below, probably scoffing bacon and egg butties to relieve the tension of waiting.

Then, just as he began to relax, the calm was split by an urgent announcement over the loudspeakers: 'Air-raid warning, red! Enemy aircraft on the starboard side and closing! Full steam ahead!'

He saw the aircraft a split second before he heard the thundering boom of their Seacat firing at the swooping Skyhawks overhead. Then the din of firing erupted all around as they trained their guns and peppered the sky. They caught one and it exploded in a blinding flash, the debris scattering on the sea. Two bombs hit the water either side of them, sending up a deluge of water that momentarily blinded the gun crews.

The jets turned and came at them on the port side. This time there was a thud and then a deafening blast as a bomb ripped through the ship just forward of the bridge. Another struck the bulkhead and there was an almighty explosion from below as a boiler blew up. Within minutes, dense white smoke began to belch up and the ship went dead in the water. The Seacat was out of action, but they carried on firing with small armaments and machine guns – anything they could lay their hands on. Mark did not know how long the attack went on, but it seemed an eternity. His gun caught the tail of one fighter plane, which moments later dropped abruptly into the sea.

But fire and thick black smoke were now engulfing the forward, below which was the mess deck where a first aid station was laid out. Mark knew that Skippy was confined in that part of the ship.

Suddenly the jets were gone, their target mortally wounded. The call came to abandon ship. Men were rushing around in survival suits, making for the fo'c'sle where they had been told to gather. Some were emerging from the inferno below, being helped to the fresh air by those above. Mark did not hesitate. He had to find Skippy. Ignoring shouts from his fellow gunner, Andy, he dived below deck, going aft.

He groped along dark passageways, the acrid smell of smoke stinging his nostrils and making his breathing laboured. The door he came to was jammed, but he heard banging from a nearby hatch. Levering it up, he found a gasping sailor on the other side, his hair singed and his face blackened with smoke. Mark hauled him out and pushed him in the direction of the stairs. He lowered himself into the darkness of the mess deck, promising himself he would just give it five more minutes to find Skippy then save himself.

He was met by a vision of hell. Part of the mess hall was flooded, with water pouring down from burst pipes above. There were wires on fire, throwing a lurid light on the horrific scene. Men were running past him with hands raised, their burnt faces bloated, screaming in agony.

Mark tried to shout at them, 'Where's Skippy – Billy Jackson?' But suffocating smoke was filling his lungs and rendering him speechless. He stumbled forward, disorientated in the half-dark and dizzy from smoke and fear at what he witnessed.

On the point of giving up and turning to go, he heard someone cry out his name. Groping towards the sound, he caught sight of a stranger pinned under a girder. His flash hood must have been ripped off in the explosion, for his face was badly burnt. Then Mark recognised the terrified eyes.

'Skippy!' he gasped in horror.

'Help me!' his friend whimpered.

Mark tore at the heavy girder like a madman, but could not shift it. He had to keep stopping for breath and it felt as if he was smothered in a heavy blanket, his actions slowed. All the time, Skippy's unblinking look beseeched him to save him.

'Shift, you bastard!' Mark grunted as he threw all his might against the iron weight that pinned his friend to the deck. Unable to budge it, he looked around in panic and grabbed at a man staggering past.

'Help me shift this!' he gasped. But the seaman did not seem to hear him and carried on sightlessly. Mark felt a sharp pain in his hand and saw that the man's smouldering overall had melted on to his plam. He winced at the burning sensation and turned back to Skippy, who was trying to say something. Mark leaned close.

'Go!' he was trying to mouth. 'Bugger off!'

Mark knew that if he did not do as his friend urged, he would die there with him in that hell-hole. The heat was unbearable and the black smoke swallowed up air like a hungry predator. Mark leaned forward and kissed Skippy. 'I'm sorry!' he sobbed in frustration. He thought his friend smiled, but it was difficult to know as his face contorted into a grimacing death mask.

Then Mark was crawling along the deck where the smoke was not quite so thick, trying to find a way out. He wondered if he was going towards the fire, for the heat seemed even more intense and he could hear metal bolts blowing off and exploding like ammunition around him. Suddenly one caught him in the leg and he slumped forward, writhing in agony.

He thought in panic that he was going to die after all and realised with a fierce yearning how much he wanted to live. Then someone was urging him forward in the smoky confusion.

'There's a hole in the bulkhead,' the man said. 'Keep crawling – follow me.'

Mark could hardly see him, though his voice was familiar. He followed, dragging his throbbing leg. Suddenly there was a whiff of clear air in the dense smoke and Mark crawled towards it, gulping at its sweetness. Next he saw daylight through the gaping hole in the ship's side, and heard the slosh of the sea twenty feet or more below.

His energy was all but spent and his head swam with light-headed thoughts. Strangely, it was Jo's face which came to him at that moment of half-fainting, half-consciousness. She was a girl again, swinging on the branch of a chestnut tree, grinning down at him.

'Inflate your jacket!' his rescuer ordered.

Dazed, Mark did as he was told, wondering how he had the breath left to do so. His throat felt raw, but he managed the job.

'Jump!' the man shouted. Mark was suddenly paralysed with fear at the thought. The sea seemed so far away. He just wanted to lie down and close his eyes for a moment. 'Jump, you bugger!' came the voice again. Mark did not feel himself pushed, but the force of the seaman's order stirred him. He crawled to the hole's gaping edge, pulled himself up and jumped.

The impact of the icy water on his scorched hands and face was agonising, yet brought him to full consciousness. He struck out in the water, away from the listing ship. His boots felt like lead weights and he did not seem to make any progress. Looking up, he could see the fire eating its way along the stricken vessel. High up, helicopters hovered, their blades beating in the dusk, the sun already retreating from the short afternoon.

Mark glanced around for his rescuer, but he could see no one near by. Looking up at the black hole in the side of the ship, he watched for the other sailor to follow. No one else jumped. As he worried over the man's disappearance, he became aware that he was sinking in the water. He must have failed to inflate his jacket sufficiently, for the weight of his clothes and boots seemed to be pulling him under. Water lapped around his ears and roared in his head. He felt a creeping numbness and knew he was drowning.

As unconsciousness claimed him, Mark was suddenly aware of two things. In his mind's eye, he could see Jo as clearly as if she bobbed next to him. 'Race you to the end of the pool!' she challenged, and started swimming. He splashed ineffectually after her, though he knew he was hallucinating. And as he fought against the frozen waters that tried to submerge him, it came to him that his rescuer was no stranger. He recognised the voice now, the familiar accent. It was Skippy's.

Chapter Twenty-one

It was Alan's birthday, and Jo had organised a meal out at an Italian restaurant in Jesmond. She had gone home briefly to shower and change, but had blasted the flat with a David Bowie tape while she got ready rather than listen to the news. Now that there was real war going on over the Falklands, she found herself listening anxiously to every news bulletin. She dreaded the telephone ringing in case it was her father with bad news of Colin – or Mark and Skippy. Jo still found it incredible that her brother and childhood friends were caught up in a war at all. It was something that happened in history – in Ivy's generation, not her own.

So on this day, Alan's forty-first birthday, she was not going to spoil it for him with worrying about her brother. She put on a peasant-style red muslin dress that Alan liked, squirted on lots of musk perfume over her long hair and dashed out again. She had arranged for several of Alan's friends to be at the restaurant as a surprise, one of whom, Frank, was to bring him there after he'd finished work.

Alan was late arriving and Jo could tell he had been drinking somewhere first. They had delayed in ordering and the restaurant was now busy, Jo felt faint from lack of food.

'Jo, darling, this is wonderful!' Alan gave her a beery kiss. 'I didn't think . . .'

'Come and sit down,' she smiled. 'I'm starving – let's order. Happy birthday, by the way!'

More carafes of wine were brought to the table and soon the noise was deafening from the chatter and laughter. Finally the first course came and Jo munched hungrily at her plate of antipasto. The talk was of Alan's latest production and the gossip surrounding some of the cast. Maya, Frank's partner, knew everything about everybody. Jo joined in with anecdotes of her own and basked in how well the evening was going. So it surprised her when Alan squeezed her knee and asked, 'You all right, girl?'

Jo smiled at him quizzically. 'Of course, why shouldn't I be?'

But he just patted her knee in relief. 'That's my Jo.'

She might have thought no more about it, but for the look of warning she intercepted between Alan and Frank. The conversation flowed on around her and Jo did not want to question him in front of the others. Yet she felt he was keeping something back. She went off to the toilet. On her way back, she stopped at the bar and asked casually, 'Has there been any news on the war, do you know?' The barmaid gave her a blank look. 'The Falklands?' Jo prompted.

'Oh, that!' she said. 'I did catch something before I came out – a ship sunk, I'm afraid, lots of casualties they said.'

Jo's heart thumped. 'Which ship?' she asked.

The girl frowned. 'Don't remember the name. Sorry. Do you know someone down there?'

Jo gulped. 'More than one.'

'Sorry,' the barmaid repeated, 'terrible carry-on, isn't

it?' Then she was serving someone else.

Jo went straight to the payphone and dialled home, her heart thumping uncomfortably, but there was no reply. 'Oh, God!' she whispered, and tried Pearl's number. Again it just rang out. If it was Mark's ship, they might have gone to be with Brenda – or Ivy. Jo wondered which. She did not feel she could ring Brenda, and Ivy was not on the telephone.

Then suddenly Alan was standing over her. 'What are you doing?' he asked suspiciously.

Jo looked at him guiltily, 'Just ringing me dad to check . . .' Then it dawned on her that Alan knew something and had not told her. She could tell by his face. 'What's happened?' she demanded.

'Come back to the table,' Alan protested. 'You're spoiling the party.'

'Tell me now!' Jo replied, anger leaping inside. 'You've heard something, haven't you?'

'I didn't see any point in worrying you unnecessarily,' Alan blustered, 'when there's nothing you can do.' But her look made him relent. 'Okay. There was a news bulletin in the pub – HMS *Gateshead's* been hit. And a landing ship went on fire with troops on board.' He looked uncomfortable. 'They won't say how many are dead.'

Jo's hands flew to her face. 'Oh, no!' she gasped. 'Not *Gateshead*!' She began to shake, unable to take it in. 'And troops? What troops?'

'It's okay.' Alan put a hand on her shoulder. 'They were Welsh Guards.'

For an instant, Jo felt a selfish wave of relief that it was not Colin's outfit, then guilt gripped her at such a thought. The dead would be someone's husband or son, someone's heartache. She thought of her brother having

273

to cope with the casualties. Then fear over Mark and Skippy engulfed her anew.

'But *Gateshead*,' she trembled, 'I need to find out – there's no reply at Dad's or Pearl's. That must be bad news, mustn't it?'

'No, it means they're out, that's all. Come on,' Alan pleaded, 'have another drink. We'll ring them when we get back. There's nothing we can do at the moment.'

Jo felt torn between wanting to please Alan and yearning to be out of there. She went and sat down, but her mind was elsewhere and she could not join in their conversation. It all seemed so trivial now. To her annoyance, Alan invited their friends back for more coffee and drinks. While he poured out large brandies and Maya took over the coffee-making, Jo went to the bedroom to telephone. Finally her father answered.

'I've just got in, pet,' he said breathlessly. 'Been down at Ivy's.'

'What's happened?' Jo asked desperately.

There was an agonising pause, then he said quietly, 'Both Mark and Skippy are missing.'

'Oh, no!' Jo moaned. 'Oh, Dad!'

'Ship's sunk, but it doesn't mean they weren't picked up,' he tried to reassure her. 'Trouble is, survivors have been taken to different ships – it'll take a while to account for them all. That's why they can't say for definite. Brenda's mam's been ringing the MoD for news. She'll let us know when they hear anything more.'

'What about Ivy?' Jo asked, silent tears slipping down her cheeks.

'Pearl's stopping the night with her,' Jack replied. 'I said I'd go down as soon as there's any news.'

'I'll come down,' Jo said at once.

'You don't need to, pet—'

'I want to, Dad,' Jo insisted. 'I want to be with you all.'

'Well, go and keep Ivy company – she needs it most,' Jack suggested wearily.

Jo put down the telephone so he could not hear the sob that welled up in her throat. She thought of the inadequate, stilted letter she had composed for Mark after Ivy's revelations, and then torn up and binned. In the end she had hurriedly bought two postcards of Wallsend library, because the corner shop had no others; one for Mark and one for Skippy. The meagre good luck she had scrawled on each seemed so inadequate now. Why had she not managed something warmer and more encouraging? she wondered. Packing a bag quickly, she ordered a taxi and went through to tell Alan she would stay the night in Wallsend.

'It's not as if it's your brother,' he complained drunkenly. 'Why do you have to be so dramatic? You weren't even speaking to those boys before they left!'

Jo winced at his brutal frankness. 'I still care,' she said tensely.

'Obviously!' Alan cried. 'I wish you showed as much concern over me.'

She gave him a look of impatience. 'Sorry if I've spoilt your precious party, but you haven't been bombed out of the sea!'

Maya intercepted. 'I understand. You just go. We'll look after this old sod,' she smiled. Jo thanked her. The taxi hooted outside, and she went without giving Alan a kiss, the knot of anger inside too taut.

The taxi dropped her off at the top of Nile Street and she walked down in the half-dark. She loved June, when it never really got pitch black at night. There was still a child out riding his bicycle at twenty minutes to midnight.

Pearl answered the door. Jo fell into her arms and they hugged silently. Ivy looked up from her vigil by the fire. Her face broke into a smile of relief. 'Eeh, hinny, I've been thinking of you. I'm that glad you've come!' Jo went to her and put her arms around her plump comforting shoulders.

'So am I!' Jo croaked with emotion.

They sat up through the night, talking and drinking tea and dozing. Ivy refused to go and lie down and Pearl kept them going with awful knock-knock jokes. Her aunt looked exhausted, her eyes dark-ringed, and Jo realised what a strain the past day must have been for her, trying to keep Ivy's spirits up.

'Why don't you go and lie down for a bit?' Jo coaxed. 'I'll sit up with Ivy.'

To her surprise, Pearl nodded. 'I think I will – just for a bit. You'll wake me . . .?'

'Course,' Jo smiled.

'She doesn't show it,' Ivy said heavily after Pearl had gone, 'but she carries the world on her shoulders, that one.'

Jo was too tired and anxious to ask her what she meant. But as she dozed on the settee, she realised that Ivy was right: Pearl was the rock on which all the family leaned. She had been a substitute mother, a glamorous aunt breezing in with foreign presents, a confidante and friend. She cheered them up, told them off and made them laugh in equal measure.

'She certainly carries us Elliots,' Jo said wryly, her eyes already closed. Then she slept.

It seemed only minutes later, though it must have been hours, when a sharp hammering on the door woke Jo.

Ivy was already standing, making toast, when Jack burst into the room.

'They've heard!' he cried. His face was contorted in either misery or relief, Jo could not make out which.

'Mark?' Ivy croaked. Jack nodded, gulping hard. Jo could tell he was struggling to get his words out. She leapt up and went to hold Mark's grandmother.

Tears spilled down her father's face. 'They picked him out the sea,' he whispered hoarsely. 'He's injured – but alive!'

Ivy let out a sob and sank on to the arm of the chair as if her legs had been felled. 'Thank the Lord!' she wept.

Jo kept looking at her father as she hugged Ivy. 'Injured?' she asked softly. 'How badly?'

Jack shook his head. 'They don't know – or wouldn't say. There was a fire on board – he's suffered burns, they know that much.'

Jo felt sick at the thought of Mark suffering and so far from home. Her father just stood there, clutching his hands, his face still twisted with emotion.

'What is it, Dad?' she asked in alarm.

'Where's Pearl?' he said fretfully.

'Lying down,' Jo answered. 'Shall I get her?' Jack nodded, his chin wobbling again. 'Dad, tell us,' Jo pleaded, going to him.

'It's Skippy,' he mumbled. 'The Jacksons heard this morning and rang Brenda.'

'Skippy?' Jo fumbled for words. 'Is he . . . ?'

'Aye,' her father rasped. 'He went down with his ship.'

Jo put her arms around him and they hugged each other fiercely. 'Oh, no!' Jo sobbed. 'Oh, poor Skippy!'

Chapter Twenty-two

Mark was moved for a second time, from the ship which had picked him up to the hospital ship, *Uganda*, a converted P&O liner. He remembered little of being pulled from the sea, only that someone had come down on the helicopter hawser, risking their life to save him, for he had passed out and been on the point of drowning. Coming round on the deck, he was told, 'You're lucky we spotted you – just saw your arms splashing at the last minute.' Then the medic had jabbed some morphine in his arm and he had blacked out again.

Now he lay in a ward with other survivors, the smell of singed flesh and sweaty bodies making him nauseous. Nurses bathed his hands and the right side of his face in Savlon solution and treated his leg. At first he had gabbled in relief with the others, each giving their story of escape, high on their own adrenaline. When he heard that *Sir Galahad* had been bombed, he questioned some of the men who had come from it.

'Me mate's a medic with Field Ambulance,' Mark said anxiously. 'Were any of them on board?'

'Yes,' a young Welsh Guardsman confirmed through cracked lips. 'But they got off before the attack. That's why so many of us were caught – all the lads – still waiting for the medical stuff to be taken off first.' His voice was bitter.

Another one agreed. 'So your friend should be all right,' he told Mark kindly. But their stories of the horrific fire on the bombed *Sir Galahad* brought back his own nightmare memories of charred corpses and the smell of burning flesh and oil. How come he could smell it all as if he were still there? he wondered in horror.

Once the euphoria of being alive wore off, his leg and hands throbbed with pain and kept him from sleep. The ship's surgeon told him they would need to operate on his leg to save it as it was becoming infected. But on the way to the operating theatre there was a red alert. Suddenly everyone was running around putting on life jackets and shouting orders. Mark found himself being covered with pillows on the stretcher and the orderlies taking cover beside him. The memory of those last nightmare hours on HMS *Gateshead* came back to him with brutal clarity and he was paralysed with fear.

'I can't go through that again!' he cried and began to scream incoherently at all the people running by. One of the stretcher-bearers told him to shut up, but the other gripped his shoulder and spoke in a quiet, reassuring voice.

'You're all right with us,' he said. 'Just lie still.'

Mark's panic subsided, but he lay whimpering at the sound of gunfire up above. When the air raid came to nothing, he was taken for the operation and blissful oblivion. After that he slipped in and out of a feverish sleep and nurses came to peer in concern. He heard doctors talking about his heart and lungs being weakened from smoke inhalation, but he was not sure if they were talking to him or whether he dreamt it. When he was finally fully conscious again, he felt shame at his cowardly reaction to the air-raid warning and withdrew into his own thoughts.

But here there was no relief, for he was plagued with guilt at leaving Skippy behind to die. The image of his friend's pleading face haunted him and gave him no peace. He felt numb with helplessness and a sense of failure.

Gradually information seeped out and spread around the injured men about the fate of their comrades. Mark had a visit from his fellow gunner, Andy, who confirmed that Skippy was dead.

'You nearly got yourself killed trying to save him,' Andy reminded him. 'You couldn't have done any more.'

'If I'd got there sooner – if I'd been there with him!' Mark was tortured with doubt.

'Best not to think too much about it, eh?' Andy said briskly.

But Mark was consumed by black thoughts. 'There's something else . . .' He stopped Andy from going, grappling with his memory. 'Someone was with me when I jumped – helped me find me way out.'

'Really? Who?' Andy asked.

Mark was hesitant. 'It – it sounded like Skippy.'

Andy gave him a pitying look. 'Couldn't have been,' he answered. 'No one else came out of there alive after you. It's a bloody miracle you're here, mate.'

Mark's look was harrowed. 'Then who was the lad that saved me?'

Andy could not answer him.

It was early evening by the time Jo and her father and Pearl made their way back to the flats. They had stayed with Ivy while Pearl kept popping out to ring Brenda for news. The reports were conflicting. First she had been told that Mark was only slightly injured, and then another phone call had come through to say he was more seriously hurt.

'Lass sounds in a bad way,' Pearl fretted. 'Worried about how badly burnt he is.'

Jo winced. 'Should I go and see her?' But no one was sure.

Ivy had then become agitated about Matty and Norma being told. 'They haven't released any names or details on the news yet and Brenda doesn't speak to them, so they'll still be worrying.'

Jo and her father exchanged looks. She knew Jack was thinking the same, that Mark's parents had shown scant concern at his going away. But Pearl was more generous. 'Of course they'll be worried. Would you like me to pop over, Ivy?'

'Oh, please, pet,' Ivy said gratefully.

While Pearl went, Jo persuaded Ivy to lie down. 'I'll take any messages,' she insisted.

Pearl had returned to tell them that only Norma had been at home and that she had wept with hysterical relief to hear her youngest son was safe. 'I've never seen her so emotional,' Pearl said in surprise. 'Matty went off to work leaving her to worry alone. But maybe even Matty will be pleased to have a son who's a hero.'

Afterwards, they had steeled themselves to go and visit the Jacksons. Pearl drove them over to High Farm, where Skippy's elderly parents lived in retirement. Jo had been to the estate frequently, especially the summer she had briefly gone out with their son. She remembered with a pang Mrs Jackson's cheerful efforts to fill her full of cake every time she visited. Both parents had always doted on their only child.

They were in shock. Mr Jackson stood by the window,

gazing out sightlessly at the neat patch of front garden, hardly able to speak, while Skippy's mother sat clutching his uniformed photograph. 'I'm that proud of our Billy,' she kept repeating, and glancing to the door as if he might walk through it at any moment.

'If there's anything I can do . . . ?' Jo offered, feeling helpless and tearful. They left not knowing what to say. By the time they got home they were completely drained. The telephone was ringing when Jack unlocked his flat but stopped just as he picked it up.

'They'll ring back,' Pearl reassured, flopping into a chair and kicking off her shoes. 'Do you mind if I stay for tea?'

'You don't have to ask, Auntie Pearl,' Jo laughed.

Her aunt gave her a quizzical look. 'And what about you? Doesn't Alan mind you being on the missing list this long?'

Jo flushed. 'That was probably him ringing. I left him having a birthday party yesterday – was it only yesterday? Seems like ages.'

'You'll not be popular then,' Jack grunted.

'Why don't you give him a ring?' Pearl said quickly, giving Jack a sharp look.

Jo nodded, beginning to feel guilty at the abrupt way she had rushed out of the flat. She had hardly thought about him since, but now that the panic over Mark had subsided, she wanted to hear Alan's reassuring voice. She had just decided that she would give him a call when the doorbell rang.

'I'll go,' Jack said.

Jo went to get a beer from the fridge before ringing Alan. 'What do you want, Auntie Pearl?' she asked.

'Anything, as long as it's not more tea,' Pearl said, momentarily closing her eyes. Jo pulled the ring off a can and poured the beer into two tin mugs. She crossed the room and handed one to her aunt. 'By, you know how to do things in style,' Pearl said drily.

'Getting fussy in your old age?' Jo teased, and perched on the arm of her chair.

They could hear a man talking in a low voice in the hallway, then Jack appeared in the doorway ahead of the mystery caller. All colour had drained from his face. The next second, Jo caught sight of the man behind. He was in army uniform. And at once, Jo knew.

Chapter Twenty-three

The officer was from the Army Medical Corps, and they sat him down in Jack's chair and offered him a drink as if he had come on a social call. There was an unreality about the calmness in the room. The captain declined the drink and tried to explain.

'Your son was on the *Sir Galahad*,' he said quietly. For a terrible moment Jo recalled the stark images of the landing ship on fire that had been shown on the news. She groped for Pearl's hand and squeezed hard. The officer went on: 'Colin made it off the boat. But he was hit on the shore – attending to the wounded.'

'Just like he was supposed to.' Her father smiled proudly. 'That's our Colin.'

Jo sat frozen in confusion. 'But he is – dead?'

'Yes.' The young officer nodded. 'I'm very sorry. The report said it was instantaneous. He wouldn't have suffered.'

It was Pearl who noticed Jack shaking uncontrollably. She got up at once, knocking over her mug of beer, and went to him.

'Oh, Jack, I'm so sorry!' she whispered.

Jo watched, stunned, as Pearl put her arms about her father and his face crumpled like a small boy's.

'He's dead, Pearl,' he cried, 'me lad's dead!' and he convulsed into sobs on her shoulder. All Jo could do was look on in shock as her aunt tried to comfort her heartbroken father.

After that, Jo was only half aware of events happening in the outside world. She remembered hearing of the advance of troops on Stanley and reports of fierce fighting to regain the hills around the Falklands capital. Names like Mount Longdon and Tumbledown registered in her mind, but little else, as she existed in a state of numbness. She stayed on at her father's flat, attempting to carry out mundane chores for him such as making breakfast, washing up, shopping for food. Jack could do nothing but sit watching the television as if the whole war was a film with a tidy ending that he was waiting to discover.

Jo wanted to talk about Colin, but her father did not. When she grew weepy or impatient with him, only Pearl seemed able to cope with them both. When Jo buried her head in her hands and wept unconsolably, over-whelmed by grief for her brother, Pearl would be the one to put her arms about her.

'I just can't imagine never being able to see him again . . .' Jo sobbed. 'And now Dad's cutting himself off from me, too. I can't bear it!'

Pearl rocked her gently. 'He doesn't mean to hurt you, pet,' she explained. 'He's just having difficulty believing the nightmare's true. We all are. Don't be too hard on him.'

A padre from Colin's unit called to offer sympathy and see how they were coping, but Jo was not sure her father took in much of the visit. That same evening, the Ministry of Defence officially released the names of the fifty-six servicemen killed or missing from the attack on Fitzroy, including Colin's. Only after that did Pearl manage to persuade Jack to go to bed rather than sleep fitfully in his chair.

'It's as if he's been on watch,' Pearl said sadly to Jo. 'But now it's official, he knows Colin's not coming back.'

'It's like a bad dream,' Jo said angrily. 'I just can't believe he won't ever come banging in through that door, shouting that he's home. Can you? If we could have a funeral even . . . !' Her look turned forlorn. 'But there's nothing. We just have to believe them when they say he's dead and buried in some bleak, far-off place we'll never see.'

Pearl put her arms around her. 'At least he's buried alongside his fellow soldiers,' she said gently. 'He was always at his happiest with them.'

'But I want him to come back alive with all the others!' Jo cried. 'I want to see him marry Marilyn, have kids – he had so much to live for!' She buried her head in her aunt's shoulder, the thought of Marilyn's shocked face haunting her.

She had been to see her friend, who had gone home to be with her parents, but it had been a difficult meeting. Marilyn had looked terrible and had hardly been able to speak about Colin. Mrs Leishman had tried to ward off Jo. 'You look that like your brother,' she said, 'it just upsets her more. Maybe you should leave it for a few days.'

Then, late one evening, there was a sudden announcement on the television. Mrs Thatcher was giving a statement in the House of Commons. '. . . *Our forces reached the outskirts of Port Stanley. Large numbers of Argentine soldiers threw down their weapons. They are reported to be flying white flags over Port Stanley.*' Jo sat with her father and aunt as the news of surrender was confirmed. They watched the Prime Minister on her return to 10 Downing Street telling the British people to rejoice at their victory. In the background they could hear crowds of onlookers cheering and singing 'Rule Britannia'.

'So it's over,' Jo said, taking her father's hand and squeezing it.

He looked haggard. 'Not for us it's not,' he said bitterly, and switched off the television for the first time in days.

The only thought which kept Jo going through late June was that Mark had been spared. News of Colin's death brought reconciliation with Brenda. Her former friend came to see Jack and found Jo there. After an awkward start, they hugged and talked about the old days when they had been in a happy group together.

'Any news of Mark?' Jo asked tentatively.

Brenda's tense face broke into a smile of relief. 'Aye, he sent me a letter from the hospital ship. Says he's feeling a lot better. Had an operation on his leg. He was hit by flying metal. I just can't wait to get him back and make a fuss over him!' Her excitement at seeing Mark again was palpable. 'We're going to organise a big welcome home party for him at the Coach and Eight. The Duggans are going to help pay for it.'

'Mark's parents?' Jo asked in astonishment.

Brenda nodded. 'They've been canny since it all happened. I don't know why Mark fell out with them so badly – they've been fine with me these past couple of weeks. And Gordon's been round to see if there's anything I need, an' all.' She caught Jo's suspicious look and added, 'Oh, I know what you think of him. But Mark being wounded has brought the family together. I like to think they might all get on again, once he's back.'

'Aye.' Jo smiled encouragingly, keeping her doubts to herself. 'That would be great.' They would need each other's support even more, Jo thought, once Ivy's secret came out. She was pleased that Mark would be made a fuss of when he returned. It would be something to cheer them all up, she thought. But Jack would not be comforted by talk of homecoming celebrations for Colin's best friend. He sank deeper into his own gloom, wrapped in grief that Jo could not penetrate.

Eventually Pearl said to her. 'Why don't you get yourself back to Alan's? You need to get on with your own life – I can keep an eye on your dad. Alan's been very patient over all this.'

Jo had to admit this was true. Alan had phoned her every day to see how she was, and had come down to see Jack. But she knew she had been neglecting him more than she should. Now, she realised, she wanted to get back to Sandyford and some semblance of normality. Brooding round her father's flat was doing none of them any good.

She gave Pearl a hug. 'You're right. Thanks for all you're doing, Auntie Pearl. I don't know what we'd do without you.' They looked at each other tearfully. 'I just can't imagine that my mam could've been any better to us than you have.'

'Get away!' Pearl protested.

'It's true,' Jo insisted. 'You're more than a mam – you're a best friend an' all!' This made her aunt cry.

'Off you go, before Eamonn Andrews walks in and tells me "This is your life!" '

So she took Pearl's advice and went back to Alan. The first few days were a relief. Alan showed his pleasure in having her back by spoiling her, cooking her special meals and taking her on long walks when she did not feel like facing anybody.

'I really am sorry about your brother,' he told her. 'I know Colin and I didn't have a lot in common, but I hate to see you so sad. It's such a bloody stupid waste of life!' he railed. 'Thatcher's great military extravaganza is just to save her own political neck. It's worked, of course. She thinks she's a reincarnation of Churchill. God, they'll elect her for evermore!'

Jo agreed, but she did not want to hear it. Her heart was sore at the thought that the lives of Colin and Skippy might have been squandered in some reckless escapade for mere political ambition. And there was Mark, who would carry the scars for ever. What would he be like? Jo wondered anxiously.

'You won't go saying things like that to me dad, will you?' Jo pleaded. 'All he's got left is the belief that Colin died doing his duty.'

Alan scrutinised her. 'And what do you think?'

'I don't know any more,' she said in distress. 'Only that I'm never going to see him again!'

In early July, when Jo was visiting her father, Brenda came to see her. It was two days before she was due to drive south to Brize Norton with the Duggans to meet Mark.

'Will you come out for a drink?' she asked. 'Please?' Jo agreed reluctantly, for she had lost the appetite to socialise, but it soon became clear that Brenda was deeply troubled.

'You must be dead excited,' Jo encouraged. Brenda gave her a nervous look. 'Tell me what's wrong,' Jo said gently.

'It's about Mark coming home,' she finally admitted. 'I'm scared.'

Jo looked at her in surprise. 'Why? Is it because of his family?'

Brenda shook her head. 'No, nothing like that.' She took a deep breath. 'It's the thought of what he's going to be like. I mean, how bad is he? What if he looks a real sight? I know it sounds terrible to worry about things like that when I'm getting him back alive. But I'm a coward when it comes to burns and that.'

Jo understood. She was sure they were all wondering what state Mark would be in but no one dared say it. 'The worst bit's waiting,' Jo said. 'It'll not be so bad once you're with him. And his letter said he was on the mend, didn't it?'

'Aye, but he might have been trying to stop me worrying,' Brenda answered.

'Then that's what you should do,' Jo said. 'Be strong for each other.'

Brenda sighed. 'I just want to get the waiting over with. Get this whole thing behind us and have a normal life again.'

Jo forced a smile of encouragement, but wondered if that was possible. How could anything ever be normal again without Colin or Skippy there? she thought bitterly.

A couple of days later, when Jo was thinking about Mark's arrival back in the country, Pearl rang her to say the celebrations were being postponed. He had arrived in Brize Norton only to be sent immediately to the army hospital at Woolwich.

'Brenda hardly got to see him,' her aunt said. 'He was off in a helicopter and the Duggans just had to come home. Brenda's going to travel down to Woolwich at the weekend with her mother.'

'What treatment's he having?' Jo asked in concern.

'Skin graft on one of his hands for the burns,' Pearl

291

said, and Jo felt her stomach clench. 'Brenda's in a bit of a state about it all.'

'Can't blame her,' Jo answered. 'But how's Mark bearing up?'

'She said he was making jokes about it,' Pearl said. 'After he got over the shock of seeing his parents there waiting for him.'

'I bet,' Jo murmured. 'Is there anything I can do?'

'Not really,' Pearl said. 'Just wait like the rest of us.'

Jo went to see Ivy, knowing how Mark's grandmother would be fretting over his delayed return. 'Maybe we could arrange for you to speak to him on the telephone,' Jo suggested. But Ivy was nervous at the idea.

'I don't like talking to someone I can't see,' she complained. 'I just want to give the lad a big hug.'

It was not until the end of the month that Brenda got word that Mark was to be allowed home and referred to a local hospital. She went south to fetch him.

Mark sat waiting for her in a small room watching a bulletin on the television of the thanksgiving service at St Paul's Cathedral for the end of the war. He scanned the screen for a sight of anyone he recognised from his ship, but glimpsed no comrades. Mark felt suddenly alone and wished he were back on the ward among the other injured servicemen. They at least knew how he felt; they shared the same experiences. Soon he would be leaving them behind for ever, along with the physio-therapy, daily dressings and games of cards that had become his quiet routine.

Part of him yearned to be back on Tyneside with Brenda and Ivy and his old friends, yet part of him feared leaving the hospital and his last contact with military life and the experience of the war. It was only four months since he had left Newcastle, less than his normal stints away, but he would be returning as quite a different man. How could he begin to describe to Brenda what he had been through? he wondered. He knew he would not even try.

Just before Brenda arrived with her mother, Mark admitted that part of his reluctance to return was that Colin and Skippy would no longer be there with him. His two closest friends were gone. News of Colin's death had reached him on the hospital ship on their way to Montevideo. He still could not believe it. As long as he stayed away from Wallsend, he could still imagine they lived, but once he was back in their home town he could no longer pretend. The protective numbness he felt when he thought of Colin and Skippy might dissolve and give way to real pain. And he would have to face their grieving families too, Mark thought with dread.

Then, thankfully, Brenda breezed into the room and took his mind off his troubled thoughts. She rushed at him with a waft of strong perfume, her black hair gleaming under a white summer hat. She wore a red dress and a pale linen jacket and gabbled at him excitedly.

'Looks like you're off to a garden party,' he teased, kissing her awkwardly, aware of the tightness on the right side of his jaw where he was scarred from burns. He noticed her hesitate just a fraction before kissing him. Her nervousness was obvious in the way she kept glancing towards his injured hands and face and then quickly away again. 'The left hand's nearly as good as new,' he reassured her. 'It's just the right one that needs a bit of attention still. I'm getting good at picking things up again, mind.'

'You'll just have to drink pints with your left hand then,' Brenda smiled.

'I intend to,' Mark grinned, 'and lots of them.' They looked at each other, suddenly at a loss as to what to say. 'I've missed you,' Mark said quietly, trying to put them both at their ease.

'Good,' Brenda replied, her eyes shining. 'I didn't like to think of you enjoying yourself here with all these army nurses.' They both laughed. 'Haway, Mam's waiting outside with the car,' Brenda said hastily, watching how he levered himself up with the aid of a stick. 'Can I do anything?' she asked.

Mark shook his head. 'We don't have a car,' he grinned. 'Or do we?'

'I borrowed Gordon's.' Brenda smiled nervously. She saw the look on his face. 'Don't worry, I've taken out insurance. Both Mam and I can drive it. Gordon offered to come down, but I told him not to take time off work.'

Mark's mouth tightened. 'Can't have him doing that, can we?' he grunted.

Brenda tried to hold his hand but he winced in pain. 'Your family's been good to me while you've been here,' she insisted. 'I'm going to make sure that you all get on in future. There's no use looking back and harping on the past. I want us all to have a new start, don't you?'

Mark wanted to laugh out loud. If only it were that simple, he felt like saying. He would give anything to have amnesia about the past few months, to not be frightened of going to sleep and dreaming of the unspeakable horrors that lay in wait for him.

He gritted his teeth in determination. 'A new start sounds grand to me,' he said, hobbling out of the room as quickly as possible. He shouted goodbye to the lads at the windows and the nurses who had gathered on the steps to wish him well. Moments later they were roaring away from the hospital and there was nothing to tell him apart from the thousands of other civilians they passed on the road, Mark thought soberly.

It was a drizzly late July evening, but the banner was out over the Coach and Eight: 'Welcome home, Mark!' surrounded by union jack bunting. Matty Duggan had a friend who played in a brass band and had organised them to play on the steps of the pub when his son arrived back. Jo murmured to Pearl as they stood in the street, 'Funny how Matty's suddenly so interested in his son since he's become a war hero.'

'Don't be like that,' Pearl chided, squinting through her instamatic camera. 'I think it's grand the way everyone's rallying round.' The local papers had been full of Mark's miraculous escape from *Gateshead* and there was a reporter and a cameraman hanging around waiting for his arrival. 'Norma says Matty's wanting Mark and Brenda to move in with them until he gets fit again. Imagine that! It's always been a squash for them at Brenda's mam's when he's been on leave, so Brenda's keen.'

Jo thought that would be a disaster. 'It's about time they got somewhere of their own,' she whispered.

'Plenty time for that,' Pearl answered distractedly. 'Let's just get him home and settled first.'

It struck Jo that they were talking about Mark as if he belonged to them all, common property to share around. She looked at her father's drawn face as he sat on a wall behind the crowd on the pavement. She and Pearl had persuaded him to come at the last minute, not wanting to leave him alone with his bleak thoughts. Painful realisation engulfed Jo. They were using Mark as a substitute for Colin, channelling their raw hurt into this homecoming. It could never be the same as having her brother back, but it was a temporary balm to their grieving. It made Jo afraid at the burden they were putting on Mark. He should not be expected to make them all feel better. He belonged to Brenda and Ivy and the Duggans and not to them, she reminded herself harshly.

Jo looked around for Alan, who was leaning against the wall with her father, looking ill at ease. He had been reluctant to come.

'You'll only get upset,' he had predicted. 'It'll just rub it in that your brother's not there.' How right he had been, Jo thought, and moved swiftly to his side. This was a mistake, she panicked.

'We'll not stay long,' she said, grateful for the arm he slipped around her shoulders.

'We can go now if you like,' Alan suggested.

But just then a cry went up from the street corner. 'They're here!' The band struck up a nervous rendition of 'Bobby Shafto' and then 'Rule Britannia'. By the time Mark and Brenda and her mother had emerged from the car, they had played them both again. There were shouts of delight, flashing cameras and tearful greetings. Jo wondered at the scene. Half these people hardly knew Mark, she thought indignantly, and wouldn't have crossed the street to talk to him before he went away.

Craning for a view, as the welcoming party of Duggans steered him into the pub, Jo caught a glimpse of Mark's bemused face. Her heart thumped to see him at last. His hair had grown. It curled around his ears, but did not hide the puckered skin around his jaw. It made his smile lopsided, but his dark eyes shone with emotion and she felt a momentary wave of relief that he looked much the same. His hands were bandaged and he walked with the aid of a stick, but he hardly limped. Strangely,

296

he looked fit, his shoulders broad, his stance confident.

'How does he look?' Jack asked nervously.

'Fine, Dad,' Jo answered, feeling a hard lump form in her throat. They exchanged looks of sorrow, each thinking of Colin and how they would have given anything for him to be sharing this moment. Marilyn had gone away to visit friends now that the school holidays had begun. She seemed unable to cope with their grief as well as her own, and Jo knew she had been desperate to avoid Mark's triumphal return.

'I'd only spoil the party,' she had cried into Jo's shoulder before she left.

This was how Jo felt now. She could not face going into the pub and pretending to be cheerful. She knew it would be awkward for Mark too.

'Let's go home,' she urged her father. 'We can see him later, when there's less of a fuss.' She saw the relief on Jack's face as he stood up.

'Aye, let's,' he nodded. 'Where's Pearl?'

'Disappeared inside with Ivy,' Alan told them. 'Doing her roving camera bit.' He took a firm hold of Jo's arm. 'Come on, let's leave this circus and get your father home.' She went quickly, before anyone saw the tears streaming down Jack's grief-stricken face.

'I'm sorry, Dad,' she whispered. 'I shouldn't have put you through this.'

Inside the pub, Mark felt dazed by all the attention. Brenda had promised him a quick drink at their local, for old times' sake, before going home. He had never dreamed of this surprise party. Now he was downing pint after pint, astonished by the number of well-wishers coming up and embracing him and shaking his hand as he sat in a chair by the bar. He felt like pinching himself as he watched his father and brother fighting over who would buy his next drink. Opposite, his mother was beaming at him and wiping away tears as if he had come back from the dead. Brenda hovered close, a possessive hand on his arm, laughing and crying with the rest of them.

Only Ivy sat with a strange expression on her plump, flushed face, as if like him she could hardly believe what was happening. He felt a mixture of euphoria and detachment, as though he was watching himself from above. Was this really his father who was speaking about him with such pride to Ted at the bar? Mark marvelled.

Gordon was apologising drunkenly to him. 'We're going to be best mates from now on,' he promised. Mark guessed he had been in the pub celebrating for a considerable time.

Mark gulped down his beer, obliterating the hollow feeling in his guts at the mention of best mates. No one could ever take the place of Colin or Skippy, he thought emotionally, but tonight he was going to do his best to forget. Glancing around the pub again for any sign of the Elliots or the Jacksons, he was relieved that they had not come. Only Pearl had been there briefly, steering Ivy into a seat beside him and giving him a tearful kiss.

'Grand to have you back, pet,' she had smiled. 'Come and see us when you're settled.' Then she had disappeared before he could ask about Jack or say anything about Colin.

Someone had put Queen on the jukebox, and another pint had been slopped on the table in front of him.

'Get it down your neck, son.' Matty was grinning. 'We'll carry you home tonight.'

Mark felt elated, the alcohol wrapping him in a delicious feeling of well-being. He had survived. He was home. Everything around him was sweetly familiar and now his family appeared to love him again. It was all too good to be true, and he was going to make the most of it, he determined. Looking at Brenda's pretty, animated face, Mark felt a surge of optimism for the future. They were going to be fine. It was his last conscious thought that night. By closing time, they had to frog-march him to the door and haul him into a waiting taxi.

Chapter Twenty-four

To Jo, it seemed as if the whole summer was punctuated with a succession of ships returning to southern ports and flag-waving celebrations caught on television. Each time she was drawn to watch the cheering crowds and emotional scenes of reunion – close-ups of hugging families and tearful sweethearts. She could feel their relief and joy and it made her feel wretched for her family and Marilyn. Yet her friend would not allow Jo to comfort her. Marilyn returned briefly at the beginning of August, but her parents took her away on a coach tour to Austria and Jo only managed a snatched telephone conversation.

'We'll meet up when I get back,' Marilyn promised. 'It's too soon just now.'

Jo was hurt that her friend did not want to see her, but she could hardly blame Marilyn for steering clear of them. Had she herself not done the same to Mark? Jo thought guiltily. She had written to him and Brenda suggesting a night out in Newcastle, but had never arranged it. She had not meant to deliberately avoid them, but the end of term was busy and she knew Alan was not keen to go out with them.

'Leave them alone,' he had said. 'They'll want a bit of peace and quiet after all the limelight. Time to themselves. You get on with your own life, girl.'

So Jo had taken his advice and kept away, only hearing from Pearl that Brenda and Mark had moved in with the Duggans. But by August, her aunt was making pointed remarks.

'The longer you leave it, the harder it'll be,' Pearl warned on one of Jo's visits to her father. 'Mark's been round to see us a couple of times. He was asking after you.'

'I can't just turn up at the Duggans',' Jo protested. 'Matty probably wouldn't let me through the door. And I don't want to run into Gordon . . .'

Pearl gave her a look. 'You know I'd go with you,' she offered.

'I'll leave it a bit longer,' Jo said uncomfortably. 'I sent him a card when he and Brenda moved.'

She was surprised that Mark had agreed to move in with his parents, but then she no longer pretended to know what he thought about anything. She could not tell Pearl that she was burdened by Ivy's secret about Mark's grandfather, that increasingly she was uneasy that Ivy had told her and not her own family. Mark might be able to guess by the look in her eyes that she was keeping something from him. But then maybe Ivy had already told Mark about Hassan. Maybe it had helped reconcile him to his father and that was why they were living under one roof for the first time since Mark was in primary school.

'How is he?' she asked tentatively.

'Still getting physio on his right hand,' Pearl said, 'and I think his leg gives him bother at times. But he seems cheerful.'

Suddenly Jack came out of his reverie by the window and spoke. 'No he's not. The lad's hurting inside,' he said quietly. 'He's not right.'

Jo glanced at Pearl. Her aunt sighed. 'It's early days.'

'What do you mean, Dad?' Jo asked. But her father just shook his head dolefully.

Pearl explained. 'Norma's worried at the amount of time he spends round the pubs with Gordon and Matty. He's drinking a lot.'

'Well, he's on leave,' Jo said. 'He's entitled to let his hair down after what he's been through.'

'Perhaps,' Pearl sounded unsure, 'but Norma says it's most nights. Brenda goes out with them too. They're spending all her wages and giving nothing towards the household expenses. Norma says that's why Brenda's mam was happy to see the pair of them move out. They're spending like there's no tomorrow.'

'Maybe they don't want to think about tomorrow,' Jack said bleakly.

Pearl's face flickered with impatience. 'We all have to think of the future some time,' she said crossly. Jo looked at her in surprise. She had not heard Pearl utter one cross word to Jack since Colin's death. Her father did not seem to notice and went on staring out of the window. Pearl shrugged dismissively and turned to Jo. 'Go and see Mark,' she urged. 'He visits Ivy most afternoons, while Brenda's working. He doesn't seem to be able to talk about Colin to us, but maybe he could to you.'

Jo finally plucked up courage to visit Ivy's towards the end of August. It was a couple of days before she was due to go on holiday with Alan. His friends Frank and Maya had taken a house in Galicia, in north-west Spain, and Jo and Alan were to join them. They both needed a break. Alan had been working punishing hours at the theatre, but now there was a lull until mid-September.

Jo had been reluctant to leave her father, but Alan had insisted. 'We need to get away, Joanne,' he said, adding pointedly, 'and give each other some loving attention.' Now that Alan had made the decision for them, Jo was looking forward to the holiday. But she needed to get this visit to Ivy's over with before she could leave with an easy mind.

Ivy answered her knock with a finger raised to her lips. Jo crept in behind her, wondering why she had to keep quiet.

There he was, curled up on the sofa asleep. He looked like a young boy, his face empty of expression, the scarring hidden by a cushion. His mouth was slightly open and he was breathing rhythmically. Now and then, his arm would flutter as if a small shock was sweeping through his body. She looked at the bandaged hand as the tremor lifted it and wondered what he dreamed about. Jo felt a wave of tenderness towards him. He looked so vulnerable, childlike. She resisted the urge to touch him or kiss his head of dark wavy hair. Why had she been so afraid of seeing him? she thought guiltily. She had been wrong to avoid him for so long.

Ivy silently handed her a mug of tea and nodded to her to follow her outside. They took two kitchen chairs into the backyard and sat in the afternoon sun.

'Comes here most afternoons when the pubs close at three,' she sighed. 'I try and sober him up before he goes back to Matty's. There's something eating away inside him – but he won't talk about it.'

'Who's he drinking with in the daytime?' Jo asked.

Ivy snorted. 'Anyone who'll buy him a pint. And there's plenty of them want to be seen with the lad now he's famous round here. One day soon they'll get tired of it and then who's going to pick up the pieces?' she asked angrily.

'What do his parents think?' Jo squinted at Ivy.

'Oh, Norma's spoiling him – making up for years of neglecting the lad, so she won't say anything,' Ivy answered. 'And Matty... oh, Matty! He thinks it's champion having someone to go out drinking with! He doesn't see what I'm worried about. Gordon's just as bad. He and Barbara aren't getting on, so he's out all the time. And Barbara takes it out on the family by not bringing Michelle to see me...!'

'I'm sorry, Ivy,' Jo sympathised. 'What does Brenda think of it all?' she asked.

Ivy shook her head. 'She goes out with them too – or with her other friends. Never in as far as I can gather. It's been one big party since Mark got home, except...'

'What?' Jo questioned.

'No one seems happy,' Ivy said heavily. 'Mark loses his temper so easily these days. He's like a rollercoaster – up high one minute, down in the dumps the next.'

'He's probably missing the Navy,' Jo guessed. 'Or maybe he's worried about going back after what he's been through.'

Ivy's look was grave. 'I think it worries him that they might not take him back. He'll have to pass all sorts of fitness tests first.'

Jo asked gently, 'Have you told him?'

'Told him what?' Ivy said, feigning ignorance.

'You know what,' Jo answered, holding her look.

Ivy said sharply, 'No, I haven't! He's in too much of a state at the moment. I don't think he could take it.'

'Take what?' said a bleary voice behind them. Ivy gasped and Jo jerked round.

'Mark, hinny,' his grandmother said in a fluster,

'we didn't want to disturb you.'

Jo stood up and smiled nervously. They stared at each other for a long moment, neither knowing what to say. Eventually she forced herself to move forward and gave him a peck on the cheek. In the harsh daylight she thought he looked terrible, much worse than when he had returned a month ago. His eyes were dark-ringed and his face was lined with pain. He could have been thirty-six, not twenty-six.

She was about to stand back, when Mark put out his arms and gave her a hug.

'I'm sorry about Colin,' he said in a low voice. Jo felt tears sting her eyes as he squeezed her to him.

'Me too,' she whispered, burying her head in his T-shirt and feeling the agony of her brother's loss anew. Standing close to Mark brought Colin back to her so vividly it was as if she could feel him there too. She had no memories of a time before Colin and Mark had been friends. It seemed inconceivable to have one without the other and Jo knew this was the real reason she had kept away from Mark. She had not wanted to contemplate a time when there would be just the one. It was too painful.

Suddenly the words were tumbling out of her. 'I miss him that much,' she cried, 'and I never got to speak to him again after that night we all rowed. I never got to tell him how much he meant to me – or how sorry I was about falling out with him! And now he'll never know. I feel so bad about it . . . !' Jo convulsed into sobbing, wondering where the words came from. She had never admitted such regrets to anyone before; she had suppressed them deep within herself.

'He knew,' Mark comforted, 'of course he knew.' But his kindness just made her all the more wretched. She shook with distress, and Mark simply held her. Eventually she became aware of his arms around her. He smelt of cigarette smoke and stale beer. She pulled away, glancing with embarrassment at Ivy. The older woman's eyes were glistening behind her spectacles.

'Eeh, hinny!' Ivy fussed, pushing a handkerchief at her. 'Sit yourself down. I'll get us some lemonade.'

'I'm sorry,' Jo apologised, 'I didn't mean to . . .' She turned away and wiped her face. Mark sat down on Ivy's chair while his grandmother went for refreshment. Jo looked at him awkwardly. 'How are you?'

He gave her a bleak, haunted look, then reached into a pocket of his scruffy jeans for a squashed packet of cigarette papers and tobacco. He began to methodically roll a cigarette. When he'd finished, he offered it to her, but she shook her head. Only when he had it lit did he speak.

'I'm alive,' he said with a bitter little laugh. 'I'm the lucky bugger, aren't I?'

'Aye, you are,' Jo answered, taken aback by his sudden change in attitude.

'Well, it doesn't feel like it,' he said in a stony voice.

She tried to jolly him. 'You've been through a lot. You just need to get yourself fit again.'

'Fit for what?' he demanded.

'The Navy, of course.'

'Look at me!' he said savagely, waving his bandaged hand at his wasted right leg. 'Who wants a screwed-up cripple like me on board?'

Jo was suddenly annoyed at his self-pity. She wanted to shake him out of it. 'So you're feeling sorry for yourself. Is that why you're drinking yourself stupid round Wallsend every day?'

His look was hard. 'I drink because it's a free country.

That's what we all fought for, wasn't it? Me, Colin, Skippy—'

'Stop it,' Jo said, frightened by his bleakness. 'Don't belittle what you all did.'

Mark gave a harsh laugh. 'So you approve of what we did now, do you? Well, that's big of you. Has your bleeding-heart boyfriend had a change of heart an' all?'

'Alan doesn't deserve that,' Jo said, offended. 'He's been very supportive over Colin's death.' Jo heard her voice tremble and stopped. Damn him for riling her like this!

'Well, I'm glad for you,' Mark said, blowing out smoke contemptuously.

Jo rounded on him. 'So why are you giving up so easily?' she demanded. 'You should wake up every day being thankful you're alive and safe at home. You've got Brenda and all your family around you. You've got the rest of your life ahead of you.'

He looked at her with narrowed eyes. 'And I should be more grateful, is that what you mean?'

'Aye, I do!' Jo sparked. 'You're not the only one suffering, you know. Have you seen the state of Skippy's parents? Have you seen how my dad has aged? He's like an old man! And Marilyn can't even bear to be around us any more. So don't you feel so bloody sorry for yourself!'

Mark lurched up on to his good leg and ground out his cigarette under a scuffed trainer. 'Don't tell me what I should feel!' he shouted. For a moment she thought he would hit her. His whole body was taut with anger. 'I saw Skippy burning to death,' he hissed in her face. 'I can still smell him. Every time I close me eyes I see him. I hear him shouting at me to save him, the poor bastard!'

Jo stared back in horror. 'I'm sorry . . .' she gulped.

'Not as sorry as me,' he said, his face contorted in fury. 'Don't you think I would have given anything – *anything* – to have saved him or taken his place? Or Colin's?' He shook as he spoke. 'What do you think it's like for me – the one who survived? Why me and not them? They were better lads than me! I'm the one who's always screwing things up. So why should I be saved? I shouldn't have lived when they didn't,' he choked. He could hardly get his words out. 'I feel guilty for living!' he rasped.

Jo was shaken to the core by his tortured words. 'You mustn't feel like that,' she gasped, stretching out her arms to him. 'It's the last thing Colin or Skippy would've wanted.' But he pushed her away.

Shaking with dry, angry sobs, he demanded, 'How do you know?'

'Because I knew them,' Jo said desperately.

His look was full of contempt. 'No you didn't. You stopped knowing us years ago. I don't know why you still hang around here. Why do you, Jo?'

She felt winded by his cruel words. 'Go to hell!' she shouted, pushing past him.

His dark eyes blazed. 'I'm already there,' he said in a hard voice.

She fled into the kitchen, nearly knocking Ivy over as she returned with a tray of tumblers fizzing with lemonade.

'Whatever's the matter?' Ivy gasped, catching sight of Jo's distraught face.

'I'm sorry, Ivy,' Jo quavered. 'I've just made things worse. I can't help any more. I can't bear to be with him!'

Clamping her hand over her mouth to smother the sob that rose in her throat, Jo stumbled for the front door and out into the warm, breezy street. Dust blew in her eyes and throat, but she rushed on, desperate to escape Nile Street. She hated Mark for his wounding words. How dare he accuse her of not knowing her own brother and one of her oldest friends! She had loved them both. She had gone out with Skippy long before she and Mark had got together. He did not have the monopoly on friendship. How could he be so cruel as to exclude her, as if she had not been close to any of them?

Damn Mark Duggan! Jo cried inwardly, as she ran up the hill on to the high street, hoping she would not meet anyone she knew. She could not face her father or Pearl after that. She could not face anyone. She rushed for the Metro station and jumped on the first train back into Newcastle. Only in the half-empty carriage, as the shipyards and docks gave way to suburban housing and office blocks, did she allow herself to weep silently, biting on her fist.

Stepping on to the underground platform in the centre of the city, Jo cursed herself for getting involved again. She had tried to help Mark, but he had thrown her friendship back in her face. She could do nothing more for him. It would be best to stay away and let those close to him cope. More than ever, Jo wished she did not carry Ivy's secret. But Mark's grandmother would have to be the one to tell him, not her, especially not now. He had hurt her deeply and robbed her of her peace of mind.

In turmoil, she walked the streets of Newcastle for an hour, until she had calmed down enough to go home to Alan. At least in two days' time she would be out of the country and away from the source of her pain. Alan would help her recover. He always did. She hurried to be with him, impatient for escape.

Chapter Twenty-five

Galicia was lush and green, its beaches busy with Spanish families eating huge picnics of spicy sausages, chicken, hunks of bread and potato omelettes. Frank and Maya's rented house was on the edge of a village near La Coruna, and they would drive into town and drink coffee at pavement cafés and argue Spanish politics. There were two other couples there: Maya's sister Susie, with boyfriend Bob, and two playwrights whom Alan had known for years. At night, they would sit under the stars drinking red wine from flagons filled up at the village bar, their talk and laughter punctuated by distant fireworks at some fiesta.

The effect on Jo of their heartiness was to make her quieter than usual, and she would slip away and sit by the village pump watching the children playing with the water. If her baby had lived, she thought, it would have been five years old by now and as boisterous as these lithe children with their high-pitched chatter. But she chided herself for such thoughts, for they brought with them painful reminders of Gordon and Mark. If her baby had lived, she would have been inextricably linked to the Duggans for ever. She would never have been free of them. Sitting listening to the splash of water on hot stone flags, Jo realised how much she wanted to be free of them.

At least the time away had given her perspective on the terrible scene at Ivy's. She now had to admit that there was some truth in what Mark had said. She had grown away from Colin and her old friends in Wallsend. Marilyn was the only one she had kept in regular touch with since Alan had come into her life. Jo had moved on, outgrown the circle of friends with whom she had grown up. But she would not be blamed for changing, and developing other interests and friendships, she decided. Just because Mark had not! Lifting her face to the warm sun and closing her eyes, she tried to find the inner calm that eluded her.

Jo was sorry for Mark in his private hell, but she could not reach him. He had made it quite plain that he saw her as an outsider now; he had changed beyond recognition from the Mark she had once loved. Yet she was still angry with him for his harsh words about not knowing her brother.

As she lay next to a sleeping Alan in their shuttered room, the thought of never being properly reconciled with Colin robbed her of sleep. She would give anything to have five more minutes with him, to explain how much she cared for him, she agonised in the dark hours. He had been her closest childhood companion, the one who had always stood up for her, her cherished older brother. But their friendship had suffered after the miscarriage. Mark had come between them. Colin had blamed her for Mark's wounded pride and their split. Yet it was not all her fault! It was they who had pushed her away, Jo realised in distress. Was it any surprise that she had forged a new life for herself? she questioned angrily.

'What's wrong?' Alan demanded towards the end of the holiday as they walked across the imposing cathedral square of Santiago de Compostela. Maya had dropped them off there for the day, sensing that they needed time alone from the rest of the household.

'What do you think's wrong?' Jo replied sharply.

Alan was not going to let her argue. He swung an arm around her. 'I know it's a difficult time. You're grieving. That's why I wanted to get you away from all that. Spoil you a bit.'

Jo relaxed against him. 'I know. I'm sorry.'

'Let's go to the hotel for coffee and cake,' Alan insisted.

It was quiet and cool in the imposing hotel on the edge of the square and Alan was in such a good mood that Jo found herself telling him about the encounter at Ivy's. His mood changed at once.

'You never told me you'd seen Mark,' he said crossly. 'Why not?'

'I was too upset by what he said,' she exclaimed. 'And he's in a terrible way mentally.'

'God, that boy!' Alan cursed. 'He's a complete head-case, can't you see that? I've always thought it – he's unstable. I can't imagine what you ever saw in him – he's just not your type.'

'Don't patronise me!' Jo flushed. 'And he hasn't always been like that. He's had a bad time – more than we can ever imagine. He saw his best friend burned alive.' She shuddered.

'Oh, yes,' Alan said impatiently, 'and there's that sob story about his Arab grandfather. I suppose that gives him the excuse to behave badly as well? Poor, misunderstood Mark.'

'Don't!' Jo protested, regretting that she had ever told Alan Ivy's secret. 'He doesn't know about all that.'

Alan looked incredulous. 'You mean the old baggage

hasn't had the guts to tell him yet?'

'Don't speak about Ivy like that,' Jo cried. 'She's right not to tell him now – the state he's in.'

'Well, I wash my hands of the lot of them,' Alan growled. 'And the Duggans don't deserve all the pity and anguish you spend on them, that's for sure. You should forget them and concentrate your efforts on getting your father out of his depression. He's the one you should be worrying about.'

Jo was stung by the rebuke. 'I do worry!'

Alan's anger subsided suddenly. He covered her hand with his. 'This is awful, arguing,' he grimaced. 'I wanted this to be a special time together – just you and me.'

'And six others,' Jo reminded him.

Alan shrugged. 'Well, I need people around me, you know that. But I also wanted you to myself – away from all those others who make such demands on you. You're only ever half with me, I can tell. I can't get close to you like I want to,' he complained.

She felt a stab of guilt at his anxious face. 'I'm sorry,' she relented, 'I know it hasn't been easy for you either.' She squeezed his hand. 'I want to get close again too,' she whispered.

He put her hand up to his lips and kissed it. 'We won't go back tonight,' he murmured. 'We'll book in here. Tonight is just for us.'

Mark had had another row with Brenda and was walking the streets late at night. She had gone on a pub crawl with Gordon and Jerry from the old rock band. He found it stifling at home with his mother sitting watching his every move and his father making opinionated remarks at the television. The nightmares had increased, not lessened, with time. Now he was getting

314

them while he was wide awake, and it terrified him. He would get flashbacks that paralysed him. It might happen in the street. One of his shipmates would pass right by him and he would reach out to grasp him, the words that he longed to say trapped in his throat. But before he could speak the man would turn into a stranger and brush him off, leaving him gasping and sweating in confusion.

Once he had frozen at the sound of a machine gun and ducked behind a car.

'What you doing?' Brenda had laughed. But the look on his face must have told her it was no game. 'They're drilling the road,' she told him. 'Get up, Mark man, people are staring.' She had walked on in embarrassment and tried to make a joke about it later when they were out with Gordon.

Increasingly, Mark did not want to venture out at all. He sat in their bedroom watching the television Brenda had brought from her mother's, or he went to Nile Street, where Ivy made no demands on him. Brenda was tiring of his moods, but he could not help them, they seemed quite beyond his control.

'When are the Navy going to get in touch with you?' she complained.

'I don't know!' he snapped. 'Stop going on about them. One buggered-up sailor isn't of any importance!'

'Yes you are,' Brenda cried. 'And we need to make plans, Mark. I can't stick it here with your parents much longer.'

'It was your idea to come here,' he reminded her.

'Keep your voice down,' she answered. All their arguments were carried out in hissed whispers; they couldn't even row properly in case Norma got upset. 'I didn't know you'd be on the sick this long,' Brenda argued. 'If you're not going back to sea, I want us to get a place of our own.'

'With what?' Mark asked in agitation. He wanted this twilight world to change too, but he did not have the energy to do anything about it. He felt lost in a fog and each day he wandered deeper into it.

Brenda had put on her lipstick and gone out for the evening. She didn't even ask him if he wanted to go any more, because he had lost the appetite for social drinking. He felt safer drinking himself into oblivion in his room, frightened of being shown up public if an anxiety attack seized him. Even the smoke in pubs could send him into a panic. It would invade his nostrils and grip his chest and in seconds he would be back below deck in the hell of that burning ship. He tried to explain it to Brenda, but she just looked at him as if he were mad.

As he roamed the riverside in the dark, the huge cranes looming over him, Mark thought he probably *was* mad. There were demons in his head that he could not control. The only person he had come close to explaining this to had been Jo. But it had come out all wrong. She had reminded him too painfully of Colin, and his guilt and anger had erupted. Jo had made him feel his weakness and despair and he resented her for it. What right had she to lecture him about his duty to be thankful and happy because he had survived and her brother had not? he thought bitterly. He had been shaken by the force of his rage towards her.

Walking until he exhausted himself and his leg throbbed with pain, Mark turned towards Nile Street. His grandmother would take him in without grilling him with awkward questions. She was the only person who seemed to accept him the way he was, even during his bouts of drunken anger. He knocked at the door and went in without waiting for an answer. The room was in darkness except for the glow from the television.

'Nana?' he said, squinting at the bulky shadow in the chair. Ivy was dozing. He leaned over the back of the chair and kissed her grey hair gently.

She woke with a start and put out a hand to him. 'Hassan?' she gasped in confusion. 'Is that you?'

Mark laughed softly. 'Who's Hassan? Some lover boy from the bingo?' he teased. But the look on her face halted his laughter. She was staring at him, clutching her throat in fear. 'It's all right, Nana, it's me,' he said, quickly reaching to turn on the light.

She let go a long breath. 'By, you gave me a fright!'

'Aye, sorry. You look like you've seen a ghost,' Mark said, easing himself down beside her.

She put out a hand to him. 'I thought I had,' she whispered. Mark felt a tingle of fear at her words. She was looking at him so strangely.

'What is it, Nana?' he asked in concern. 'You've not been having nightmares too?'

A little sob caught in her throat. 'For longer than you can imagine,' she said in a desolate voice. She clutched his hand tighter. 'Oh, Mark, hinny, I've got to tell you. It's on me mind all the time these days. It can't make you any unhappier than you already are – and maybe it'll make you feel better about yourself.' She gave him a desperate look.

Mark asked in bafflement, 'Tell me what?'

Ivy hung on to his hand as if it were a lifeline. 'About your grandfather and me. Your grandfather Hassan.'

Chapter Twenty-six

September 1982

Jo did not know what to wear for the memorial service. It was being held at the cathedral and was a joint one for all the forces. Would it be like a funeral? Or would it be an excuse for victory celebrations? she wondered. That was what Alan had thought and that was his reason for not going with her.

'It'll be triumphal – flags and uniforms and hymns about the sea,' he said dismissively. 'It won't be about Colin.'

'Maybe it won't, but Dad wants to go,' Jo said defensively. 'At least I can go there and think about Colin. And if Dad finds it a comfort, then I'm happy to go.'

'I think you'll both get very upset – not comforted,' Alan predicted. 'You'd be closer to Colin going for a walk in Wallsend Park.'

'You're not making it any easier for me,' Jo snapped, discarding the black skirt in favour of the green. The late-September day was too warm and bright to be dressed in black. She was dreading the afternoon ahead and angry at herself for arguing with Alan. They had ended the holiday being much closer and happier together and she missed the teasing intimacy of those last sunny Spanish days. But on returning, the aftermath of the war had come between them again. As she hurried through the streets of Newcastle, with their normal bustle, she wondered if anyone else even thought about the Falklands any more.

She found her father and Pearl waiting on the corner of the Bigg Market as they had arranged. She slipped her arm through Jack's and gave him an encouraging smile. Pearl seemed distant, her face pale and thin in the sunshine, and Jo suddenly wondered how well her aunt was bearing up. She had taken the strain of Colin's death on her shoulders, coping with Jack's overwhelming grief and worrying over Mark. Jo realised that no one ever asked Pearl how she was feeling, and yet she had been like a mother to Colin. This was the first time she had seen Pearl since going on holiday and she noticed how her fair hair was lacklustre and her eyes glassy. There was a ladder in her tights and her make-up had been slapped on in a hurry. It was not like Pearl to let her appearance slip.

'You all right?' Jo asked.

'Course I am,' Pearl answered in her no-nonsense way. Jo gave her aunt a quick kiss and determined to pay her more attention.

They filed into the cool interior of the cathedral with its ancient tombs and memorial stones, its stained glass and solid pillars. It was filling up with mourners and people in uniforms representing all the forces. Officers from Colin's regiment were present, and there was the captain of HMS *Gateshead* and some of the crew in the procession. As music boomed around the church and the voices of hundreds rose to the vaulted ceiling, Jo looked around for sign of Mark. She knew he must be somewhere there, but she could not spot him in the crowd.

Having gone full of reluctance, Jo found herself moved by the service. There was no glorifying of the war, just short prayers of remembrance and simple words offering comfort. She felt drawn to the other people in the pews, strangers mostly, who cried silently or listened and held each other's hands. Although she did not know them, she felt close to them, taking comfort from their shared sorrow. Some of the time her mind wandered and she realised she had kept herself frantically busy since her brother's death to avoid having too much time to think. Only on holiday had she had moments of contemplation, but even then she had been afraid to be left alone with her thoughts. Now she let them drift up with the music.

The war had always seemed so far away and unreal for those who did not have loved ones out there. It struck Jo that this was why she and Alan saw things in such a different way. He had never been emotionally involved in the war. He could analyse it objectively, talk about politics and the immorality of killing. She could agree intellectually, but in her heart there was no such objectivity. She understood that there were hundreds of soldiers' sisters in Argentina who felt as bereft as she did. But she would have traded in the life of the pilot who dropped the bomb on Colin to have her brother alive. That was the difference between her and Alan. Up until her brother and Skippy were killed, she had been passionately pacifist. She had performed anti-war sketches at the gates of military bases. She still knew that war was wrong. But now it was more complex. Her feelings were mixed and conflicting. Were there times when it was necessary to fight to prevent a greater injustice? she questioned.

Mark had been so sure of this before he went and she had been envious of his straightforward conviction. Colin and Skippy, Jo knew, had just gone because they had been sent. Their motivation had been simple loyalty to their mates, wanting to do their best and not let anyone down. But Mark had seen it as standing up to the Junta, the playground bullies. And, Jo reflected, he had had experience of bullies, not just in the playground but in his own home. Again she looked around for him, hoping that he was finding some solace from having old shipmates there. Soon they were streaming out again into the mellow afternoon sunshine and exchanging quiet greetings with those around. The captain and padre who had visited them at the time of Colin's death sought them out and shook their hands.

Afterwards, Jo asked, 'Would you like to come back to the flat for a cup of tea, Dad?'

Jack looked at Pearl for guidance, but her aunt shook her head. She looked flushed and ill at ease. 'No, I'd rather just head home,' she said, sounding breathless.

Jo put out a hand. 'Are you sure you're all right, Auntie Pearl?'

Pearl brushed off her concern. 'I'm fine. I just need to get me feet up for a bit.'

Jo looked at her father, but he did not seem aware of her aunt's discomfort. 'Perhaps you're coming down with something?' Jo puzzled.

'No, I'm not,' Pearl said in irritation. 'Don't fuss.'

'Well, I'll come back with you then,' Jo insisted.

'There's no need,' Pearl began.

'Please,' Jo said. 'I'd rather spend the rest of the day with you both.'

★ ★ ★

Mark had intended to go to the service. He had set out in his naval uniform, encouraged by the thought of seeing Andy and some of the other survivors of his old ship. He was to meet Brenda and his parents at the Metro station and they would travel into the city together. He had just gone out to buy a newspaper. Passing the Coach and Eight as it was opening, he went in knowing it would be quiet. Just one for Dutch courage, he told himself.

Three drinks later he left and wandered down to the riverside. He thought about going to see Ivy. But he had not spoken to his grandmother since her shocking revelations about his real grandfather, a Yemeni sailor he had never heard about. So the mystery was solved. His dark skin had nothing to do with his mother's affair – his blackness had come from his *father*! Mark had been stunned by the news. He was not upset by it, for in a strange way it was a relief to know why he looked the way he did.

But he had been furious with Ivy. He had bawled and shouted at her and picked up the photograph of himself in uniform and smashed it in the fireplace. How could she have let him suffer all his childhood from his father's prejudice and abuse knowing what she did? he had accused.

'All me life I've been made to feel different and not known why!' he had cried. 'And all the time you knew! You let me mam take the blame. It could've just as easily been Gordon who looked different, but you let me brother pick on me too. You've ruined all our lives, you cowardly old bitch!'

Ivy had sobbed hysterically. 'I knew I should have kept it to myself, but she said I had to tell you! Now it's just made things ten times worse!'

323

'Who said?' Mark had asked in fury. 'Who else have you been blabbing this story to before you told me?'

'Jo,' croaked Ivy.

Mark had felt humiliation flood over him at the thought of Ivy confiding in Jo. Her of all people! Try as he might to rid his world of her, he could not. Now she had another hold over him, this explosive knowledge about his family.

'How long has she known?' Mark demanded, shaking his grandmother roughly.

'After you sailed for the Falklands,' Ivy wept.

All this time Jo had known about his past and yet said nothing. She could have written to him on Ivy's behalf. But all she had sent was an almost blank postcard with a begrudging 'good luck', he thought bitterly. He imagined Jo discussing him with that boyfriend who looked old enough to be her father. He would be an interesting case for their dinner parties, the Geordie with an Arab grandfather who went to fight for Britain, just like Hassan had done. Poor old Mark, discriminated against just like his foreign grandfather, having to prove himself more British than the British. The thought of their patronising pity was just as bad as the callous remarks of the casually racist. 'He looks more like an Argie than the Argies, that one!' he had heard it said by onlookers in Plymouth and seamen in Ascension Island. Well, he did not want Jo's pity or the curiosity of her middle-class friends.

Mark had stumbled out into the night and spent it curled up on the railway embankment under a hedge, his mind in turmoil. Now he was too ashamed to face his grandmother after all the vile things he had said to her. She had begged him not to tell his father yet, but he felt armed with a new weapon against his family and one day he would use it, he determined.

There was still time for another drink before catching the train, and he needed to numb himself to the ordeal ahead. For as the time drew nearer, the thought of seeing old comrades and of being packed in close to all those people in the cathedral made his heart hammer and his palms sweat. He needed to get away from menacing faces on the street who were staring at him as if he were the enemy. Mark hobbled back to the pub and stayed there all afternoon. At one point he vaguely remembered Ted trying to get him to go home, and eventually the landlord must have rung Brenda. Suddenly all his family were there, dressed in their best clothes, shouting at him. Even Gordon had taken the time off to attend the service.

'You're a bloody disgrace!' Matty fumed. 'We were stood on the platform an hour.'

'I checked in here, but Ted said you'd left ages ago,' Gordon added.

Mark grinned. 'I came back, didn't I?'

'We had to go without you,' Norma said in agitation. 'Your father said we should.'

'You missed all the lads from the ship,' Brenda said impatiently. 'People were asking for you and we had to pretend you weren't well.'

Mark laughed mirthlessly. 'Pretend! You wouldn't have to do that, would you?'

Matty cuffed his head. 'You've no respect for anyone – not even your old comrades. Call yourself a hero!'

Mark's temper flared at once. He shoved his father back. 'I've never called m'self a hero. It's you lot who've pushed that on to me!' Gordon tried to steady him, but Mark flung him away too.

Brenda joined in angrily. 'Mark! Stop showing yourself up.'

He turned on her. 'Sorry to be such a disappointment to you all, but I didn't do anything special – I just survived. The heroes are the dead ones – sorry I messed that up for you.'

Norma stretched out a hand. 'Don't do this,' she pleaded in tears. 'You *were* brave. Why are you punishing yourself?'

But Matty said with contempt, 'Let the little beggar stew in his own misery. We've done all we can for him.'

'No,' Norma quavered, 'we're not going to turn our backs on him, he needs help. Come on, pet,' she coaxed, 'come home.'

But this seemed to annoy Matty more. 'Don't pander to him – you always were too soft on him. That's why he's gone to pieces now. Look at all those tough lads at the service – none of them were in the state he's in and they've all come through as much or worse! Why does everyone else's son cope with the war except for this one!'

Mark lunged at him and grabbed his jacket. 'And what do you know about war? From *Boys' Own* comics?' he ridiculed.

'Let's go home,' Brenda urged. Mark threw off her hold.

'No, I want to hear him. What gives you the right to sneer at me, eh?' he demanded of his father.

Matty flushed and pushed him back. 'The Duggans have a proud history of fighting for their country. I never had the opportunity – but I would have gone like a shot and not whinged about it afterwards. No Duggan ever cracked up like you have. You're—'

'Go on, say it,' Mark goaded. 'I'm not really a Duggan?'

'Well, look at you!' Matty cried.

Norma sobbed, 'Stop it, both of you. He's your son, Matty, whether you like it or not!'

'You're both right,' Mark said, glaring at his father with savage triumph. 'I'm not a Duggan – but I *am* your son.'

'What you talking about?' Matty barked.

'You're not a Duggan either! You're just a pathetic bully—'

Matty seized hold of Mark and pushed him up against the bar. Ted hovered behind, wondering whether to call the police. 'Steady, lads,' he pleaded, 'I should have closed ages ago.' But everyone ignored him.

'Don't you bad-mouth me!' Matty shouted.

'You're not a Duggan,' Mark repeated with a savage smile. 'None of us are. You're the son of an Arab sailor. All these years you've blamed Mam for the colour of me skin, but I got it from you all along.'

'Of all the bloody lies!' Matty cursed, and knocked him to the ground. Gordon leapt to intervene.

'Leave him alone, Dad,' he ordered, coming between them and fending Matty off.

Brenda stood and stared, but Norma went to help Gordon haul Mark to his feet. 'What do you mean? What Arab sailor?' she asked.

'He's lying! It's an insult!' Matty blustered.

'Ask Nana, she told me everything,' Mark said, his head reeling. 'She married a Yemeni before Duggan.' He glared at his father. 'So don't you ever look down on me again. And don't you lift another finger against Mam, or I'll kill you. 'Cos it wouldn't bother me if they lock me away for murder. I've done plenty of that already.'

Mark felt nauseous with drink and anger. He turned and staggered towards the door, leaving them staring after him in disbelief. He was vaguely aware of his father ranting behind him.

'You're not coming back to my house! Do you hear? You're out for good this time!'

Mark did not care. He felt light-headed at having told the secret. Somehow the power of it had lessened by its telling. Fear of his father had been diminished too. Never again would Matty be able to dominate, hurt or undermine him in the way he had in the past. He was free of him, Mark thought as he stumbled out into the glare of daylight and fled.

Chapter Twenty-seven

Jo was making paella in her father's kitchen while he watched the evening news with Pearl. She was worried about her aunt's tired tetchiness and had rung Alan to say she was going to stay the night. She was determined to get to the bottom of what was bothering Pearl, for her father did not seem to notice there was something wrong. She would make her go and see the doctor if necessary. Jo would not contemplate how her father would cope if Pearl were ill, he relied on her so completely these days.

As she stirred in the rice, the doorbell rang. Nobody moved to answer it. It rang again. Jo turned down the gas ring and dashed across the sitting room with a look of annoyance. But Pearl had fallen asleep and her father was staring at the local news coverage about the service.

She opened the door to see Mark standing there. He was dressed in naval uniform, but was dishevelled and reeking of beer. His look was startled, then hostile.

'I didn't think you'd be here,' he said. 'I'll come back another—'

'Did you want to see Dad?' she interrupted, not wanting an argument. 'He's here. Come in,' she insisted, reaching out to stop him going. 'It might cheer him up to see you.'

Jo smothered her resentment that her father seemed

to find more comfort in seeing Colin's old friend than he did in her. She knew from Pearl that Mark often came round to see Jack. They would sit and play cards or read newspapers, saying very little. 'They don't even talk about Colin,' Pearl had said in bafflement. 'Still, if that's what your father wants . . .'

Mark's look was wary, but he nodded and stepped inside. Jack brightened to see him.

'Memorial service is on,' he said, indicating for Mark to sit down. Pearl stirred as he did so, squinting at the visitor in confusion.

She put out a hand to him. 'We didn't see you there, pet. Did you meet up with some of your mates? Looks like you did,' she said pointedly, taking in his bleary-eyed appearance.

Mark hung his head. 'I didn't go,' he answered.

'Why not?' Jo asked at once. 'It was wonderful. I kept thinking how it would be helping you – being with the other lads, all the support.'

'Well, I wasn't there!' he snapped. 'I couldn't face— Oh, what's the point of it all? It doesn't bring Colin or Skippy back, does it?'

'But what about the others? You've got other mates who are still alive,' Jo reminded him.

'How can they be me mates when I don't know if I'll ever go back on board a ship again?' Mark said angrily.

'You've got to give yourself time,' Pearl said wearily. 'You'll not have those injuries for ever.'

Mark gave a look of desperation. He touched his head. 'But what about up here?' he asked. 'It's what's up here that's stopping me going back,' he admitted. They all looked at him in silence for a moment, not knowing what to say. Jo was aware this might be the first time Mark had talked about having a problem.

'You need to get help,' she said quietly. 'Talk to someone professional.'

He shot her a hostile look. 'Is that what you said to Ivy when you got her to spill the beans about me grandad?' he asked savagely. 'Interfering in other people's business, thinking you're doing them a favour. Well, you haven't. Now all the family knows, and me Dad's chucked me out for good. I'm not even speaking to Ivy – I said some terrible things . . .'

He covered his harrowed face with his scarred hands, the euphoria of half an hour ago having dissolved into depression. Pearl and Jack looked at Jo for an explanation.

'What have you done, Joanne?' Jack demanded.

'Nothing!' she defended herself. 'I was just there for Ivy when she needed someone to talk to. I never forced her to say anything – she wanted to. For years she bottled up a secret about Matty's father, and it was destroying her. I'm glad it's out and that all your family know. If I interfered at all it was to encourage her to tell *you*, Mark, because I thought it would help you come to terms with who you are. You had a right to know.'

'Know what?' Pearl asked.

'Tell them, Mark,' Jo urged.

'Why don't you?' he said with a resentful glance. 'You're the psychologist.'

Jo got a whiff of burning from the kitchen. 'Oh, hell, the tea!' She leapt up. 'It's your story, Mark, you tell them.' She left the room, wondering if it had been right after all for Ivy to tell Mark about his grandfather. Mark seemed so angry about it all. Listening from the kitchen she could hear him begin to speak about Ivy and Hassan in a faltering, embarrassed way. Jo salvaged the meal and busied herself until she heard him finish. Then she carried a tray of cutlery and plates into the room.

Jack broke the silence first. 'Well, you come from a line of old salts then, don't you? The sea's well and truly in your blood.'

Mark smiled for the first time. 'Aye, I suppose it is.'

Then Jo caught sight of Pearl's tear-stained face and stopped. She had never seen such an expression on her aunt's face before. Pearl looked consumed with resentment. Jo waited for her to say something comforting and encouraging, but she just sat there, struggling with some deep emotion.

'Mind you,' Jack went on, 'I'm one for letting sleeping dogs lie – not like Jo. I'm not sure dragging up the past doesn't do more harm than good.'

Jo turned on him in annoyance. 'Don't you think Mark had a right to know about his real grandad?'

Jack waved a hand at her. 'You and your rights! Look where it's got him. All his family have fallen out with him just when they'd got back together again. I can't imagine Ivy's any happier now with her family at each other's throats over it. Sometimes it's better to protect people from the truth – suffer in silence.'

Suddenly Pearl cried out, 'Aye, that's always been your way, hasn't it, Jack? Covering up and pretending! Going through life like some suffering martyr! But it's not for any noble reason that people keep secrets – it's usually to protect themselves, not the innocent ones.'

They all gawped at Pearl. Her face was livid and tear-streaked, and her body trembled. Jo put down the tray and rushed over to her.

'Auntie Pearl, don't upset yourself.'

But Pearl ignored her niece and turned to Mark. 'Tell me what you think. You've done nothing but criticise our Joanne for interfering, but what do you think now that you know?' Mark looked taken aback and Pearl went on before he could answer. 'Your real grandfather sounds a grand man to me, and I admire Ivy for having the courage to stand up to her mother and marry him. They didn't have long together, but I bet she doesn't regret one short minute of it – because they loved each other. Matty was born out of love – it doesn't matter two hoots what colour his father's skin was. And you should be proud of your grandfather – he stood up for his rights and his community and he loved your grand-mother. And why do you think you're so special to Ivy? You don't just remind her of her first husband because you look like him. I bet it's because she can see the potential in you to be as great a man as Hassan was. So do you wish you'd never known about him, or are you glad of the chance to know about your real past? Because it's thanks to Jo that you do.'

Jo gawped at her, and Mark looked stunned by the outburst.

'Leave the lad alone,' Jack remonstrated.

'Go on, tell us!' Pearl insisted.

Mark was visibly shaken. He looked at Jo and Jack and then back at Pearl. 'Aye,' he answered hoarsely. 'I'm glad I know – even for all the upset it's caused. I am proud of me grandad – very proud,' he said fiercely. 'I'm just angry at Nana for not telling me years ago.'

Pearl looked triumphant. 'There!' She rounded on Jack. 'That's what secrets do, they spread into other people's lives like a poison.'

'Why you shouting at me?' Jack asked.

'You know why,' she answered. 'You damn well know!'

His face went ashen. 'That's enough, Pearl,' he warned.

'It's time, Jack,' she insisted. 'It's time to come clean about your past – *our* past.'

'Stop it,' he growled, 'don't say any more. You always promised—'

'I don't care what I promised!' she snapped. 'I haven't anything to lose any more. Colin's gone. Jo's got her own life with Alan and you just sit here like a zombie who's only interested in the dead! Well, I've had enough of it! I drag myself down here every day wondering why I bother, wondering when you're ever going to notice. And you know what? I've finally realised you're never going to.'

'Notice what?' Jo asked, seeing how her father was dumbstruck.

'That I'm getting old – past it!'

'No you're not,' Jo began.

'Yes I am!' Pearl cried. 'I'm forty-eight and I've got to have a hysterectomy.'

'Oh, Auntie Pearl!' Jo flung her arms around her aunt. 'I'm sorry. I knew there was something wrong. I should've noticed sooner.'

Jack found his voice. 'Why didn't you say anything?' he demanded. 'I didn't even know you'd been to the doctor's.'

'No, you never notice anything where I'm concerned,' Pearl quavered.

'That's not true.' Jack flushed. 'It's not my fault if you keep me in the dark about things. You should've told me. When is it happening? What's wrong with you?' he asked in fear.

'It's not life-threatening, if that's what you mean,' Pearl said, her fierce eyes filling with tears.

'Thank God for small mercies,' Jack breathed.

'What then, Auntie Pearl?' Jo asked.

'Fibroids. Non-malignant, they think.'

'That's good then, isn't it?' Jack said with relief.

Pearl looked at him in fury. 'Good? They're going to rip out my womb!'

Jack turned puce with embarrassment. 'But it's not as if . . .' he floundered.

'Say it, Jack,' she hissed. 'A woman of my age has no use for that any more. You have no idea what it means to me, do you? That I'll only feel half a woman. What do you care?' Pearl accused. 'It doesn't bother you that I'll never be able to have my own bairns – as long as I've brought up yours!'

'I didn't know you wanted bairns,' Jack protested. 'I wouldn't have stood in the way if I'd thought there was someone else . . .'

'There wasn't anyone else!' Pearl cried. 'There was always just you, Jack. I've wasted me life on you. And to think of all these years I've stood by you after Gloria died, pretending she was such a wonderful wife and mother.'

'Don't,' Jack gasped. 'You've said enough.'

'Can't have anything said against your precious Gloria, can we?' Pearl said bitterly. 'How long are you going to let her memory rule you, Jack? A false memory an' all. It's blighted my life. I've always hoped that one day you'd face up to what happened and let us get on with living. But I can see that's never going to happen. Colin dying has shown me that. I thought it would bring us closer – I needed your comfort too. But I never got it! I've wasted my whole life waiting . . . !' She broke down sobbing.

Jo exchanged uncomprehending looks with Mark. 'What does she mean, Dad?' Jo asked tensely. 'What's all this about my mother?'

'She's just upset – she's not herself,' Jack stammered.

'Tell her, Jack,' Pearl sobbed. 'That's all I'm asking of you.'

Jack looked horrified. 'I can't, he whispered. 'Don't make me go over all that again.'

'Tell her, or I'll walk out that door and never come back,' Pearl threatened.

'Please, Dad,' Jo pleaded. She did not know what was happening between them, but Pearl had come to the end of her tether.

Suddenly Mark made a move. They had almost forgotten he was there. 'I think I should go.'

But Pearl put out a hand to stop him. 'No, you might as well hear it too. You've been brave enough to confide in us.'

'Aye,' Jack said at last, seeming to draw strength from Mark's presence. 'You're the nearest I've got to Colin. Please stay.'

Chapter Twenty-eight

1958

'I want Pearl to come with us,' Gloria insisted, her fair face twisted into a tired frown. Pearl thought how her sister seemed to be permanently tired and fraught these days, her life one of relentless domestic chores. Joanne was nearly one and crawling at speed, while Colin at two was walking and bumping into everything. Gloria complained constantly about Jack been away at sea and Pearl was growing resentful at her older sister's reliance on her to care for the babies or help with the mounds of washing. Yet again, she regretted Aunt Julia dying and depriving her of a modest independence. Gloria had seized the chance to move back in with Pearl, along with her expanding family.

'Aunt Julia's flat is bigger than ours and you can't afford the rent on your own. You're family and I'll not see you fending for yourself.' This was her older sister's way of telling her that she would keep an eye on her.

A year and another baby later, Pearl had been pressured into taking the boxroom, so that the second bedroom could be turned into a nursery for Gloria and Jack's three children. At least it was a small haven from her sister's demands, although three-year-old Joy now managed to open the door. But Joy lived up to her name, for she was a constant source of chatter and fun and even the harassed Gloria melted at her charm. Jack doted on his eldest child too. Now that he was back home for a month, he had suggested a trip to Blackpool to relieve the tension in the household, and Joy was squealing with excitement as he tickled her.

'And there'll be donkey rides and tram rides,' he promised, 'and as much ice-cream as you can eat. We'll go for the start of the illuminations – be back in time for Joanne's first birthday.'

'She's not going to know the difference if we don't,' Gloria said shortly. 'Why don't we leave her with Pearl and just take Colin and Joy? The baby's too young to know any difference.'

Jack looked scandalised. 'We can't do that. I hardly get to see her.'

'Well, that's not my fault!' Gloria snapped.

'We can't expect Pearl to spend her holiday looking after our Joanne.' Jack was adamant. Pearl listened, not wanting to intervene until she had to. It struck her how Gloria never referred to Joanne by name, as if she still did not accept her as one of the family. The third child had been unplanned and was resented by her sister as a burden they could have done without.

'Well, we can't manage all the bairns on our own – not with the amount of luggage we'll have to take on the train,' Gloria protested. 'If we can't leave the baby, I want Pearl to come with us.'

Jack hesitated, then said, 'That's up to her.'

They both looked at Pearl. She wanted to say no. It would do Gloria good to have to cope without her and to have some time with Jack and the children, as a proper

338

family. At times she felt like hired help, and then felt guilty for her ungrateful thoughts. Gloria had been more like a mother to her than a sister as they grew up and had always been a strong support for her until the pressures of young motherhood had reversed the situation.

'You will come, won't you?' Gloria pleaded.

'Auntie Pearl come too!' Joy chanted, slipping from her father's knee and rushing over to her aunt. 'See the donkeys!' She started doing donkey noises with Jack and falling in a giggling heap.

Pearl laughed. Perhaps she would meet someone on holiday who would help her escape from their claustrophobic household. 'All right, I'll come,' she relented, against her better judgement.

Gloria's face relaxed into a smile. She picked Joy off the floor and gave her a hug. 'That's grand, isn't it? Auntie Pearl is such a help.'

Then the baby began to fret and wail to be released from her pram out in the backyard, where she had been strapped in for a sleep. Gloria grimaced, her nerves frayed at the very sound of her crying.

'I'll go and fetch her,' Jack said quickly. 'We're all going to have a grand holiday, don't you worry.'

The train journey seemed to take for ever and tempers were short with the effort of trying to keep the children entertained and fed and nappies changed in the cramped compartment. Pearl felt sorry for the elderly couple who had to share it with them. 'Don't worry, the nightmare's nearly over!' she told them cheerfully as the train finally pulled into Blackpool.

They disembarked, Joy in a frenzy of excitement to catch her first glimpse of the beach. 'I want to go now!'

she cried, pulling on her mother's hand. Jack beckoned to a porter to come and help them with the luggage. Pearl stood holding Joanne, who was trying to wriggle out of her arms. It had been her suggestion to book a guesthouse that could provide a pram for the younger two. Colin climbed on to the trolley, thinking it had been brought over specially for him.

'You'll need a taxi for this lot,' said the porter at a glance, and led them off to find one. They squashed into the taxi, and soon the fraughtness of the journey dissolved into excitement as they drove through the resort.

'Look at the Tower, isn't it grand?' Jack exclaimed, holding Colin on his knee so he could see.

'There's the beach!' Joy squealed. 'Please can we go to the beach?'

'Soon, pet,' her mother promised, smiling for the first time that day. 'Tomorrow, it's the first thing we'll do.'

'No, now!' howled Joy, her nose pressed up against the window as they passed the bustling promenade and the crowded beach below.

'We could take a walk after tea,' Jack suggested, eager to placate his daughter.

'They'll need an early night after the journey,' Gloria snapped. Joy burst into tears of frustration.

Pearl sat in the front with Joanne in her lap, thankful to be removed from the argument in the back. A double-decker tram clanked past, packed with trippers, and there were stalls selling everything from spades to china ornaments. She looked out of the other window and gawped at the sights of the famous Golden Mile. It was one long ribbon of shops, attractions and hotels stretching into the distance in gaudy splendour.

'Wait till you see it lit up at night,' the driver said, seeing her amazement.

'I can't wait,' Pearl smiled. 'I'm dying to see a show or go dancing.'

'Charlie Drake's been popular this year,' he told her, 'and that young Eric Morecambe – he's even funnier, I reckon. There's plenty for the children too.' He nodded towards the Tower. 'They feed the fish at half past eleven at the aquarium, and there's the chimps' tea party in the zoo.'

As they trundled slowly through the traffic and hordes of pedestrians, Pearl received a stream of useful information about what to see. They passed Roberts' Oyster Rooms, and the North Pier, jutting out like a jewelled finger into the blue-grey sea. There were people everywhere.

'I've never seen so many folk in one place!' Pearl gasped.

'It's always packed for the switch-on,' the taxi driver grunted. 'The world and his mother come for the illuminations.'

An hour later they were installed in Mrs Hugo's neat boarding house in a quiet Edwardian terrace away from the grander hotels on the front. They were lucky to get anywhere this close to the attractions, Pearl realised. The landlady welcomed them warmly and fussed over the children, giving them the window seat in the cramped dining room, with Joanne perched in a wooden highchair looking on in astonishment. They were revived with ham salad and a pot of tea, but it was the cake stand full of scones and fairy cakes that made Joy's eyes widen in delight. Gloria was a good baker, but she never seemed to find the time any more, and they all tucked into the home-made fancies.

Fortified by the meal, Gloria relented and they bundled the two youngest into the pram and set off back to the front. The babies were asleep in minutes and Jack walked with Joy riding on his shoulders, calling out the sights she could see and giggling to be up so high. It took twenty minutes to walk to the North Pier and they wandered around until the sun dipped, taking in the sights of the merry-go-rounds and the smell of seafood and fish and chips. As Joy got her way and rode triumphantly in a gilded carriage behind a white horse, Pearl peered at the diners sitting in the windows of grand hotels, eating under glinting chandeliers.

'That could be you one day.' Jack winked, catching her look of longing. Pearl glanced away with a self-conscious smile.

'It just makes me realise that there's a lot out there in the world I've never seen,' she answered softly, rocking the pram, 'and I want to see it all.' She laughed. 'Maybe I'll go to sea like you.'

Jack grinned. 'It's a grand way to see the world, if that's what you want.'

They looked at each other for a moment and Pearl felt her heart skip a beat at the sight of his lively green eyes and slim, expressive face under the Brylcreemed black hair. In the glow of the sunset, the recent lines that marked his face did not show, and he looked younger than his thirty-two years. She remembered the first time she had met him, in the dance hall during Race Week, and how he had walked her back to Aunt Julia's. It had been the warmth of his smile and his bashful boyishness that had attracted her. But her aunt had been scandalised that she had slipped away from her friends and brought home a man at the tender age of nineteen.

'You're too young to be courting,' Julia told her censoriously, but Pearl had shrugged off the rebuke.

She thought Jack Elliot probably was too old for her, and she had no desire to 'settle down', so she discouraged Jack from calling for her again. There were plenty more where he came from, was Pearl's attitude. She had thought no more about the merchant seaman and danced with many young men on nights out with her friends to the Oxford in Newcastle. Several of them called to ask her out to the pictures or the coffee bars. Sometimes she went and sometimes she said she was washing her hair. If she could persuade them to take her to a variety show or a musical, then Pearl's interest in them lasted longer. Gloria was disapproving. She was eager to be courting, but, burdened with looking after an increasingly frail Aunt Julia, did not have the opportunity. She fretted over her sister's cavalier attitude to boys.

'No one'll want to settle down with you the way you treat them,' Gloria warned.

'Suits me,' Pearl would answer, maddening her sister with her lack of interest.

Then, to her surprise, Jack called on his next leave when she was out at work. By the time she got home, Gloria had made him stay to tea and paid him so much attention, that it was she whom he asked out that Saturday. Pearl pretended not to mind, especially when her sister's courtship developed quickly and she became engaged to Jack before he went back to sea. She could see how happy he made Gloria, and how her sister made him feel special and cared for, so Pearl told herself she was glad for them both. Once they were married and starting a family, Pearl had seen much less of her sister, and Jack was often away. For a while she continued her active social life, despite the extra demands of having to look after Aunt Julia more and more. She would get up early and prepare her aunt's meals and call home in her lunch hour. Sometimes Gloria would pop in and check on Julia during the day, but it was Pearl's job to put her frail aunt to bed. Sometimes she would pay a neighbour to sit with Julia while she went dancing, until Gloria found out.

'You selfish little madam!' her sister scolded. 'How could you leave Aunt with a stranger?'

'Not a stranger,' Pearl protested, 'a good neighbour. Besides, Mrs Potts can do with a few extra pennies, she's happy to help out.'

'It's your responsibility,' Gloria declared, 'not Mrs Potts's. That's just typical of you to think of yourself all the time. You and your Elvis Presley records and your obsession with dancing and theatres!'

'If you were so concerned with Aunt then you would have stopped here instead of rushing into marriage with Jack,' Pearl retaliated. 'So don't criticise me for the way I run this household. You moved out – I'll do things as I see fit!'

'That's not fair!' Gloria said tearfully. 'You know I'd do more, but I've Joy to cope with and a second bairn on the way.' She dissolved into tears. 'I find it so hard on me own . . . !'

Pearl's indignation had subsided quickly and she went to comfort her sister. It was then that it struck her that her sister might not be as happy as she professed to the outside world. She went out little, except to the shops, and did not seem to have made friends among her new neighbours.

'You could bring the bairns round here more often,' Pearl had said kindly, 'and stop over here with me when you want.'

After that, Pearl's nights out had dwindled and she

had begun to lose contact with her partying friends. Gloria came over more and more frequently and Pearl found herself coping with them all until Jack came back on leave and they became a family again for a short happy spell. Pearl would feel relief at having the place to herself once more and was determined to have a strong word with Jack about Gloria's gloomy moods. Then Aunt Julia had died and Pearl had weakly agreed to let Gloria and family move in permanently with her. But with the coming of the third baby, her sister's black moods had increased.

'It's just the baby blues,' Jack had said, falsely hearty. 'It's expected for a bit.'

'What's your name, Dr Spock?' Pearl had snorted.

Jack had escaped to sea again and gradually Pearl's life had become one of carer to them all. She found it increasingly hard to manage the household as well as her job at the shipyard office. Things, she knew, would have to change.

Looking now at Jack in the Blackpool sunset and catching something dangerous in his eyes, Pearl determined she was going to do something radical when they got home. She was frightened by the sudden feelings he stirred in her that she had not realised were still there. Suddenly she found herself saying, 'Aye, I do want to see the world. I've been thinking of getting a stewarding job on one of them cruise ships. They've been advertising in the papers for single lasses.'

Jack gawped at her and Pearl realised he thought she was joking. 'Cleaning out the "heads" for rich Americans, you mean?' he smirked.

'If that'll get me on a ship, then yes,' Pearl said indignantly. 'I'll wipe their bottoms an' all!'

Jack laughed incredulously and repeated the joke to

Gloria, who had just walked over with Joy in her arms. But Gloria's face crumpled as she looked at Pearl. 'That's not funny! You wouldn't go off and leave us, would you?'

Pearl looked in horror at her miserable sister and the look of confusion on Joy's round, glowing face. She realised that she was going to be trapped for ever in this situation if she did not break out soon. She steeled herself to reply. 'I've got me own life to lead. I'm serious about going away.'

It spoilt the end of the evening, and they trudged back to the guest house without saying much at all. But the next day it was as if nothing had been said. Mrs Hugo gave them a hearty cooked breakfast and they set out into the early September sunshine for the beach with spirits revived and Joy filling the awkwardness between the adults with her constant chatter.

They spent the morning on the beach, riding donkeys and paddling in the sea, until it was time to go back to the boarding house for dinner. Mrs Hugo filled them full of oxtail soup, steak and kidney pie, potatoes and cabbage, followed by apple crumble and custard. Afterwards Pearl felt so sleepy that she went for a lie-down while the others sallied out again to the amusements of the Pleasure Beach. By evening, Pearl was revived and raring to dance.

'I couldn't drag myself out again if you paid me,' Gloria announced. 'I'm going to bed with the bairns. They wake that early in a strange place.'

Pearl was disappointed. 'Haway, Gloria, it'll do you good to get out without the bairns. Mrs Hugo said she'd keep an eye on them for an hour or two. You could have a lie-down for an hour first.'

'I don't like dancing much – never have done,' her sister answered irritably. 'Jack'll take you if you're that keen to go out. Won't you, Jack?'

Jack looked embarrassed to be caught between the two of them. 'Well, if that's what you both want . . .'

Pearl felt uneasy at the suggestion, but she could hardly go on her own. Maybe just this once it would be all right, until she made friends with some of the young women staying in the guest houses round about and could go dancing in a group.

That night, they were both awkward with each other to begin with, walking stiffly apart and saying little, as if they hardly knew each other.

'You don't need to stop all evening,' Pearl said hastily as they approached the Tower. She was longing to see the newly refurbished Ballroom, which had been damaged by fire three seasons before.

Jack gave her a quizzical look. 'I'll not stand in the way of the rush of young lads to dance with you, if that's what you mean.'

Pearl blushed and laughed. 'No, I didn't mean that! But perhaps you shouldn't leave Gloria on her own for too long.'

Jack glanced away. 'She'll be asleep by now. She'll not notice if I'm there or not.'

They said no more about Gloria, and soon Pearl's attention was transfixed by the glories of the Tower Ballroom. Its vast ornate golden ceiling and balconies glittered under sparkling chandeliers and the hall pulsated to the sounds of the wurlitzer and the band. The Ballroom floor was already packed with dancers as Jack showed her to a seat and went off in search of drinks. Pearl was still gawping at the painted, gilded ceiling and the magnificent stage when he returned. Intoxicated by the music, she soon had him twirling across the floor. It was the most romantic setting she

347

had ever seen and she felt a twinge of guilt that she should be sharing it with her sister's husband. But the music was so good that she did not want to stop dancing and Jack seemed happy to be holding her in his arms.

It was harmless fun, Pearl told herself, but the evening sped by and neither of them mentioned again about going home early to be with Gloria. When they finally emerged from the dance, Jack pulled at his tie and undid his collar.

'I feel hungry now,' he said, his face glistening and hair ruffled. 'Fancy fish and chips?'

Pearl agreed, and they bought fish suppers and carried them to a bench along the promenade. The conversation was light-hearted, until Pearl said, 'I've really enjoyed myself tonight. I can't remember the last time I had that much of a laugh.'

'Me neither,' Jack said softly, and looked at her searchingly. 'It made me think of that night we first met, at the dance in Wallsend. Do you remember?'

'Aye, I do,' Pearl answered, feeling her heart begin to hammer.

He touched her cheek with his hand, and when she did not draw away, he leaned towards her and kissed her gently on the lips. Pearl felt light-headed and her pulse raced.

'Oh, Jack,' she whispered, 'we shouldn't . . .' But she let him kiss her again, this time more urgently. When they stopped, he was breathing hard.

'I knew it then and I know it now,' he said. 'I married the wrong sister.'

The words were out before Pearl could stop him saying them. They hung between them, explosively.

'You don't mean that.' Pearl tried to laugh it off.

Jack clutched her shoulder. 'I do,' he rasped. 'I think

it every time I look at you. Me and Gloria aren't happy together, you must know that. She hates me being at sea and she hates me being at home. She blames me for Joanne. She only ever wanted two bairns, but you can't always plan it that way, can you?'

Pearl blushed at his words. 'She's under a lot of strain at the moment,' she tried to defend her sister. 'It'll get easier as the bairns grow. You'll be close again.'

'We've never been close,' Jack declared. 'We just both wanted to be wed to someone more than staying single. And we both wanted bairns.'

Pearl grew agitated. 'Well, you've got them – and you've got a responsibility towards them no matter what you and Gloria think of each other right now.' She drew away from him and the grip of his hand on her shoulder. 'They're lovely bairns, Jack. Don't spoil things for them. You're lucky to have them – and so's Gloria. You have to make her see that too.'

Pearl stood up and wrapped the remains of her half-eaten chips in the newspaper, then walked quickly to a nearby bin. She heard Jack follow her.

'I'm sorry,' he said contritely. 'I must've had too much to drink. I should never have said such things to you. Will you forgive me?'

'Aye, of course,' Pearl smiled, steeling herself against the turmoil of feelings inside that cried out for him to kiss her again. 'I know you didn't mean it – just the beer talking.'

'Aye, that's right,' Jack said hastily, throwing his rubbish into the bin too. 'You'll not say anything to Gloria?'

Pearl gave him a sharp look. 'Of course not. Neither of us meant anything by it. Let's just forget it, Jack.' She turned and walked on briskly, and hardly another word was spoken between them all the way home. By the time they reached Mrs Hugo's, Pearl was overwhelmed with regret at having been so foolish as to kiss Jack, and she sensed he felt the same.

The next morning they both avoided looking at each other and Pearl kept out of the way for a day, taking herself off to look round Louis Tussaud's waxworks. For a while she was diverted by the amazing likenesses to famous figures such as Attlee and Eisenhower, and thought how Joy would love the depictions of Snow White and Little Miss Muffet. She determined to take her niece there the next day. That evening they all went out for the switching-on ceremony and Pearl was relieved to see Jack being extra attentive to Gloria and the children. They spent a happy couple of hours taking trams up and down the promenade and gazing at the spectacular illuminated tableaux.

Joy clapped in wonder at Pantomime Land depicting fairy tales such as *Aladdin* and *Cinderella*. There was a beautiful scene of *Swan Lake*, with a ballerina illuminated among giant swans, and tableaux displaying the four seasons.

'Look! They're on holiday like us!' Joy cried at the scene of summer.

'Do you like being on holiday?' Jack asked her.

'Yes. I want to stay all the time,' Joy grinned. Gloria kissed her head affectionately.

'We'll come every year if that's what you want,' Jack announced impulsively.

Gloria flung him a look. 'Don't promise what you can't keep,' she reprimanded. But Joy was already throwing her arms round her father's neck in excitement.

'Yes, yes! Can we come again next week?' she cried.

'No, of course not,' Gloria answered.

'Auntie Pearl, you take me,' Joy demanded. 'I like you best.'

Pearl caught Gloria's dashed expression and quickly shook her head. 'No you don't. You'll have lots of grand holidays with your mam and dad in the future. I'll be off to sea, so I'll not be around.' She saw the child's face crumple. 'But I'll sail past Blackpool on me ship and give you a wave,' she added with a quick kiss. But Joy cried anyway, while Gloria sank into one of her bad moods, and Pearl realised she had spoiled things yet again.

After that night, Pearl contrived to go out in the evenings with a widow and her daughter from the same guest house so as to keep out of the way. During the day, she would volunteer to take one of the children out for a walk and keep them entertained while Jack and Gloria had the other two. Invariably she would be left with Joanne, but she enjoyed spoiling the lively baby with her riot of auburn curls and ready toothless grin.

Finally, towards the end of the week, she persuaded Gloria and Jack to let her babysit while they had a night out at a show. Once the children were in bed, Pearl played cards with Mrs Hugo and some of the other guests in the downstairs lounge. She went to bed before her sister and brother-in-law returned, and in the morning Gloria seemed in better spirits and decreed they would spend their last full day on the beach with the children.

'We'll take a picnic today,' she told Mrs Hugo, who packed them up some salmon paste sandwiches, cake and bananas, with a flask of tea.

It was a gloriously sunny day and the beach was packed with trippers enjoying the last of the summer. Joy was in particularly high spirits at the thought of a day on the sands armed with a special red metal bucket and spade that her father had bought her. Gloria insisted that she keep her bonnet on so as not to burn in the sun, but apart from that was content to let her dig in the sand with Jack and splash in the sea. As the tide began to turn and people were packed even more tightly together on the shrinking beach, Jack announced that he would take Joy to see the Punch and Judy show for the last time. She had been badgering him all day.

Colin and Joanne had fallen asleep in the pram after the picnic and Gloria was feeling drowsy. 'You take Joy,' she yawned at Jack. 'I'll have a nap.'

'Do you want to come?' Jack asked Pearl. There was something in his eyes that pleaded with her to say yes, but Pearl distrusted such a look. She did not want to be left alone with him again and give either of them a chance to weaken.

'No, I'll keep an eye on the babies,' she said, glancing away from his frustrated expression.

'Watch out for the tide,' was the last thing Gloria said, calling after them. 'And make sure she keeps her bonnet on!'

Pearl must have dozed off too, for she woke to find Jack standing over her, his shadow blocking the sun.

'What time is it?' she asked, disorientated for a moment.

'I've only been gone ten minutes,' he laughed quietly. 'Joy forgot her spade. Come back with me – I want to talk.' Pearl glanced over to see that Gloria was asleep. She sat up and squinted at the crowded beach.

'Where's Joy?' she asked.

'Sitting watching Punch,' Jack assured her, pointing over towards the pier arches. 'I told her I was coming for the spade.' He reached down and grabbed her hand, trying to pull her up. 'Haway, Pearl, we need to talk,' he said urgently. 'You're not enjoying this any more than I am, are you?'

Pearl felt her heart beating rapidly at his touch. 'Not here, Jack. We can't talk here,' she whispered nervously.

'It's driving me crackers having you around and not being able to . . .' He broke off, giving her a desperate look.

'Please don't say something you'll regret later,' Pearl urged, glancing anxiously at her sleeping sister once again.

'I won't regret it – I don't regret what happened the other night,' Jack whispered recklessly, trying to pull her nearer. 'I don't think you minded either. Tell me you feel the same!'

Pearl knew that if she kept on looking into his fierce green eyes she would weaken and confess her love for him. But that would cause untold havoc and she could not do that to Gloria and the children.

'No, I don't,' she forced herself to say. 'I don't feel anything for you. The other night meant nothing – I just enjoyed the dancing, that's all.'

She saw the wounded look in his eyes and the hardening of his mouth in disappointment. But he did not leave go of her and Pearl feared he did not believe her words.

At that moment, Gloria opened her eyes and saw them. She stared at her husband gripping her sister, Pearl half-raised off the sand. They looked at her guiltily. For a long moment she said nothing. Jack tried to explain.

'Joy wants Pearl to make a sand castle with her,' he gabbled. 'I've come back for the spade – and Auntie Pearl.'

It suddenly occurred to Pearl that he might have deliberately left the spade in order to have an excuse to come back for her. Please don't let that be true! she thought. But seeing Gloria's distrustful look, she wondered if such suspicions were racing through her sister's mind.

'Where is she?' Gloria demanded, looking round. 'Where's Joy?'

'Over there, at the Punch and Judy show,' Jack repeated, a defensive edge to his voice. 'She knows not to wander off.'

In an instant, Gloria was on her feet. 'She doesn't know anything of the sort! She's still a baby! Jack, how could you leave her alone in this crowd?' She flung an accusing look at Pearl too.

Pearl felt suddenly ashamed that she had only given Joy a glancing thought these past minutes. She had taken Jack's word for it that the small girl would be safe, but only because she could think of little else but herself and Jack.

'Sorry, Gloria . . .' she began, but her sister's glare silenced her. Without a glance at the other two children, Gloria hurried off into the crowd, hopping in bare feet along the sand, weaving in and out of deckchairs and legs and playing children.

Pearl and Jack exchanged guilty looks, and then Pearl said, 'I'll keep an eye on the babies, you go with her.' Jack sprang after Gloria without another word.

It seemed an eternity waiting by the pram and the ruffled towels. Pearl smoked one of Gloria's cigarettes, even though she disliked the taste. Ten minutes passed, then twenty, but no one returned. They could easily have walked to the Punch and Judy show and back again several times, but neither parent appeared to reassure her. Colin woke up and was instantly wanting to explore. He threw a tantrum when Pearl tried to restrain him and she kept him distracted with Joy's forgotten spade.

'Wait till Mammy gets back,' Pearl said, pulling him back yet again. Colin burst into tears.

'Mammy! Mammy!' he wailed. This woke Joanne, who began to struggle to be out of the pram too.

Finally Jack came pushing his way back to their picnic spot. Pearl only had to take one look at his ashen face to know Joy was missing.

'I thought she might have found her way back here . . .' he gasped. 'Has she? Have you seen the bairn?'

Pearl shook her head. Behind them the tide was fast approaching and people were beginning to pack up and head on to the promenade. The donkeys were being led away.

'She wasn't where you left her?' Pearl whispered in fright. Jack shook his head, his face haggard.

'It'll be easier to find her once the crowds thin out,' Pearl attempted to reassure him.

'I'm going for the police,' Jack said, full of panic. 'Gloria's searching along by the pier.'

'Shall I start looking along the other way?' Pearl asked. 'She might have wandered off to see the donkeys.'

Jack looked torn. 'Aye – no – I don't know! Just stay where you are in case she looks for us here.' Then he was gone again.

Nearly an hour passed, the longest in Pearl's life. Eventually the incoming tide chased her off the beach with the fractious infants. Seizing towels and the half-eaten picnic, she tossed them into the pram and took refuge on the promenade. She bought ice-creams for the children and sat waiting on a bench, while Colin whined about wanting to see the chimps in the zoo. Finally Jack reappeared with an hysterical Gloria. Her sister was screaming and crying, almost incoherent with panic and anger.

'You should never have left her!' she yelled at Jack again and again, while a policeman tried to calm her.

Pearl saw Jack's harrowed look and knew that Gloria's words stung him with agonising guilt.

'We'll keep searching until we find her,' the constable assured them. 'I really think you should go back to your guest house and rest. We'll bring word as soon as we hear anything. Mr Elliot's given us all the details we need.'

'No! I can't just wait around there,' Gloria cried. 'I'm staying here.'

'But the other bairns . . .' Jack tried to reason. She looked at him with hatred.

'I can't think about them! Not while Joy's out there lost and looking for me – she'll be so frightened!'

'Let me take the babies back to Mrs Hugo's,' Pearl said gently. 'You and Gloria can wait at the police station for news. Don't worry about Colin and Joanne.'

She saw Jack's eyes glint with tears as he put out a hand to touch her. 'Ta, Pearl,' he said hoarsely. But Gloria just gave them an accusing look, as if they had somehow contrived the terrible situation between them. Pearl hastily pushed the fretful younger children away in the pram, glancing back only once to see Gloria hurrying ahead of Jack beside the policeman.

Mrs Hugo and the other guests were full of concern when they heard of Joy's disappearance. 'Someone will have found her,' the landlady said. 'She can't just have vanished.' But that thought made Pearl even more anxious. What sort of person took charge of a small child and did not deliver them straight to the police? she fretted. Maybe someone had watched and waited for a restless, inquisitive child like Joy to be left unguarded for a few moments. Joy was so friendly she would talk to or go with anyone who showed her kindness or promised her treats. Pearl was plagued with monstrous thoughts and felt wretched to think how Gloria and Jack must be suffering.

After tea, she put Colin and Joanne to bed. Once they were asleep she hurried down to the police station for news. On the way, she saw that the tide was now high and the beach completely submerged. What if Joy had wandered off under the pier with her bucket and got stuck on some sand bar with the incoming tide racing around her? Pearl agonised. Arriving at the station, she found Jack and Gloria waiting tensely, smoking in silence. When Gloria saw Pearl, she stubbed out her cigarette and got up.

'The bairns are asleep,' Pearl reassured her. But Gloria ignored her.

'I'm going out again,' she said shrilly. 'I can't bear this sitting around.' Pearl knew that what she really could not bear was to be near her or Jack.

'I'll come too,' Jack said.

'No!' Gloria shouted. 'I don't want you with me!'

When she had gone, Jack broke down. 'It's all my fault,' he whispered in turmoil.

'Don't say that,' Pearl protested.

'It's true,' he went on relentlessly. 'I left her – on purpose,' he said very low.

'Stop it, Jack!' Pearl said in alarm. 'Of course you didn't.'

'I wanted an excuse to come back and fetch you,' Jack said, his look agonised. 'I couldn't get you out of me head – all this week. I left my little lass on her own.' He looked at her in desolation. 'You know what the last thing she said to me was?' he almost sobbed. ' "Don't go, Daddy, stay and watch the funny man!" '

Pearl covered his mouth with her hand. 'Shush! She'll turn up,' she insisted. 'Don't think the worst.' But her mouth filled with bile at the thought that she had been the reason why Jack had left Joy alone, even for such a short time. She should have discouraged his feelings for her much sooner, she accused herself. Joy must be found! she thought desperately.

It grew dark. Pearl left Jack and went back to wait at Mrs Hugo's. Neither Jack nor Gloria came back that night. Pearl sat up, dozing and smoking in a chair, listening out for the front door. Joanne woke at six and was hungry for a bottle of milk. Soon afterwards Colin was awake and demanding his mother.

'She'll come soon,' Pearl tried to comfort the perplexed little boy. 'Let's go and have breakfast.'

When neither parent arrived, Pearl busied herself packing their bags for the journey home. She did not know what else to do, and they were due to leave at noon. Eventually she bundled the children into the pram, unable to contain them any longer, and walked them down to the police station. The good weather had broken. The sky was a low blanket of grey cloud and the sea a choppy cauldron of foaming waves, crashing against the pier supports. It was hard to believe this was the same place as yesterday, when hot sun had roasted the beach and its hordes of holidaymakers. Today, fewer people braved the sands, though the promenade was full of trippers wrapped in coats against the threatening rain. Blackpool had an air of autumn in the brisk westerly wind.

Suddenly, deep down, Pearl had a dreadful feeling

that Joy would never be found. She tried to banish it, but when she reached the station the news was grim. Searches of the beach areas had begun again at first light, but no trace of Joy had been found. The police were widening their enquiries around the town, and coastguards were out combing a wide area.

When Colin spotted his mother he scrambled out of the pram and almost fell over himself to reach her. 'Mammy, mammy!' he whined, stumbling at her knees and clutching on. Gloria picked him up distractedly, but his boisterous clambering wearied her quickly.

'Come here, bonny lad,' Jack said, picking up his son and trying to divert him. 'Let's go and see if the nice bobby has a biscuit for you, eh?'

Pearl glanced at Joanne sitting contentedly in the pram, sucking her hand and gazing around in interest with her large green eyes, so like Jack's. She did not look remotely like her missing sister, and Gloria seemed to derive no comfort from having her younger daughter there. In fact the baby's wide-eyed placidness seemed to irritate her mother.

'There's no point you hanging around here with the baby,' Gloria said tersely. Pearl could see by her dark-ringed eyes that she was completely exhausted.

'Why don't you come back to Mrs Hugo's and lie down for a bit?' Pearl suggested. 'You're all done in.'

'Do you think I could get a wink of sleep while Joy's still out there?' Gloria cried. 'I'll not sleep again till they find her!'

'Well, come outside for some fresh air – stretch your legs,' Pearl replied.

Gloria gave her a helpless look. 'No, I must stay here in case any news comes in. I must be here for Joy when they find her.'

Jack returned and Pearl gave him a beseeching look. 'What do you want me to do with the bairns? The train goes in two hours.'

'I'm not going back without my lass!' Gloria said, her voice rising hysterically. 'You'll not make me!'

Jack said gently. 'No one's going to make you. We'll stay here in Blackpool till she's found,' he promised.

Pearl looked at Jack. 'I should be back at work on Monday,' she said quietly. 'Do you want me to stay?'

Jack gave her a longing look, but shook his head. 'No, you must go home. You've done all you can. I'll look after the bairns here.'

Pearl was struck by his words. He was taking responsibility for the younger children, knowing that Gloria was incapable in her present state. She looked sadly at her broken sister, wanting to put her arms about her but knowing she would be rebuffed. In Gloria's eyes, Pearl had betrayed her. Gloria knew that something had happened between her sister and Jack, and because of it, Joy had been left alone – lost, abducted or drowned. Gloria no longer trusted her and might never do so again.

So Pearl kissed the children briefly and said a stilted goodbye. 'You'll ring me if you hear . . . ?'

Jack nodded, his look following her as she moved towards the door. But he did not come out after her or attempt to speak to her alone.

Pearl rushed back to the guest house and took a quick farewell of Mrs Hugo. She could hardly speak and her last views of Blackpool were blurred by tears. Part of her could not wait for the train to pull away from the station, while another part felt she was dying at having to leave Jack and the children to fend without her. She tried to swallow her sobs as she sat staring out of the window, handkerchief jammed against her mouth.

Even after the seaside town had disappeared from sight, Pearl's mind was branded with images of the lively Joy. She saw her awestruck face raised in delight at the cascading lights of the laburnum trees along the illuminated carriageway. She remembered their trip to the waxworks and the grasp of her small hand tighten as she asked in excitement, 'Are those pirates real, Auntie Pearl?'

But most vivid of all was the sight of Joy hopping along the sand, hand in hand with Jack, turning with a broad smile to wave at them one last time . . .

Chapter Twenty-nine

Pearl could hardly bear the emptiness of the flat those first few days back on Tyneside. She was thankful to get back to work and busy herself in her job. Yet, strangely, she could not bring herself to tell anyone about the trauma of the holiday or that her niece was still missing. She bottled up her anxiety and talked to no one about it.

When Jack did not ring her, she called Mrs Hugo for news of the family.

'Sorry, chuck, nothing to tell,' the landlady said unhappily. 'There've been no sightings – and nothing found . . .' Her voice trailed away, and Pearl could picture the grim watching of the tides to see if any body or clothing had been washed up. 'But that means it's not definite she got taken out to sea. So there's still hope, isn't there?'

'Aye,' Pearl gulped, unconvinced. 'How – how's me sister?' she asked cautiously.

Mrs Hugo sighed. 'Not good, I'm sorry to say. Thin as a rake – won't eat enough to keep a mouse fed. Spends the days out looking and the nights sitting up smoking, waiting.'

Pearl gripped the receiver tighter and swallowed hard. 'And the children?'

Mrs Hugo's voice brightened. 'They're being very

good, bless them. Mr Elliot takes them out for a walk every day – keeps them occupied. He's a good father to them. I think they help take his mind off it all. They're out now – sorry you can't speak to them. But you'll ring back?'

Pearl felt her throat tighten. 'Just tell them I rang and was asking after them.' She was glad Jack was out, for she did not think she could speak to him without breaking down.

All through that week, and the next, Pearl went around in a twilight world of waiting and existing from day to day. She knew that by the end of the second week, Jack would have to come to some decision, for he was due to join his ship in a few days' time. But whenever she rang the guest house, he was never there.

Then, abruptly, without warning, two weeks after Pearl had returned home, Jack and Gloria arrived back with the two infants. Pearl got home from work to find them in the flat. Colin beetled over to greet her with one of his lungeing hugs and Joanne beamed at her in recognition and threw her arms about in excitement.

Jack looked at her warily. 'Gloria's lying down. The doctor's been and said she must have complete rest. I'm not going back to sea till she's on the mend,' he said in a dull, tired voice.

Pearl stood rooted to the floor, staring at him. 'You never rang,' she quavered. 'Does that mean . . . ?'

Jack's eyes looked empty of emotion. 'Nothing,' he said in desolation. 'They don't expect to find her now – not alive. Most probably a strong current pulled her right out to sea . . .'

Pearl groaned in horror and moved towards him, flinging out her arms to comfort him. He looked so bowed and beaten. 'I'm that sorry!' she cried.

But he did not respond to her embrace and held himself stiffly, not pushing her away, but not wanting her to touch him. She knew then that everything had changed between them in the two weeks apart. The way he spoke and looked at her – or rather, did not look at her – told her that his feelings for her had died along with his beloved daughter. She knew that the memory of his desire for her would always be tainted by that terrible afternoon on the beach and the endless, bitter searching for Joy. By loving Pearl, he had betrayed not only Gloria but, unintentionally, Joy. Pearl knew such thoughts were unfair, but she could do nothing to dispel them. She felt just as guilty.

Guilt seemed to hang over the whole flat during those next gloomy days. Pearl saw it eating into Jack like a disease. She felt it following her like a ghost when she went into Gloria's room to bring her something to eat. Her sister took the food meekly. She was strangely vacuous, all her energy spent. Her anger towards Jack and Pearl seemed to have vanished too, which just made Pearl feel more shamed. What Pearl only realised gradually was that Gloria had turned the blame inwards on herself.

'If only I'd taken her to watch Punch and Judy myself,' she fretted one day when Pearl had persuaded her to get up. She refused to go out for fear of people asking after Joy. Only Mrs Potts had been told of the tragedy, and they all colluded in a wall of silence. While there was no body to bury, they could still hope.

'Don't say that,' Pearl answered as she spoon-fed Joanne, thankful that Jack was out with Colin. He had taken the boy to watch the ferries down at the docks. 'You couldn't possibly have known what would happen – no one could.'

'It was just laziness not taking her myself,' Gloria continued as if Pearl had not spoken. 'If I hadn't felt so sleepy . . . ! But the baby always made me so tired, waking in the night!'

Pearl grew concerned at this train of thought. Gloria was twisting things round to blame Joanne. If anyone was innocent of the whole tragedy it was the baby. 'Joy disappearing had nothing to do with Joanne,' Pearl insisted.

'No?' Gloria questioned, her look straying back to the photograph of Joy in her hands. Her face suddenly crumpled. 'No,' she admitted, 'it was my fault. I let her down, my little pet. I should never have trusted her to anyone else. I'm her mother—' She broke into dry, racking sobs.

Pearl rushed to her and put her arms about her thin shoulders. 'Of course you are. You always will be,' she said gently. 'But you've got the other two to think of as well. They need their mother too.'

She had meant to comfort her sister, to show her she was still loved and needed by her other children, but it seemed to have the opposite effect. Gloria gave out a desolate cry like a wounded bird and clutched the photograph tighter.

'She's still out there somewhere,' she sobbed. 'I know it. I'll never believe she's gone until they find some proof.' She looked up at Pearl with wild eyes. 'Joy still needs me.'

Pearl coaxed her back to bed, seeing how the conversation was making her agitated. She thought her sister quite deluded. She did not believe that Joy was still alive and the sooner Gloria came to terms with this the better. Pearl was due back at work in ten minutes, but she did not like to leave her sister alone. Glancing outside, she saw the sun lighting up the coppery leaves of the horse chestnut across the road and was reminded of the false illuminated trees of Blackpool. She shuddered, suddenly longing to be out of the house.

'I've got to go now,' she told Gloria, plonking Joanne on the bedroom floor with some wooden bricks. 'Jack'll be back shortly. Will you be all right?' Gloria was sitting on the edge of the bed, staring at the wall. 'The baby's fed and changed,' Pearl added.

Gloria looked up and nodded. 'Time to be off,' she acknowledged.

'Aye,' Pearl said. 'I'll see you at teatime.'

She saw Joanne look round and grin. 'Da-da!' she gurgled, putting down the brick she had been chewing and stretching out her arms.

'Ta-ta, pet.' Pearl blew her a kiss. But when Joanne saw she was going, she pulled herself up on the bed-covers and tried to totter towards her. Pearl closed the door quickly behind her so the child could not escape. She heard Joanne wail in protest. But Pearl did not have time to placate her. Gloria would have to see to her daughter for once, Pearl determined. She would have to tell them soon that she had handed in her notice and signed up with an agency for a stewarding job. If all went to plan, in a month's time she would be going south to join a cruise ship. She felt her spirits lift at the thought.

After work, she detoured round the high street to buy sausages from the butcher's, and some cooking apples from the greengrocer to stew into a purée for the children. When she got home, she was startled to find Mrs Potts minding Joanne and a tearful Colin.

'He's gone out looking for Mrs Elliot,' the neighbour answered Pearl's anxious look.

'Mammy's gone!' Colin bawled, rushing at his aunt's legs.

'Where?' Pearl asked. 'Has she left a message?'

Mrs Potts shook her head. 'Mr Elliot thinks she's taken a change of clothes – and the housekeeping money he kept in the dresser's missing. He's gone to the police. It's a terrible business,' she tutted. 'Mr Elliot came back to find she'd left the baby on her own – screaming the place down she was, poor little lamb. Mrs Elliot's not in her right mind, if you ask me.'

Pearl sank down, all strength drained from her legs. She pulled Colin into her arms and hugged him tight. 'Daddy will find Mammy,' she crooned, trying to placate the distressed child. 'Please God he does,' she added in a whisper.

Jack came back late that night without Gloria. 'I'm going to Blackpool tomorrow – I'm sure she's gone there. You'll look after the bairns for me, won't you?'

Pearl bristled at his off-handedness, as if she was just some skivvy whom he now took for granted. For too long she had been a prop to both Gloria and Jack. If she had stood up for herself sooner and lived a more independent life, none of this might have happened, she rebuked herself. She felt like telling him to let the police do the searching, but she didn't.

'Aye, I'll look after them,' she said shortly, 'but just this time. They're not my bairns and they're not my responsibility! When you come back, I'm packing in me job and going away. I've got a stewarding job.' She stopped, seeing his look of amazement, and sighed, unable to be angry with him. 'I'm sorry, Jack, but I can't go on like this. It's no good me being around. You and Gloria have to sort things out between the two of you. I'm just making things worse being here.'

He looked at her hard for a long moment and Pearl could not fathom if he was angry or sad. 'Aye, you're right,' he said at last.

They said nothing more on the matter, and the next day Jack prepared to leave for Blackpool. But Joanne, who had been listless and whiny since the night before, developed a sudden temperature and Jack went racing in a panic for the doctor.

'Just keep her cool,' the doctor advised, 'and I'll call in again this evening.'

'I can't go while she's poorly.' Jack was adamant, and Pearl was secretly thankful, not wanting the responsibility of nursing a sick Joanne.

The fever was gone a day later and Jack prepared once more to leave. This time he was more hesitant. 'Are you sure you don't mind being left?' he asked.

'No, you go,' Pearl assured him. 'Mrs Potts has offered to help me out.'

'I'll fetch Gloria back and talk some sense into her,' Jack determined, putting on a brave face. 'We've two canny bairns still alive and we'll get over this somehow,' he said stoutly.

Pearl was encouraged by his fortitude, but shortly after he had left for Newcastle's Central Station, there was a long ring at the door. Annoyed in case it woke the napping children, Pearl peered down from the sitting room window. Her heart stopped to see a policeman standing there. She raced downstairs, her mind in turmoil. Had something happened to Jack, or had they news of Gloria? Could they possibly have found Joy at last?

The officer asked for Mr Elliot, so she knew that he at least was safe. 'Can I come in?' he asked, when hearing she was Mrs Elliot's sister. Pearl led him upstairs, heart pounding.

'I'm very sorry, Miss . . .?'

'Rimmer,' Pearl croaked. 'Pearl Rimmer.'

'Miss Rimmer.' He cleared his throat. 'We've heard from the police in Blackpool. Your sister . . .'

'They've found her there?' Pearl asked in hope.

'Yes,' he answered, 'but I'm afraid there's been an accident. Mrs Elliot's been knocked over by a tram. The driver claims she just stepped out in front of him, he didn't have time to slow down.'

'Is she alive?' Pearl whispered.

The officer shook his head. 'I'm sorry. She was killed instantly.'

Pearl covered her face with her hands. 'Oh, dear God!' Then she looked at him in horror. 'Jack's catching the train to Blackpool now. He was sure she'd gone there.'

'We'll ring through to the station to stop him,' the policeman said at once with a sympathetic look. 'We know about their missing daughter. Did you suspect she'd gone back there to carry on looking?'

Pearl nodded, hardly able to speak. 'She believes Joy is still alive somewhere. Believed . . .' She broke off.

'I know this is painful, Miss Rimmer,' the man said diffidently, 'but did she leave any note – any indication that she meant to take her own life?'

Pearl looked at him in horror. 'No!' she insisted. 'There was no note. I told you, she was convinced Joy was still alive. She took money to live on – and photographs of her. That belief was keeping her going.'

The officer shook his head sadly. 'Yes, I'm sorry, but we have to ask. Do you have a neighbour who can be with you until Mr Elliot gets back?' he asked, standing up. She nodded. 'I'll get on to the station right away and see if we can stop him.' Pearl's insides twisted to think of this further blow to Jack. On the point of going, the policeman asked. 'There's just one other thing. Mrs Elliot was found carrying something when she was knocked over.'

'What?' Pearl asked numbly.

'A child's spade. A red one,' he answered. 'And she was crossing the carriageway towards the beach.'

Pearl's heart squeezed to think of a weakened and dazed Gloria heading back to the beach where they had last seen Joy, clutching the girl's spade. Her mind must have been so preoccupied with searching once more for her lost daughter that she wouldn't have noticed the tram bearing down towards her.

'That proves it wasn't suicide. She was still looking for Joy – it was her spade.' Pearl said, her eyes brimming with tears at last.

Within a week, Gloria's quiet funeral had been held and her remains cremated. By the end of October, Jack had paid a month's rent up front on a small terraced house in Jericho Street, the other side of Wallsend.

'I don't want to stay here any longer,' he told Pearl bluntly, 'even if you weren't going away. I can't bear this place. I want to start somewhere fresh with the bairns. They're all that matters to me now and I'm going to bring them up properly – like Gloria would've wanted.'

Pearl flinched. She had had second thoughts about leaving since Gloria's sudden death, worrying about how Jack would cope with the children. If he had asked her to stay, she would have done, even at this late stage. But he had not. Instead, he had made the decision not to return to sea at all. He was looking for a land-based job and would employ help while the children were still young. Once Aunt Julia's flat was sold, there would be money to pay for such care from Gloria's share.

But Pearl could not get Jack to talk about how he really felt. He never mentioned Joy any more, and began to talk about Gloria to Colin as if she were some tragic saint. There were pictures of Gloria about the house, but any with Joy in had been removed. It was as if by denying Joy's very existence Jack could stop blaming himself for her disappearance. Pearl knew there was something unhealthy about this attitude, but she saw that it was Jack's way of coping with the recent horrors. She managed to salvage one photograph of herself standing with Joy at a local fair, the two of them beaming, ridiculously happy at some joke of the photographer's.

When Pearl finally came to leave, she found it much harder to say goodbye to Colin and Joanne than she had imagined. Colin climbed all over her and whined about her going, while Joanne grinned and dribbled against her cheek, not understanding. Pearl clutched them to her, breathing in their babyish smells.

'You'll come and visit us in Jericho Street, won't you?' Jack asked awkwardly. 'You're always welcome – the bairns would like it.'

Pearl nodded, realising that now the flat was sold, she could make her home anywhere in the world. 'And thanks for agreeing to store me things for me in the meantime.'

She felt ridiculous shaking hands with him when she really wanted to fling her arms around his neck and cry. But she had been unable to comfort him these past few weeks; he had kept her well at arm's length. Whatever he had felt for her in the past, she knew the feeling was now dead. He wanted her to leave and start a new life for herself, perhaps blamed himself that he and Gloria had stood in her way for so long, demanding too much of her.

The taxi she had booked hooted below. 'I'll write,' she promised, tearfully handing the children over to their father. He nodded, swinging Colin up into one arm and Joanne in the other, jollying them.

'Auntie Pearl's going to sail the seven seas – and send us postcards of faraway places,' he told them. 'And we're going to live in a brand-new house, with lots of bairns in the street to play with. Won't that be grand?'

Pearl smiled, thinking of the dowdy area that would soon be their home. At least Jericho Street was near the park, and Jack was right that it was probably full of children playing out in the street, not like here, next to the busy dock traffic. Pearl was suddenly moved by the sight of Jack holding on to his two remaining children. She knew in that moment that they would be all right with him, that he would dedicate his future to caring for them and bringing them up the way Gloria would have wanted. She chided herself for her recent day-dreams that she might become a part of it. With painful realisation, she saw that Jack did not need her. She could not begin to be a replacement for Gloria and Joy, even had she wanted to be.

With that thought weighing in her heavy heart, she turned and hurried out of the flat and down to the waiting taxi. As she climbed into the cab, she glanced up and saw the three of them gazing down from the upstairs window. She waved quickly and then scrambled into the back seat. Only when the taxi had turned the corner did she allow herself to weep.

Chapter Thirty

1982

Jo stared at Pearl, tears streaming silently down her face. In the end it had been her aunt who had told most of the painful story. Jo was shattered to discover she had had an older sister that no one had ever told her about. But worst of all was the discovery that her mother had never loved her, had cared only for this Joy she would never know. Gloria had died, distraught and alone, still trying to find the daughter she really loved and could not live without. The saintly, gentle mother in the fairy-tale wedding dress, whom Jo had fantasised about as a child, had never existed – or at least not for her.

'Did Colin know about any of this?' Jo croaked.

Pearl shook her head. Jack seemed unable to speak. He just sat trembling on the edge of the settee next to Mark, his eyes bloodshot from weeping. Jo wanted to go to him and hug him, but she could not move. She wondered whether she really knew him at all. How was it possible to live all your life with someone and not know such fundamental things about them? she thought in bafflement. But her mind was bursting with un-answered questions.

'Did – did they ever find Joy's body?' she whispered.

For the first time in several minutes her father spoke. 'No, never.' He looked old and haggard, sitting there, lines of pain creased around his mouth. Jo felt confused. She experienced sympathy as well as anger at the mess he had made of things.

'Oh, why did you never tell me the truth?' she demanded. 'How can I trust you about anything when you've kept me in the dark all these years? It's as if I don't really know you!' But her father just hung his head in shame.

Mark suddenly spoke. 'That's how I felt about me nana – really angry and let down. Why didn't she say something sooner?'

Jo looked at Mark, suddenly realising how hurt he must have been by the truth about his grandfather. It had seemed easy from her point of view to accept Ivy's story and sympathise with the older woman, but then she had not been affected by it. Now she could under-stand Mark's resentment and contradictory feelings.

Pearl said quietly, 'Ivy thought she was protecting you by not saying anything, but really she was making it much worse in the long run.' She leaned over and squeezed Jo's hand. 'Your father thought the same. That's why I went along with the secret. It wasn't deliberate at first – we just didn't mention it. Then after you'd moved to Jericho Street and none of the neighbours knew about Joy anyway, it seemed impossible to talk about it. I was only around from time to time. The secret just grew.'

'So that photograph of you and the little girl you showed me . . .' Jo gulped. 'That was me sister?'

'Yes, it was,' Pearl admitted.

Jack looked winded. 'I had no idea until now that you'd kept a photo of her.'

'I had to,' Pearl said defensively. 'At times it was the only thing I had to remind me she wasn't just a figment of me imagination!'

'I don't blame you,' Jack said hastily. 'It's just – I – I'd like to see it,' he said with difficulty. Jo could see he was struggling not to weep again. Suddenly her heart went out to him and she was overwhelmed by the tragedy and futility of it all. However shattering it was to discover that her mother had resented her, the fact remained that her father had always loved and cared for her.

'Oh, Dad!' she cried, rushing over to him. 'I'm sorry . . . !'

She felt his arms go round her in a hug of relief. 'I'm the one who's sorry, pet!' he rasped.

'You shouldn't have punished yourself all these years,' Jo insisted.

'But I was to blame,' Jack said stubbornly.

'No, you weren't – it was all a terrible accident,' Jo tried to reassure him. Jack just shook his head.

'He'll not be told,' Pearl said wearily. 'He wants to go on blaming himself – he feels guilty when he's happy.'

'That's not true!' Jack protested. 'I just didn't find it as easy to get over the deaths as you did.'

'How dare you!' Pearl snapped. 'You have no idea how I felt 'cos you never asked me. You've been punishing me all these years, because of your guilty feelings towards me!'

'Well, maybe I have!' Jack replied, stung by her bluntness. 'Maybe I did love you once. But you never returned it. You told me at the time you felt nothing for me, so why are you angry with me now?'

Jo saw the looks of accusation that flashed between them.

'For goodness' sake!' she cried. 'Why are you still

377

fighting? It's obvious you both care deeply for each other – any fool but you two can see that!'

'Your father doesn't love me,' Pearl said bitterly. 'He's never dared to love me since Joy and Gloria died.' She glared at Jack. 'To love me would've been disloyal to the wonderful Gloria, wouldn't it?'

'Of course he loves you!' Jo intervened. 'I know – I lived with him long enough. The excitement when a postcard came from you, the preparations for you coming home. He was always like a cat on hot bricks. Me and Colin never doubted he loved you. We all knew.'

Suddenly Mark backed her up. 'It's true. I used to love coming round your house when you were home from sea,' he told Pearl. 'It was like being with a proper family – you all got on together, loved each other.' He flushed as he added, 'I used to imagine you and Jack were me real mam and dad.'

Pearl pressed her hand to her mouth to smother a sob. Jo felt a lump form in her throat at the memory of the lively young Mark forever at their door, yet they had never guessed at his loneliness and deep longing. She turned to her father and challenged him with her look.

'Tell her, Dad,' she urged. 'Tell her how you felt – how you still feel. Don't lie about this!'

For a moment Jack said nothing as he struggled to compose himself. Jo thought he was still too angry to speak. Then he stood up and went across to Pearl.

'I love you.' He forced out the words. 'I've always loved you.' His eyes swam with tears. 'But you're right, I've always been too afraid to let it show. I believed for so long that I didn't deserve to be happy after what I'd done. I could pretend I didn't know how you felt about me, but it wouldn't be true. At first, maybe, I thought you didn't care. But over the years I grew to know it –

the way you loved the bairns, the things you've done for me, the way you've kept me going after Colin was killed . . . I haven't deserved it—' He broke off.

Swiftly, Pearl put out a hand and reached for him. At once they were in each other's arms, holding on tightly, making up for years of misunderstanding and missed opportunity. Pearl cried with relief, while Jack kept repeating, 'I'm sorry, forgive me, please forgive me!'

'I do!' Pearl wept happily.

'Promise you won't leave me?' Jack whispered hoarsely.

'Promise,' Pearl said, and kissed him on the lips for the first time since that distant night in Blackpool, dissolving the hurt between them.

Jo forced back her own tears which threatened to spill over. She glanced at Mark, still smiling. They exchanged looks and she saw that his haunted dark eyes were glistening with emotion too. She wondered what he was thinking, but could not read his pensive expression.

Mark stood up quietly. 'I'll go,' he said softly, already making for the door. Pearl and Jack hardly seemed to notice, so Jo followed him out into the hallway.

He turned at the front door and they looked at each other awkwardly.

'So we both have to come to terms with our pasts,' Jo murmured.

Mark nodded. 'Suppose so. I'm glad things look like they're working out for Jack and Pearl. If anyone deserves happiness, it's those two.' He reached for the door.

'And what about you, Mark?' Jo challenged. 'What are you going to do about your future?' She wasn't sure why, but suddenly she needed to know. Seeing her father and aunt reconcile their differences and express their feelings after so long had stirred up some of her old feelings for Mark. She cared what happened to him.

He looked at her hard. 'I have to work out if I've got a future,' he answered in a low voice. He hesitated. 'Seeing Pearl and Jack making it up between them – well, it makes me think I might be able to an' all. Maybe I haven't tried hard enough.'

'Oh?' asked Jo, holding her breath. Her pulse was beginning to quicken.

'I need to get me head together first,' Mark said, looking embarrassed. 'But I'm going to see if me and Brenda – you know – can give it another go.'

Jo nodded, but inside she felt strangely empty at his reply.

'Of course.' She smiled in encouragement. 'Good luck.'

Then he was gone through the door and out of the building, without glancing back.

Chapter Thirty-one

Jo spent October throwing herself into as many projects as possible. She was working in schools, rehearsing a small part in a pantomime at Alan's theatre and at weekends taking off to Greenham Common to give support to the women's peace camp protesting against the proposed siting of US Cruise missiles.

'I feel I have to do something,' she told Alan when she first decided to go. 'Sometimes I get these huge feelings of powerlessness – like nothing I do will ever count for anything. It's frightening what they're doing – it's more likely to provoke war with the Soviet Union than stop it.'

'I quite agree,' Alan encouraged. 'I think you should go. It'll help you move on. And it's something positive you can do in Colin's memory – make sure other people's brothers aren't sacrificed to imperialist wars.'

'Maya said she'd come with me,' Jo smiled, glad of his support.

'Really?' Alan sounded surprised. 'Didn't think she'd be the type to camp out.'

'It's hardly just a camping trip,' Jo bristled. 'Anyway, she's arranged to meet up with her sister – Susie's already got a tent there, we just have to bring sleeping bags.'

Alan kissed her. 'Sounds cosy,' he grinned, 'wish I could come.'

'Well, you can't,' Jo smiled. 'We're not going to let the men hijack our protest.'

Her father was less sure. 'I don't want you getting yourself arrested or anything daft,' Jack fretted. 'Why do you have to go?'

'I'm doing this for Colin and Skippy,' Jo tried to explain. 'They're victims of war. We want to make sure there won't be any others.'

'You'll never stop people fighting,' Jack was sceptical. 'We'll always need weapons and soldiers to protect us.'

'We have to start somewhere,' Jo replied. 'Some country has to be brave enough to make a stand. We want nothing less than world peace.'

Jack shook his head and sighed. 'Colin wouldn't have agreed with you. He believed in protecting his own kind first and foremost.'

Jo was instantly angry. 'That's the morality of the caveman!' she said scornfully. 'Anyway, none of us know what Colin would've thought,' she added bitterly. 'He might have come home a raving pacifist after seeing real combat – like half the Great War veterans did. Look at Mark! He's a mental wreck. He doesn't believe in anything any more. Ask him if he thinks what he went through was worth it!' She glared at her father, hurt by his rejection of what she was doing. 'All I know is that my brother was robbed of the best part of his life, because of some senseless war the other side of the world. And that's what I'm going to Greenham Common to protest about!'

She had not given him a chance to answer back or talk about anything else, for she had slammed out of the flat and kept away. She spent her days in a state of semi-rage that goaded her on to work relentlessly. More and more her mind was filled with thoughts of war and death. The further the Falklands War receded, the more she seemed to think of it. At times, in the middle of a workshop or rehearsal, she would be seized with a sense of panic about the world and about the future. Anxiety gnawed away at her insides and robbed her of sleep. The only way she could keep her dark thoughts at bay was to work, to keep on the move and not to stop for a minute.

Jo found herself most at peace among the campaigners keeping vigil at Greenham US Air Force base. There she enjoyed the companionship of shared meals around the campfire and warm friendship from complete strangers who did not question her motives or demand anything more than the snatched days she could offer. If she could not sleep there was always someone awake with whom she could talk.

After Jo had returned to Newcastle one weekend, the honours list for Falkland veterans was published and Pearl rang her up in excitement. 'Mark's been awarded the Distinguished Service Medal. Listen to this: ". . . *for courage, steadfastness and total disregard for his own safety*." Isn't that grand? Brenda's over the moon, her mam says.'

Jo felt a twisting in her stomach. 'Aye. What does Mark think?'

'I'm sure he'll be pleased,' Pearl said, sounding less sure. 'We haven't seen him for a couple of weeks. He and Brenda have moved in with Gordon while they look around for their own place.'

'Gordon?' Jo repeated in astonishment.

'Yes, he's being very supportive since all that business came out about Ivy and Hassan. Matty's not speaking to anyone, according to Norma. But if it brings Mark and Gordon closer together, that's something at least.'

'Yes, it is,' Jo agreed, still flabbergasted by the thought of Gordon and Mark choosing to live under the same roof. 'Ivy will be pleased at that.'

'So when are we going to see you?' Pearl asked.

'I'm very busy just now,' Jo said evasively.

'You're not staying away because of that silly tiff with your father?' Pearl questioned bluntly.

Jo flushed but denied it. 'I'm travelling around the area a lot this month – and spending the weekends at the peace camp. But I'll be there when you go into hospital, Auntie Pearl.'

'It'll be grand to see you whenever you can manage,' she answered.

The next day, after work, Jo caught a glimpse of the triumphal Victory Parade through London that the Government had organised to coincide with Columbus Day. She watched Thatcher take the salute beside the Lord Mayor as rank after rank of Army, Navy and Air Force filed past. The commentator was describing the luncheon in the Guildhall that followed. Jo quickly switched it off before Alan came in, and sat down feeling suddenly depressed by the sight of all the pomp and regimental splendour. It was so easy to be caught up in the pageantry and forget what the reality of the war in the Falklands must have been like.

'They weren't wheeling on the maimed ones like Mark at their great parade, were they?' she fumed to Alan later. 'That's what war really boils down to – dead brothers and burnt corpses and young men with scarred memories.'

'Okay, okay,' Alan replied with an impatient sigh, 'You don't have to go on. You're preaching to the converted, remember? Can't you just drop the subject for one evening? I thought we could go out and see a film. I still haven't seen *Sophie's Choice* with Meryl Streep. Fancy going?'

Jo was eventually persuaded, but the evening was a disaster. She got very upset at the flashbacks to the Second World War and the Nazis and cried uncontrollably for an hour after the film had ended. She slept badly that night, her mind continually dwelling on the tragedy of the film, and Alan ended up sleeping in the spare bed, complaining at her restlessness and her keeping the light on to read.

'I think you should go and see the doctor,' he told her the next day. 'Get something to help you sleep.'

'I don't need drugs!' Jo snapped at him. 'I just want peace of mind and I can't get it around here!' The words were blurted out before she had consciously thought of them.

'What's that supposed to mean?' Alan asked irritably.

Jo sighed. 'I'm sorry. I seem to have no patience with anyone these days.' She looked at him helplessly with dark-ringed eyes. 'I think I need to get away for a bit. Maybe I'll spend the whole of half-term at the camp . . .'

Alan's mouth drew into a tight line.

'I know we'd thought of going to Scotland for a couple of days,' Jo remembered guiltily, 'but I don't think I'd be very good company in my present frame of mind, do you?'

'No,' Alan agreed, turning away to fill the coffee pot. 'You do what you want. We're not joined to each other at the hip.'

Jo said nothing more, knowing that when she had offended him it was best just to keep quiet and not make it worse. She went off the following weekend and stayed away all week. The only reason she came back was to visit Pearl in hospital, for her aunt had her operation at the end of October.

Pearl looked tired and her face was lined with pain on the first visit, but the next evening she was brighter and sitting propped up in bed. Jack was there, and Jo went over and gave him an awkward kiss on the cheek. She hadn't seen him since their disagreement weeks ago, but he smiled as if nothing had happened and said he was pleased to see her.

'I'll be in hospital till the end of the week,' Pearl told Jo.

'I've got two of the others to cover me workshops in November, so I can help nurse you when you get home,' Jo replied brightly.

Pearl glanced at Jack and he nodded. Her aunt stretched out a hand to her. 'That's canny of you, Joanne, but you shouldn't have cancelled your work.'

'No, I don't mind,' Jo smiled. 'I want to be able to help. It'll make me feel I'm doing something useful.'

Pearl looked embarrassed. 'The thing is – well – it's not necessary.'

Jo said, puzzled, 'But I thought you wouldn't be able to do anything for six weeks? And the doctor said you'd probably have to take it easy for the next six months.'

Pearl nodded and threw a beseeching look at Jack. He cleared his throat.

'You see, pet,' he said, his thin face flushing, 'I'm going to look after Pearl when she gets out. She's going to move into my flat.'

Jo felt herself blushing too at his bashfulness. 'Oh, I see. W-will you manage?' she stammered.

Jack grinned. 'Course I will. I've spent a canny few years looking after others, haven't I?'

'Aye, you have,' Jo admitted. 'Well . . .' She was at a loss as to what to say.

Pearl spoke. 'Your father's never one to explain things

clearly,' she laughed weakly, and then winced and put her hand on her body. 'Oh, me stitches!'

'You all right?' Jack sprang from the chair.

'Tell her, Jack,' Pearl urged, 'tell her properly.'

Jack faced Jo. 'Your aunt has not just agreed to live with me. I've asked her to marry me – and she's said yes. We're planning to get wed in the spring, when she's feeling better.'

'Aye, when I can get round the shops for a decent outfit,' Pearl smiled.

Jo leaned forward and gave Pearl a hug. 'That's fantastic!' she cried, feeling suddenly tearful. 'Congratulations – it's about time!' She turned to her father and threw her arms around his neck and kissed him too. 'I hoped this might happen – after everything came out . . .' They grinned at each other.

'You're pleased then?' Jack asked for reassurance.

'Course I am,' Jo said, hugging him again. 'Do I get to be bridesmaid or best woman?' she teased.

'Both if you want,' Pearl laughed, and then closed her eyes in pain.

Jo looked at her father. 'Colin would've been that chuffed,' she said, her eyes swimming with tears. 'At least we'll have a family wedding after all—' She broke off, unable to speak, her mind filling with images of Marilyn waving away frantically to Colin on the dockside. She had been bubbling with happiness at the thought of them marrying at last. Now her oldest friend had moved away from Tyneside and was teaching in London, trying to start a new life. Jo had not seen her in two months and her letters asking her to meet up at Greenham Common had gone unanswered.

Then Jack had his arms around her and was hugging her in sympathy. 'I know, pet. It's hard for us all. But having you there with us on the day – it's all Pearl and I could ask for.'

'Thanks, Dad,' Jo whispered in gratitude.

At first, Jo was buoyed up by the good news and Alan seemed genuinely pleased at the news of the engagement.

'Good to see them moving on, getting it together at last,' he commented, opening a bottle of red wine to celebrate.

A few weeks previously, Jo would have railed that no one could move on from the death of someone as close as Colin, but she said nothing. She knew that keeping her thoughts to herself was the way Alan wanted it. As long as she steered clear of the subject of the Falklands, he was happy and things were good between them. He was already looking ahead to next year, talking about going back to Spain.

'We could go away after your dad's wedding,' he suggested. 'Things are bound to be a bit flat once it's all over.'

Jo just nodded. It suddenly dawned on her that she did not want to think about the wedding and having to be cheerful when inside she felt she was dying a little bit more each day. So she listened to his day-dreaming with half her attention and thought impatiently of getting away south again. For as the days wore on and Pearl came out of hospital, she felt more alone. Jack and Pearl at last had each other, and Jo had a month off with nothing much to do but her bit part in Alan's pantomime. Deep down she admitted she was hurt that they did not need her to help out. She did not want to hang around Newcastle with not enough to do and risked Alan's temper by pulling out of the pantomime.

'Honestly, Jo! I thought you needed the work?' he said in exasperation. 'There are scores of actors out there who would give their eye-teeth . . . !'

'Then you won't find it hard to replace me,' Jo answered irritably.

'Well, just don't expect any favours from me again, if you can't be reliable,' he criticised, as if scolding an irresponsible child. She felt indignant at the suggestion that the only reason she got the part was because of her relationship with Alan, but she did not care enough to keep on arguing about it.

So she prepared to take off again for Greenham with a stock of thick clothing, thermal underwear and her sleeping bag. Maya declined to come this time and Jo suspected she did not want to become embroiled in her row with Alan. But she knew Susie would still be there.

On the day before she left, still smarting from Alan's dismissiveness, she went down to Wallsend to see Jack and Pearl. On the spur of the moment, she went to visit Ivy too. She had hardly seen her since the summer. Ivy was delighted to see her and said how pleased she was to hear of Jack and Pearl getting married. Yet Jo soon became aware that something was preying on her mind.

'It's Mark,' Ivy admitted without much probing.

'I thought things were going better for him and Brenda?' Jo said. 'That's what Pearl heard from Brenda's mam. Said they were living with Gordon – planning to get a house of their own. And he got that award—'

'I know all that,' Ivy interrupted fretfully. 'He's better in a lot of ways. His hands have healed up champion and you'd hardly notice there was any weakness in his leg now. But he's still very moody. I don't know how Brenda puts up with it half the time. He'd argue with his own shadow. And he's refusing to go to London for the medal ceremony. That's upsetting everyone.' Ivy gave her a look. 'Though you'd probably approve of that, with all your peace camp business!'

Jo looked at her sadly. 'It doesn't matter what I think. I'm sorry for all of you. Why won't he go?'

Ivy shrugged. 'Says he doesn't deserve it – that they should chuck it in the South Atlantic for the real heroes who died there.' She sighed. 'I kept thinking maybe he doesn't want to see all the other servicemen who are fit and back at work.'

'You're probably right,' Jo agreed.

Ivy looked perplexed. 'Aye, but it's more than that – it's as if he's really afraid of something, but I don't know what.'

A memory came back to Jo of that terrible argument she had had with Mark in Ivy's backyard. He had said something about being guilty for living when his friends had died. It struck her that that was how her father had reacted to the loss of Joy and Gloria all those years ago. Jack had wrapped his grief in guilt and punished himself for years because he was still alive.

'Maybe he's afraid of being *happy* again, because Colin and Skippy aren't there to share it with him,' Jo said quietly. 'It's like he's being disloyal to them. He's stuck with his guilt at being alive and can't move on. He won't let himself imagine a future without his friends.' She shrugged, wondering if she was right.

'Do you think so?' Ivy asked worriedly. 'What a terrible burden to carry.' She looked at Jo pleadingly. 'So what's the answer?'

Jo gave a bitter smile. 'I wish I knew! I don't have answers any more, just lots of angry questions.'

Ivy stretched out and squeezed her hand. 'Look after

390

yourself, hinny. Don't get into any bother. It would worry your father that much.'

Jo smiled, but felt her heart sink. She too had a burden to carry these days that the war had bequeathed her – that of being the family's last surviving child. She hurried away from Wallsend and thoughts of such heavy respon-sibility. She had a right to live her life as she chose, she determined angrily, and she was going to choose action.

Chapter Thirty-two

Jo gazed around her. As far as the eye could see there were thousands of protesters ringing the high chain fences of the air base. They were all wrapped in waterproofs and boots and hats against the bitter December weather. Since before dawn, women had been arriving, some drifting out of the makeshift tents, others pouring in from far and wide.

She felt a great stirring of pride at the numbers who had responded to the call for the December 'embrace the base' protest. They were going to completely surround the American Air Force base with peaceful protesters. Quite a few of the women had brought their children with them. One woman with a baby told her, 'I see everything differently since I had Ben. I have sleepless nights – not just from feeding either! It's the thought of nuclear war – it's really terrifying.' She stroked the nose of her baby, muffled in layers of clothing, and smiled tenderly. 'It's his future world I care about – that's why I'm here.'

As the day wore on, people pressed forward to pin baby clothes and toys to the wire fence. Huge cobwebs of cotton where woven into the wire to represent their campaign symbol of a tiny missile trapped in a web. Some children came forward and stuck a crumpled piece of paper in the mesh.

'It's our poem,' one of them said proudly. 'We don't want them to bring big bombs here. They're dangerous. We have to tell them, don't we?'

Jo smiled and nodded. She fumbled with cold fingers inside her jacket pocket and pulled out an old black and white photograph she had been saving for this occasion. It showed a group of children about the age of the ones beside her now. Three cheeky-faced boys laughing and two girls leaning on each other, grinning at the camera. The background was Wallsend Green, with a long-forgotten summer fête going on outside the imposing building in the background. On the back of the photograph, scribbled in fading pencil, was the date, 1965, and the names: Colin, Skippy, Mark, Joanne and Marilyn. Pearl had taken it with her box Brownie camera and they had posed for what seemed like ages while she lined them up in the glass.

'Keep still and stop giggling!' Jo remembered her aunt shouting. 'Colin, look up – and Marilyn, don't put your hand over your mouth. That's it. Oh, Mark, you're moving again. Skippy, put your tongue away!'

'Haway, Auntie Pearl!' Colin had complained. 'We want to gan round the stalls.'

'Fête'll be over by the time she's finished,' joked Mark. 'Is that the sunset behind you?'

'Ha, ha. Now smile and stop breathing!' Pearl had ordered, and finally clicked the camera, catching them in various degrees of merriment.

Jo's eyes swam with tears as she stared down at the lively group of friends, so happy and carefree, living for the moment and innocent of the future. She kissed it quickly and secured it to the fence with a paperclip.

'Who's that?' the young girl with the poem asked.

'My brother,' Jo said quietly. 'He's dead. So's one of

his friends. That one there.' She pointed at Skippy. 'Killed in the Falklands.'

The girl looked puzzled. 'But they're just children.'

'We all were once,' Jo said, with a pang of memory. 'They grew up. Colin joined the Army, his friends the Navy.'

'Then they must've known they might get killed,' the girl answered.

'I don't think they really thought about it,' Jo reflected. 'It was a job, a way to see the world, a big adventure.'

The girl touched the photograph. 'What about him? He looks nice.'

'That's Mark – he fought in the Falklands too.'

'Is he still alive?'

'Aye,' Jo sighed, 'but he wishes he was dead.'

The girl looked shocked. 'That's terrible. Why does he wish that?'

'Because his two best friends were killed in the war,' Jo answered, feeling her anger stir.

'He must be very sad,' she said simply.

Jo was struck by the girl's words. Sad was not how she would have described Mark to a stranger. Angry, embittered, depressed, self-pitying, mad at the world or just plain mad. But the girl was right. Underneath all the protective armour of his fury and punishing guilt, Mark must be unutterably sad, she realised.

'Is that you?' the girl asked. Jo nodded. 'You all look really happy.'

'We were,' Jo said, her eyes stinging with tears.

'Well, at least he's still got you as a friend,' the girl said, turning to her.

Jo felt a stab of guilt at the child's trusting bright eyes. If only she knew what a useless friend she had been. To her relief, at that moment the other children pulled on the girl's arms and tugged her after them impatiently. She smiled and waved at Jo and then was gone into the crowd. But the feeling of emptiness and failing remained, and as the throng of supporters grew and more police appeared to contain them, Jo's unhappiness turned to angry determination and she joined in with the anti-war songs and lit candles as the circle was completed.

At this point the police moved in to clear them away from the gates. When talking to the children, Jo had become separated from Susie and the other friends who shared her tent, and she had no idea where they now were.

'Sit down!' someone shouted at her in the mêlée. 'We'll be harder to move. Keep singing!' Jo plonked herself down on the tarpaulin at once and linked arms with the women on either side. Others around them did the same, some of them lying stretched out. They continued to sing, keeping a watchful eye on the police.

It didn't take long to discover the police's plan. Scores of them began to pile out of vans and march towards the throng of women near the gates. They pushed and trampled their way through the passively resisting protesters until they had cut a swath through the crowd and reached the fence. Then the men linked arms like a dark-blue chain cutting off the women behind from those around the gateway. The same was done on the other side. Jo could see how those of them sitting in front of the entrance were now to be targeted. She could hear police radios crackling and orders being shouted above the sound of the singing.

'Hang on to me,' she urged the woman beside her. 'They'll have to carry us out together!'

Dozens of police came towards them and began to

haul the women off the ground, stepping on them with their heavy boots in order to reach the ones nearest the gates.

'Ah-ya! Watch it!' Jo howled, as one of them stood on her hand.

The constable just laughed at her and gibed, 'You should be home looking after your husband and kids.'

Another one gave them a look of disgust. 'Bunch of lesbians – don't imagine they've got husbands. Just look at them – stink something rotten.'

Jo grabbed his coat, furious. 'Have you got kids?' she demanded.

He looked at her as if she had some contagious disease. 'Yeah. And a wife at home looking after them. You lot aren't normal.' He tried to shake her off, but she clung on to him.

'And you're thick and ignorant!' she shouted. 'We're the ones protecting your family – protecting their future – not you! When the nukes start flying it'll be too late.'

He gave her a kick. 'Go home and don't worry your little head about war,' he sneered.

Jo's fury ignited. She half rose and pushed at him.

'Steady!' the woman beside her warned. 'Don't let him get to you.'

But it was too late, Jo could not stop. 'I know all about war, you patronising bastard!' she yelled. 'I've lost me only brother and a best friend to war. Don't tell me not to worry. You don't have the first clue what war can do – or you wouldn't be doing the dirty work for the warmongers now!' She grabbed him round the legs and tried to bring him down.

He took a swipe at her and caught her on the side of the head, sending her toppling backwards. 'Right!' he barked. 'We'll have you!' He seized her by the arm and yanked her up, kicking her again in the side as she tried to resist.

The woman beside Jo attempted to hang on to her, but the first constable who had taunted them jabbed her out of the way and then grabbed Jo by the other arm. The next minute they had her on her feet and were dragging her away towards a van. Jo's head pounded and she felt sick and winded, but still she fought to stay behind. She was vaguely aware of passing someone with a camera and then she was being shoved through a van door and thrown on to a seat. The door slammed shut.

She crouched where she had landed, sore and breathless and full of rage. Outside she could hear the women still singing in the cold air, their defiant, hope-filled voices rising up above the din of shouting and struggling. Moments later, the door banged open again and two other protesters were bundled in beside her. At first they talked animatedly and indignantly about their arrest, but by the time the van lurched off, they had fallen silent. Jo was suddenly exhausted, her anger spent. Without knowing why, she put her face in her hands and started to cry.

Mark was at Ivy's, sitting drinking from an endless pot of tea, when the scenes from Greenham Common came on the news. It was dark outside and bitterly cold, but inside it was cosy and the fire was glowing. Ivy had already put up her ancient decorations on a silver imitation Christmas tree and stood it on the sideboard.

Ivy clucked, keeping up a running commentary. 'Look at them all! They must be frozen in this weather, living rough. Eeh! See the way the police are going in. I hope Joanne isn't anywhere near them. Jack's that worried about her.'

'At least she's doing something,' Mark said impassively.

'You don't agree with them, do you?' Ivy asked in surprise. Mark gave a shrug of indifference. She went on, 'Mind, you've got to admire them, whatever you think of them. It's like the suffragettes, isn't it? And look at the way the police are handling them – just the same.'

Mark lurched forward and stared at the screen. 'Look!'

'Whatever's the matter?' Ivy asked, startled by his sudden interest.

Mark jabbed a finger at a figure in the background being frog-marched away. 'It's Jo!'

Ivy squinted. 'No it's not! It's someone much older.' Then the clip finished and the newscaster was talking about Britain agreeing to send troops to Lebanon as part of a peace-keeping force. Ivy quickly switched off the television, knowing that Mark became volatile with any mention of British forces.

He sank back. 'It was her – I'm sure of it.'

'I hope for Jack's sake it wasn't,' Ivy fretted. 'I warned her not to go getting into trouble.'

Mark almost smiled. 'Well, she's always done the opposite of what folk tell her to do – you should know that by now.'

Ivy snorted. 'I hardly think she's doing it just to spite me.' She picked up the empty cups. 'Do you know what she told me? She said she's doing it for all the future Colins – but I can't help thinking it's because she can't come to terms with losing her own brother.'

Mark looked at her uncomfortably. 'What d'you mean?'

'Well, all this rushing about! She has to be doing something every minute of the day. Stops her having to think about life without him, I reckon.' Ivy sighed. 'But what would I know? I suppose she's spent her life dashing at a hundred miles an hour.'

Mark thought about it. There was Jo pitching head-long into protest and action while he sat vegetating, paralysed and fearful to do anything. Yet perhaps they were more alike than he cared to admit. They were both trying to escape the past which haunted them, the ghosts that followed them and would not let them go. A sudden moment of clarity came to him. It was not just the ghosts of Colin and Skippy that would not give them peace, but the ones of their childhood. Both their lives had been overshadowed and blighted by family secrets – his by his grandfather Hassan and Jo's by a lost sister and a mother who had rejected her. All those years, without even knowing it, they had shared a similar burden. Was that why they had been drawn to each other as children, sensing that they were somehow different from the others? he wondered. Was that why they had understood each other so well?

Then his heart hardened again. Their understanding and tolerance for each other had long vanished, he thought savagely. Watching her being arrested for peace protesting made him realise they had never been further apart. It was a rejection of what he had been through in the Falklands – a slap in the face for those who had stood up against aggression. By demonstrating against the military, she was as good as saying that he and his mates were the real enemy, Mark thought bitterly.

He got up quickly. 'Best be off,' he muttered.

'How's your new flat coming on?' Ivy asked tentatively.

'Brenda's still painting,' Mark grunted.

'Be canny to have your own place for Christmas,' she encouraged. 'Fresh start, eh?'

He gave her a bleak look, wishing he could summon up an ounce of her enthusiasm. It was causing endless friction with Brenda that he would not motivate himself to help decorate their council flat. But he felt disembodied, watching himself from far off – and he did not like the irritable, nervy man that he saw.

'Aye, perhaps it will be,' he answered, pecking her on the cheek as he passed. She put out a hand to touch his face, but he flinched away. He still could not bear anyone to touch his disfigured jaw, he was so self-conscious about it.

Ivy let her hand drop. 'Take care, hinny,' she said worriedly, watching him escape into the dark.

Chapter Thirty-three

Jo spent only a night in the cells and was let go without being charged the following day. She felt deflated, as if they had cheated her out of her moment of glory. They had belittled her protest by treating it as too trivial to bother the courts with. She returned to the camp to find Susie feverish and unwell.

'You should go home,' Jo told her in concern. 'I'll take you back to London if you like.' Susie accepted her help without much argument and Jo found herself nursing her friend for a week through a bout of flu. Susie's boyfriend Bob chose that moment to break off their eight-month relationship and go abroad, so Jo stayed on longer. As Christmas neared, she knew she ought to go home, but was alarmed when she rang Alan to discover that she had been seen on television being arrested, and that everyone was talking about it.

'Jack's been on the phone daily,' Alan laughed. 'You've really put the cat among the pigeons.'

'I had no idea,' Jo gasped in embarrassment. 'They never charged me.'

'I know,' Alan said, sounding amused. 'I made enquiries – to get your father off my back. I told him you'd be fine and could look after yourself. I'm very proud of you, girl.'

'I'll ring Dad to tell him I'm all right,' Jo said hastily,

encouraged by his friendliness and feeling an urge to go home.

'Are you staying down with Susie for Christmas?' Alan asked. 'I'm up to my eyes here with the pantomime – it's going very well. But I'll not be around much.'

Jo was disappointed at this. 'Well, I could go to Dad's for Christmas if you're tied up with things . . .'

'Whatever you want,' Alan said easily.

Jo made her mind up quickly. 'That's what I'll do then.' Perhaps she had stayed away too long. 'Have you been all right without me?' she fished.

'Been too busy to pine for you, girl,' he teased. 'But I've missed you, of course.' Jo was not sure he sounded very convincing, but at least he was no longer cross with her for dropping all her commitments and running off to the camp. Soon she would have the chance to catch up with his news and pay him some attention. She rang her father and got Pearl, who was full of concern, but relieved to hear she was safe in London.

'How are you, Auntie Pearl?' Jo asked.

'Canny,' Pearl assured her. 'I'm getting out again and your father's fussing round me something wonderful!' She laughed, but added, 'It would do both of us good to see you, mind.'

After that, Jo made plans to return north. She could not afford the train fare, so booked herself on a coach and managed to get a seat on an overnight bus on the twenty-third.

'Why don't you come with me?' Jo suggested to Susie, who was beginning to venture out of the flat again but was still weak. 'See a bit of Maya and Frank.'

'Oh, she's not with Frank any more,' Susie declared. 'I thought you knew.'

Jo shook her head. 'When did that happen?' she asked in surprise.

'After that time you both came down to the camp, I think.' Susie shrugged. 'Maya said they were just creatures of habit – should have gone their separate ways ages ago.'

'I'm sure they came round together the last time I saw Maya,' Jo said, trying to remember.

'Probably did – they're staying good friends,' Susie said. 'Just not living together any more. Anyway, Maya'll be too busy with the panto over the holidays. Not much point in going there.'

'Well, you could come and stay at Dad's with me,' Jo suggested.

Susie smiled weakly. 'Thanks, but I think I'd rather just take it easy and slob around here. I don't think I'm up to an all-night bus journey. I'll probably invite myself over to Heather's for Christmas Day.'

Jo knew that their friend Heather from the peace camp would spoil and mother Susie, and she could not persuade her to change her mind. On her final night in London, Jo attempted to contact Marilyn again. There had been no reply all week and Jo thought she might have already gone north to be with her parents. But just as she was about to give up, someone answered. It was a man's voice, and Jo wondered fleetingly if she had dialled the wrong number.

'No, this is Marilyn's, I'll just get her. Who's calling?' the cheerful voice asked.

'Her old friend, Jo. Jo Elliot, tell her.'

There was a slight pause, and then the voice said, 'Just hang on.' It seemed to Jo that Marilyn took a long time to come to the telephone.

'Hello?' Marilyn said finally.

'Hi, it's me, Jo,' Jo answered brightly. 'I've been trying to get in touch all week. I'm in London at Susie's. You know, Susie? Maya's sister, the one—'

'I know,' Marilyn cut in, 'the one from the women's camp.'

'Aye,' Jo said, sensing a coolness. 'I wondered if we could meet up tonight? I'm going up north on the bus tomorrow and there's loads I'd like to talk about.' She held her breath. 'It's ages since we've had a proper chat.'

After a silence, Marilyn said, 'I'm sorry, Jo. I can't tonight. I'm going to a party.'

'Oh.' Jo was disappointed. 'Does it need any gate-crashers?' she asked hopefully. They had often just turned up at people's houses as teenagers if there'd been a rumour of a party.

'No,' Marilyn said quietly but firmly, 'it's a dinner party, they'd notice.'

'When can we get together then?' Jo asked in frustration. 'Are you coming north for Christmas?'

'No. Mam and Dad are coming down to me.'

Jo was surprised. She protested, 'You can't avoid me forever, Marilyn! I'm Colin's sister. I want to talk about him to you. You'll have to face up to what's happened some time, for God's sake!'

'I have faced it!' Marilyn lost her patience. 'But I've coped with losing Colin in the only way I know how – getting on with my life! It doesn't mean I don't think about him – I do. But it doesn't help to keep thinking about what we would've been doing now if he had lived. And I can't cope with you harping on about the old days as if there'll never be any good times again!'

Jo began to shake at the harshness of her rejection. 'I don't harp on!' Her voice rose. 'But there's so much I need to tell you – things that I've found out about me

406

mam and a sister I never knew I had – that Colin never knew!' she said in panic. 'I need to tell you, Marilyn, because you're the nearest thing I have to Colin. You were so close. Please don't turn your back on me now!'

'You've got to stop treating me like I'm your sister-in-law,' Marilyn entreated. 'I'm not and I never will be – not now!'

'You've got someone else,' Jo accused. 'That's it, isn't it? You've already got over Colin and replaced him with someone else. That didn't take long!' She knew it was a hurtful thing to say, but she felt hurt too and could not stop herself.

'Yes, I am seeing someone else,' Marilyn answered defensively, 'but I don't feel guilty about it. Colin would've been the last person to stand in the way of me finding happiness. He was too kind and loving to begrudge me that. No one will replace Colin for me and I resent you saying that. I know that I would have made him happy and that he loved me. No one can take that certainty away from me. That's why I don't feel guilty at moving on.' She broke off a moment and murmured to someone in the background. Then, 'I'm sorry for you, Jo, if you still feel guilty about the way you fell out with Colin. But that's something only you can come to terms with.'

'*Me* feel guilty?' Jo was indignant.

'Yes, you,' Marilyn insisted. 'You just want to meet me so you can hear me say that none of the falling-out mattered, that he loved you really, despite the arguments. But I wouldn't be helping you in the long run. Only you know what your relationship was really like with your brother. All I know is that he was angry at you for siding with Alan and patronising him and the other lads for going to war. He was hurt by the things you said. So was

407

Mark. Brenda says you've screwed him up good and proper. She blames you for Mark refusing to go and receive his medal in person – says it's all your pacifist talk that's done it.'

'You and Brenda talk about me like that?' Jo gasped.

'We keep in touch,' Marilyn admitted. 'We're both of the same mind, that it's the future that's important – not dwelling on the past like you and Mark do.'

'But it's not true, Marilyn! Brenda can't blame me for what Mark chooses to do. We're not even friends any more – he's more likely to do the opposite.' Jo felt her head reeling. 'But are you telling me that Colin was still angry with me right up until his death? I like to think I'd made it up with him – that he understood me.'

'He loved you, Jo, but he never understood you. He would've been ashamed of you getting yourself arrested on television in the name of peace. He thought CND were a load of dangerous cranks. The army was his life.' Marilyn sighed impatiently. 'But you know all that. I'm sorry if this isn't what you want to hear, but maybe it's time you faced up to the truth. Stop trying to recreate a cosy past that doesn't exist any more – probably never did. Our childhood was never that great. It's time you let go of Colin and me – and Mark and Brenda – let us get on with our lives. Your father and Pearl have moved on, why can't you?'

Jo gripped the receiver, stunned by the attack. Although her throat felt tight, she forced herself to speak. 'I'm trying to!' she cried hoarsely. 'That's what joining the peace camp was all about – something positive to do after Colin's death, to make his dying less futile. Don't rubbish that!'

'I didn't mean to,' Marilyn replied. 'I think it's great if you're doing it for yourself – for the next generation or whatever. But don't kid yourself you're doing it for Colin, because he wouldn't have wanted it. He was a soldier. He believed in fighting to protect people. The army to him was all about "fight the good fight" – like that hymn in Sunday School we were always singing. He'd have done anything for the glory of the regiment and love of his mates – as well as love of those at home. That's what going to war was all about for Colin – love and glory. Peace came afterwards – and only if those two had been satisfied.'

Jo asked hoarsely, 'And what do you think of peace? Does it rank a poor third with you, Marilyn?'

Marilyn dropped her lecturing tone. 'I admire you and the others who put yourselves on the front line for peace,' she admitted. 'And I envy your conviction – your simplicity of view. Because I don't see things in such a clear-cut way any more. I learnt as soon as Colin left Portsmouth that I couldn't believe in pacifism and still support him wholeheartedly. I had to believe in what he was doing – and for him to know that.' She added more gently, 'That's why I avoided coming down to Greenham Common when you asked me to. You and those other women are far more courageous than I ever will be. Don't lose that courage, Jo, I've always admired that in you. But try to find some peace of mind too.'

A man's voice called to her in the background to hurry up. 'I'm coming,' she said quickly. 'Sorry, I've really got to go. Take care of yourself, Jo.'

'Aye, and you,' Jo managed to say.

Jo put down the receiver and stood over the telephone, not moving for several minutes, Marilyn's words thumping in her head. *Harping on the past . . . Colin would've been ashamed . . . I'm sorry if you still feel guilty . . . he was*

*a soldier... stop treating me like I'm your sister-in-law...
love and glory...*

Susie found her staring at the wall, quite unable to
move. 'That was a weird conversation,' she commented.
'You hardly said a word. Is everything all right?'

Jo shook her head, unable to speak. She felt as if the
floor had disappeared from beneath her and she was
teetering in mid-air, groping for something solid to hold
on to. The world seemed to have shifted focus during
those past minutes of Marilyn's tirade, and she felt dizzy
and disorientated. Marilyn had called her courageous,
but had left her feeling terrified.

'I think you need a drink,' Susie said in alarm.

Jo suddenly blurted out, 'Can I stay here for
Christmas?'

'Of course,' Susie said, puzzled. 'But why?'

Jo's mind echoed with Marilyn's reproach. *It's time
you let go of Colin and me – and Mark and Brenda – let us
get on with our lives. Your father and Pearl have moved on,
why can't you?*

She whispered, 'I don't think I can face going home
just now.'

Chapter Thirty-four

Jo cancelled her bus home and got Susie to ring her father and say she had flu and could not travel. She hated making excuses, but she was so rocked by what Marilyn had said to her that she could not speak about it. She felt guilty for not being with Jack and Pearl this first Christmas without Colin, but it would all be too painful, she realised. She was not strong enough to face it. She salved her conscience with the thought that at least they had each other.

Strangely, she did not immediately think of rushing back to Alan, which was what she usually did if she needed to feel better about something. She spoke to him on the telephone, saying she thought he would be so busy that she would hardly see him.

'Susie is going to be on her own, so I thought I'd stay and keep her company,' she told him. To her relief, he put up no resistance to the idea.

On Christmas Eve, Jo and Susie went on a pub crawl then on to a candlelit midnight service where they sang off-key. On Christmas Day they walked over to the house of their friend Heather and her three lively children, clutching several bottles of wine, and stayed for two days. In between drinking too much, Jo went out to the park with the children and played football, or sat and watched any film that came on television.

On the last night, her friends coaxed her into talking about what was bothering her and Jo found herself telling them what Marilyn had said. They sat up late with a bottle of port and several cans of beer, discussing peace and war and families. Jo veered between anger and indignation and confusion and guilt.

'The only thing I'm sure of now is that I'm not sure of anything,' she said, feeling drunk. 'Marilyn's made me question everything I believe in – even who I am! I thought we had a happy childhood and now I discover that me best friend didn't think it was. I thought I was close to me brother, but Marilyn says he never understood me. She said I'm always harping on about the past. Am I?' she asked.

Susie drew on her cigarette. 'Well, you are at the moment,' she teased.

Jo laughed at herself. 'Sorry,' she said sheepishly, 'I'll shut up about it.' She lay back on the comfortable sofa, feeling overwhelmingly weary.

Heather leaned over and touched her arm. 'I can tell you're mixed up about it all. But it's not surprising, considering what you've been through this past year. I can't imagine what it must be like to lose a brother and a good friend, just like that,' she sympathised. 'But I think it would make me feel more strongly pacifist. Don't let Marilyn undermine your beliefs – it's only her opinion against yours. Who's to say she's right?'

Jo sighed. 'I know. I think I am still a pacifist. But at the same time, I feel I'm letting down Colin's memory – because he believed in the opposite. I'm belittling his sacrifice – that's what Marilyn was getting at, I think.'

The others were silent. Jo went on thinking aloud. 'And I keep remembering something Mark once said, about standing up to the bullies. He was always more

412

political than Colin. I think he saw the Argentinian Junta in the same light as the Nazis or other fascists. He knew all about discrimination; he's been on the receiving end before. Doesn't he have a point?' Jo questioned. 'Where would we be today if the Allies hadn't stood up to the Nazis?'

'People will always find reasons for justifying going to war,' Heather answered. 'And I can't blame Mark for his. He had to act the way he did because he was part of a militarised system – he had no choice. What we're trying to do is break the mould – create a world where cooperation and peace are the norm, not a sign of weakness. We can't look back to the past for role models – we need to build a new vision for the future where armies won't be necessary.'

'Yeah,' Susie agreed, 'and the vast amounts of defence money can be spent on health and education and pensions.'

'All we need,' Heather said with conviction, 'is enough people in enough countries to stand up and say no to the arms race. We're not alone in thinking the super-powers have got it wrong – ordinary people all over the world want to live without the fear of war. I bet there are millions behind the Iron Curtain who think the same as we do. We need to reach out to them and give them the courage to say no to Russian missiles – tear down the Iron Curtain!'

Jo grunted. 'Can't see that happening in our lifetime.'

'It will!' Heather was optimistic. 'If a few more people have a bit more courage and faith in human nature.'

'I wish I was like you.' Jo sighed again. 'I don't feel courageous any more. Anything I do counts for nowt. I feel like a tiny ant who could be stood on and squashed at any minute.'

Susie squinted at Jo through the cigarette smoke that hung in the air like gauze. 'You need to get your confidence back, Jo. You know what you should do?'

'Shut up and go to bed?' Jo suggested wryly.

'Yes,' Susie smiled. 'But after that, you should do what you do best – acting. Why don't you write down what you feel? Put it into a play and then perform it? Get to the bottom of how you feel about losing Colin.'

'That's a brilliant idea,' Heather enthused. 'What better way to pay tribute to your brother and his friends! And say something positive about peace at the same time,' she added with a smile.

Jo felt a spark of interest stir in her groggy head. Maybe they had a point. Right now she was too exhausted to think about it, but tomorrow . . .

'Will you remind me of this conversation when I'm sober,' she smiled, and sank back on the cushion. Within a minute she was fast asleep.

Jo stayed on at Susie's all that January. While her friend went back to work for a temping agency, Jo hibernated in her flat, thinking and writing and acting out her thoughts. Some days she would be paralysed with anger and guilt as she thought about her past: the mother who had failed to love her, the sister who had inadvertently torn their family apart, the brother who had never really forgiven her for hurting his best friend. She began to accept that some of what Marilyn had said must be true.

The shock of losing Colin had been so great, and the discovery of her unhappy origins had followed on so swiftly, that her only response was to take refuge in a happier past. Steadily, her obsession with reinventing her childhood had grown. For too long she had harked

414

back to a golden age when she and Colin and Mark had been the centre of their group of friends, deliriously happy through long hot summers that never ended.

Yet that had been a distortion of the past. They had fought just as much as they had played. She had been excluded from their games as well as included. Colin had neglected her as well as taken brotherly care of her, and many were the times when she had disappeared with Marilyn not even thinking that Colin or her father would be worrying about her. They had loved, bickered, laughed, fallen out and made up countless times.

Theirs had been an ordinary childhood. Instead of romanticising it, she should just have been thankful for its normality. And she should not be bitter about her unknown mother, Jo came to realise. Gloria had failed to love her because she was mentally ill after her birth. That was not to say that she wouldn't have grown to love her as much as she had Joy, given time. The tragedy lay in her mother not receiving the help that she needed.

Gradually, as she worked on her play, Jo began to feel an easing of her deep loss and pain. She and Colin had always seen things differently. He had always preferred Paul McCartney to her John Lennon. He had supported Newcastle United, while she had chosen Sunderland, probably just to annoy him, she couldn't remember why. So it was nothing out of the ordinary for them to argue over the war or the world. It would've been unusual if they hadn't; suspicious even, Jo thought wryly. That was something that Marilyn, as an only child, had never understood. When Marilyn saw Colin and Jo arguing, she thought they'd stopped loving each other. But Jo was certain now that Colin had never stopped loving her, no matter what she had said. She had still loved him, despite past hurts, so why should it be any different the other way round?

'How's it going?' Susie would ask each evening.

Sometimes Jo would answer, 'Okay, I think.' At others she would just show her a binful of crumpled-up paper.

One night Jo said tentatively, 'I'm thinking of making it a one-woman play – doing all the parts.'

Susie nodded in approval. 'Sounds interesting – and cheap. More likely to get someone to put it on.'

Jo looked at her in alarm. 'You don't think anyone will actually want to watch it?'

Susie laughed. 'Well, there's no point spending all this time and effort on it just to show me and Heather in the sitting room! Alan will help you there, won't he?'

Jo wondered. She had hardly been in contact with him in weeks. She had rung him at New Year to tell him she was staying on in London to work on a play about the Falklands and the peace camp. He had sounded interested but distracted, and said he would try and get down to see her when the pantomime finished.

Jo rang him that evening but there was no reply. She tried for three days but never caught him in and so gave up. Maybe he had gone away for a few days' walking in Scotland after the Christmas season had ended. She would encourage him to come down for a weekend in London when she had something to show him.

The more she worked on her idea, the more auto-biographical it became. She had to change some of the characters in case it became too personal. Increasingly, her thoughts dwelt on Mark and the effect the war had had on him. At first she made him into a character who went off to war full of idealism and came home virulently anti-war, like some First World War veteran. But then she abandoned the idea as having been done too many times before. What was she trying to say when she thought of Mark? she agonised.

Jo went for long wintry walks around Clapham Common and sat in cafés over mugs of coffee thinking about him. How did Mark feel now? she wondered, ashamed that she did not know. She had been too quick to criticise him for his self-pity and not listen to why he was hurting inside so much. But wasn't it obvious? In a world where people were too quick to judge him by the way he looked – the colour of his skin – he had felt safe among his childhood friends. Then he had lost both Colin and Skippy overnight, and for some reason felt responsible for Skippy's death.

For all his outward show of toughness and devilment as a boy, Mark had been the most sensitive and idealistic of them all. Even as a child, he had railed at his father's brutality towards his mother and refused to be bullied himself. He had been a true grandson of Hassan, who had stood up for injustice against black sailors, and had also inherited a strong sense of fairness from Ivy's father, the liberal Mathias.

But Marilyn had warned Jo to leave Mark and Brenda alone to get on with their lives, so she might never really know what ate away inside him. They did not want her inquisitive interference. She would always be a reminder of Colin and the past that Brenda was eager to forget. Maybe it was best if they did forget, Jo concluded. But even if she never saw Mark again, she could pay tribute to his bravery and the values for which he had stood up all his life.

Jo sat up late, writing and tearing up her work and starting again. In the end, she abandoned the idea of describing the war at first hand and set it all at home. She created a group of women characters who saw the war through their own eyes and the way it affected the men who went. At the heart of it was the unresolved debate about peace and whether it was right to fight and die for it, or braver not to fight at all.

On Colin's birthday, she rang her father.

'I was thinking of you, pet,' he told her, and she could hear the tears in his voice. 'I'm glad you rang.'

'Me too, Dad,' she answered.

'When are you coming home?' he asked plaintively. 'We miss you that much.'

'Soon,' she promised, 'when the play's finished.'

'Pearl's wanting to arrange the wedding,' Jack pressed her. 'She needs to know when you're going to be back. You won't miss that, will you?'

'Course not,' Jo said hastily. 'It'll be the highlight of the year.'

There was a silence while both of them remembered.

'Dad,' Jo said cautiously, 'I've been thinking a lot about the family while I've been writing – a lot about Mam too.'

'Joanne, don't think too badly of her – don't upset yourself,' he panicked.

'No, Dad, I don't blame her any longer,' Jo broke in quickly. 'There's no point getting angry. She might have loved me without it really showing. Anyway, I had you and Auntie Pearl giving me more than enough love – still have – and that's what matters to me now. When I come home, I'm going to spoil you both – make up for not being there for you these past months.'

At first she heard nothing, then her father's croaky voice said, 'You're always with me, pet, wherever you are. And I thank God for you every day of me life.'

Jo put her hand to her mouth to stop herself crying. Gulping down tears, she said, 'Give me love to Auntie

Pearl. I'll see you soon.' Then she quickly rang off.

Finally, at the end of February, Jo felt she had something to show for all the weeks of struggle. She gave it to Susie to read one night. Her friend came rushing through to where she was sleeping on the sofa, tears streaming down her face.

'It's – it's brilliant!' she cried. 'It's so powerful – right from the guts.'

'Do you think so?' Jo asked, feeling her insides lurch with excitement. She had been so afraid that Susie would reject it for being open-ended, raising more questions about peace and war than it answered.

'Yes,' Susie assured her. 'Heather probably won't like it. She'll say it's too sentimental – that you let the military off the hook. But it's so moving,' she enthused. She clutched Jo's arm. 'It's just you. You've given everything of yourself – it's all here.'

Jo felt a wave of relief. She had put everything into the play and was exhausted by the effort. But even if Susie was the only person who ever read it, it had been worth the agony.

Susie sat clutching the manuscript, the duvet pulled over her knees. She looked reflective, then turned to Jo. 'You must love him very much still,' she said softly.

Jo felt a pang as she nodded. 'He was me only brother; of course I'll always love him.'

Susie gave her an odd look, and then laughed as she realised the confusion. 'No, Jo, not Colin,' she answered gently. 'The other character, the one you call Greg. Mark – is that his real name?'

Jo flushed. 'W-why do you say that? How can you tell? I mean, it's only fiction!' she stammered.

Susie gave her a disbelieving look. 'Listen, Jo, I think I know you pretty well by now. It's obvious to me. The

419

way you write about him – it's very beautiful and touching. You shouldn't be embarrassed.'

Jo put her hands to her burning face. 'But I am. He's married. He doesn't even like me any more! No, of course I don't still love him. I'm just using his case to make a point,' she blustered.

Susie did not press her. 'If you say so.'

Jo did nothing for a few days, except walk and sleep and listen to the radio. She wondered whether she should rewrite bits of the play. The main character lost her lover to the war. Was the lover really based on Mark, and if so should she change him? she fretted. Then she determined to empty her mind of the play and relax. Susie had never even met Mark, so how could she know? The Greg character was just a vehicle to express Jo's ideas on freedom and loyalty and love.

Her state of quiet limbo was brought abruptly to an end by a telephone call from Pearl.

'We've booked the registry office for next Friday afternoon,' her aunt told her firmly, 'and a meal at Georgio's in the evening. We've taken a room upstairs. So you get yourself home sharpish. I want to take you out and buy you a nice outfit.'

Jo was suddenly full of nervous excitement. 'Just don't say frock, Auntie Pearl,' she teased.

'Well, you're not coming in old jeans,' her aunt insisted. 'And the other thing. You won't go on calling me Auntie once I'm married, will you?'

'No, I suppose not,' Jo said, not having given it any thought. But the relationship would be different. 'You don't want me to call you Stepmother, do you?'

'Course not!' Pearl exclaimed. 'You know what I mean.'

'I'll practise,' Jo promised. '*Pearl*. Is that okay?'

They both laughed. 'Eeh, it'll be grand to have you back home,' Pearl said. 'Alan's invited, of course.'

Jo felt herself blushing. She had hardly thought about him for days. 'Thanks,' she answered. 'I don't know what he's doing next Friday . . .'

'You sort it out and let us know,' Pearl said. 'And Jack wants to know when we're going to see this play of yours.'

'I'm not sure.' Jo was evasive. 'I'd thought of contacting my old friend from the Dees Theatre, Martha Jones. Do you remember?'

'Course I do,' Pearl said. 'I was at a production of *The Dumbwaiter* there before Christmas. I saw Martha and she was asking after you. She's not acting any more, but she's still one of the trustees.'

'Could you look her number up for me?' Jo asked excitedly. Pearl came back after a couple of minutes with the numbers for the theatre and for Martha's home. 'Thanks, Aun— I mean Pearl!' she grinned. 'I'll be up next week.'

'Make it early next week,' Pearl warned.

By the time Jo boarded the coach for Newcastle on the Tuesday, she had already spoken to Martha and arranged to meet her and show her the play. Her old friend and mentor was as encouraging as always and delighted to hear from her. They had a lot of catching-up to do.

It was difficult saying goodbye to Susie after all their time together.

'You've been so good to me,' Jo said gratefully. 'I don't know what sort of mess I'd be in if you and Heather hadn't sorted me out over Christmas.'

'I was glad of the company,' Susie told her. 'Stopped

me moping around thinking about Bob.'

'You'll come up and stay soon?' Jo urged.

'Love to,' Susie said, giving her a direct look. 'Will I get you at Alan's or your dad's?'

Jo pulled a face. 'Not sure what I'm going to find. Better let me ring you.'

Susie hesitated, then decided to say it. 'It might mean nothing. But that time you couldn't get in touch with Alan. Well, Maya was away then too. Could just be coincidence . . .'

Jo flushed. 'They've always been good friends,' she said defensively. 'It doesn't mean—'

Susie hugged her quickly. 'No, of course it doesn't. Take care. Hope the wedding goes really well. Have a few drinks for me!'

Moments later, Jo was on the bus with her bulging bag made out of patchwork leather and suede, finding a seat. She slept a lot of the way, but as they neared Newcastle she craned out of the window for familiar landmarks: the crescent shape of the Tyne Bridge lit up in the winter dusk, the solid castle tower and the delicate thistle dome of the cathedral. Jo felt a strange hunger at the sight of the river below. There was a naval ship docked at the quayside. Her heart began to beat faster as it made her think of Mark and Skippy. She glanced downriver towards the cranes of Wallsend and suddenly could not wait to be there.

Instead of taking a taxi to Alan's flat in Sandyford, Jo went straight to the bus station and climbed on a bus for Wallsend. In twenty minutes she was ringing the bell on her old doorstep. Her father opened the door and squinted over his reading spectacles at the figure in the dimly lit hallway. Jo hardly gave him time to throw open his arms as she flung herself at him.

'Dad, it's me!' she cried.

'Joanne!' he answered and hugged her to him in delight.

'Haway and bring her inside!' Pearl commanded. 'Let's have a good look at her!'

Jo grinned at the familiar words. Her aunt had said them every time she had come home from abroad and could not wait to see how she and Colin had grown. This time Jo herself was the returning wanderer, but it felt just as good.

Chapter Thirty-five

It was Pearl's idea. She made the suggestion the next day when Jo went to talk to Martha about putting on the play at the Dees Theatre in March or April. Jo gawped at her.

'You're not serious? Do the play at your wedding reception? But I haven't learnt it—'

'I bet you have.' Pearl gave her a look. 'Anyway, you could do it as a reading.'

'But it's not suitable for a wedding.' Jo made excuses. 'It's not a happy play.'

'Susie said it was uplifting,' Pearl answered. 'Didn't she, Jack?'

'Aye,' her father agreed.

'You've been speaking to Susie about it?' Jo gasped. 'What else did she say?'

'Just that she's coming up for the wedding,' Pearl smiled. 'She's been that good to you we thought it would be a nice way to thank her. And she said she'd definitely come if you did a performance.'

'Dad, are you in on all this?' Jo asked, dumbfounded.

He looked at her guardedly. 'Aye, in a manner of speaking. It was Pearl's idea, but we're both curious to see what's been keeping you in London all this time.'

'But you'll probably hate it.' Jo cringed at the thought of those closest to her seeing her work. It was much easier to perform in front of strangers, especially when she had written it herself. It would be like exposing herself in public, she thought in embarrassment.

'Go on,' Pearl encouraged. 'You know how I love a good play. Doesn't matter if you make us cry or laugh, it'll be special because it's you doing it on our special day.'

'Oh, Pearl, I don't know . . .' Jo said, covering her burning cheeks with her hands.

'Haway, there won't be many there,' Jack coaxed. 'It would be a grand wedding present for us to see your work, pet.'

Jo was suddenly fired by the idea. 'If you're sure it won't spoil your evening,' she said with a bashful smile.

'We've got the weekend in Edinburgh to recover if it does,' Pearl joked, with a kiss on her cheek.

'I'll need to get some music taped.' Jo began to plan at once. 'I'll go over to Alan's tomorrow and sort that out. I left a message at the theatre to say I was back.' She stopped. They were both looking at her. 'What?'

'He rang while you were out at Martha's,' Pearl said quietly. 'Said he couldn't make it to the wedding – wished us all the best.' Jo felt herself go hot.

'Think it's time you sorted things out there,' Jack said, unusually forthright.

'Aye,' Jo said stiffly, 'it is.'

The next day, Jo and Pearl went into Newcastle to buy the promised outfit. Pearl forbade black. They laughed like teenagers as Jo tried on various skirts and tops, but in the end she settled for a long purple dress and black boots. They parted at the bus station, Jo bracing herself to go back to Alan's.

'I'll see you on Friday, then,' Jo smiled, kissing her aunt affectionately. Pearl was suddenly emotional.

'I can't wait!' she sniffed. 'I feel as excited as a young lass.'

'You still are,' Jo grinned.

Pearl caught her hand. 'If things get awkward – you come straight home.'

Jo nodded, realising that they both still thought of Jack's flat as her home. The nearer she drew to Sandyford, the more she felt that she no longer wanted to be there. It had suited her to have excuses to stay away, and she imagined Alan already knew that. She had hardly been back since she had left for the peace camp in October.

Alan was not there when she let herself in, so she busied herself taping the pieces of music that she needed for the play, from his large collection of LPs. She could not help herself nosing around for signs that Maya had moved in or was a regular visitor, but there was nothing to suggest it. In fact, the place had an air of neglect about it, as if it had ceased to be a home to anyone. The fridge was empty, apart from some ancient Brie and a few stalks of withered spring onions. The newspapers lying around were several weeks old, and dust lay thick on everything.

Jo shivered and switched on the gas fire, made herself a cup of black tea and settled to read through the script while the music played. Later, she got up and drew the curtains against the dark, then decided to pop out to the corner shop for some milk and fresh bread before it closed. By the time she had bought provisions and chatted to the grocer, whom she had not seen in months, half an hour had gone.

Fiddling with her key in the lock, she heard a familiar voice shout, 'It's open!'

She staggered in with two carrier bags and dumped

them down, looking across at Alan. He looks old, she thought with detachment. 'Hi. I've got some stuff to make a curry.'

He smiled at last and came forward to give her a kiss. It was brief, without enthusiasm. 'Welcome back at last. Wasn't sure if I'd see you again.'

'Sorry,' she said awkwardly. 'I wasn't sure if I'd come back.'

'That's honest,' Alan answered evenly. 'So I'm going to be honest with you. Glass of wine?'

Jo got the impression she was going to need to sit down for what was coming next. She flopped into an armchair and undid her coat while watching Alan pour from an already opened bottle.

'I haven't been here much myself – not since Christmas,' he told her, handing her a large goblet of red wine. She took it and sipped, her heart hammering, but her face composed.

'You've been at Maya's,' she said.

He gave her a look of surprise. 'Yes. Who told you?'

Jo shrugged. 'Just put two and two together, I suppose.' She could not believe how calm she sounded.

'She's always been a good friend,' Alan said as if they were discussing a play, 'and I felt I'd lost your interest a while ago. Am I right?'

'Yes,' Jo said quietly, feeling a flood of relief at having admitted it at last. She was almost grateful to Maya for stepping into her place, though her pride felt bruised.

Alan looked relieved too. 'I imagine you've been seeing someone in London,' he said, studying her.

Jo put down her wine in surprise. 'No,' she declared. 'I've been living like a nun. Well, a nun who drinks too much maybe – but there's been no one else.'

'Sorry,' Alan said quickly. 'Just my big head. Didn't think you'd simply go off me.' He smiled in self-mockery.

'It's not like that—' Jo began.

He stopped her. 'let's not talk any more about it. As long as we both know where we stand.'

'Are you going round there now?' Jo asked. 'Is Maya expecting you?'

'If that's all right?' Alan looked sheepish.

Suddenly they were both laughing. 'Why are you asking my permission?' Jo giggled.

'I've no idea!' Alan said, shaking his head. He put down his glass. 'I thought this would take longer. Oh, girl! I think I might miss you more than I imagined.'

'Don't start that,' Jo grimaced. 'No you won't. There is one thing I'd be grateful for, though.'

'Go on,' Alan said, sitting down opposite.

'Will you read the play and tell me what you think?' Jo asked, feeling her stomach knot with nerves.

'Of course,' he agreed. 'Show me.'

She handed him the manuscript and refilled his glass. He raised his eyebrows. 'It's that bad, is it?'

'Read!' she ordered, and went into the kitchen, unable to bear watching him read it. She began to prepare a curry and then remembered she would be eating it alone, so gave up and went back to the sitting room, putting on her tape of music softly in the background. Alan was absorbed, but his face was stern and she feared his criticism. They might have proved incompatible, but she still valued his judgement when it came to theatre. She tiptoed restlessly around the flat like a child waiting to hear if she had passed some test. Eventually she went back in the kitchen and carried on making a mound of curry that would probably never be eaten.

After half an hour she poked her head round the door, wondering if he'd fallen asleep. He sat with the play on his knee, his wine glass empty. He looked up at her sombrely and shook his head. Her heart sank.

'You hate it, don't you?' she said for him. 'It's a load of emotional rubbish.'

He put out a hand for her to sit down beside him. Only then did she notice that his eyes were glistening.

'It's certainly emotional,' he said, clearing his throat. 'I'm impressed, Jo,' he said simply. 'I had no idea you could write.'

'I don't think I can,' she said, her heart thumping in excitement. 'I just couldn't keep this stuff in any longer.'

'That's obvious.' He nodded. 'It's very powerful. I had no idea how much you were grieving for your brother. I'm sorry, it's very humbling. I was pressing you the whole time to forget and move on, without really thinking how you felt. But this is very good.' He ran a hand through his greying hair. 'I'd like to do something with this. Can I copy it and show it to Maya?'

Jo coloured. 'I suppose so.'

'She could give advice on the publicity,' Alan urged. 'She'd like this.'

'Ask her round for curry,' Jo suggested. 'There's loads of it.'

'Are you sure?' Alan looked taken aback. Jo nodded. He sighed. 'You really have got over me, haven't you?'

'Don't fish,' Jo warned him. 'Go on, give her a ring. I don't mind if she doesn't.'

Alan got up. 'By the way,' he added, 'is Greg based on someone we both know?' He gave her a quizzical look. When she shrugged, he nodded. 'Yes, I thought it was him. Poor Jo.' He gave her a pitying look. 'You've never stopped loving him, have you?'

Jo looked away, her heart squeezing painfully at the thought of Mark. Alan had seen it as clearly as Susie. The play had brought out all her deepest feelings and longings for Mark, but that was where they must stay – contained in the play.

'No, I haven't,' she whispered.

Alan nodded. 'Some of it reads like a very beautiful love letter. Pity it'll be wasted on him,' he added drily.

On the day of the wedding, Jo went with Pearl to the hairdresser's and kept her occupied until it was time to get ready. Alan was coming to the wedding after all, to be a witness with Jo, now that they had agreed on an amicable friendship. Jack was quite baffled by their relationship, but Pearl seemed to understand. 'It's nice you'll have an escort for the occasion,' she said.

Alan was to meet Susie off the train and bring her to the registry office. Jo's stomach twisted with nerves at the thought of doing the play. Pearl had suggested that Martha come along in the evening to the restaurant and help her with the music.

'At least you'll all be anaesthetised with champagne,' Jo joked.

They met Alan and Susie on the steps of the registry office and went quietly inside. Jack and Pearl wanted no one else there, for it was an emotional moment without Colin and they wanted no comparisons with Jack's grander wedding to Gloria. Jo remembered the photograph, now put away in a drawer, of her mother in an elaborate white dress and veil outside a church, clutching a large bouquet of flowers. But when the time came for Jack and Pearl to make their promises to each other, her thoughts were only for them and how happy they looked together. She knew with all her being that they were doing the right thing at last.

Afterwards, they went home for a celebratory cup of tea and Alan produced a bottle of champagne. Jo felt quite euphoric by the time they arrived at the restaurant and were shown upstairs to the small function room. She had been there the day before to gauge where she would perform, and Martha was already there to help.

Then the small band of friends that Pearl and Jack had invited to celebrate with them began to arrive. Marilyn's parents were the first, Jo noticed.

'The Leishmans love a free meal,' she whispered to Alan.

'Stop bitching,' he smiled at her.

Then Skippy's parents came in and Jo went over to greet them, knowing that it was still an effort for the Jacksons to come out in public. There was a friend of Pearl's from her keep-fit circle, Nancy from the Coach and Eight and a former workmate of Jack's with his wife. A couple of friends from the Seamen's Mission followed, and then Ivy came in, escorted by Mark.

Jo's heart thumped in fright. She had not expected to see him. Ivy had been invited, but Pearl had explained that they were restricting it to close friends of their generation to keep it small and intimate. When Pearl saw Mark, however, she waved him in. 'You'll stay for a drink, won't you, pet?'

Mark came over, looking long-haired and gaunt. 'I just came in to wish you well,' he said, bending to kiss Pearl, 'and to see Nana got here safely.'

'Pull up a chair, lad.' Jack was effusive. 'Is Brenda with you?'

Mark's look flickered towards Jo as he shook his head.

432

Jo wondered if he blamed her for them not being invited. Maybe her father and aunt had decided that it would be awkward for her if they were. She would have said hello, but he did not look in her direction again, slipping off to talk to the Jacksons.

Ivy came over and greeted her quickly, but she was seated at the far end of the long table and Mark pulled up a chair next to her. Jo wondered how long he would stay. She tried to forget about his presence at the opposite end of the room and enjoy the meal, but she could not eat for nerves and kept a check on what she drank, determining to keep a clear head. She must not make a fool of herself or let her father and Pearl down.

Towards the end of the meal, Alan gave her hand an encouraging squeeze. 'It's time you got ready. Go and do some deep-breathing exercises in the ladies',' he smiled, and kissed her lightly on the cheek.

Jo nodded, heart hammering hard. As she got up she noticed that Mark was watching her. She panicked that he was going to stay for the play. Suddenly she was not sure if she could perform it in front of him. She would be mortified if he guessed that Greg was him.

As she passed close to him on her way to the door, she realised she had been hiding from the truth. The whole play was about Mark. Susie and Alan had seen it plainly enough. Her words might be fiction, but they spoke of her love for him. He was the hero of her drama.

Ivy called out to her, 'I hear you're going to put on a bit of a play, hinny!'

'Aye, Ivy,' Jo smiled, 'so no snoring in the cheap seats.' Ivy chuckled and Jo rushed out for fresh air.

She stood at the back entrance, breathing in the cold, drizzly night air. There was no hint of spring yet and she knew when that came, it would remind them all of the time of year that Colin and Skippy and Mark had gone away, one long year ago. Jo closed her eyes and took deep breaths to calm her nerves. She turned as she heard footsteps thumping down the stairs behind her. Mark loomed out of the doorway and looked startled to find her in the dark.

'Are you going?' she asked him, her heart sinking.

'Aye,' he grunted. 'I've stayed longer than I meant.'

'Oh,' Jo said, wondering why she was suddenly stuck for words. Damn it! She must think of something.

'Your dad looks happy,' he added, 'and Pearl.'

'Aye, they are,' Jo agreed, nodding as inanely as a toy suspended in a car window.

'Well, I'll be off,' he said. But she stood in his way.

'And how about you?' Jo asked quickly. 'Are you feeling any better?'

He gave her a quizzical look. 'Less screwed up, you mean?'

'Sorry,' she said, feeling gauche and helpless. 'I didn't mean to sound like a doctor.'

He gave her the glimpse of a smile. 'Some things seem clearer now,' he said in a low voice. 'I had a visit from me shipmate, Andy. His new ship was in at the quayside last week. I went on board.'

Jo was surprised. 'What was that like?'

'Strange,' he admitted. 'I was dead scared.'

'But you did it?' Jo asked softly.

'Aye, and it wasn't that bad once I got on board,' he reflected.

'So are you going to go back in the Navy?' Jo dared to ask.

He gave her a hard look with his dark eyes and she saw that the pain was still there. 'No,' he answered.

'That's one thing I've come to accept. I'm taking a sick pension. I realise I'm not fit enough to gan to sea again – I'd be a liability.'

She wanted to protest that he would not be, but stopped herself. He went on defensively. 'But I don't need anyone's sympathy. I'm not bitter about it. It's just something I've come to a decision about.'

'What will you do?' Jo asked.

'Bewick's widow is giving me a bit of gardening work.' He shrugged. 'One step at a time.'

'What does Brenda think?' Jo dared to ask.

His look hardened again and his mouth twisted. 'She's given up on me,' he said. 'We're splitting up.'

Jo felt her heart lurch. 'Oh, Mark!'

'No, it's a bit of a relief not to pretend any more,' he admitted. 'She's wanted to leave for ages, but she's felt too guilty to go – me being wounded and that. So I made the decision for us – I'm moving back to Ivy's till it's sorted out. We're going to divorce.'

Jo stepped forward. She reached out her hand and touched him gently on his puckered jaw. She felt him flinch, but he did not pull away. 'Stay for the play,' she pleaded softly.

'Why? Still trying to make a pacifist out of me?' he joked.

She shook her head. 'I'm not trying to change you at all. I started by writing the play for Colin,' she confessed, 'but I ended up writing it for you.'

He gave her a look of disbelief, '*Me?* Why me?'

Jo swallowed and forced herself to admit out loud, 'Because I care for you, Mark. I always have done, even when we've been worlds apart or not speaking.' She pushed back his tousled mane of hair from his scar and leaned close. 'I've kidded myself for so long that I didn't care. But that's been my problem all along. I've never been able to tell you how I really felt deep inside.' She swallowed hard and forced herself to confess, 'I've loved you all me life. And I still do love you.'

For a moment he stared at her as if she had hit him, and she feared she had made a fool of herself. He must feel nothing of the deep desire that she felt for him, she panicked. She recoiled, but swiftly Mark pulled her back, gripping her arms.

'What do you mean?' he demanded. 'I thought you hated me guts. I thought you resented me for coming back and not being Colin!'

'No, Mark, never!' Jo exclaimed. 'How could you think that?'

'Because you were so angry about your brother!' Mark cried. 'You seemed to hate me for not being grateful that I'd survived, when all I wanted was not to have come back at all – not without Colin and Skippy!' He looked deep into her eyes for reassurance. 'But all the time you say . . .'

'Yes, I love you,' Jo repeated, not caring whether she was making a fool of herself, just knowing she had to tell him.

'But that man up there?' Mark jerked his head towards the restaurant. 'You're with him!'

'Alan?' Jo questioned, having forgotten all about him. She saw now how it must look to Mark. 'No, no,' she insisted quickly, 'he's with someone else now. He came as a witness. We're just friends.'

'Oh, Jo!' he groaned, as if a great burden had been lifted from him. 'I thought I'd lost you for ever!'

Jo silenced him with a fierce kiss. 'Now do you believe me?' she asked, her pulse thumping. He pulled her closer and answered her with another kiss, hungry and lingering. They gripped each other tightly, as if both were afraid to let go again.

Mark whispered into her hair, 'You're the only one who can see me through the darkness. I need you!'

'I'm here for you now, Mark,' she promised. 'I'm never going to leave you again.'

He held her away suddenly. 'I have to tell you something,' he said desperately, 'but I'm afraid you might think me mad.'

'Go on,' Jo urged.

'I've never spoken about this to anyone – not since the hospital ship. But it's been haunting me ever since . . .' He swallowed, and Jo sensed his fear.

'Tell me,' she whispered, holding on to him.

'When I was down below deck,' Mark said hoarsely, 'looking for Skippy – I found him trapped under a girder. I couldn't move it!' Jo could tell by his face how he was reliving the agony. 'I tried! But I had to leave him – he told me to go and save m'self. I heard him screaming, Jo, dying . . . !'

She gritted her teeth against the nausea she felt inside and nodded for him to go on.

'I was alone in that hell,' Mark rasped, 'but then someone led me out of it to the hole in the bulkhead. He told me to jump and I did. He saved me life.'

'Who was it?' Jo asked, with a tingle up her spine that told her what he was going to say.

He looked at her, afraid of her disbelief. 'It was Skippy's voice – I'd know it anywhere. Do you think I'm mad?'

They stared at each other, speechless. Jo knew that if she poured scorn on the idea that Skippy had saved him, then she would shatter his trust for ever. She might even destroy his cautious gropings towards sanity and peace of mind.

'You're not mad,' Jo answered gently. 'Who's to say that Skippy didn't save you?' She took his tortured face between her hands. 'And if he did, then it was done for a purpose. He wanted you to survive. It was his final gift to you, Mark. You tried to do as much for him, remember?' She looked at him tenderly. 'Take his gift, Mark, your second chance at living. Anything you do from now on will be living proof of the friendship you both had – and with Colin too.'

She saw tears well in his handsome dark eyes and his drawn face soften in relief.

'Thank you,' he said hoarsely, and buried his face in her neck. 'I can't believe you've come back to me.'

'I have,' she assured him.

'Do you know what my last conscious thought was in that freezing water?' he demanded. 'Do you know what kept me going?' He looked at her lovingly. 'It was you. I was half drowning and I saw you swimming ahead of me, like at Wallsend Baths, telling me to keep me head above the water!'

Jo smiled, exultant. 'Interfering to the last, was I?'

'Aye,' he grinned. 'And I'm bloody lucky you always do!' He kissed her again. 'I love you!' he whispered.

There was a noise on the stairs behind them, and Pearl's voice demanded, 'What you doing out there in the dark, Joanne? Are you ever going to come up and do the play? Everyone's waiting.'

They looked round guiltily, their arms dropping from each other, but Pearl had seen. 'I'm coming,' Jo said quickly.

'I've interrupted something, haven't I?' Pearl said. 'You look as guilty as if you'd been caught pinching apples from Bewick's orchard.'

They both laughed, and Jo felt Mark take her hand possessively, as if he didn't care who saw them together. 'You never did miss much, did you, Pearl?' he teased.

'I'm not going to ask any awkward questions now,' she declared, 'not on me wedding day. But I can't say I'm sorry to see you two making it up,' and she winked a little tipsily.

'Come on, then.' Mark pulled Jo after him. 'Let's see this play.'

Jo followed them both, bubbling with nervous excitement again. This was going to be the most important performance of her life, she realised. She looked around the room, at her father and Pearl, at Mark sitting with Ivy, never taking his eyes from her. She was doing this for the most important people in her life too.

Martha was ready with the music. Jo stepped forward, shaking inwardly, but feeling a calm strength coming from somewhere, filling her with courage.

'This is a one-woman play called *For Love and Glory*,' she announced. 'I dedicate it to Colin and to Skippy who will always be with us.' She gulped, catching sight of the Jacksons' emotional faces. 'I can feel them close to us today especially. We're all thinking of them.' She exchanged emotional looks with her father and he nodded in encouragement.

Jo took a deep breath and directed her look at Mark. 'But most of all, I give this play to Mark. For being the survivor, for being a loyal friend and for having to carry all our grief as well as his own.' He blurred in her vision for a moment as she fought down her tears. 'Mark, this is for you, because you're special to me,' she smiled, 'with all my love.'

She saw him grinning back at her with that look of

tenderness she had not seen in years and feared never to see again. It gave her a surge of strength and conviction.

'For Love and Glory!' she declared boldly, and with pride.

she never would had but known what he had found in her, nor
how it gave him a sense of strength and power in
his own being, and an self-assured in woman and wife
again.

Now you can buy any of these other bestselling books from your bookshop or *direct from the publisher*.

FREE P&P AND UK DELIVERY
(Overseas and Ireland £3.50 per book)

My Sister's Child	Lyn Andrews	£5.99
Liverpool Lies	Anne Baker	£5.99
The Whispering Years	Harry Bowling	£5.99
Ragamuffin Angel	Rita Bradshaw	£5.99
The Stationmaster's Daughter	Maggie Craig	£5.99
Our Kid	Billy Hopkins	£6.99
Dream a Little Dream	Joan Jonker	£5.99
For Love and Glory	Janet MacLeod Trotter	£5.99
In for a Penny	Lynda Page	£5.99
Goodnight Amy	Victor Pemberton	£5.99
My Dark-Eyed Girl	Wendy Robertson	£5.99
For the Love of a Soldier	June Tate	£5.99
Sorrows and Smiles	Dee Williams	£5.99

TO ORDER SIMPLY CALL THIS NUMBER

01235 400 414

or e-mail orders@bookpoint.co.uk

Prices and availability subject to change without notice.